ADRIAN COLE

BOOK ONE OF THE OMARAN SAGA

A PLACE AMONG THE FALLEN

D1026284

AVON BOOKS ◆ NEW YORK

AVON BOOKS
A division of
The Hearst Corporation
105 Madison Avenue
New York, New York 10016

Copyright © 1986 by Adrian Cole
Front cover illustration by Kevin Johnson
Published by arrangement with Arbor House Publishing Company
Library of Congress Catalog Card Number: 86-28752
ISBN: 0-380-70556-7

First Avon Books Printing: March 1990

AVON TRADEMARK REG. U.S. PAT. OFF. AND IN OTHER COUNTRIES, MARCA REGISTRADA, HECHO EN U.S.A.

Printed in the U.S.A.

RA 10 9 8 7 6 5 4 3 2 1

Contents

Blood from the earth,
And blood to earth return.
                The Abiding Word

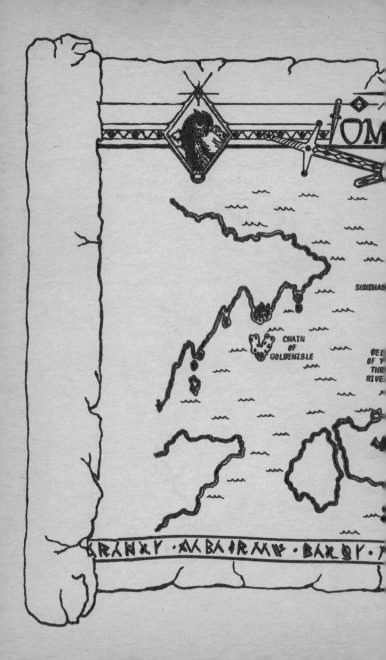

SUNDMAS

CHAIN
OF
GOLDENISLE

DEL
OF T
THR
RIVE

CRANXY · MBAIRMY · BAXDY ·

Part One

AUGURIES

1
Sea Borne

EACH NIGHT for almost a month, the man's face had haunted the girl, Sisipher. At first, asleep, she was barely aware of the intrusion, but slowly the features of the face took shape, floating on the surface of her dreams. It was a strange face, full of contradictions, for though it was the face of a comparatively young man, it was somehow not a young face. Some private agony had aged it; its torment was evident in its eyes, but they also held a resolve, a remorselessness of purpose, so that it almost seemed as though the man could step from dream to reality without effort.

As if bursting from a pool, Sisipher woke, crying for air. Beside her it was not the intense gaze of that face that hovered, but that of Brannog, her father. He reached out at once with a sponge and gently dabbed at her forehead. Not seeing him, she did not respond, her mind clouded. He was about to speak, but he realized he would not reach her. Let her sleep if she can, he thought. In a moment her eyes closed and she sagged back among the twisted sheets. The face was no longer waiting for her. She seemed at peace.

Brannog, turning in the candlelight, motioned to another girl who waited by the door, her face white. Cautiously she came forward and took the proferred bowl. Her eyes were fixed on the now inert Sisipher as if expecting her to wake in confusion. The girl, Eorna, had watched Sisipher convulse with this fever (if fever it was) on several

3

nights recently. It seemed unusual to her that by day Sisipher behaved as if nothing was wrong with her, yet by night there was an element of madness in her fever. Yet Eorna shared none of her conjectures with Brannog: he cared too much for his daughter.

"It grows worse," he said quietly, his anger muted.

Eorna studied his broad back as he spoke. Even sitting his height was obvious; his arms were well muscled, his hands calloused with years of working with nets and ropes. He had a weatherbeaten, solid face, his eyes like the eyes of an eagle, always alert, and to Eorna (as to many others in the village) he stood out from others around him, a dominant but gentle man. And yet what warmth there was in him seemed to be directed solely at his daughter.

"What will happen to her?" Eorna whispered, drawing closer to his side. She wanted to place a hand upon his shoulder, but instead gripped the bowl tightly as if it gave her comfort.

"The dreams that troubled her as a child were never like this." It was true, for she had often gabbled to him, sitting on his great knees as a child, speaking nonsenses about other realms which she conjured so vividly. Such things had never concerned him in those days.

Beyond the tiny window of the attic room the night winds raced down off the mountains and into the bay. For three days and nights the winds had gusted with uncanny strength, even for this stark coast in the winter months. Just as the winds raged, so Sisipher's nights worsened, as though the storm outside perfectly balanced that within. Brannog shut out the thought. Absurd. Coincidence. But Sisipher's invisible nightmare raised up in her father's mind ghosts that were never at rest. He could feel the power of the elements about his home and village, as though there was a purpose in their violence, yet he knew there was nothing beyond the raw power of the storm. Like the sea, it had no being, no divine will. Such things were not held within Brannog's world. There was no power, no magic, no gods. Yet he shuddered as he listened to the snarl of the wind, an echo of his daughter's turmoil.

Is this your mother's gift, curse of her blood? he wondered, thinking of her mother. He had found her in a coastal village far to the north, where she had lived in an isolated community, a remote village that clung grimly to its independence. In Frostwalk there had been an almost unique will to shut out the world. A squall had forced Brannog into its harbor, where the fishers had admitted him reluctantly.

He had been young then, hot-headed, and had defied his father by insisting on wandering the seas for a while before settling to the life prepared for him. Inexperience and poor weather had left him no alternative but to shelter in Frostwalk, where he had met Sisipher's mother. At once he had fallen in love. While her people were never hostile to him, they gave him no encouragement to stay. But the girl had. Later she told her people that she would have no one but Brannog for her husband. I can never leave Frostwalk, she told Brannog. You must remain here if you want me for your wife. He had argued, of course, but his love had been intense enough to triumph over duty to his home village. He had married and had stayed, masking what it had cost him, though his wife had understood such things and had loved him the more for his sacrifice.

The chain that bound him to Frostwalk was strengthened by the birth of Sisipher, and for a few years he had felt secure in the company of the taciturn inhabitants. He fished with them, never far from land, his skill and strength much envied, for he was shaped by the power of the sea, and he had laughed with them. Even so, their secretiveness sometimes disturbed him, as though they behaved differently when he was not with them. His wife shared this twilight secret of Frostwalk, though never fully with him. He could not touch this thing, but it touched him with fear.

Eventually his wife had told him that she had been born with a gift, rare but not unique. It was, she said, the gift of telling, though she had repressed it since birth. It is only because I love you that I tell you this, she said. *Power.* The impossible, his mind cried. Yet nothing could divert his strong love for her. Frostwalk, she had told him, had a claim upon her gift that she could not deny. He remained

sceptical until the day she predicted the death of a child
beneath a miniature avalanche: the child was made to take
another path than the one it had chosen to play along, and
later there was a fall that would have killed it as prophe-
sied. To Brannog, the gift was a curse. To view tomorrow
could not be right, natural. No good could come of such
a thing, even though it had saved the child's life. His dark
belief was vindicated on the day that his wife confessed to
him that she had foreseen her own doom. He scorned both
her tears and her insistence. Frostwalk had become eerily
withdrawn, as if already in mourning. The fishers had
known.

When his wife fell to the sudden sickness, Brannog's
heart had frozen. In two days she had died. The elders of
the village had covered her and taken her away for a secret
burial, though not at sea, as was the custom with Brannog's people. Devastated, Brannog had shut himself away
and had wept. He had never seen her again. Afterward he
was told nothing, but the people of Frostwalk shared his
grief. Sisipher had been three years old. Her mother's final
words to Brannog had been that Sisipher, too, had the gift
of telling, which had been handed down over many generations, though for what real purpose, no one knew. You
have a choice, she told Brannog. Stay in Frostwalk and
help your daughter to fulfill whatever purpose calls her, or
return with her to your father's home. Perhaps the gift
within her will die if you leave. Brannog knew that it had
cost Sisipher's mother much to say this, the final evidence
of her unwavering love for him.

A few days after her death, he took the infant Sisipher
to his boat, quietly murmured a farewell to the fishers of
Frostwalk and set sail for his first home. No one had called
him back, but he had read their unexpected deep sadness,
for his going as much as for the child's. At home he had
been welcomed heartily, and if his father's people had had
any misgivings about his past and his new daughter (a
Frostwalk child, no less!) they did not let them show. Very
soon his people had made him one of them again, as
though he had been away but a few days, and already the

young bloods looked to him for guidance in times of decision.

He never spoke of the gift within his daughter to anyone, and said nothing to her. Fifteen years ago he expected it to wither and die, but the thought of it tormented him even now. This past month it had done so increasingly.

"What does she see in her dreams?" came Eorna's voice beside him. Her plump figure brushed him deliberately as she leaned forward, her bosom like an offering. She wanted to help, to please him, but he so rarely smiled, and gave her no encouragement. At least there was no other woman in his life, save Sisipher. Eorna felt the familiar stab of jealousy.

Brannog had been aware of Eorna's desire for some while. It needed no gift of telling to see it. But he did not want her. It was not possible for him to love any woman as he had loved his wife. Casual physical love he would not consider, not with a servant girl like Eorna. She was not beautiful, nor alluring, yet perhaps it would have been good to take her. But she wanted things he could not give her, and he had no wish to cause her pain or shame.

"See? If I knew that," he said, "I would put an end to whatever troubles her."

Eorna nodded, eyeing the girl. Sisipher was a young woman, yet no more than a year younger than herself, pale-skinned and slender—not quite beautiful (and Eorna's eye was honest, not marred by spite) but attractive in a subtle way that could, if she used it, turn the head of many a man. Her eyes were immediately arresting, like no other eyes seen in these lands, betraying her lineage. It was known that in her past the secrets of mixed races were buried, but no one ever dared speak frankly of this to Brannog.

"You have been with her for many hours, Brannog. Will you rest now?"

His eyes remained on Sisipher. "Aye. You should not have roused yourself."

"I do as I am bid," Eorna sniffed, meaning, I am a hired servant, no more. It was true, for in return for her keep here, she worked with the other girl, Harla. Both girls had no other homes. Harla's parents were dead, as were Eorna's, whose only relative was her sister, who could not keep her. Brannog's home was an inn, though rarely used as such now except as a place for the men of the village to gather and to drink. Travelers were rare so far north, even in the summer months. The two girls kept the inn for its host.

Brannog ignored Eorna's pointedness, and she sensed that this was no time to press herself upon him. He turned to her, but movement on the bed alerted him at once.

Sisipher had opened her eyes. She gave the impression of someone looking vaguely across a landscape and seeing something in the distance. Her hand gently tugged at her father's sleeve, and as she spoke he heard the laughter of the storm.

"He's coming," she said, but there was no hysteria, no frantic movement now.

"Who?" said Brannog at once.

For a moment she seemed anxious, frowning, but then her eyes closed. She was asleep again, if indeed she had been awake. Brannog turned abruptly to Eorna, who looked puzzled by what she had overheard.

"Another dream," he said, getting up. "This is some fever. I have seen such things before. Say nothing, girl, eh? It has no meaning. Don't speak of it beyond this room. You know how men will talk." He gently gripped her arms and she made no attempt to move away, even though his fingers hurt her.

"As you wish," she nodded, knowing that he could no longer ignore her and what she wanted for them both.

Even so, he loosed her, turned quickly and straightened the sheets. "Go and rest. It is late."

Dismissed, she withdrew. Something in Sisipher's words had worried him, she had seen that. But she smiled. At least she had something, a tiny hold. He wanted her silence. She became so preoccupied with trying to devise a way to use her fragment of power that she did not wonder why he should be so anxious not to have his daughter's words repeated outside.

Brannog's shadow danced on the wall and he glared at it. Who would be coming? What had his daughter seen? For years he had lived with the dread that someone would come from Frostwalk to claim her back, to demand the right of the village to her gift. Now the girl had been terrified, but of what? Brannog bunched his fists, straightening up his great frame as if preparing for a physical conflict. The storm roared, ignoring him. The village would have to sit out its rage. It could not last. He thought of the sea beyond the harbor, unchained, ruler of them all. No one could survive it in such a mood.

It had been a hard, cruel winter, far worse than any other that Sundhaven could recall. The stone houses, built into rock ledges that had been hewn from the lower skirts of the mountains, were safe enough from the excesses of wind and driving sleet and snow that alternated in gusts from the heights, or beat in from the sea beyond the jetty breakwater. Men of Sundhaven had died this winter, their fishing ships not returning, the small fleet decimated. It was rare to lose a single man of their hardy breed to the weather, for they had a strength of will to match the ferocity of the elements. Yet something in this cold season had turned upon them like malice.

Under the brow of sheer cliffs, the houses of Sundhaven were embedded in shadow, blending into the grayness like boulders. Only the arms of the breakwater and the sweep of cliffs on either side of the cove had checked the cutting edge of any seaward gale enough to have permitted Sundhaven's survival. As dawn fought for birth, the windows rattled, faces peering out at the attacking sea, the lash of waves. The thoughts of each man and woman who could not sleep for the din were that it must end soon. For three days the fishers had not been out on the water, and already the fish harvest had been a disastrous one. The warehouses behind the quay were not large, but were yet less than half full. Without fish—the coin of Sundhaven—the men would not be able to trade with the other ports for fuel for their fires, or for candles, or for clothes, or for food with the farmers of the coastal estuaries to the south. True, a subsidy might be negotiated, but it would have to be repaid

in time. The promise of spring was not good. The threat
of hunger swirled around the village with each freezing
gust of the wind.

Brannog held up an oil lamp to a window of his drinking hall, scraping the frosted glass with his nails. He would
not be returning to his bed this night. He stared out
through the jagged hole he had made. The night was not
pitch, but gray, half-lit, the white spume falling like snow
beyond the walls of the quay. This was no place for Sisipher. She had never said so, but she was not content here.
In a way, they were all penned like sheep on a mountainside. Brannog had left once, but his duty was to the fleet
here now. He had no spirit remaining to try for a new life.
What, then? Submit to Eorna's eagerness? She worked
hard, and would doubtless be capable of bearing many
children. He would never love her, which did not seem
fair. But what of Sisipher? It was not too late to find her
a better life. Small wonder she was visited by nightmares
in this desolate place. Perhaps in the spring he should take
her with him to the south on one of the trading voyages.
Possibly she would find a cause in one of the towns to
draw her, some better purpose. But he scowled. A girl
alone in a place like that would be prey to many dangers.

Something raced across his vision. He squinted out at
the jetty that ran around one arm of the cove. There were
men there, bent over, buffeted by the wind which threatened to cuff them over the side into the boiling water beyond. At once Brannog made for the door. He tore back
the thick bolts, set down his lamp, and thrust his huge
head into the icy blast. It was almost as though he had
pushed it underwater as the shock of the cold hit him. His
eyes narrowed to slits, but he could discern the men, fishers of the village. They were pointing along the curling
arm of the jetty.

"A prow!" came a shout, heard only because of a freak
twist of the wind which flung it back into the snarl of
another great gust. Brannog withdrew, but quickly prepared himself for a dash into the tumult outside. Dressed
in thick, fur-lined skins, he stepped outside and fought
hard to slam the door against the wind's determination. A

dozen men were running now, and Brannog grimaced at the knowledge that others had not slept, but had been watching the play of the storm. But what had they shouted? A prow? A *ship*? Out in this madness?

Brannog felt himself hurried by the wind, as if it were eager to show him its spoils, his steps quickening along the slippery quay and on to the jetty. He joined the group of men and like them tried to study the heaving swells of open sea beyond. Each wave that rose up obscured that behind it, dashing itself at last into countless jewelled fragments against the jetty wall. The men felt the wall shake, and the salt spray stung their eyes, but they ignored it as they had done since childhood.

"Who called prow?" shouted Brannog, his arm gripping that of a companion.

"Yarnol," came the reply, almost a snarl. The man pointed. "Out there!"

"Have you seen it?"

"Aye!" came a shout beside them. "I swear it. A prow! No mast. Torn away, likely. But she floats."

"She'll never make shore," Brannog cried, and with the wind streaming like a torrent in spate off the land, the men all knew he spoke the truth. But they were fishers and could not help but search with their eyes for this doomed vessel, even though it would be sudden death to put out a ship to help. After a moment the distant prow rose up like a knife, slicing apart a rolling crest, black and glossy as a seal, and the men marvelled that it should be pointed toward the land. A freak gust must have sent the rudderless hull twisting around. Minutes later the prow rose up again, battering through the swells, and still it faced the cove. The faces of the watchers were intent with disbelief. Brannog heard a voice within him, the calm voice of Sisipher as she spoke from her dreams. *He's coming*.

Brannog jolted, watching for the prow as a bird of prey watches the ground beneath it when sensing a kill. That prow could not sail into this wind, could *not* reach the cove. No man among them would have said otherwise, and when the black prow rose yet again, still aimed unerringly at them, they drew back in uniform amazement. Nothing was said now. Words were not necessary. Each man understood that something outside their knowledge approached. A deep fear stirred in them all. They were not superstitious, for they had no time for supernatural concepts and believed only in what was around them. As the prow drew on, heedless of the battering of wind and wave, the men craned their necks, searching for a sign of life within it. They saw none, yet willed the ship to survive.

With a final surge, the small ship rode through the jaws of the stone jetties and bobbed into the cove. Along the quayside there were now gathered some score of villagers, and storm lamps flickered. Brannog was one of the first to race along the jetty, all the time watching the dark boat as it was flung about by the waves. Even here it defied the wind, but as it reached the pebble shallows it dipped, disgorging two distinct figures like sacks of ballast. Brannog scrambled down a flight of slick steps, almost slithering into the harbor. He splashed through the shallows. The water was like ice, but he surged through it with other men close behind him.

Now upon the shingle, the two figures rolled as if drowned, half floating as a wave dragged them back into its embrace. Like weed they eddied, floating outward.

"Hurry!" yelled Brannog, even though he knew they must be corpses. No man could live through such a voyage. The rescue party, hampered by the water and furious wind, came to within twenty yards of the bodies. One of them was again discarded upon the shingle. Incredibly it stirred, then rose to its feet, groggy as a man fuddled with drink. Somehow it waded to its companion and dragged him laboriously ashore. Brannog and the fishers had jerked to a halt, watching this without moving, held back by the same irrational fear that had gripped them as the boat tumbled into the harbor. The first man hauled his heavy catch up the beach, until, far enough from the clutching foam, he collapsed.

Brannog's gaze was diverted by movement on the water. The black-prowed vessel had swung away, and now that it had brought its sinister cargo ashore, seemed prepared to let itself fall prey to the wind that had sought to destroy it for so long. How eagerly the storm leapt upon the offering! Within moments the waves had dashed the ship against the rocks beneath the far cliff wall, and the sound of the structure breaking up was completely lost in the mirth of the wind.

Another party of men had come around the shore from Sundhaven, also having witnessed the eerie drama. They stood off from the two fallen men, seeming to wait some word, some permission to go to them. Brannog urged his own party on through the swell. Biting back his fears, the big fisherman bent over the man who had so miraculously pulled his companion from the sea. He was alive. Brannog reached down and with remarkable ease lifted him, supporting him around the waist. He found himself looking into eyes that were lucid, aware, almost immune to the terrible cold that surrounded them all. Yet the man felt warm.

Others crowded in now, helping Brannog to get the man ashore, but in their anxiety for him they neglected the other man, who remained prone where he had fallen. No one gave a thought to his being alive. The man that Brannog held coughed violently and thick pelts were wrapped around him. They had to get him inside quickly or the cold would kill him, they felt certain.

Brannog turned abruptly. "See to the other," he began, but his voice trailed away. No one had seen the other man move, but he now stood as if completely recovered, as though, in fact, he had never been through the rigours of the voyage and the frigid immersion. He was not looking at the villagers, but studied instead the open sea. Its frenzy beyond the breakwater had not subsided. Frozen in a tableau of bafflement, the villagers stared at the back of this grim figure. The man was tall, taller even than Brannog (by a head) and had a thicker, more massive girth. Even with his clothes plastered to him by the sea, his frame was huge. His hair was pale gold, smeared down now like weed over the back of his neck, and the arms that hung at his side were thick, sheathed from elbow to fingers in long black gloves. No one had yet seen his face, so that his age remained a mystery.

The wind died suddenly. One moment it raged as vociferously as it had done for days, and then, like a great shout expiring, it had gone. Silence came down like an avalanche and the fishers gaped in awe at the sky. Hanging over them, seemingly listening, the mountains waited. The man that Brannog had tugged from the water watched the sky as if it were his enemy. "The lull," he said. "Afterwards the storm will be worse."

Scarcely had he finished speaking when the tide sighed, drawing back, as it often did when on the turn, releasing itself in a last surge of spray. But it was not yet time for the ebb. Brannog knew this, as did all his companions. The sea was their life, and they felt it as they felt the beating of their hearts. Every eye was upon the water. Quickly it slipped away from the beach, too quickly. Brannog expected the land to lurch, to betray their footing, for how was it possible for the waters to race away like this? Within minutes the cove had emptied, leaving its bottom bare, its mud and pools gleaming in the first searching beams of dawn. Crabs scuttled indignantly for cover, and here and there a small fish wriggled in desperation. Beyond the jetties the water retreated still further. Never, not even at the lowest of the summer tides, had the sea drained itself so far from the shore before.

No one spoke. They remained locked by amazement, stupefied by the bizarre terrain that had been uncovered. The man with his back to them turned now, showing his face partially. There was no amazement there, only a glimmer of what could have been fear. His voice came up to them as crisply as ice, cold, insistent. "Get inside your homes. Quickly! There is no time to delay. Guile!" Apparently he was addressing his companion. "Go with them. Hurry now! I may not be able to protect you from this."

The man Guile nudged Brannog. "We had better do as we're told. He has the scent of something dire."

There was no time for argument, not here, where so many impossible things had already happened. Brannog liked none of this, but the echoes of his daughter's nightmare still ran along his nerves. *He's coming.* This dark man, who sensed power? The fishers would call upon him to answer that. Brannog motioned his people away. They were glad to follow him. Guile went with them, seemingly recovered for the most part, though he could not control his shivering. Brannog glanced back once, and to his horror (he would not have described it otherwise) saw that the man beyond was again facing seawards, and now walking down the slope of the cove that led through the weed and cloying mud to the gap between the jetties. Brannog watched briefly, but then moved on, suddenly anxious to get inside and to attend to the roaring blaze of a fire. The fishers and the man called Guile reached the quay, where others held out more skins to the man from the broken ship. He was glad of them.

"Brannog!" cried a voice in the stillness. The big man swivelled. For the second time that dawn he found himself peering out to sea. A distant roaring announced the coming of yet another storm, no longer off the land, as if it had blown itself out to sea, turned, and now came back upon them. But it was not the storm that filled the fishers with terror. On the close horizon a wave was gathering itself like an army. Thundering like doom, it bore down upon the land voraciously, and by its sound the men gauged its height to be nigh on a hundred feet.

All around Brannog men were shouting, confused, racing this way and that, spilling into the houses, slamming doors and sealing the windows from within. Brannog did not move. He was transfixed. He was staring with the intuition born of certainty at his death. It bore down upon him just as surely as the death of his wife had come reaching for her. His eyes were hypnotised by the onrushing wave, but for a moment they caught sight of the remote figure out on the mud flats. From here it looked no more than a few inches high. What could the stranger possibly be doing there? He had chosen for himself an abrupt death, for the mountain of water would pound him to pulp as it fell.

Sundhaven will perish, Brannog thought, yet somehow

the realization did not leave him numb, and a strangely dispassionate mood took him. He watched the lonely figure that had chosen to sacrifice itself. Vaguely he saw it raise its black-gloved hands, the fists balled. Brannog did not see the smile upon the face of the shivering man beside him, the man who had made no move to flee the impending destruction, though he had been warned to.

As the wave's long brow curled in under itself like an immense fist, the figure in the bay stood its ground. It should have been inundated, buried alive, but it was not. Brannog's deepest fears shot to the surface of his mind as he saw the wave split open, as though passing either side of an invisible rock. Before the two shimmering curtains of water could reform and break as one over the man and twin jetties behind him, both fronts veered aside, becoming two separate waves. The gap between them widened rapidly and they raced away from the cove. All that swirled into the cove was a light wash of surf, no higher than a man's knees. Already the figure was returning. The two huge waves boiled toward the cliffs on either side of the coast, hidden from view, exploding on contact with a concussion that made the rocks blur in Brannog's sight. He dropped to one knee. Even then he expected the spume of backwash to rush into the channel between the jetties, but it never came. Somehow it swirled past, sucked back out to seaward. Brannog knew as he saw it go that Sundhaven was safe. From the sea at least.

The man beside him nodded as though to confirm that no more had happened than he had been expecting. Brannog rose and clawed at his arm. "Your companion. He divided the wave! You cannot deny it."

"Yes."

"He will have to account for this. My people will be terrified."

"And are you not?"

Brannog was watching the man in the cove. He was climbing the steps up the jetty. He looked from his movements to be spent, but he had turned his back upon the sea as if it were some once fierce animal that had been tamed and which no longer presented a threat.

"I have seen power," Brannog muttered softly, but as the wind had not returned, Guile heard him quite clearly. "I have seen the storm race to meet your ship, yet the vessel ignored it, as a living creature might have. And I have seen all the force of the sea scorned. Yet there is no power that can do this." But as he said this, he thought again of the village of Frostwalk, where the harvest had always been plentiful, and of the secrets that lurked there, power that had led its people to shut themselves away. And he thought of his daughter and the gift of telling, and of her prediction that the man now stumbling toward him across the quay would come. There was no doubt in his mind that it was this creature to which she had referred.

The man Guile sighed, waiting for his huge companion. "This world does not accept power, or high magic, or gods. They do not exist for you. But Korbillian is not a man of this world."

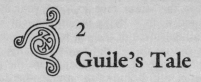

2
Guile's Tale

BY THE TIME Brannog and Guile had helped Korbillian into the inn, the huge man had succumbed to his extraordinary ordeal with the sea and had collapsed, unconscious, in their arms. There was now a blazing fire: Eorna had seen to it at once, having observed Brannog on the quay almost from the moment he had gone out there. Now she busied herself bringing logs into the long room and keeping a stock of peat blocks in readiness. Korbillian was stretched across the pelts before the hearth and Guile began stripping the wet clothes from him at once. Eorna made to help, reaching for the long gloves, but Guile gestured her away. For a second his look scared her and she looked to Brannog for guidance, but he shook his head.

"Fetch something warm," he said. "Soup."

She obeyed at once. Brannog had already tossed fresh clothing and skins down at Guile's feet. "You'd be wise to remove your own sodden clothes. A man can die of a chill like that."

Guile satisfied himself that his companion had been made comfortable, however, before he stripped. His body was pale, lean, hardly a muscle visible beneath that taut skin, and his joints stood out in the flickering firelight. Where had his amazing strength come from that he had withstood that terrible cold? No man of Sundhaven would have survived it. Brannog saw before him a gangling figure that looked as though a strong wind could either pick it up and fling it effortlessly aside, or at least snap those

18

brittle-looking bones in a single gust. Yet the key to the man's obvious reserves was his face. The eyes were piercing, the features finely cut, as if wrought by a skillful artist bent on emphasizing character. Intelligent, alert, even now, with exhaustion hovering at his elbow, Guile exuded a natural aura which strangely served to put Brannog on his guard. And Guile somehow had about him a confidence bordering on the insolent, although Brannog had wit enough of his own to allow that this could be his own unfair judgment. Certainly he felt at a disadvantage, yet Guile could surely not match him for strength.

As Eorna returned, Guile finished wrapping himself up in Brannog's welcome furs. Guile eagerly began on the hot soup that the girl placed upon a table beside him. Korbillian remained unconscious, curled up like a huge hound asleep beside the blaze. While Guile ate, the door opened from time to time and the room half filled with fishers, invited by Brannog, their shapes materializing like phantoms from the storm. Outside it had returned, the wind redoubling its efforts to uproot the village and fling it into the sea, just as Guile had said. The air in the hall moved, trembling with draughts that found out each minute chink in the defenses of the building. Dawn had broken, but the men yet needed oil lamps to see by: their wavering flames threw elongated shadows around the room.

"Your name is Guile," said Brannog, so that everyone could hear. He had seen that all the men of the village were now here. He spoke the name in a way that emphasized its peculiarness.

"That is so. It is how I have been named by men who consider themselves to be amusing. Even so, I have adopted it, as it amuses me."

"Are you comfortable enough to speak, or would you prefer to rest before you speak to us?" No one would question Brannog's right to offer this, not in his own home. By bringing the two strangers here he had accepted responsibility for them and for their actions. There were those present, however, who wondered why he had done so.

"I will sleep later, if you will permit me. First, I feel that we owe you certain explanations." Guile said this with more than a hint of a smile on his lips. If it had been meant to set the gathering at ease, it had failed. Guile did not react to their evident suspicion.

Brannog saw no point in prolonging matters and replied bluntly. "Where are you and your companion from, and what is your purpose? When we have heard that, we will decide if we are prepared to act as hosts to you."

"You will hear my companion's side of things when he is well enough to tell you. I give you my word that he will hide none of it from you. As for me—well, I will attempt to explain. My thanks for the broth. It has put back much of what the storm took away." He pushed the empty bowl away, wiping at his mouth with a crooked finger. Leaning back, he eyed the company before him. Other men would have flinched under their combined stares. They could quite easily have torn him limb from limb, these hardy northerners, Guile knew, and yet Brannog had said they would be terrified. They hid that well, Guile noted, but he could sense their fear. Like woodsmoke, it hung heavily on the air.

"You are men of the sea," he told them. "More at home upon it than upon the land, I would surmise. Some of you must have voyaged far out across that ocean outside."

No one as much as intimated that his statements were accurate, but Guile was completely undeterred. He knew that his ease would work to his advantage. "Some of you may well have heard of the Chain of Goldenisle. It is a complex cluster of islands, some of them minute, others quite the reverse. Legends have it that the Chain was once one island, a vast continent, in fact, that the forces of nature saw fit to pull apart." The implication that the elements had acted with a will of their own was not lost on the fishers. Brannog wondered why Guile should couch his words in such a way as to arouse potential derision. He was, however, a stranger.

"I digress. The Chain of Goldenisle. Is it known to you?"

Brannog answered for them. "By word of mouth only. We have no need to fish so far afield. And we could not know if we would be welcome in so remote a place."

Guile chuckled. "Ah, wise! You are probably quite right. To sail unannounced into any of the ports of the Chain (even the tiny southern isles) would probably reap you an unwanted reward. Strange days are upon the Chain. The Emperor, who has taken the liberty of bestowing that grand title upon himself (for he was born a king but could not rest content with that) is at war. Or so he believes. Quite with whom he is at war, no one is sure. But it is considered imprudent to inquire of the Emperor. It is, indeed, less than wise to seek the Emperor's advice on anything. Quanar Remoon, you see, is quite mad. At least, I am convinced of it, as are more than a few of his high-born retainers. However, Quanar Remoon, Most High Descendant of the Bloodline, Emperor of the Chain, and so on, is also extremely powerful. There are those in his court who enjoy a large share in this power, and it well suits them to keep him happily raving atop his priceless throne."

As his rambling tale unfolded, Guile was quite aware that his audience, hostile though it may have been initially, was secretly warming to his words. They were fishers—he had their mark—and it was in their blood to sit beside a fire and weave tales. Instead of cursing him and calling for a swift accounting of himself (which was what they desired foremost) they were ready to listen to his full account. Yet they remained like men hewn from forest oaks.

"The Emperor, in keeping with the peoples of our world of Omara (as far as is known, and much *is* known of Omara in the Chain, for we are a traveled race) does not believe in the existence of gods, and of course, if he did, he would resent having to pay homage to them. Children speak of such things, of course, just as they speculate upon ghosts and other mythological fantasies. But the Emperor has made it quite clear that gods are not to be tolerated. Nor is any belief in magic, high or low, or power of any kind."

"We are not bound by his decrees," cut in Brannog. "Yet these are also strongly held beliefs in Sundhaven."

"Indeed, as they seem to be over much of Omara. Quanar Remoon, however, reserves the right to invest certain amounts of power in himself. He has not yet gone so far as to declare himself a god, although given suitable encouragement, I am certain he would do so. Fortunately he has no magic powers, otherwise he would have worked some ghastly fate upon the whole of Omara. He is as petulant as a child, with no more self control. Well, I have painted a brief picture of my Emperor. I was born in the shadow of the inner citadel's walls, and I have to say here that my people should not be despised, as, for the most part they themselves are not mad. (Possibly some of them are, for I cannot claim to share the acquaintance of them all.) Yet the Emperor is a lunatic, enforcing laws that need no enforcing (being held in common belief) and being repaid with obedience. There is, of course, the war, but as the Emperor is the only one who knows much about that, little is said of it. We do have a most impressive army, and navy, but I have heard no reports of battles.

"Now, I have no great wish to recount my own dull history in any detail. Once I was a man of some position at court, but like all such men I had my enemies, and suffice it to say they found a way to discredit me (a despicable business, a fabrication of lies built around alcohol and certain young ladies) and I was demoted far down the ranks. I became a mere clerk to one of the Administrators, whose task it was to keep an eye on me. I was as good as a prisoner, for my movements were restricted. As a clerk, I did have access to certain information, most of it exceedingly dry and boring, and I was required to keep ledgers and records by the score. My only compensation was that I was able to place my not inobtrusive nose into places where, had it been discovered, it would not have been welcomed." This remark brought not only a rash of smiles from the listeners but a distinct chuckle or two from the half light. "It was from such a position of opportunity that I first learned of the arrival in the city of the man stretched out before you." Guile nodded at Korbillian.

"He comes from afar," he went on, with a deliberate glance at Brannog. "You will hear that tale from him. So, to my own again. It was quite clear from gossip that I managed to glean from the halls of the court that the stranger was, how can I put it? A heretic? His views were, to say the very least, unorthodox, as you shall hear. At any rate, it was murmured that a man had come ashore on one of the lesser isles to the west of the Chain and had declared himself possessed of certain powers. Naturally he was assumed to be a simpleton. Had he chosen another country (if indeed he chose the Chain, I am not sure) he would very probably have been dismissed. Politely but briefly indulged, but ignored soon enough. However, word of this man of supposed power reached the ears of Quanar Remoon. He was unable to resist meeting him. No sooner had the imperial decree been uttered (the Emperor does not make requests, nor issue orders: each gesture is an imperial decree) than the stranger was brought to court. According to my informant's report, there was a guard of some hundred fighting men sent to act as escort. This suggested to me that Quanar Remoon rather took the man's claim to power seriously.

"I could not have hoped to be present at the interview between Emperor and stranger, but something of that auspicious occasion did come down to me. The entire court buzzed in contemplation of the event. Again I must excuse myself from speaking for Korbillian, as he would prefer to do so himself (and I assure you he is far more eloquent than I in unveiling his cause) but I can say that he inspired great consternation. He openly professed to be able to unleash certain powers. How should a nation react to this? With laughter? Or with death? Whatever the choice, none would accept such a thing. And yet the Emperor (believing himself to be possessed of power) confused his subjects by tolerating the stranger and claiming to understand him. He went so far as to hold private conversations with the man, and I am sure that he hoped to learn from him the secrets of the power that he secretly believed him to possess.

"At the time of Korbillian's sojourn in the citadel (although it was incarceration in truth) I was a man of open mind. I had no reason to go against the grain of public belief, the common holding that gods and power are mythologies. By power I speak of magic power, you understand. What some would call sorcery. Not power of position, power over others, control, military power. Oh, I understand all these things. Indeed, yes. Social stature, riches. I had dreamed of them all often. I had none of them, so not unnaturally I was envious of those who had them. My position was now intolerable. Having once been so much better off, I craved a means of reinstating myself. I strove to better myself, though I wondered if the Administrator who watched me was in the keep of my enemies. My curiosity for the stranger was intense, and grew more so. If he *did* possess power, if such a thing were truly possible, then how could someone like myself turn it to my advantage? It was, I agree, a foolish contemplation, but my nights were often taken up with such longings.

"Yet how could I, no more than a clerical menial, hope to meet this closely guarded stranger, much less borrow from him such arts as I could to better myself? I considered countless ways, but discarded each as hopeless. I took to enlisting the help of cheap wine to assist my plans, but in truth the potent stuff (which I was not used to) only enhanced my bitterness and resentment. To reach the stranger, I would need to reach the Emperor first, and this would entail such a complicated chain of command that I could have no hope of getting even close to the inner court. I despaired and drank even more wine. And yet one idea grew in my mind. It was a high risk, but wine makes one laugh at risks.

"One night, quite drunk, I summoned the most superior Administrator that I could (although his rank was not especially high) and I let it be known, quite loudly, that I had been the recipient of a vision. Not a dream, mark you, but a *vision*. It came, I insisted, from the stranger. I would divulge its details to the Emperor alone. My principal fear was that nothing more would be said and that the Administrator, Angat Fulwat, would dismiss the incident at once. At first he sought to drag the secrets of my vision from me (not by torture, as he was anxious that no word of my supposed vision reached other ears and brought officials running, dripping curiosity). I held resolutely to my desire to speak of the vision only to the Emperor.

"Angat Fulwat was equally resolute. Quanar Remoon did not speak to lowly clerks, much less discredited ones. 'It is for your own good that you are kept away from the inner court,' he told me stiffly. 'I doubt that he knows of your indiscretions personally, but if he did so, you can imagine what he would have done to you. He can be extremely unpleasant when it suits him.' That sobered me. I saw at once the strong argument of his words and realized I had allowed the wine to speak for me. 'Forgive me,' I told the Administrator. 'I overreach myself.' He seemed suddenly very thoughtful. 'Mind you,' he said at last, 'you do have a point. This vision may be of vast importance. The Emperor is anxious to solve the riddle posed by the stranger.' 'I will describe it to you atonce,' I told him, but he shook his head. 'You will not! As you rightly say, the Emperor alone should hear of it.' With that he left me, now a very sober man, to my thoughts. I had trapped myself.

"Word was sent to the Emperor, unfortunately bypassing my enemies who would have snuffed it out, and he sent a dozen of his Imperial Killers to fetch me. Their title had always seemed rather pompous to me, as I doubted that any of them had ever killed anything larger than a cockroach, but when they confronted me, complete with armoured regalia, I promise you, my bowels almost betrayed me. The Killers were most awesome, and it struck me then that every one of them had doubtless been chosen as he had killed in his time, likely beginning with the least favorite member of his own family.''—Again there were chuckles among the fishers. Brannog would have smiled, but the business of the vision, however spurious, bothered him. Even so, he liked the man's honesty, although there were still many disturbing things about his arrival here that had to be resolved. He had said nothing of the man he called Korbillian, and yet had told Brannog privately that he was a man of another world. Such things were not possible.

"I was taken directly to Quanar Remoon, and although I had glimpsed him from time to time, this was the first occasion on which I had faced him close to. He was remarkably young and handsome, but his eyes spoke quite clearly of his madness. They never seemed to fix upon anything for more than a few seconds, as if he spent his waking hours gazing deeply into a world that no one else knows existed. Again, he would smile at unexpected moments, scowl inappropriately, or sigh or chuckle entirely at odds with conversations or events around him. Fortunately I was presented to him on a night when his humor was predominantly good. Angat Fulwat, to my undying gratitude, had seen to it that nothing of my past history had reached his ears before my interview. He would, Angat told me, otherwise have assumed me an assassin.

"It was only when I stood before him that it came to me that I must be at least as insane as the Emperor, otherwise I would never have let my tongue drag me into the situation I was in.

" 'Ah,' said Quanar Remoon, with a smile that I felt in my stomach, 'I perceive the man of vision.' You note he did not use the plural, thus totally obscuring the meaning. Again my stomach curdled. What, precisely, was he expecting of me? 'I am most interested in what you have to say.' He was, incidently, paying considerable attention to a fly, and I wondered at any possibility of his addressing it rather than myself. There was no one else present.

" 'I must crave forgiveness, Lord Emperor, for having disturbed you with my dreams, but I thought it most prudent that you hear their content as you are known to be highly astute.'

" 'I was not chosen as Emperor purely because I was my father's son,' he commented, as though a great philosopher propounding a vast theory of life. I retained sufficient sanity not to argue. 'Well,' he went on impatiently. 'We are alone. I will hear more.' He sat and involved his hands with a bowl of rich fruit, so that again I could not be sure that he was listening to me. 'In my dream,' I began, 'I saw a man, a strange man, not of your Empire, who came out of the western darkness, wielding strange powers. He was making his way to your very gates, Lord Emperor. I feared that he would sunder them and advance upon your city.' I said no more for the moment, hoping to assess his preliminary reaction.

" 'Powers? What powers?' he replied, words muffled by the peach he was sucking.

" 'This man is lying,' came a cold, stern voice, and I shuddered as if someone had cast a bucket of icy water over me from behind. The strange man I had heard of (I had no doubt at all that this was the very same) had stepped from behind a pillar, quite brazenly, and now stood menacingly before me. Oddly, it was not his face that drew my eyes (although I had never seen its like before) but his arms. He had placed them on his hips, and from elbow to fingertip they were sheathed in gloves, as though dipped in midnight.'' Precisely as Guile had intended, every eye in the room went to the arms of the man stretched before the fire. The unusual gloves were clearly visible.

" 'Why do you say so, Korbillian?' demanded Quanar Remoon casually.

" 'Kill him at once,' was the retort. 'He is no more than an ambitious menial, seeking to impress.' As I heard this death knell, tolling my demise, as it were, I could already see my head adorning some high parapet of the inner courtyard. The Emperor rose at once but turned his back on both of us. He paced away, seemingly lost in thought, just as though his next decision would have repercussions the length and breadth of his Empire. As he moved away, Korbillian brushed past me, and his voice was a silken whisper.

" 'I have just saved you from death,' he staggered me by saying. 'The Emperor likes to make decisions for himself. No one else is allowed an original thought. Keep your wits, man.'

" 'What do you want?' I whispered back, my eyes fixed on the Emperor's back. He could hear nothing of our secret exchange.

" 'I am a prisoner. I must not remain here. Trust me, as I will you. You must get me away.'

"The Emperor turned around, took a deep breath, then emitted a weighty sigh. 'No, Korbillian. I have read his mind. Oh yes, a shock to you both. But I have already hinted at the powers I possess. And this man does not lie. He saw you in his vision, lusting for my city and for my power. It is time to dispense with subterfuge.'

" 'I am not your enemy,' replied Korbillian in such a way that it was evident that he had spoken the words many times previously. 'I came here to warn you.' I was naturally intrigued, but Korbillian did not elaborate.

"The Emperor waved his words away. 'My man,' he addressed me (as a father addresses a son almost) and beckoned me to him. I went nervously. 'Kill you? Absurd. A trick. No. Now tell me about this strange man. Who is he? What is his purpose? Your dreams can unlock the truth he has hidden from me.'

" 'My dreams, Lord Emperor, were so confused, so disjointed—.'

" 'No matter. Reveal them. They will not confuse your Emperor.' His arm was about me (though I would have preferred the embrace of a constrictor) and his eyes closed in anticipation of I knew not what. But I chose the easiest course. I recited several dreams (all totally fabricated) which were as grotesque and obscure as my imagination could make them, riddled with symbols and splintered actions. At the end of my exhaustive confession, the Emperor nodded and began pacing about. He looked at Korbillian with a knowing smile. 'These are things you did not tell me,' he said. 'Things you sought to hide from me.'

" 'They are the ramblings of an idiot,' said Korbillian, quite correctly, I have to confess, but he had the measure of Quanar Remoon, who seemed to believe exactly the opposite of anything the stranger told him. In a while I saw that jealousy was the reason for this.

" 'What do my visions mean?' I asked innocently. 'Have I done right in confiding them to you?'

" 'Indeed!' laughed the Emperor. 'Yes, indeed! Quite

clearly this man has come here to poison me, usurp my throne, cast down my loyal Administrators, replace them with his own men (men who lurk within the city already, your dreams suggest) and carry war to the whole of Omara. You deny this?' he flung at Korbillian.

"Korbillian stared at him, and his coolness amazed me. 'Quanar,' he said after a moment, 'you said those very words to me when I first came to you. I denied them then; I deny them now. I am here to serve you.'

"The Emperor turned back to me. 'Tell him!' he laughed. 'Yes, tell him!'

"I gaped. 'Lord?'

" 'The dream—the final dream! Tell this upstart what happened in your last vision, the climax to your gaze into the future. Tell him the fate meted out to him.'

"My mind was racing like a rat trapped by fire, but a shaft of inspiration stabbed at me. 'Oh, Lord Emperor!' I cried, dropping to my knees dramatically. 'It was you, *you* who sent the visions! Your power cannot be denied. You sent these visions to me.'

"He scowled down thunderously, and if he had been holding a sword, I am sure he would have split my skull in two with it. Then his smile returned. 'Of course,' he agreed gently. 'You understand. *I* sent the visions. I will not explain why; the mystery is too deep for you.'

" 'And the final vision—the fate of Korbillian—that too. You showed me how you had decided not to kill the stranger, but to grant him a fate much worse than that, more painful, more enduring.'

"Quanar Remoon's smile faded. Had I overplayed my part? 'Was the stranger not executed?' he demanded. 'His pieces not scattered throughout the Empire, one to every island in the Chain?'

" 'You are too cunning, too far-sighted,' I bowed. 'You banished him to the eastern lands, Lord, placing upon him your curse, that he would tread their wastes for a thousand years.' It was the first thing that occurred to me, for in the city we had heard only the faintest rumor as to what lies in the interior of the great eastern land mass.

" 'You have recalled every detail precisely, save one,'

corrected the Emperor. 'It was for a hundred thousand years.'

" 'Ah, even so,' I bowed again.

"Korbillian had listened to this without a flicker of emotion, yet somehow I sensed his amusement. 'I salute your genius,' he told Quanar Remoon. 'To kill me would have brought my followers out from their holes like locusts. But to banish me,' he sighed. 'Too clever. Now my followers will never find me, though of course you will have it announced that I have left. Doubtless you will not tell them where you have sent me?'

" 'You are wrong. I will announce that I have sent you, under escort, to toil in the quarries of the far western archipelagos. Your followers can spend their time digging for you there.'

"Korbillian bowed to this seeming masterplay. 'No one but you will know the truth,' he told the Emperor. 'Except, of course, this man.' His words chilled me. I had assumed, for some reason, that we were allies, as we had been teamed against our mad ruler. But now I was unsure, I knew nothing of the man's true purpose. 'Unless you kill him, as I have already suggested,' he added.

" 'What pleasure it would give your enemy, Lord,' I hastily cut in. 'To see you kill the man who has unmasked him.'

"Quanar Remoon frowned. 'And yet you would have the truth, the location of his banishment. One indiscreet word and his followers would find him. I cannot risk that. Ah, of course! I will have your tongue cut out. And your hands will have to be struck off.'

" 'I would rather die, Lord Emperor!'

" 'And have this traitor laugh? I'll not permit it.'

" 'Then I must make the necessary sacrifice, Lord,' I babbled on. 'The one hinted at in another dream, that I had not connected with this business, and yet which now, clearly, I see—'

" 'I do not recall having sent any further dreams,' retorted the Emperor, and my heart shrivelled under his gaze. 'And yet, you speak of sacrifice?'

" 'Yes, Lord. I have done what little I can to serve you.

Now I have become a burden to you. Let me depart, therefore. Let me leave the Chain of Goldenisle, not to wander in exile, but to find a home elsewhere, where the secrets known to me can never fall into the hands of your enemies.'

" 'I can recall the dream now,' said the Emperor. 'Of course I do. The remote shores of the eastern lands.'

" 'And for me?' I asked.

" 'I have said.'

" 'I thought you meant that for him, Lord Emperor?'

" 'Indeed. But the details have come back to me. Since I am to send a ship to the remote east, I must place on board some apparent representative, otherwise people would wonder at the ship's going. You will be that man. I will invest in you some wondrous cause, the conversion of the wild people of the interior. The formation of an outpost of Empire. And down in the hold of the ship will be this wicked man. Of course, once you have landed, you may both go your separate ways. Was not that the essence of the dream?'

" 'The minutest detail is precise,' I agreed at once, although I was not a happy man.''

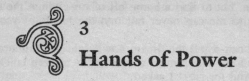

3
Hands of Power

WHATEVER UNEXPLAINED POWER had given Guile the strength to survive the storm and sit before the gathered villagers to deliver his tale was at last beginning to drain out of him, and he began to look drawn. As he had reached what appeared to be a natural break in his tale, Brannog stepped forward and leaned across the table.

"Perhaps you will give us what remains of your tale after you have rested," he suggested.

Guile sighed gustily and slumped back, though it was no theatrical gesture. "There is little more to tell. Quanar Remoon put us on a ship and we left the Chain the following day. His sailors had no liking for either of us—we might have had some grim plague for the way they treated us—so that when we came within first sight of your continent, they put us in the smaller craft and set us loose. The storm had already begun. I think they expected us to drown." He gave a prolonged yawn, rubbing at the salt that coated his face. "Aye. Sleep would be most welcome."

"I will find you a bed."

"No need. This is all I require. What a relief it is to have land beneath me again. I could sleep upon marble!" Almost at once he had crossed to one of the bare benches before the fire, curling up on it, and like a cat had fallen asleep, though it was evident that his sleep was no cat-nap, but more like that of a man drugged. Within moments a murmur had broken out among Brannog's folk.

"He weaves a pretty tale," said Gronen, one of the elders, his face creased even more by consternation than by age. "But I for one am full of misgivings. You speak as the host, Brannog. What do you say to this strangest of tales?"

Brannog shrugged. "It is a half-finished tapestry. It presents us with more mysteries than it solves. The Emperor that he spoke of may well have been mad. If he believed himself to possess powers—magical powers—there would have been grounds to call him mad. But this man Korbillian also claims power. Are we agreed on what we saw outside?"

With the coming of dawn beyond the windows and the sudden bright sunlight on the sea, the storm had finally abated. Yet the echoes of its fury remained. "There was much talk," said another of them, Hengrom, a man of Brannog's age, "of dreams. Could it be that what we have seen was illusion?"

"I know what I saw," protested Yarnol with a sneer, and there was mutual agreement. It had been a shared experience.

Hengrom was determined, however, to put his point of view. "The man Guile spoke of visions sent to him by his Emperor. It was a trick of the tongue to baffle him, and a good one, but is it possible that a man can have the power to send dreams or illusions into the minds of others?"

Gronen snorted. "I know of countries where you would be executed for even speaking such a thing."

"But I beg you to consider," went on Hengrom, with respect for the elder, "if no illusion, then how are we to account for the breaking of that wave? Sundhaven should have been swept away by it—every last stone."

"I, too, would seek natural answers," said Brannog. "Otherwise we would see the fabric of our beliefs tearing before us. All I would say for now is, let us at least prepare ourselves for the possibility that this man Korbillian has tapped some source about which we know nothing. We must hear him speak before judging him."

Gronen nodded. "I am not sure that we have the right to judge him. Perhaps we should allow him and his companion (I am not sure that Guile is not his servant, even his slave) to go from here unhindered. Be done with them both when they are recovered.''

Yarnol agreed noisily. "Aye. Guile claims the Emperor is mad. But perhaps Quanar Remoon was no more than furious that these men should claim power between them. Perhaps they fled the Chain of Goldenisle and the wrath of the Emperor. In which case, it would be foolish to harbor them.''

Hengrom was not so easily persuaded. "And yet, if they have saved our village from destruction, are we not in their debt?''

Brannog listened to the discussion mounting, and after a while put a stop to it. "The least we must do is hear them out. I feel they owe us the truth, no more. When we have that, we must consider what to do. Guile has said that he and his companion wish to explain themselves. For the moment, we must admit, they have thrown themselves on our mercy. Would it not be easy to kill them where they lie?''

"I agree,'' nodded Gronen with a dignified cough that was meant to imply that these had been his feelings from the beginning.

Quietly the men dispersed, knowing that Brannog would send word to them all when the strangers were refreshed and ready to deliver up more of their history. As Brannog bolted his door (though there was no longer a need to do so) and turned back to the silent hall, he saw Eorna watching him. She offered him food and he nodded, sitting near the sleepers.

"My thanks,'' he breathed, looking into the fire. For a moment Eorna lingered. He knew that she had listened to every word that had passed here, but did not begrudge her that. It was right that the women of the village should know. As the girl withdrew, he felt himself shiver. Dreams. All this talk of dreams, and of sendings. Sisipher's dreams worried at his mind anew. She had known Korbillian would come. Why had he, Brannog, not told his fellows this? Why had he not confessed? They would have believed him. But he knew why. Fear. Fear that they would recognize in

Sisipher the gift of telling, the curse. They did not believe in such things, and so when they appeared, they were to be destroyed. Abruptly he turned—Eorna. But she had gone. What must she be thinking? Had she read anything into Sisipher's words? It angered him now that she had been there.

"Eorna," he said to a moving shadow, but as the light struck it, he saw the face of his daughter. He felt guilty at once.

She came to him and touched his shoulder, as if healing some wound. His arm encircled her. "Is she your lover?" she asked him lightly.

He bristled and she regretted having said it. "She is not," he said, but then smiled. "You should have slept on."

"I am awake now, father. I heard voices. Who are these men at the hearth?" She studied the recumbent figures without alarm, but seemed puzzled. Travelers were rare in Sundhaven, especially in winter.

"Cast up by the storm and fortunate to be alive. We must leave them to rest." He stood up, preparing to shepherd her from the hall, but she had slipped past him. She looked briefly at Guile, seemingly unimpressed by him, but as her eyes fell upon the face of Korbillian she recoiled.

Brannog was beside her at once. "A face of rare anguish," he said, but he knew the truth.

"I have seen him, father! That terrible face. In my dreams—"

"Nonsense, girl. You imagine such things." He pulled her to him and could feel her trembling.

"No. I somehow knew he would come to us."

Brannog lacked the strength to deny what was within her. If there was some kind of poison there, it must be drawn out. He stroked her hair gently. "Sisipher, what do you know of him?" he said very softly. "Has he brought harm to us?"

Slowly, as if dazed, she shook her head. She was trying to see through a veil. "I somehow think not, father. But he will speak of evil, I am sure. I think he comes to warn us.''

He shuddered and she reacted at once. ''What is it, father?'' Her hands dug into his arms, but again he soothed her.

''His companion claims that he is a man of power. You must know that such a thing cannot be.''

She nodded, though with uncertainty. ''I don't understand such things. But I have a strong feeling that we must help him.''

''Of what can he wish to warn us? What evil?''

''It is only for him to tell us. But father, I think it is not of our world. Oh, I know you still think of me as a child, with a child's wild fancies, but I sense things sometimes. This man is true.'' Her eyes searched his for anger, for disbelief, yet found an unexpected understanding. ''Am I mad to suggest this?''

Grimly he smiled. ''No. Not mad. There may be something in what you say.''

''But how can I know these things?''

This time he did not lead her away. ''It is a mystery,'' he lied. ''But it is our secret, too. Let the man speak for himself, when he is ready. The men will hear him out.''

''Of course, father. Where's Eorna? I'm famished.''

It was not until well into the afternoon that the two sleepers by the fire stirred. Brannog had decided to send to his fellows later, rather than subject the two men to questions at once. For some reason—possibly Sisipher's attitude—he was prepared to accept the men as not being hostile. Korbillian awoke first, and a moment later Guile sat up. Brannog was near at hand.

''More food?'' he asked.

''You are generous,'' said Korbillian. ''Whatever you can spare will be appreciated.'' He reached into a pocket and placed coins upon the table.

Guile chortled. ''Quanar's money is no use here! Even I can see that. Or am I mistaken, host?''

Brannog waved the money away. ''We are fishermen. What we have, we trade for what we need. I could exchange your coins down along the coastal lowlands, perhaps. But there is no need to pay."

"The winter has been hard," said Guile, apparently for the benefit of his companion. "You can have little to spare."

"Is this true?" Korbillian asked Brannog.

"Accept my food. There is enough." He looked at the face of this stranger, quietly shocked by it. It seemed to be the face of a man—a man who had been young until recently—who had undergone some dire ordeal and failed. It seemed exhausted, drained, and yet still retained some spark, some dogged resistance to whatever knowledge it carried, almost like a man who is sure that today he will die, but even so will cling to the hope that he will not. "What is it that you want from Sundhaven?" Brannog asked.

"Since you ask," said Korbillian, "maps."

"Maps? Of what?" The reply had taken Brannog by surprise. He noticed Eorna hovering in the background and felt a pang of anger. Curtly he snapped at her to fetch some food and water.

"My goal lies in the east, somewhere at the heart of this continent," said Korbillian. "I need maps to show me how to get there. Have you any?"

"We are fishermen," repeated Brannog. "We look to the west and the open sea. Our charts are in our heads. We have nothing written down. No books. I have seen such things at southern fairs, but we have none. As for the east—firstly there are the mountains and the glaciers. I know of no one from this village who has gone beyond them, or even climbed high into them. I heard once that there are forests beyond, but to the south east nothing but desert."

"I see," mused Korbillian. "Can anyone guide me up into the mountains? Is there a pass, nothing more?"

"I will ask. Some of the youths like to test themselves against the strength of the mountains. But you have chosen winter to travel in. I doubt that anyone of Sundhaven would wish to climb now, whatever you might offer him."

"Not for gold," said Guile, with a broad grin. "But for a good sea harvest, perhaps?"

Korbillian turned a look upon him of such heat that he looked away at once, the smile melting. "Do not speak for me," Korbillian told him curtly.

"I will ask," Brannog said.

Korbillian drew back as Eorna brought food and the big man was careful to keep his gloved hands beneath the table, as though they offended him. Brannog saw this, but said nothing.

Guile seemed anxious to restore a better mood. "I have explained something of our past," he told Korbillian, and briefly sketched for him the tale he had given to the villagers.

Korbillian ate slowly and thoughtfully. He turned to Brannog. "Very well. Call your people. I must explain myself. I am anxious that they do not assume us to be enemies, or dangerous."

Brannog spoke to Eorna, and silently she left to go and spread the word. Brannog unlocked his door. As he turned to speak, Sisipher entered. Her expression betrayed her anxiety. Before her was the face that had haunted her dreams. It seemed even more pained in reality. When Korbillian saw her, he ceased eating at once and rose, inclining his body politely. He was huge, dwarfing Guile, who also stared at the girl, though his expression was very different. Guile saw before him a beautiful creature that took his breath away; he had lost count of the dreamy, empty-headed thralls of the Emperor's palace that had swarmed about the imperial chambers. None of them, for all their cosmetic skill, could compare with this sweet innocence. Sisipher, however, had eyes only for Korbillian, though it was not with love or admiration that she looked upon him, but with trepidation.

"My daughter," said Brannog, tensing. Did Korbillian already know of her gift? Did he know of Frostwalk, or have kin there? Brannog found himself unable to resist the admission, "She is from Frostwalk."

"Where is that?" said Korbillian courteously, and Brannog felt sure it was no act. He knew nothing of it,

and could not have been there. The fear that he had somehow come here to find Sisipher partially drained from
Brannog.

"Father!" protested the girl. "I've lived in Sundhaven
most of my life." Why ever did he say that? she was
wondering.

Korbillian seemed to interpret something in the exchange, but he did not comment.

"Have you eaten and rested sufficiently?" Brannog said
after a pause. Guile and Korbillian nodded. Brannog
wanted to send Sisipher away, still unsure of her safety,
but he did not seek a scene. He hoped that she said nothing of her dreams and of her gift. In fact, no one said
more than a few words until the men of the village began
to arrive. They eyed Korbillian with open uncertainty,
standing shoulder to shoulder in the hall. Every man had
come, even the very old. They each nodded to Brannog,
who at last established that they were ready. He turned
again to Korbillian and Guile.

"You must forgive us if we are blunt, but you have
brought much confusion to Sundhaven."

Korbillian nodded. "Guile has told you how we came
here. It is for me to explain other things to you. Things
that may anger you, though I will accept that risk." He
took a great breath and stared at them. For a moment he
looked like a man who has reached a critical point in his
challenge upon life, and who has found that he has not
got the strength to persevere and must admit defeat. But
he stirred himself and began. "I must ask you to reverse
your ideas, your concepts of your world, question your
security, all this and more. I do, truly, bring confusion to
you, but at least I can promise you nothing but truth, and
I ask you to remember these words. All that I am to tell
you is truth. I am a man who *must* deliver the truth to you
and all your world, though I know that so few will believe
it. Guile has come to believe me. So far, he is the only
man of Omara who has. Yet I am sure of my purpose and
will not waver from it." His strength seeped back into
him as he spoke, and his eyes met theirs evenly. "There
is an evil in your world, a terrible evil and I have come to

destroy it. That is the prime truth. If you can believe that, then there is hope for its eventual destruction.''

Yarnol cleared his throat and spoke as firmly as the stranger had. ''Who told you to bring us this truth?'' He looked directly at Brannog, remembering that it had been him who spoke of truth earlier.

''No one has instructed me,'' said Korbillian. ''I have no master, and like the men of your world, I owe my allegiance to no gods.''

''Our world?'' said another of the elders. ''You speak of this part of it, or of all Omara? From which part of Omara do you come? It has not been made clear.''

Korbillian looked directly at the old man. ''I am not from Omara. There are other worlds. That is another truth you will have to accept.''

''And if we do not?'' said Gronen tersely.

''You must.'' It was Sisipher who had spoken, and at once the room fell absolutely silent. Brannog could feel a sheen of perspiration on his forehead. He could neither move nor speak, though he wanted to cry out in protest. Never before had he been more acutely aware of his daughter's uniqueness, and of the villagers' wariness of it.

Korbillian looked at the girl, then back to Gronen. ''If you do not, then I must begin again, as I have done before.''

''Begin what?'' challenged Hengrom.

''Let him speak!'' snapped Brannog before his daughter could say anything more.

''You all live,'' went on Korbillian, ''in a peaceful world, a world without gods or power. Such things do not exist here; or rather, they did not. Yet I am here, a man from another world, a world which you would find incomprehensible, for in it everyone has a degree of power. I speak, for convenience, of magic. Each man and woman of my world, Ternannoc, has power. Some have a little, some much, and a few have vast power.'' He paused to let them consider this. They did not react openly, but Brannog could feel their minds rejecting the idea. Even in his own mind there was a strong doubt. Sisipher *knew* Korbillian spoke honestly. He was no madman, not as

Quanar Remoon was mad. And they had all seen a demonstration that he possessed power, even if it had been illusion, which he refused to believe.

As though Korbillian had heard Brannog's very thought at that moment, he held up both gloved arms. "I possess power, I will not deny it. I see you flinch before it. Part of you believes the truth. You have seen me use it. It is not something I would have chosen to do, because I know what fears it must hold for you. But it was necessary. The wave would have destroyed your village.

"In Ternannoc such forces of nature could be tamed by certain men, but not by all. Most powerful of all the men of my world were the Hierarchs. Individually they were men who wielded power with great skill, and there were women also who possessed such skills." He glanced at Sisipher as he said this, and his look was not lost on Brannog. It was as though a clouded part of the big fisherman's mind was slowly clearing. Eorna was there, too, eager to hear this tale, but Brannog had not noticed her. "Individually, I repeat, the Hierarchs were very strong. They operated in different parts of our world, working mostly for the benefit of all. Ternannoc was no perfect world, for there was strife, even war in places, but it was a good world."

"Strange," said Yarnol quietly, though everyone heard him, "that you have left it."

Korbillian's face seemed even more anguished, almost as if he had been stabbed. "I had no choice," he breathed. "Ternannoc is dead. The Hierarchs destroyed it." If anything convinced the men that he was being honest, it was his face. No man could act out those lines of despair. "At a gathering of the Hierarchs, one of them spoke about other worlds that he was certain existed. He did not speak of the stars, for the skies of Ternannoc were no less spangled than the night skies of Omara, spangled with worlds impossible to reach across the frozen immensities of space. He spoke of worlds around us, aligned in some way to our own. It would be possible, this Hierarch promised, to open gates to these worlds, and in time he persuaded the gathering that it must be so. I will not try to explain this. It is another truth you must accept.

"In order to open these gates, the Hierarchs were told, it would be necessary for them to combine their power in a working that would release more power than had ever been released before. There was a great deal of argument over that. Yet in the main, the Hierarchs were in favor of this working, for the possibilities were too intriguing to ignore, though some talked of the dangers of releasing such power. Surely, they argued, too little was known of what could happen. For days the debate raged, but the lure of other worlds was great. So, a decision was reached. The working was to be effected." Korbillian shook his head despondently. "They should have been content. Ternannoc was a fine world, with beauty enough."

"This working," said Brannog, "it failed?"

Korbillian shook his head again. "It opened the gates to other worlds, but it was like an explosion that throws out gouts of molten fire, volcanic and destructive. Ternannoc died, slowly, like a mortally wounded beast. Such gates as were opened were like wounds in the worlds beyond them, wounds into which poison flowed. Power, but blackened power, like disease. Some worlds perished along with Ternannoc. Others were not harmed. The gates held, some for a long time, but in the end they all closed again, as flesh closes over a wound, so that the paths between the worlds were sealed once more.

"During the time that the gates were opened some of us managed to flee our world. I cannot say how many of us survived. For many years our scattered people settled on other worlds, adopting them and starting new colonies. It is long in the past, this first migration from Ternannoc. Many generations have passed since it happened. But not all of those who first fled Ternannoc have died. It is a gift of our world that some of us, and I am one, live far longer than normal men. And it seems that the passing through the gates somehow prolongs or alters the power. When I left my world, knowing there was nothing more that could be done to save it, I traveled through several gates. I found worlds where the power of the working was eating into the heart of those worlds, destroying them as surely as a canker destroys its victim. My task was clear. I determined to use my power to try to destroy the power of the Hierarchs' working. A mad dream, perhaps.''

He paused and did not seem to be aware that he had an audience. Instead of the faces, he saw before him some ravaged landscape, or some violent destruction. He shook himself wearily. ''On four worlds I attempted to reverse the effects of the power. Each time I failed. The grip was too strong for me alone. I moved on into another world, and behind me the gate decayed and died. I knew there would be no more gates, no more time.''

''Omara,'' said Sisipher.

''Omara,'' he nodded.

''The evil is here?'' gasped Gronen.

''At first I thought not. I was far to the west of here, and in southern lands I searched. But over the years I have spent in your world, I have felt it. I must find it. It grows stronger, but is not as strong as the power I have tried to beat before. There is time for me to succeed here. But,'' he went on, ''I must have help. I must win the belief of the people of Omara. People such as yourselves. I have tried. I thought that in the Chain of Goldenisle, a strong Empire, I would find help, but when I sought to impress its Emperor, I found a man without reason.''

''So Guile has told us,'' said Hengrom.

''Did he tell you also that without his own quick wit, I would be a prisoner of Quanar Remoon yet?''

''If you have power,'' said Yarnol, ''why did you not use it to win free of him?''

Korbillian smiled, but it seemed to take an effort. The question was predictable, but reasonable. ''Even without power, I could have killed him. He was like a child. I could have slipped a knife into him, for we were often alone and there were weapons about his palace within reach. But if I had slain him, I would have had to have done the same to half of his palace. I had no wish to indulge in such slaughter. It seemed to be exactly the reverse of what I came to Omara to achieve. Also I was sinking into a despairing mood, fearing that it was pointless to attempt my grand dream. It was only when Guile arrived that I decided to steel myself. His tongue proved stronger than a knife.''

Guile bowed, and for him the smile was effortless. ''And so to sea. By now the Emperor will not even recall us.''

''Our captors listened to what I have told you of Ternannoc,'' Korbillian told the fishers. ''I tried to enlist their help, but they held only derision for me. I think they would have killed both of us had they not been a little wary. Some dozen leagues from your shores, they cast us adrift.''

''We should have perished,'' said Guile. ''Just as the Emperor's ship must have.''

''They drowned?'' said Brannog.

''Perhaps,'' admitted Korbillian, and for a moment there was silence, for the fear of drowning hung over all the fishers.

''But you survived,'' said Brannog. ''How?''

''By my arts,'' said Korbillian, as if describing the simplest of acts. ''I deflected the storm, though the power behind it was awesome. I have wondered about that. Is your coast familiar with such blasts?''

Brannog scanned the faces of his people. None of them would have denied that the storm had been out of proportion to the worst of that winter's excesses.

''And the wave,'' said Korbillian, ''the wave that came not from the east as the storm did, but from the *sea*. What of that?''

''There has never been such a wave before,'' said a youth who had pushed himself to the fore of the watchers. His eyes were alive with excitement. The men would have cuffed him for daring to speak out of turn, but his words were perfectly accurate. None denied them. The wave had been beyond anything seen before.

''I thought not,'' said Korbillian. ''It required much power to divert.'' He considered this in silence.

''This evil of which you speak,'' said Gronen. ''I have been alive more years than most of Sundhaven's children, but have heard almost nothing of the inner lands. No word has ever reached us here of an evil beyond the mountains. What is the nature of this evil?''

"Just as a disease runs in the blood of a man, just as a poison courses his veins, so does this black power run beneath the earth. Omara is like a man with an evil growth in him. It is mindless power, with no purpose, but it spreads. Only when it has consumed Omara will it cease, for it, too, will perish with its host."

"How are you to destroy it?"

"I must find as many people as I can who have either power, or remnants of power, or who will lend me the strength of their arm or heart. Power comes from the earth. There must be power in Omara."

Brannog again felt himself going cold. "You say there are people with power? Who are they? Men of Omara?"

"There must have been many people of my world who fled its destruction and came here before the gate closed. I suspect that their descendants now abjure power and will have nothing more to do with it, word of its potential having been passed down through time. Now they would welcome the Omaran belief that there is no power."

Yes, thought Brannog, and so I see the picture clearly. He speaks of people like the reclusive villagers of Frost-walk, descendants of these runaways. Like my own wife, and our child, Sisipher. Is it from this that I have sheltered her? Is this to be her destiny?

"So long ago," said Korbillian. "The legends of these people will be faint. They may not even be aware of the power within them. Even so, I have to search for them, to persuade them."

"How will you know them?" said Gronen.

Korbillian looked impassively at the elder. "I will know them," he said, and to Brannog it was as if he had already pointed a finger directly at his daughter.

4
The Gift

THEY HAD LISTENED PATIENTLY to Korbillian for an hour before he concluded his story. He seemed tired, as if talking had taxed him even more than his actions in the harbour. When he fell silent, no one seemed sure what to say, or how to react.

"I think," said Brannog, "Korbillian and Guile should retire for a while. I have a room I am willing to let them use. Gronen? Hengrom? Yarnol? What do you say?"

There was no disagreement. "We must discuss these matters," the elder told Korbillian. "Though it will not be for long," he added pointedly.

"Come with me," Brannog told his guests and they followed him to the stairs. Their host took them up to an unused bedroom. There were pelts and blankets on the wooden bed. Brannog held his lamp high as they entered, for the late afternoon was already darkening the sky.

"They believe very little," said Korbillian.

Brannog knew that he was expected to reply. "I think none of them will help you. How could they?"

"Tomorrow I must begin the ascent of the mountains. Will none come with me? You, Brannog?"

"To what end? I have never been there, and would lose us. There is that young puppy, Wolgren. Little more than a boy, but he boasts to have scaled some of the heights. You understand how young men must parade their prowess. How far his boasts are true is arguable."

"Would he come?"

46

"I will not speak for him. But the others, well, they are men of the sea, as you said. Our lives are simple enough, oh aye, hard. But we struggle this winter to live. Our existence here is threatened by the cold, and by starvation. That is what we fight. We have little time for your unseen evil. You must understand that." Brannog spoke calmly and reasonably.

Korbillian nodded tiredly. He had heard such words before, many times. "Yes, of course. But you can help."

"I?"

"Your daughter."

Brannog felt again the cold clutch of his fears. He had known this would come, but it still felt like the turn of the knife. "How can she help?"

"Surely you must know."

Brannog considered denial, but only for a moment. He nodded.

"She has power," Korbillian went on. "Have you masked your knowledge from her as well as from others?"

"It is true," Brannog sighed, knowing that he had to relieve himself of the burden of hiding it.

"Does the girl realize?"

Brannog shook his head. "No. No one is aware of it. Bad dreams, they know that much, no more."

"She has the gift of telling."

Brannog was not shocked by Korbillian's simple statement. He had known that the stranger had seen it as soon as he met the girl, but still it frightened him. He could feel his grip on his daughter slipping. "She has. But she has never used it."

"Will you allow her to try?"

Brannog flinched under Korbillian's gaze. It had become desperate. "I will not force her. If she chooses not to—"

"That is good," said Korbillian. "I would do much harm if I sought to bend the power of others. It must be freely given. Listen, after your people have gone, we must talk. And any others that will stay."

"Very well."

"If your daughter consents, will you allow her to open her eyes on tomorrow for me? I do not have her gift."

Brannog hesitated. He put the lamp down for them. "Aye, if she is willing. But no harm must come to her. If it does, power or not, I will seek vengeance."

"No harm," agreed Korbillian.

"No harm," echoed Guile from the shadows, but Brannog could not see his face. Brannog left them, and as he returned through clinging darkness to the gathering below, his mind churned. He felt a sharp premonition that he would lose Sisipher, but shrugged it off. As he rejoined his fellows, he saw at once that more than a few of them had already gone. They wanted no more of this stranger and the confusion he had brought. Gronen remained at the forefront of the fishers.

"Well?" he said clearly, and it was a challenge.

"Why must you look to me?" Brannog growled at them. "I am not your custodian. You are responsible for yourselves! You all heard this man from another world."

"You believe that?" said Hengrom, whose face indicated that he, too, believed it. "And in power? A world where *everyone* has that power?"

"What reason can this man have to lie? I told you that all we should ask of him was the truth. I do not consider him to be mad," said Brannog. Why am I defending him? He seeks my daughter, and yet I seem to be supporting him! If I spoke against him now, the village would throw him out.

"It seems," said Gronen, "that he asks for things which are not to be found in Sundhaven. Maps. There are none. And no one to speak of the interior. Had he asked for sea passage, perhaps I would have considered helping him. But not now. Who wishes to die in a land that has not been heard of?"

Many voices were in agreement, just as Brannog had guessed.

"Tomorrow," he said, "they will leave us. This Korbillian has promised me. He is intent upon crossing the mountains and will not be dissuaded. I will give him what provisions I can spare."

"Let us wish him well," said Hengrom. "Whatever his cause. He has not harmed us. I, too, will give provisions. But I think the man is foolish to leave Sundhaven, particularly for the mountains. Who could live up there?"

No one was prepared to act as guide. The youth, Wolgren, kept silent, and Brannog tried to read his eyes, but could not. He knew, though, that he would discreetly ask the boy to remain. "And what are we to say to other men we meet, on the seas, or at the spring fair?" he asked the fishers. "Are we to warn them?"

"Of what?" grunted Gronen. "Men of power? The death of Omara? Who would believe us?"

Brannog sighed. "It is a grim task this wanderer has set himself. Omara will laugh at his plea for help."

"I think we must help him with our silence," said Hengrom. "We should say nothing. Perhaps we will meet with the spies of Quanar Remoon upon the seas. I've traded with the ships of the Chain. Let us lead them to believe Korbillian has gone to the south. If the Emperor does seek to kill him, well, let him look elsewhere."

"Well said," agreed Brannog. "I see no reason to betray him."

Gronen coughed. "Then I will go home. I have no more to add, though I wish the man Korbillian safe crossing."

Slowly the fishers took their lead from the elder and departed, until only two remained, Wolgren and Hengrom. The latter grinned at Brannog. "Had I not a fine wife and two sturdy sons aching for a chance to sail their own craft even though they are yet children, I would think hard on this crossing."

Brannog was stunned by his friend's confession. "You would go with Korbillian?"

Hengrom nodded. "I will not sleep easily with so many mysteries brought to our door. It grieves me that I am not to know the answers. I have never been far from the village, not by land. You, though, had your adventures, eh, Brannog? I envied you then. So, my thanks for your hospitality." With a last grin, he was gone. In the vacuum he left, Wolgren rose steadily to his feet. He was a tall lad for his age, usually taciturn, but with boundless energy locked within his wiry frame, as Brannog knew well.

"And what will you do, young man?" said Brannog with a smile. "Your father was here. Does he not act for you both?"

Wolgren glanced quickly at Sisipher, who had never been far from her father's back. "He does not. I am his son, but my own man."

"And?"

"I have climbed high above Sundhaven. No one else knows the way. I have seen the pass of the Mountain Owls."

Brannog frowned. "You are serious?" The youth spoke of a pass that was more of a legend than reality. No one had ever been there.

"I have seen the great Owls."

Brannog's scepticism grew. "I see. What are you saying? That you will escort Korbillian?"

"I am the only one who can help him," agreed Wolgren proudly.

Brannog studied him, but at last chuckled. "Well. We will see. There is yet much to discuss." He turned more soberly to his daughter. "And you, Sisipher. You spoke of Korbillian's needs. What do you say now?"

She gripped his hands. "I believe him, father. As much as I believe anything."

"Then will you help me, girl?"

She twisted around to see Korbillian and his shadow, Guile, at the foot of the stairs. Sisipher looked askance at her father.

"Every man has spoken for himself," he told her. "You, too, must give your own answer. I thought I would order you to remove yourself, but could not. Fear moved me, that is all. I am still afraid."

"Of what?" she cried.

"I cannot say. A premonition. Since we are asked to believe such powers exist, then call it that. Your mother—" He stopped, face drawn.

"What?"

"She had the gift. Perhaps there is a residue in me."

"You have power?" said Korbillian, coming forward.

Brannog shook his head. "No. Unless a father's instinct is a form of power."

"Who was the girl's mother?"

Brannog told him. There seemed no point in concealing it.

"Then there may be a little power in you," said Korbillian.

"Even so, I will not go with you."

"Father, I do not understand—" began Sisipher.

"You will," replied Brannog. First, he told Korbillian of what had been said by the fishers. Then he called Wolgren from the shadows. The youth was sturdy for his age, yet beside Korbillian he was dwarfed. "This youth claims that he will guide you to the passes."

Korbillian studied the boy. He had a shock of raven hair, bright eyes and hands that spoke of labor. "How can you help me?"

"Sir, I've not crossed the mountains, but I know the pass of the Mountain Owls. I can lead you there. It is the only way through the range."

"Indeed?" Korbillian brightened. "And what is this pass?"

"It is said," put in Brannog, "that the Lord of the Mountain Owls is human, though I fear he is a myth."

"Who is he?"

"He sends out his Mountain Owls," said Wolgren, quite seriously. "They see everything that happens in the mountains. They would know the way through them."

"And you could find their master."

Wolgren smiled. "Put me to the test."

Guile laughed, clapping the youth on the back. "That we will, boy!"

Wolgren's smile changed to a scowl. "I am fifteen, a boy no longer!"

"Then you will be a welcome companion," Guile went on. "But what of your family?"

"I've already asked him," said Brannog. "He assures me he speaks for himself. He is no weakling, eh, Wolgren? If the pass can be reached, he will find it for you."

Korbillian already seemed to be contemplating a meeting with the legendary keeper of the Mountain Owls. "Our thanks," he murmured to the youth.

Sisipher held her own head proudly. "And what must I do?"

Korbillian looked to Brannog, but then away. "It seems you have your mother's gift. Can you use it?"

"I don't know. What is the gift?"

"Will you try?"

"To what end?"

"If you can open tomorrow and beyond. Allow some glimpse of the future, some hope. It will guide us as surely as Wolgren."

"Father?" She remained baffled.

"It is your gift," said Brannog. "You must bestow it or withhold it. Korbillian makes no demands upon you, he has given his word. It is the gift of telling that your mother had, and with it you can see into the future. I should say this; that your mother told me that her village had a claim upon her gift."

"What must I do?"

Korbillian breathed a sigh of relief. "I will show you. Brannog, can we use this hall?"

Brannog nodded. If this was to be done, then it should be here.

Korbillian issued instructions at once. The windows and door were secured, the curtains drawn so that the hall became just as dark as it would be in the depths of the night, lit by the fire. Korbillian sat himself at one end of the central table, with a lamp placed in its center. He asked Sisipher to sit opposite him and told the others to keep out of the circle of light. Brannog had noticed the ghostly figure of Eorna watching and he quietly dismissed her.

Sisipher sat as requested. Brannog could see that she was trembling. Was he right not to have forbidden this? She put her slender hands before her on the table, but withdrew them instinctively as Korbillian stretched out his own gloved hands face down, toward the lamp. "Do as I do," he said. "But do not touch my hands." He need not have warned her, for she looked at them as she would have done at serpents. Nevertheless, she slid her hands toward the center of the table. "You must concentrate," he told her. "Look at me—look into me if you can. Take your time."

She studied his tired face, the face that had so troubled her dreams, fixing on the eyes, and in the silence she seemed to sink back into her dreams, with no more than the face hanging before her like a continent. Brannog and Guile stood motionlessly, their own eyes shifting from face to face. Wolgren's hands were restless, for he had fears for the girl. One move to harm her, and there was a knife hidden at his belt. Power or not, he would use it without a second thought to protect Sisipher. How fitting, he thought, that she should have power! As if she needed power other than the power of her beauty, which to Wolgren was more intoxicating than the crude mead of Brannog's inn.

Sisipher found herself surrounded by darkness, but the lamp seemed to illuminate a terrain beyond the table. The face had gone, and in its place she could see a mountain side and a snow-blocked path. It was as though she looked down from a great height with the eyes of a bird. There were figures trudging wearily along the path. As she studied them, her eyes must have indicated that she could see something other than the room.

"What do you see?" came Korbillian's gentle voice. She described the detailed snow scene, fascinated by it. "Can you see the figures?"

"Yes! Wolgren is leading, although the way ahead is not clear. The snow comes, whipped by a strong wind. Behind him is Guile, and then two others." By its size and clothes, one of these figures was plainly Korbillian, and she said so.

"And the fourth?"

All of them strained their eyes into the dark, as though they, too, would see the remote procession. Sisipher saw the fourth face and broke her concentration at once to turn to her father. He wanted to go to her. "What have you seen?"

"You must be still!" snapped Korbillian, but the images had gone. Sisipher could not recall them. "What did you see?" Korbillian asked.

"It was me. I was the fourth figure."

Brannog shook his head. "It means nothing." But he had no confidence in his words. His mouth felt dry and bitter.

"Again," said Korbillian.

They stared across the lamplight at each other, and within moments she had slipped into another vision. Several broken images passed before her and she described them falteringly: odd landscapes, flashes of movement, people, but nothing that coalesced into a positive picture that Korbillian could give meaning to. After a while a recurring image began to fill her vision: that of a huge hill, a great mound, and in the melée of her mind it seemed to be growing, pulsing as if alive, like some impossible creature burrowing up from below the earth. Her description of it chilled Korbillian, though he pressed for every detail.

"There is a city upon and around it," said the girl.

"Inhabitants?"

"I don't think so. It is dark, night perhaps. But no lights. I can see movement. The houses are like graves." Abruptly her head slumped and her hands went limp. Before Brannog could reach her, she shook her head and looked up, seemingly unharmed. "A strange place," she said.

Korbillian looked greatly disturbed. "A city. Around the mound. This is very bad."

"Do you recognize it?" Guile asked his master.

Korbillian shook his head. "Not the city. But that mound, that hill. It is my goal. The power flows from it, and the mound grows."

Brannog seemed impatient to end the telling. "Have you learned enough?"

Wolgren spoke up. "If we can find the Lord of the Mountain Owls, he may know of this place."

Korbillian agreed. "It is the first real hint I have had."

Sisipher broke the following silence. "I will try again."

This time her father demurred. "There is no need."

"But I can feel something more. A last seeing," she told Korbillian, and Brannog could see that there was no turning her. He stepped back. Why, he asked himself, had she seen herself in the first vision? She could not mean to go with them? He could not permit that. In spite of his intentions, he would have to insist.

Again Sisipher studied Korbillian, and through his eyes found herself searching another unknown landscape. It was obscure, mist-hung, and as she sank into its embrace, Wolgren's breath caught. He sensed something amiss.

"Can you feel the air?" he asked Brannog, ignoring the others.

Brannog looked at the fire, but it blazed freely. Yet the hall was cold. Sisipher's breath had begun to trickle from her mouth in tiny white streams. "What is wrong?" Brannog whispered to Guile.

Guile frowned. An unnatural stillness surrounded the building as the coldness within it constricted like the coils of a serpent. Sisipher's eyes widened, her face white. Brannog wanted to snap her out of this, for a terrible foreboding was upon him. Something stayed him. Guile's face creased in anxiety. Wolgren pulled out his knife and the lamplight gleamed on its blade. None of them acted for fear of harming the girl.

"What do you see?" came Korbillian's voice, cracking the frozen air like a whip.

Sisipher was shaking her head, seemingly unable otherwise to move. Around her the shadows were writhing, trying to lend substance to the dark. Beyond the walls a far wind was keening, beginning its swirl high above Sundhaven that would bring it down upon the village in a rush. They listened to it as though it were a harbinger.

The lamp went out. Complete silence fell again. The wind had ceased, but after a moment it began again, only now curling around the houses, feral and hungry. Wolgren leapt to his feet, stepping toward the girl as though sure she was threatened.

"Keep still!" hissed Brannog, tensing as if about to fly at something he could not see. The air of the place ached.

There was a final frozen moment, as though time had locked. Then the door burst, its frame shattering, a blast of splintered wood and snow racing in on them. A pale light washed over the threshold as the wind howled in, bringing with it a further flurry of dancing snow. Sisipher stared at the glowing opening in horror. No one moved to the door. From the unseen night beyond it a figure appeared, coalesced, it seemed from nothing. It was too dark to identify, shrouded in a cloak, the head lost within a deep hood.

Sisipher screamed. Brannog tore his rooted feet from the floor and stepped forward, but Guile held him back with hands like ice. The figure did not enter. It raised its right arm beneath the cloak. Folds of material parted and the hand appeared, no more at first than a silhouette. Light caught it, trapped it in a ghostly halo. It was not flesh and bone, but seemed to be glimmering like steel, one edge of it a sharply curving crescent. This opened double and clashed shut like the jaws of a trap.

Wolgren acted in the darkness. He flung his knife with all his young strength. Before the knife could strike its mark, it glowed in the air as though molten, and then seemed to burst, as did the figure. Embers of light exploded into the room, sending the onlookers to their knees. As the sound died away and silence rushed in once more, Brannog was first to recover. He felt dizzy, eyes half-blinded by the flash, but as he grew accustomed to the room's proper glow, he saw that the lamp on the table burned as it had done before.

"Sisipher," he called. He found her beside the table and helped her to her feet. She seemed groggy but otherwise unharmed. Korbillian stood beside them, concerned.

"The door!" cried Wolgren. As they squinted at it, they saw that it was whole, as if the vision of its disintegration had been a dream.

"Illusion," said Brannog.

"No," said Korbillian. "Not quite. Sisipher saw into the future. She has great power. She was able to present her seeing to all of us."

"But the explosion," gasped Brannog. "Is that to happen here? Is that creature to visit Sundhaven?"

Korbillian looked bemused. "What we saw was a part of her vision, probably distorted. She can shape the images herself, or possibly her own mind interprets the images that come to her and projects them in her own way. The figure is something we must watch for."

"What was it?" said Wolgren. He had not moved, but was searching for the knife.

"I cannot answer," said Korbillian. "Brannog?"

"Nor I. Has Guile seen the like in the Emperor's lands?"

"No one I have seen dresses in that way. Quanar Remoon's Administrators have their robes of office, but none so grim as those we saw."

Sisipher had recovered, though she sat at the table. "Who was he?" she asked before they could ask the same of her.

"Perhaps," suggested Brannog, "it was no more than an image from your mind. A nightmare."

She shuddered. "No, father. It is out there, and real."

Brannog turned to Korbillian. "Then does it have power?"

"When I meet it, I will know."

Wolgren had now gone to the door, and had found his knife. It was, like the door, intact. He sheathed the blade and touched the wooden panels. There was no indication that the incident had occurred. As he turned away there came a loud rapping from outside, and Wolgren spun away as if scalded.

Sisipher broke the ensuing silence. "It's all right. Open the door."

Wolgren hesitated. Brannog strode to the door. "Who's there?" Yet there was no reply. He threw the bolts and opened the door wide. It was murky beyond, and snow was falling softly, but there was no sign of life. On the threshold there were a number of sacks. Brannog reached for one and opened its neck cautiously. He turned to the onlookers. "Supplies," he breathed, then dragged the sacks inside. He locked the door once more. "The men

of Sundhaven have sent you provisions,'' he told Korbillian. "Food, clothes.'' Something rattled in the sacks, and
when Brannog investigated, he found two swords. "Well,
well. A rare gift. Not the works of a master craftsman,
but you are fortunate. The men of Sundhaven do not equip
themselves for war, but neither are weapons given away
lightly. You have made an impression.''

Korbillian looked at the supplies in amazement. "Your
people are in danger of starvation, yet they do this. I am
grateful. But I never carry a sword.''

"I'll take one!'' cried Guile, jerking to life. "I've nothing but my wits to protect me. I'm no swordsman, but I
can learn.''

Brannog tossed him a weapon, and he almost dropped
the unfamiliar object, but then hefted it with a will and
sliced at the air.

Sisipher came forward slowly, her hand outstretched.
"I will need the other sword,'' she said simply, her eyes
searching her father's face.

He scowled at her, his anger glowing. "No.''

"Yes, father. Like Guile, I have to learn.''

"You cannot mean to go with them?''

"But I must, father. They have no hope alone.''

Korbillian looked grave. "In truth, it will take an army.
The city will not be undefended.''

Brannog stared at him in amazement. "You cannot mean
to enter such a place?''

"I must reach the mound.''

Sisipher took the sword from her father's limp hand. "I
saw myself with them, on the mountain. They have a claim
upon my gift. It is not mine to deny.''

Brannog sighed. "This is madness. None of you will
survive the mountains! How can I permit you to go?'' He
wanted to oppose Sisipher more vehemently, but already
knew that he had lost her. It was as though her going had
been ordained, even from birth.

"I have to go,'' she said, and he had no answer.

"You have my thanks,'' said Korbillian. Brannog flared
and pointed at him. "Protect her, stranger! Guard her life
well.''

"Be assured."

Wolgren stepped forward. "By me also."

Sisipher smiled at him. It was impossible to mistake the look in the youth's face. She had seen it before and had teased him for it. And yet she took it now as a compliment, not something to be scorned. "My thanks," she said, and Wolgren colored.

"It will be best," said Korbillian, "if we left by the first light. Will you speak to your people on my behalf? I would rather be gone when the village awakes. It is how they would wish it."

Brannog nodded.

"What of the hooded man?" said Wolgren.

"It is our destiny to meet him," said Korbillian. "I understand nothing of his mystery. Do you, Sisipher?"

"No. I had no control over what I showed you."

"It must be a part of the evil you seek to destroy," said Brannog.

"Yet that has no mind, no direction."

"Are you sure?" persisted Brannog. "Since you have convinced me that dark powers must exist, I am wondering about the storm. When your ship forged through the sea to our shore, you came against wind and water. A storm from the east. Yet the wave was from the west, as though the storm had by some miracle turned upon its axis. Seeking not the village, but you. As though it had a mind."

Korbillian looked mortified. "It is what I feared."

Guile had paled, and for once there was no trace of humor in him. "What do you mean?"

"Something seeks me."

"The power of the mound?" said Guile. "How can that be?"

"And the hooded man?" asked Brannog. "Is he part of this search?"

Korbillian again turned to Sisipher, but she was shaking her head. "For now I see only the present. Another time there may be more."

"But the mound cannot have developed sentience,"

murmured Korbillian. He seemed unable to say more as he contemplated such a grim possibility, and for some time sat apart from the others, his ravaged face clouded with fear.

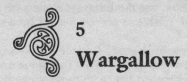

5
Wargallow

BANNOG STARED at the embers of the fire. On the table beside him were the remains of the last breakfast he would share with his daughter. He could still hardly credit that she had gone with them. Dawn had barely broken when the party of four had set out. Brannog had fed them and helped them load their packs. They had gone along the quay toward the mountains, and Sisipher had turned to wave briefly, not wishing to prolong her father's sorrow. He wondered if she knew how deep the sorrow went, how hard it was for him to accept that he had lost a second time. In some of the windows faces had withdrawn as though anxious not to witness Brannog's pain. And then the street was empty. Like an illusion of something that had never been, the party had gone.

He had come to terms with the fact that she could never stay in Sundhaven, but what would she have to face now? Should I have gone with them? he asked himself. But he would not interfere. She had chosen her own path and he must not make himself an obstacle along it. He stood up, collecting the plates. At least the skies had cleared and it seemed as if it would be a mild day. It might not last, so he must take the boat out and fish. Many of the others were already preparing for the tide.

Behind him he heard a familiar rustle of skirt, and he turned to see Eorna, carrying fresh logs. She wore a look of concern for him. "Have you slept?" she asked him.

"A little."

She put down the logs and automatically took the plates from him. Leaving them on the table, she groped for his hand. "Brannog, you think you are alone now. You needn't be," she said, unable to prevent herself from speaking her mind.

He withdrew his hand. "Leave me," he said softly.

She gripped him again. "Don't send me away."

Angrily, he pushed her, with more strength than he had intended. She stumbled, bruising herself on the table behind her. "Leave me!" he barked. "I treat you no better than I should for the work you do. Have the place tidied. I have to take the boat out." He stalked past her, face thunderous. She bit her lip and snatched up the dishes. Quickly she took them away.

Outside, in the crisp air, Brannog cooled and admitted to himself that perhaps he had been too hard on Eorna. He would speak to her again, more gently. For now he wanted no one's company.

"Putting to sea?" called a voice. Hengrom was striding toward him.

"Aye," Brannog nodded, shouldering a hawser.

"So they've already gone. The girl, too?"

"Aye. She took it upon herself as a duty."

Hengrom studied his friend, seeing the anguish on his face. "It could not have been an easy decision."

Brannog saw Hengrom's genuine concern. "No. Was I wrong to let her go?"

"A bird must fly, Brannog." Hengrom studied the high walls that towered over the village. "It will be a dangerous quest. I have not slept."

"They were glad of the swords," Brannog told him, forcing a grin.

Hengrom returned the smile. "See, the weather has turned. We must make amends for the poor catches so far this season. Perhaps our strange friend has brought us luck. We need the harvest."

Luck? thought Brannog. Or is this a gift? He went back to the hall to make final arrangements. When he was satisfied, he looked again for Eorna and found her in one of the kitchens with the other girl, Harla. He sent Harla outside for something, but Eorna would not look at him.

"Eorna, I spoke unkindly. I was distressed."

She looked up at once. "I understand."

"I should not have scorned you."

She moved toward him, but he turned away. "Perhaps when you return," she said softly, "you will let me teach you that you are not alone."

He stiffened. This was not what he meant. "No. I am glad of your concern for me. But you must expect nothing. I do not love you, Eorna."

Eorna smiled. "I do not ask you to."

"You must find another man," he said quickly, not wanting to prolong this, knowing that he would flare again.

She studied him, but did not respond.

"You need not work here if you wish to leave," he told her.

His words horrified her. "You wish to dismiss me?"

"No! But I ask nothing more of you than that you work for your keep. Nothing more. I will provide for you, but if you need a man, you must find another."

She looked down, shamed by his cold words. "Very well. Will you give me time to find work elsewhere in the village?"

"If you must leave. There is no need." He left her, wishing he had not confused matters by coming back to apologize. Instead it seemed as if he had compounded his earlier actions.

Soon afterward, Eorna watched him board his boat and leave on the tide, together with other Sundhaven craft. Hardly a man was left in the village. For a while Eorna let her tears flow. With Brannog's daughter gone, she could have filled the gap in his life. But he had nothing but contempt for her. She had spoken openly to him, made herself vulnerable, but he had rejected her cruelly. Her tears ceased. She hardened herself. Very well. If I am to be cast out, she told herself (for she would interpret it no other way) I will remain no longer. And the silence you demanded of me, Brannog, you will not have. Your precious daughter's good name will be no better than mine.

Already I am shamed by the tongues of the women, who think of me as your bed-mate. Since you will not look with favor on me, I will not remain. She went to the tiny room that had been allowed her, and collected together the few things that were her own.

The fleet moved out into deep water swiftly. The sea was kind and the harvesting began. Each man put the visit of the stranger to the back of his mind, except for Brannog, who wondered again about the lull in the weather, and about power. Korbillian had said that in Ternannoc, men had controlled the storms. In Sundhaven the women worked cheerfully, thinking of the possible harvest. They gossiped about the night, speculating on the things their husbands had guardedly told them. There were more than a few dark clouds that had dispersed.

It was a boy-child, idly fishing from the rocks at the far end of the harbor by the crab pools, who first saw the riders. There was a narrow path (it could not be called a road) that wound up and along the coast to the south, rarely used and in the summer overgrown. The boy saw horses picking their way down this path, some score of them, and sitting stiffly upon them were figures cloaked in drab gray, with muffling hoods against the cold. Frightened and fascinated, the boy could not move; his make-shift rod fell into the water.

When the leading rider threaded the part of the path that neared the rocks of the harbor, the boy was trembling. He could feel but not see the man's eyes searching every inch of him. Another rider pushed back his hood and addressed the boy.

"What village is this, child?" His face was severe, gaunt, and there seemed no warmth in him, like one sent to chastise or punish. His expression seemed to say to the boy that already he had been judged and found in need of a good hiding. The boy found it hard to speak. The other rider, who had led the party, had not moved, but the boy could feel the eyes, as if a huge bird of prey hovered over him.

"Sundhaven," the boy managed to say at last, his voice trembling.

"Go, little rabbit," came the voice of the leading rider. It was deep, but without malice. "Skip to your people. Tell them the Deliverers are here. You are in no danger."

"Thank you, sir," squeaked the boy, then tore away just as if he were indeed a rabbit, fleeing the shadow of a swooping eagle.

The second rider scowled after him, as if the flight of the child offended him. "Will they know about us, sire?"

"I doubt it. But they will have no reason to challenge us."

"Will we find transgressors here?"

The hooded man laughed shortly. "You are too eager, Djemuta. Ours is a crusade into remote lands, and I expect little or no trouble. Exercise restraint. I know well enough your desire to serve our cause. You do not have to impress me." Without a sideways glance, the man edged his horse to the lead, making his way along the edge of the harbor toward Sundhaven. He had noticed the lack of boats. On such a calm day, the fleet would be out. He had wondered at the weather, for not long since, a storm had forced his men into a sea cave for three days. Yet today was almost freakish. The man paused. There was something in the water. He pointed.

At once Djemuta dismounted and went to investigate. "Wreckage," he called, with little interest. In the storm, any number of boats could have been destroyed.

"Bring what you can carry to me," was the command.

Djemuta reached from within the sleeves of his robe and used not a hand but a steel, sickle-shaped claw to retrieve a fragment of wood from the shallows. He took it to his leader and held it up for inspection, the metal of his false hand gleaming.

The man on horseback made no attempt to take the proferred wood, nor did he push back his hood. "It is part of a ship," he said.

Djemuta instantly referred to the storm. "The wood—do you know its type?" asked the other.

Djemuta's face clouded. "I have no skill in these matters, sire."

"Of course not. Forgive me. I recognize the wood. You

note how dark it must have been even before the sea got at it. There are no trees of that type in these lands. The fishermen get their wood from southern foresters at the fairs. That wood is from the islands to the far west, from Goldenisle. That ship was a long way from its native waters." Satisfied, he moved his steed away. Djemuta tossed the wood aside and remounted. Very little escaped the eyes of his master, Simon Wargallow.

The party moved on in silence to the first of the houses. No one had come out to greet them as they assembled at the quayside. Djemuta turned to another of the riders and nodded to him. The latter produced a curled brass instrument and gave three long blasts on it, and the sounds raced up and along the coastal heights. Gulls answered in noisy clouds, flocking out to sea, but in the village nothing stirred. Then a door opened and the aged figure of Gronen stepped out into the pale sunlight, squinting up at the gathered riders.

"What business do you have here?" he called.

The leader inclined his head and spoke politely, though he did not reveal himself. "I have to ask a few simple questions."

"Who are you?" snapped Gronen, who had had a bellyful of strangers. These looked as if they could be fighting men. They had a military bearing. If so, they had no business here. The Emperor's men? No, not dressed in the drab gray. They were not seamen either.

"We are Deliverers," said their spokesman. "We perform works in the name of peace and goodwill."

"What works?"

"Merely to ascertain that all is well in such places as these. Sundhaven, is it?"

"Aye." Gronen knew the boy had told them.

"Your men are at sea? Have you a leader?"

Gronen did not answer.

"Perhaps you act for him, old man. We will not remain long. All that I ask is that you allow my men to rest their horses for a while. The recent storm tired us greatly. My men have their own provisions, and will not ask of yours. Water, perhaps?"

"Of course," agreed Gronen. If that was all they sought, it would be impolite to refuse them. But he wished the men were here. This hooded figure troubled him. Why should the man so cover himself? Was he diseased?

"I would like to talk with you," he told Gronen. "Will you admit me into your home?"

"Talk about what?"

"Simple things. I am a man of the law."

"What law?"

"The common law of the land. The unwritten law."

"Who do you serve?"

"All men." The figure dismounted. Gronen liked his words less each time he spoke, but he ushered him into the house. If these men brought trouble, they would act at whim, effortlessly superior. Without the fishers, Sundhaven was at their mercy.

Inside the house, Gronen motioned the man to a seat. The latter accepted with a bow, and at last removed his hood. His face differed greatly from the familiar faces of Sundhaven. In particular he had large, liquid eyes, deep brown, and a smooth complexion that spoke of the sun and not the winds of the north. His hair was jet black, cut short to his head, the angles of his face sharp in the interior lighting of the house. His lips were too full, exaggerated a little by the flattish nose, and his mien was a little pompous if not arrogant, as though most things around him afforded him a degree of amusement.

He asked for and was given water. "I know nothing of this law you speak of," said Gronen. "But the men of Sundhaven have no crimes to confess to."

"I am sure you are right. Tell me, though; I have heard from a passing source (and an idle one, possibly) that gods are worshipped in these mountains. Can this be true?"

The question was totally unexpected. Gronen frowned. "Gods? But these are creatures of myths, no more, surely. I know of no village within say, a hundred miles of coastland, where gods are spoken of. But the range is a long one and stretches well beyond our regions."

"None are worshipped in secret?"

Gronen laughed dryly. "Grown men do not dally with such ideas!"

"And what of powers? Strange powers?"

Gronen felt the abrupt coldness pumping into his old veins. "What powers?"

"Unnatural powers. Peculiar happenings. Word, perhaps, of travelers making claims that would be scoffed at."

The room was silent. So this was it, thought Gronen. The truth. They had come for Korbillian, like hounds upon the scent. But why? If Guile had told the truth, the Emperor's men were glad to be rid of him. Gronen remembered the vow of the fishers. No matter how reasonable these Deliverers were, Sundhaven owed them nothing. "I do not understand. There are no such powers."

"No magic?"

"Your questions are strange. Have you come so far as to ask about things that do not exist? Forgive me, but there are places where you would be abused for speaking of magic."

The man laughed. "Indeed, old fellow! But you misunderstand me. *I* keep the law. When I find men who preach magic, or gods, when I come across such transgressors, I have to act. But I have heard enough. I am satisfied." He stood up slowly, innocently, and made for the door. Gronen followed him outside. Could that be all? Surely not.

"There is power in the sea," he said. "And the storm that came gave us many sleepless nights."

"In such a storm, I imagine that ship must have been wrecked in your bay," said the man, again with his hood drawn up. His back was to the elder, but somehow there was a grim menace in his words now. Gronen did not answer. So he knew about the ship?

"I saw the remains," said the Deliverer.

"A terrible business. None survived."

"I see. Men of Sundhaven?"

"No. We never saw them. The sea swallowed them and left us only their broken ship. From the far south, by its lines."

The Deliverer turned. "How distressing. Death at sea. An unfortunate omen for a seafaring village. And you saw no one?"

"After the storm, we searched, of course. But the waves had been such that they must have dashed any survivors to pulp."

"I am sure you did all that you could." He turned away and met Djemuta.

"Shall I order the men to question the villagers, or shall we move on while the weather holds, sire?" asked the latter.

"Ask the people about the boat," was the soft reply. "But instruct the men to be discreet. There is a truth here I must uncover. But softly. These people are like stone."

Djemuta whirled away, speaking to each of the Deliverers in turn.

"There are places in Omara," the leader told Gronen almost affably, "where gods are worshipped and where men seek unnatural powers. I have known evil practices to flourish, but it is the sworn duty of the Deliverers to seek them out and to put an end to them. False gods and power are not to be tolerated. They create unrest, strife, war. Here in your lands you find it hard to believe such things exist. I have seen them, old man. Seen them and fought them. I use only the strength of my purpose and the will of my Deliverers."

"Why are you here?"

"We have to search, to guard against such things. I don't expect to find evil in these mountains. Men must be too busy getting on with their lives, which are hard enough hereabouts from what I have witnessed. No matter. We will shortly leave you in peace." He moved away, about to dismiss the old man. He paused. "I should say that if we are needed, word will always reach us."

Gronen yet did not trust him, nor his cause, but said no more. The village had agreed on its course; Korbillian would not be betrayed.

BRANNOG HAULED in his net for the third time that morning. It bulged with life and his hold was already well stocked with fish. If the other boats had trawled as well as he had, they would easily survive this winter after all. It was enough to raise his spirits. At a time of omens, perhaps this meant that all was better than it had seemed. He had wanted a good life for Sisipher—perhaps she would discover a way to fulfillment on Korbillian's quest. He made himself think so, just as he made himself believe that the fish were indeed a gift from the man of power. If he could control the sea as he had, surely he would be able to protect the girl in his charge.

As Brannog prepared to return to Sundhaven, shortly after midday (with more fish than he had netted in the previous month) he reached over the side of his craft with a curved gaff to drag aboard a struggling fish that had been hooked by one of his lines. He swung the wriggling monster aboard by its gills, then deftly loosed the gaff, turned it and used the back to beat the life from the fish with one hard but merciful blow. He held up the weapon. Blood ran from the point, down the steel, and for a cold moment Brannog saw again the grim spectre of Sisipher's vision, the hooded figure with the hand of steel. His eyes went to the horizon, beyond which lay Sundhaven. He made all haste now to return, and soon found himself in the company of other craft from the village. The fishing, it seemed, had been good for all of them, and Brannog used the knowledge to bludgeon back the dark thoughts provoked by the blood.

Two hours later the fleet sailed into Sundhaven harbor, and it looked as though most of the village stood upon the jetty. There was cheering, but not the excitement of better days. Brannog assumed they were afraid that the catch had been a poor one again. Hengrom and others stood in the prows of their vessels and called out loudly that there were fish aplenty. Yet even this did not seem to raise the spirits of the villagers appreciably. The shadow over them remained. It darkened Brannog's mood. Where was Gronen? He was not to be seen, yet was usually the first to catch a mooring rope, for all his years. As Brannog climbed the jetty steps, his fears were confirmed. Some tragedy had come to pass.

"Gronen is dying," the women told him and at once he ran to the old man's home. Gronen's family were arranged around his bed. He had no sons, but the youth, Borgir, his nephew, was there, and must have been even more quickly away from his boat than Brannog. They made way for Brannog as the old man stretched out an arm to him, anxious to speak to him. Brannog knelt beside him and took his hand. Gronen had aged noticeably since the events of the night.

"Have they told you?" the elder wheezed.

"Only that you are ill. Is it bad?"

"I will not see the next dawn," said Gronen. "Would that I had not seen today's!"

"We have had a magnificent harvest," Brannog encouraged him, but he knew that the elder spoke the truth. He was close to death already.

"They came," coughed Gronen, ignoring the good news. "I did not trust them."

"Who came?"

The elder found it hard to speak, so one of his daughters described the Deliverers to Brannog. Brannog gasped: the description fitted perfectly the figure that Sisipher had conjured from the night. He hardly heard the girl speaking about the questions they had been asked.

"We were true to our word," said Gronen. "We told them nothing of the man Korbillian and his companion, but they found his broken ship. Still we said nothing, and would have cheated them of the truth."

"And yet?"

Gronen winced as pain shot through his chest. "Eorna."

"What of her?"

"She told them."

Brannog's fingers gripped the old man hard before he saw the pain and withdrew them. "What did she tell them?"

"Of Korbillian, and of his journey up into the mountains. And of your daughter."

"Why were these creatures seeking Korbillian?"

"Because of power. They search for believers in power

and gods. They call them transgressors. They deliver them from the error of their beliefs, so they say!''

''Where is Eorna?'' Brannog snarled at the family, but no one would answer. The eyes of the women were cast down, yet they knew.

''They repaid her for giving them the truth,'' murmured Gronen. ''Their leader, Wargallow, spoke to us as if we were children. 'You have done wrong in hiding the truth from me,' he told us. 'Yet it was fear of this evil man Korbillian that moved you, so I am merciful. Know this: he is already dead and given back to the earth. And all who travel with him.' He said that, Brannog, 'And all who travel with him.' ''

''When did they leave?''

''Some hours gone. After they dealt with Eorna.''

Brannog's face clouded. Why had she betrayed them? Surely—not because he had spurned her? For that she had broken the vow of the village, compromised so many lives? ''What did they do to her?''

''Do not trouble yourself, father,'' insisted the oldest of Gronen's daughters, Ursa. She drew Brannog away and to the door. ''It was horrible. Wargallow told us that blood is the earth's. He spoke of Omara as if she were a person, a mother who had given birth to all life. Eorna, he said, was tainted. We all were, because we had not set upon and killed Korbillian for his wickedness. Therefore we must be cleansed. They took Eorna to a place away from the village. We did not see. Afterward, each of the Deliverers came back. They—'' Ursa faltered, her hand going to her mouth.

Brannog hugged her gently, as her father would have. ''In your own time. But I must know. The men must be told.''

Ursa nodded. ''They came back. Brannog—they do not have hands.''

He closed his eyes. ''I understand. It was the steel?''

She looked only momentarily surprised. Tears welled in her eyes as though she still could not believe the things that had happened. ''Steel, yes. Like claws. Each one returned, his claw slick with blood, and they wiped them clean before us.''

''So they killed her.''

''They said they had given her to the earth, to atone for our sins. After they had gone, we found the burial place. Gronen ordered no one to touch it. Eorna was not be taken to the sea. She had betrayed us. Oh, Brannog, what must we do?''

''Eorna is not to be moved. Her grave will be a reminder to Sundhaven that there are enemies abroad. Is the place marked?''

''No, but it can be found.''

''We will erect a cairn.''

Gronen died within the hour, and no one pretended that it was his age that had killed him. He was taken to sea as the Sundhaven dead traditionally were. Afterward Brannog supervised the building of the promised cairn. He stood to one side when it was done, shaken by differing emotions. Sisipher would be in real danger now. Eorna was dead. He had never loved her, but she should not be dead.

''Who speaks for Eorna?'' came a voice. Brannog jerked up to see a plump woman standing beside the grave. It was Eorna's only relative, her slovenly sister, Anar. ''Well?'' Behind her stood her husband, a weak and cowardly man, for whom the village had little respect.

''You must speak for her now,'' said Brannog.

''Oh? Must I? Was I her keeper? Did my husband feed her and provide her with work in return for a roof? Did he warm her bed?''

Brannog flinched, but other villagers murmured their disapproval. Anar was out of order. Overwrought, perhaps, for though she had never been close to Eorna, the death had shaken her.

''Were you not her man?'' Anar challenged. ''Will you let her lie there without seeking out her killers?''

In Sundhaven, such a responsibility rested upon the shoulders of the next of kin, or in the case of lovers, on the one left. Brannog was faced with a choice. He could, truthfully, deny Anar's charge. If he did so, no one would doubt him and no one would require of him a reckoning of the Deliverers. There would be no one to raise a party to pursue them. If Brannog decided to pursue them in order to prevent them from harming Sisipher, none of the villagers would be duty-bound to go with him. None of them had sought to go with Korbillian. Sisipher had chosen to. Brannog considered his second choice. He could accept that he was Eorna's "man." As her keeper he was not obliged to avenge her, but as her lover, he could demand support for a reckoning. Good men would follow him into the mountains without question.

He knew already that he would follow. Sisipher was in obvious danger. Since these Deliverers were sworn to root out power and destroy its sources, it followed that they would seek her death. Whatever Korbillian's strength, it may not prevail. And Sisipher had foreseen the coming of the Deliverers. Brannog was certain that she would meet them. He must be there. And Eorna? Should he let her lie unavenged? Perhaps if he had encouraged her, taken her to his bed, she would have said nothing to this Wargallow, and would be alive. He had never loved her. She had been nothing to him, he could not force himself to make her otherwise. Perhaps her betrayal of the village did merit a bed of earth. But the idea filled him with revulsion.

"Yes, I was her man," he heard himself say, and there was no one present who saw shame in it.

"You were silent about it," said Anar coldly.

"I had no reason to speak of Eorna to you." Brannog returned with equal coldness. "Since you absolved yourself of any real kinship to her years ago, what did it matter to you, Anar? How long will you mourn your neglected sister?"

"If the dead could hear," said one of the elders, "Eorna would be weeping."

Brannog straightened. "You are right. It is a disgrace to argue before her grave. I must collect what I need. Where is Hengrom?"

"Here." Hengrom came forward, and in a moment walked with his friend back to his home.

"You wish me to go with you?" he said. "I doubt if

any of the men will refuse." No one would wish to leave Sundhaven, but this was an affair of honor.

Brannog shook his head, knowing already that Hengrom had no desire to leave his family. "I must go alone."

Hengrom protested, but Brannog would have none of it. "I will not drag good men into this, Hengrom. Sundhaven must not suffer. And besides, I have reached a decision. I think I must have made it long ago, but have never had the courage to act upon it."

"I don't understand."

"I will leave Sundhaven, and I will not return. My home, my stores, my ship, I give to the village."

"You are mad! What sort of talk is this from a man so loved and respected? You cannot be thinking of death—"

Brannog snorted. "We have lived with it at our shoulder throughout this winter. But no. I have no intention of dying."

"Has the death of Eorna pained you so much?"

"No. I was never her man, but the village must not know that. You will say nothing."

"Very well, but—"

"I am sure this man Wargallow will be dangerous, but alone, with surprise as my agent, I will deny him his goals."

"Then why do you talk of not returning?"

"It is something I feel. I have no plans other than to avenge Eorna and stand by my daughter."

"Her path lies with Korbillian, to pursue his strange destiny. You will go with them?"

"No, I will not tread another man's path. I must find my own."

"This is wild talk, Brannog."

"I left Sundhaven before, my friend. In Frostwalk I found love and a mystery. Korbillian has reopened the old wounds. My own daughter has filled me with premonition."

"This is no more than your fear for her, surely."

Brannog shook his head. "In Sundhaven I would be old within a year. There are no ghosts, Hengrom, yet the dead are not still, are they? They are here." He touched his head.

"You have not seen your future?"

"In a way. To remain in Sundhaven would make that clear. Each day would be mapped out. But beyond the snow, I see nothing."

"Hah! There may be nothing for you. A grave of earth, like Eorna. Up there, you will not even hear the sea. At least she has that."

Brannog looked out at the harbor. "There are things that one always hears." He was silent for a few distant moments. "Now, I will prepare. I leave at once."

PART TWO

CROSSINGS

6
Ratillic

THE EARLY MORNING WAS CRISP but without wind or piled cloud, promising a day that would be like an oasis in a desert of tempests this winter. As Korbillian, Guile, Sisipher and the youth, Wolgren, left Sundhaven, a few villagers watched secretly. Sisipher felt a stab of regret as she waved to her father, but soon the snow-hung mountains rose before her, not daunting, but somehow enticing her. Wolgren picked his way like a goat along sloping tracks up into the scree and snowdrifts, watching for boulders and outcrops that he read as clearly as signposts along the way. Guile whistled cheerfully to himself, but Korbillian was silent. The terrain did not trouble him, but his thoughts did.

Sisipher found herself wishing that the gift she possessed would allow her to read minds, to understand the truth of Korbillian's quest. She knew that there was a great fear in him, a dread that this path he had chosen would lead to ruin. Even so, she had been unable to refuse to go. As the wind came back gently from above, reminding her of the bleakness of the task, she clung to her intuitive faith in her own course. Something, she knew, waited beyond the mountains for her. Her only regret was her father's sorrow: her going must have seemed like a betrayal to him, yet he understood, or seemed to. Now I have cast my lot with a stranger, a man from a place of which I have never heard. I trust this power, yet why should I? She looked ahead at Wolgren. He, too, had thrown in with the stranger without a second thought. With a smile to herself, Sisipher recalled that the boy had done this before he had known that she would be going. She knew that she could rely on his help during a crisis, although he was so young!

Little was said on the ascent, as every effort was needed for the arduous climb. However, by mid morning Wolgren had successfully guided them high up the mountain, following paths they would not have seen or expected to find here. When the party elected to pause briefly, they looked back to see low cloud veiling most of the coastline and sea. Sundhaven was hidden by a shoulder of rock. Wolgren found a cluster of boulders that he considered safe and he motioned them to sit, evidently enjoying his position as guide.

"If a storm comes upon us," he told Korbillian seriously, "or if there is a heavy snowfall, I fear we will not reach the pass of the Mountain Owls."

Surprisingly Korbillian did not seem at all perturbed by the boy's anxiety. "We need not fear the weather," he said as he sat. He did not amplify his odd remark, gazing instead out into the cloud.

Sisipher, who sat beside Guile, was not so sure. "Can he predict the storms, or is he able to control them?"

Guile grinned. "Can you not see ahead for us?"

He was teasing her, and she turned away, not sure yet if she liked or disliked him. She ought to be fair, she thought. "I can't see everything. Just fragments, and not always when I choose."

Guile saw that he had offended her and sought to make amends. "Korbillian is no sorcerer. Such gifts as he has he controls adeptly, it is true. Though I am determined to help him and take up his cause, I know very little about him. I joined him by instinct, just as you have. But I trust him."

Sisipher softened a little and turned back to him. "We must all be a little mad to follow him."

Guile chuckled. "Yes. Best not to brood on the darker side of our quest. The eventual goal is so remote that I won't allow it to worry me yet. Besides, we must find allies! Perhaps when we at last reach this place of evil, we will have enough support to make a formidable force of ourselves.''

"I think we will grow, yes," she nodded, as though trying to reach far ahead with her mind.

"I'm sure we will not find the elements against us. If they come, as they did at sea, they will hit a wall, for Korbillian seems immune. He and I should be drowned, or frozen. Even here, though, I do not feel the cold as I ought. And you?''

She shook her head. "No. Not cold."

"Korbillian has told me a little about power as he knows it. He says that Ternannoc and Omara, and the other worlds are all alive, like single organisms. All life on each world is no more than a part of that world, the common bond being power, the life force. Korbillian had power on Ternannoc, for its people had attuned themselves very closely to their world and were able to draw on its life force at will. Here he has found it harder, for he is not of Omara, but he has learnt to attune himself to it.''

"And I?" she said softly. "What am I?" She was almost too frightened to ask.

"From the words spoken last night, it seems you have your mother's gift. You are from another village.''

"I've never seen it since we left it. I was three. I hardly remember my mother.''

"If I make a guess about her, will you not consider me rude?'' For once his face was serious. She shook her head. "Many people came here from Ternannoc as refugees. Your mother was probably—almost certainly—descended from them. Thus you would have the life force of Ternannoc in you, as well as that of Omara, through your father. You are, in some ways, stronger than Korbillian, and far stronger than I am.''

She looked away, not angry but afraid. Had her father known this? Why had he not told her? But he would have feared for her and could never have foreseen what her future held for her.

A cry from Wolgren alerted her. Guile drew his sword awkwardly as he jumped up. Wolgren was pointing at the sky, visible through a gap in the clouds. They could see what appeared at first to be a dark cloud, passing quickly, but parts of it swirled and detached from it so that they realized in a moment that these were birds, countless thousands of them.

"Is it not early for migrations?" said Korbillian to the youth. Both were amazed by the sheer numbers, as the cloud streamed endlessly by.

Wolgren was scowling. "I've seen many flocks this winter, but this is the largest. Some of the birds are unlike any I've seen before."

"Where do they go?"

"Out to sea. After that, who can say? This is the first winter they have come."

"From the east?" said Korbillian, but it was not really a question. Wolgren nodded and the party moved on. It was a long time before the cloud of birds had gone.

High up in the mountains, the visibility restricted, they wound between jagged peaks, Wolgren still sure of the way. The winter night fell upon them quickly and they selected an overhang and made themselves as comfortable as they could. They ate sparingly and said little. Sisipher wondered about the youth. He seemed very sure of himself and his knowledge of the terrain was surprising. To her each mountain looked alike, each valley a replica of the next. By the time she fell asleep, Guile was snoring and Wolgren's head had dropped onto his chest.

It seemed no more than a moment before she woke again, and yet it was daylight. The weather had still not broken. Wolgren was beyond the overhang, gently exercising and studying the white landscape. It was not easy to see far ahead as cloud covered nearly everything. Sisipher was struck by the absolute silence, conscious of the lack of whispering sea. The party seemed very closed in.

"The pass is like a saddle," said Wolgren as they chewed a fish breakfast. "I've never been far into it, but it should be passable if the snow hasn't drifted too badly. Usually the wind sweeps it clear. It's more exposed, so if a storm does come, we may have to turn back."

Korbillian shook his head. "We cannot go back. Time now is against us." He turned to say something to Sisipher, but she was very still, her face white. "What is it? What have you seen?"

She was breathing heavily as if she had been running. "We can't go that way," she gasped, pointing up the valley.

"We have to," said Wolgren, dropping down beside her.

"No," she insisted. "There's blood up there."

"Has there been a fight?" said Guile, also beside her. Wolgren gripped his knife. "An ambush?"

"It hasn't happened yet," Sisipher told them. "But there will be blood spilled."

"Whose?" said Guile, exchanging a worried look with Wolgren.

"I don't know."

"Do animals hunt here?" asked Guile.

"Mountain Owls do," Wolgren nodded.

"It's human blood," whispered Sisipher.

They turned to Korbillian. "Do not press her," he said. "We must prepare, that is all. The way ahead for us will always be dangerous. Look to your weapons."

Sisipher nodded. "Yes, we must go on. I cannot see the way back to Sundhaven, but there is a strangeness about it. All is not well, I sense it."

None of them really wanted to know more: her knowledge was too disturbing. Instead they shouldered their packs and kept their weapons to hand, moving on with additional caution.

After an hour they had made good progress up the valley toward a gap in the peaks. The snow was much harder underfoot than Sisipher would have expected; it was packed and firm and she thought about Guile's words of yesterday. How much control did Korbillian exercise? Again, the cold did not seem to bite as it should, and the day, though full of cloud that drifted mistily around them, was mild.

They reached a dip in the valley and an exposed, flattened area. Sisipher stopped, her blood running cold as she looked around her. It was a bizarre feeling, for the future superimposed itself over the present. She could see patches of blood, shreds of cloth, feathers all around, and yet it was not *now*. "Wait," she called, and at once was ringed. "It is here," she said, describing the scene.

"Let us get away quickly," urged Guile. "It may not happen to us."

"Can you see anything on the slopes below us?" Sisipher asked. Wolgren ran back a little way at once, but when he returned, declared there was only the mist.

"How far to the pass?" Korbillian asked. The cloud had dropped over them and visibility closed in. Now the cold did come, like the sea.

"Not far," promised Wolgren, eagerly leading on. They moved as fast as they could without exhausting themselves, aware that exhaustion would be their most dangerous adversary.

They had left the place of blood some distance behind when a sound made them look up as one. It was the beating of wings, several pairs, and all of them evidently very large. Quickly they drew together, dropping their packs and gripping their weapons. They could see no more than a few yards into the drizzling cloud, but the wings could be heard on all sides. Silence came again.

"Mountain Owls," whispered Wolgren. "No other bird is so large."

"Are they dangerous?" said Guile softly.

"I've never been close to one. They're not said to attack people, but then again, they are said to be imaginary, like your master's powers." Wolgren grinned as he said it, and Sisipher wondered if this was why he had come, to show them that he *had* been here, and did not lie about things he had seen. In Sundhaven, only the young children had believed his tales.

Korbillian admonished them to be still, but Wolgren, surprisingly, ignored him. He moved out of the tight circle and spoke to the silence. "I am here again, Lords of the Sky. You've watched me before. You know I mean no harm. Will you let me pass?" He deliberately sheathed his knife. Sisipher shuddered—the boy was an open target for any attack.

In a moment, the beat of wings returned, and from the

mist came what appeared at first to be a huge shape. It flew over them and then back, alighting on the snow a few yards before Wolgren. Now that it could be plainly seen, they realized that it was not huge, although it stood half Wolgren's height, the largest owl they had ever seen. It was almost pure white, with a tightly curved beak and wide, staring eyes which looked at them with an expression that suggested extreme shock. It spread its magnificent wings, shot with gold, turning its head almost arrogantly to study each of the four humans. Those deep eyes blinked, and it settled, just as though preparing to sleep. Sisipher noticed its sharp talons, but there was no blood.

Wolgren was about to speak to the bird as if he thought it would understand him, but Korbillian gently moved a step ahead of him. "It's quite safe," he breathed, then turned slowly to the others. "I know these birds. They are not native to Omara."

"Ternannoc?" said Guile.

Korbillian almost smiled. "I think so. And I think I know who brought them here." He turned back to the great Mountain Owl and stared at it. Its eyes opened and fixed his eagerly. Then it spread its wings and gave voice to a sudden piercing cry, taking to the air and swooping around the group in tight circles. Guile ducked instinctively, wary of sudden deadly talons, but Korbillian was moving again, untroubled. "They are not here to harm us. We must follow them."

If Sisipher had looked on the bird in wonder, Wolgren considered it worthy of worship. He could hear the beat of wings around them and his heart leapt. To think that these glorious birds could be allies! Eagerly he followed, and though the owl that led them was mostly out of sight above, they could hear its cry.

They travelled quickly up into the high pass, and the way became even more obscured. Wolgren said they seemed to have taken a branching gulley upward from the main pass, toward the highest part of the range. "To the Lord of the Mountain Owls?" he asked.

"Yes," said Sisipher. "Korbillian, isn't that what they're telling us?"

Korbillian nodded. "It must be. It is he who brought them. Their kind have served him for many years, as once others served him."

"A Hierarch?" ventured Guile.

Korbillian seemed aggrieved. "No, no. And not a man who had respect for them."

"Will he help us?"

"Perhaps." But the word had the weight of despair.

An hour later they were above the cloud, with jutting peaks on all sides. A dozen huge Mountain Owls circled them like guardians, and the leader dropped, perching on a boulder that partially obscured a fissure in the rock wall behind it. For a moment the bird watched them, then gave another sharp cry. Behind it, from the tall crack, emerged a figure. Dressed in a long cloak that was made of a strange light pelt, it was very tall and thin, and its face was narrow with a beak-like nose that was immediately comparable to the beak of the owls. It was difficult to guess the man's age, but he moved with jerky steps, very light and agile, and seemed nervous, ready to spring away at a second's notice. Somehow there was an air of anger about him, a coldness.

Korbillian moved forward, but the owl cried out as if in a warning to him. "Ratillic," he said. "It has been a long time."

"When I knew you were coming, it was not easy to decide whether to have my children lead you over a precipice, or bring you to me." He had not even glanced at the others.

"I am on a mission of peace."

"I have no interest in your mission."

"Then why did you bring us here?"

Ratillic's claw-like hands closed tightly on themselves, just as the owl's claws would grip their prey. "I see everything in these mountains," he said, apparently changing the subject. "Why are you here? I cannot believe you have chosen to exile yourself, as I have."

"I have to pass through to the east, and quickly."

"The east? Why?" He seemed suddenly interested, suspicious.

"There is work to be done there. I may need your help."

Ratillic's derisive laugh unsettled the owls about him. "Mine? Spare your breath, Korbillian. Oh, it may suit me to have you guided through to the other side of the mountains, but that's all. You'll get no further help from me."

Korbillian seemed to accept that, but Guile looked angry. "What makes you so averse to us?" he snapped. "You know nothing about us or our intentions."

Ratillic's hands clenched and unclenched. "You are Guile, from the Chain of Goldenisle."

Guile grunted as if he had been punched. "Yes, but—"

"And I see Wolgren of Sundhaven. And Brannog's girl. Strange company you keep, girl."

"The owls told him," said Sisipher.

Ratillic looked at her and snorted. "They are my eyes, my ears."

"And they speak to you," she added.

He seemed to respect her for her observation. "After a fashion."

"You have not lost your old skills, then," commented Korbillian.

"No. Have you? I see your hands are sheathed. Do they frighten you?"

Korbillian winced, and Sisipher intervened, sensing a harsh exchange. "If your owls are wise," she said, "then they'll know you have no reason to fear us."

"Is that so!" Ratillic snapped.

"Ratillic," Korbillian cut back. "The past is gone. You must think of the future. Ternannoc is dead. Would you see Omara die, too?"

The Lord of the Mountain Owls looked horrified. "Omara? What are you saying? Why should Omara perish?"

"The shock waves of Ternannoc's death still break, even on these far shores. There is a city in the east, built on a great mound that has thrust up from the earth there. Under it festers the dark power that took root there when Ternannoc's masters opened the world-gates.'' Korbillian did not need to say more. Ratillic looked appalled.

"Here?'' he gasped. "Even here? But it was so long ago—''

"I am sworn to destroy this evil,'' said Korbillian.

Ratillic gazed at him as if he had not heard. "With what?'' he growled when he had recovered a little of his composure.

Korbillian turned to his companions. "There are four of us. We need far more. Without help, Omara is doomed. And there are no more gates, Ratillic, no exits from this world. This time we either stand and help each other, or it is the end for us all.''

Ratillic's face darkened, as if he had been deeply insulted, and Sisipher thought that he would set the owls upon them all. Yet he seemed to wilt under Korbillian's challenge. "I see,'' he said quietly. "An ultimatum. We are all responsible, is that what you are saying? Ternannoc could have been saved if we'd all poured power into her to stop her wounds?''

"We can never know that. But Omara will die if I cannot gather enough to help save her.''

Ratillic closed his eyes, but opened them again, having come to some private decision. "You cannot cross the mountains yet. There is another storm coming. From the east. Which means it will be bad. My eyes are turned to the east for much of the time. I should have guessed. Disease, storms, rumors of lurking evil. Well then, come inside.'' He said something to the white owl, and at once it flew off, calling to its fellows.

Ratillic led them into the mountain and they went down a smooth sided shaft and rough-hewn steps. Sisipher wondered who could have cut them. Ratillic had power, perhaps, but somehow the steps seemed incredibly old. There was a door beyond, and after that, to their surprise, what appeared to be more of a hall than a cave, and it had been kept in immaculate condition. There were tapestries, rugs, exquisite furniture, all of a quality that would not have been misplaced in a palace. Wolgren in particular looked amazed, but shielded his reaction quickly. He accepted that there must be powers at work here beyond his understanding.

Above them, sleeping silently on beams that were as thick as a man's waist, were owls, and although they evidently spent much time here, there was no mess, and everything was tidy and organized. Ratillic motioned his guests (Sisipher was still not sure if the word was accurate) to some of the splendidly carved seats, and they sat. Korbillian followed Ratillic to a large chest beyond which several strange globes illuminated the hall.

Sisipher turned to Guile. "He hates Korbillian, doesn't he?"

"So it would seem. There are many things about Korbillian I know nothing about. I have often wondered what part he played in the fall of his world. I don't know the real story."

"Do you think he was a Hierarch?"

"I have thought that, but have never asked him. Some things weigh him down like lead. Guilt, I think."

Korbillian returned to them while Ratillic disappeared. The owls above automatically opened their eyes and watched the people below.

"He is arranging some food," said Korbillian.

"Can we trust him?" said Wolgren unexpectedly, and his right hand fiddled with his knife hilt.

Korbillian made a dismissive gesture. "He could have killed us all easily if he had wanted to. But I think he will help. He told me he had felt something was very wrong in the east. I have merely confirmed his fear. The evil has to be opposed. What differences there are between us have to be put aside. He is wise enough to understand that."

When Ratillic returned, he had a large dish of meat. It was raw. "I assume you will want this roasted?" he said. Nobody answered, and he grinned unpleasantly, deliberately pulling a small piece of meat off the rabbit carcass and chewing it slowly while they watched. "It is good. Fresh," he told them. "Taken by the owls this morning." He pointed to the remains of a fire by one of the walls.

"Make what preparations you will. I cannot offer you wine, but there is fresh spring water if you need it."

Sisipher asked Wolgren to help her with the food and he leapt to her aid at once. In minutes he had a fire going, the smoke curling up the flue behind the wall, and Sisipher had the meat turning nicely in the flames. Guile watched her avidly, marvelling at the lines of her face, careful not to let her see him.

"What do you know of the east?" Korbillian asked Ratillic as they all sat around the large table.

"My owls do not go there anymore. Only one has ever been beyond the Silences, the great deserts. How he managed to return here in his condition is a mystery. He died soon afterward. He was unable to say much about what he saw there, but it would trouble the dreams of a stronger man than me. Yet still I did not suspect the truth."

"You speak of lurking evil," said Korbillian. "Does it have a name, a shape?"

"I think not. But like a disease, it contaminates all who go near it. If there is life in the east, it has changed."

"Can you teach us the way to this eastern city? Have you maps?"

Ratillic smiled, but the air of contempt had not left him. "My maps are unique in all Omara. Unique and priceless. I would be a fool to pass on the gift of the owls, the mapmakers. But I can show you how to reach the city."

"Is that the only help you will give us?"

"And what else should I give you? Provisions, weapons?" Again he laughed. "The power to destroy?"

"I am no warrior," said Korbillian levelly. "Yet this blight has to be razed."

"I've nothing to give you."

"The maps. You have detailed maps. I have to find as many allies as I can. Your maps will be as detailed as your fabled maps of Ternannoc. That was your skill, your power, was it not? To use the birds of the air and the creatures of the land? Pity that you had so little use for men!"

"I did not *use* them! I make no demands. I am not their master."

Korbillian nodded patiently. "But the maps."

"And should I give them to you freely and bless you and say, 'Here, Korbillian, go out and use these wisely. Free Omara. Return them to me when you are done?' "

"Are there no copies?"

"Copies! Each map takes years to compile! Who has time to make copies? No, there are none."

"Then I need the originals."

"And if I refuse?"

"That is your choice."

Korbillian glared at Ratillic. "You seem to care about Omara."

"Of course! But what can one man do against that place in the east. Ternannoc was not saved."

Wolgren's stare was even more angry than the girl's. "Let me persuade him," he said to Korbillian.

Ratillic chuckled. "So the cub has fangs, eh?"

Korbillian shook his head. "No, that is not the way. But consider, Ratillic, if you know the extent of this evil, you must see the wisdom in opposing it."

"I have only your word that you oppose it. Perhaps you are its servant."

Korbillian's face darkened, even in this dim light. "That remark was not worthy even of you, though I should have expected no better from someone who has spent a lifetime cowering away from his responsibilities." There was an edge to Korbillian's voice which spoke of the hidden power he could command, and his companions sensed danger in it.

Ratillic looked no less angry. "Very well. Since you insist. I have considered. I will give you what you ask— for a price."

"Which is?"

Ratillic looked deliberately at Sisipher. "Leave the girl with me."

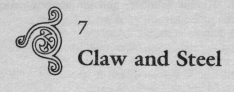

7
Claw and Steel

WOLGREN LEAPT UP and in a second had his knife at Ratillic's throat. He had moved with astonishing speed, and Sisipher was astounded. The youth used his free hand to wrench Ratillic's head back, and Korbillian had no time to move to stay the youth. Wolgren tightened his grip, but the knife was poised, the killing blow withheld.

"Wolgren!" hissed Korbillian, appalled.

Ratillic managed a single cry. Immediately there came a flutter of wings above as the owls stirred.

"You'll die before they reach me!" snarled Wolgren.

"Then you'll all die with me," gasped Ratillic.

"Release him!" ordered Korbillian.

Wolgren scowled at him, but at last did as he was told. Ratillic coughed, massaging his shoulder where the boy's fingers had dug into him. He said nothing, but the owls fluttered down. Three of them perched on a chair behind Ratillic, their huge eyes watching the youth, as if in readiness for a kill.

"You have no claim on the girl," Korbillian told Ratillic. "She has chosen to come with me, and is far more valuable than your maps. You are worthy of contempt, nothing more. I may have been wrong to ask Wolgren to free you."

Ratillic stared at them with renewed hate. As the moments seeped away, the air became charged with the promise of violence. Another movement from above them almost broke the silence. Korbillian raised a fist as if to ward off a blow or to discharge some grim force.

"Wait!" cried Sisipher, and the attention focused on her. "The owl comes with news."

"How can you know?" demanded Ratillic.

Sisipher pointed. A huge owl landed opposite them, holding its great wings out as it alighted. Its chest seemed to be splashed with blood, but it was a rusty bib of down. Ratillic studied the bird, his expression becoming one of horror.

"What does it say?" asked Sisipher, who understood that some kind of silent conversation was ensuing.

Ratillic ignored her, listening. Then he nodded, sagging back. "Damn them!" he spat. "They are here."

"Who?" said Sisipher.

"The Deliverers. And there is blood on the snow."

Korbillian looked sharply at the girl. He did not need to question her. "It is as I foresaw," she nodded.

Korbillian turned back to Ratillic. "What are these Deliverers?"

"They belong to a distant fortress city called the Direkeep. They are sworn to wipe out power and any worshippers of gods. Like plagues they drift across Omara, even to its remotest parts. Now they are below us in the pass."

Korbillian held out a gloved hand. "And are their hands clawed like steel?"

"Oh yes," agreed Ratillic. "So I am told. When they achieve full status, their training complete, their hands are struck off and replaced with the killing steel. The purifying steel, they call it."

"They kill?" said Guile, shuddering.

"It is their so-called duty to give blood to the earth, the blood of transgressors."

"Why are they here?" said Sisipher.

"Why indeed?" Ratillic smiled, and the girl felt herself crawling as his eyes watched her. She had tried to escape the implications of his earlier unpleasant suggestion.

"What's happening outside?" she asked.

Ratillic's mood changed. His eyes held a fresh anger. "My owls met them. There was a fight. Claw and steel.

Two of the owls are wounded, but Kirrikree says they will heal. Several of the Deliverers are also wounded. One of them is dead.''

"The owls killed him?" said Guile, surprised.

"No. The man was blinded. Such things happen in a fight. He would have lived, but Kirrikree says he was executed by his leader, who will not be burdened with cripples."

"Can they be after us?" Guile asked Korbillian.

"Possibly."

"They have your scent," confirmed Ratillic. "You have drawn attention to yourself, Korbillian. And this is no simple follower of the Abiding Word, the law of the Deliverers, who seeks you. Kirrikree says it is Simon Wargallow." Though Ratillic's lips twisted in a sardonic smile, he pronounced the name as though it were a sentence.

"The name means nothing to me," said Korbillian.

"Take my advice. Go out into the snow and kill him," said Ratillic. "There are about a score of them. Kill them all. They are no better than vermin. Omara has no need of their kind. As well destroy the Direkeep as your eastern city. It is as great a source of evil."

Korbillian shook his head. "By no means. The place you call the Direkeep can harbor only a fraction of the evil of the mound. I will waste no time on these Deliverers. Do they know where we are?"

"No. Nor will they find my haven. Kirrikree's owls will lead them far off. Since you will not destroy them, let the mountains do it."

"Do they possess power?" asked Guile.

Ratillic laughed. "They terrorize. They have that sort of power. Otherwise, no. Korbillian could fell them all—"

"No!" snapped Korbillian. "Power should never be misused. I have always insisted as much. If your owls will lead them astray, so be it."

"By the time the storm has come and gone, Simon Wargallow will be lost, perhaps even dead, though I doubt that. Then you can leave here in peace. But not with my maps," Ratillic added contemptuously. "You can find your own—" But he stopped, his eyes locked with those of the great owl, Kirrikree. He was silent for several moments, and it became obvious that his anger was mounting. He directed a look of fury at the silent bird. "No!" he snarled at it finally.

Kirrikree opened his wings and beat the air in defiance. His unblinking gaze fixed Ratillic, unmoved.

Sisipher clapped her hands together and gave a delighted cry. "You hear him, Ratillic?" she laughed. "He doesn't obey you anymore."

"Can you communicate with the owl?" gasped Korbillian.

Sisipher stared at him as if she had only just realized. "Oh! Yes, I can. Kirrikree and Ratillic are arguing."

"You imagine things," cut in Ratillic.

"No!" Sisipher laughed. "I know what Kirrikree thinks."

"Tell us!" cried Guile. "Why were they arguing?"

"Kirrikree," said Sisipher, "is opposed to Ratillic's hostility toward us. He wants to help."

"He will lead the Deliverers away, that is all," insisted Ratillic, but Sisipher was still laughing, delighted at the unspoken understanding of Kirrikree that she had discovered.

"No! That is not all. After that he will come with us. He will be our map, Korbillian. He will guide us across Omara!"

"But why?" said Korbillian in disbelief.

Sisipher's smile died. "Because he knows what lies in the east. And because it killed his brother. He agrees with you, the evil must be opposed at all costs." She could feel the warmth within the bird, the bond, sensing that it would grow between them, but beside it she could sense also the sorrow, and the fury.

SIMON WARGALLOW watched the skies. The clouds had parted and he felt that the owls had mercifully lost an ally. Their attack had been sudden, well-ordered. How long had they been watching us? he wondered. Did they know we were coming?

Beside him, Djemuta secretly studied him. Nothing

evaded his master's suspicion. He seemed to consider every man, every creature a threat until it proved itself otherwise. To him, every boulder, every crag, stood deliberately in his path, a challenge. Like all the servants of their ruler, the Preserver, Warden of the Direkeep, they were sworn to deny power, yet Djemuta feared its presence in every stone. If he failed, Wargallow would be hard. His reputation as the principal killing arm of the Preserver was established. Had the Preserver *known* that this man Korbillian, this agent of evil, was in these bleak mountains? The Preserver's eyes saw far across Omara, his gift from the earth. What did he know of Korbillian? I am certain, Djemuta mused, that he knows enough to have sent Simon Wargallow so far from the walks of men, placing this charge upon him, to keep Omara untainted by the evils of men, the earth-harm they might do.

There were smears of blood across Djemuta's robe, and a scored line across his cheek where the claw of an owl had almost found an eye. One of the others, Carmund, had been unlucky, rendered sightless by the owls. Himself eager to serve the Preserver, Djemuta had despatched him swiftly. As usual, Wargallow had noted the kill, but had said nothing. He shared his thoughts, his goals with no man. Djemuta knew that when he was hunting transgressors, he was singleminded and unremitting. Yet there now seemed about him a greater desire for success, as if all his past victims were stones along the path to this particular killing, when it came.

Wargallow again searched the sky. Time was an enemy now. There would certainly be another storm, and they would have to lie low. Tracking the man Korbillian would be difficult enough. Time! Wargallow growled within. If I had had more, I would have coaxed more from those wretched villagers. But had I stayed, the enthusiasm of Djemuta would have demanded more than the serving girl's blood. And yet there is plenty of time. Korbillian is the greatest prey I have yet hunted. I should savour that. Wargallow allowed himself a smile, relaxing. Even if this takes me a year, I will find him.

"Will the owls attack again?" came Djemuta's voice.

The Deliverers had defended themselves well, but had not been able to match the speed of aerial assailants. Steel and claw rang together, but several of the Deliverers had received deeper wounds than Djemuta. They did not complain, but there was an air of apprehension hanging about them all. Wargallow remained aloof from it.

"No doubt. But we will endure."

Djemuta thought of the battle. The owls had been organized, and had not fought randomly, but with deliberation. Strangely, they had not seemed to be attacking with the intention of killing for food. Rather they had fought to spite the Deliverers. Protecting, perhaps, something here in the mountains.

Wargallow looked over his men. They were close together, ready for his command. He was pleased: they were well disciplined. With a gesture he moved them on, and as a single body they rode up the pass. Their horses were small and sturdy, chosen for the arduous journey and battle-trained. A few had shown signs of panic when the owls came, but now they were relaxed. Wargallow smiled grimly to himself. The owls, he suspected, would not harm the horses.

They had not traveled far when the flutter of wings came to them and they saw the white heads of the owls among the higher snows. Wargallow reined in and the men tightened ranks. They had fought mounted previously, but the snow underfoot was deepening and so now they dismounted, reining the horses together as the first of the great white owls came swooping down. Why, thought Wargallow, do these birds attack by day instead of night?

The cries of the birds were designed to terrify, to freeze their prey, but the Deliverers raised their steel hands, unmoved. As the owls came among them in a sweeping wave, steel flashed and claws ripped down. Feathers fluttered like snowflakes, and the horses snorted, tossing and ducking, although Wargallow's guess proved accurate. The birds would not harm the horses. Wargallow's men fought in silence, but they moved with speed that would have dumbfounded ordinary men. Still it was not enough to cut the owls from the sky, for the birds were far quicker, able to turn and maneuver with stunning dexterity for such large creatures. They did not attack quietly. The first wave of them flew away, immediately followed by a new attack, and Wargallow frowned at the organization. There was nothing random about this assault, and he had known soldiers who were less well disciplined.

Gradually the Deliverers had to give ground. Their horses were not, after all, able to remain calm for a prolonged attack, and as if sensing this, the owls dived at them in mock assault. It was enough to cause confusion and reins snapped. Several horses got loose and backed away. Following up this advantage, the owls prized the horses apart and the Deliverers found themselves similarly split. Djemuta was frantically warding off an attack and trying to see where the horses were. Wargallow thought he understood the tactic of the owls—they were trying to force his men back toward one of the walls of the pass. Yet perhaps it would be better to have the solid rock behind them. He chose his moment to shout an order, and the men fell back.

"Leave the horses!" Wargallow yelled. "We can collect them after this." As he suspected, the owls did not try to prevent them reaching the rock wall, and they got there quickly, able now to rest. The owls soared high overhead, circling, waiting. It would not be long before they came in again.

Wargallow scanned the snows. Out in the scuffed blanket was a figure, alone, the only Deliverer who had fallen. He did not move. The horses had retreated down the valley. Wargallow knew they would not have gone far. The smell of blood would not deter them from coming back to their masters, though the owls were vigilant.

"Any injured?" Wargallow asked Djemuta. A quick inspection revealed nothing serious, but every man had been marked.

"How many of the creatures are there?" Djemuta wondered. "I had thought owls to be solitary hunters. And so large!"

"There is a powerful evil here," said Wargallow. "Just as the Preserver warned."

"Sire!" came a shout and one of the men waved to them. Wargallow went cautiously to look. "A cleft in the wall, sire."

"A cave?"

"Yes, sire."

Wargallow considered. "Exercise great caution." The owls were far more intelligent than he had expected, and there was now every reason to expect a trap. "See what lies within."

The man obeyed instantly, disappearing into the darkness.

"The owls are returning," called Djemuta, and at once the men readied. Wargallow motioned them into the tall cleft, making as small a target as possible for the owls. He saw no danger in that. Possibly the birds had defeated themselves. Now they were unable to reach the defenders, yet still they swooped by beyond them. While this continued, the screeches of the birds ringing off the rock walls, Wargallow's man came back from the dark. "Not a cave, sir, but a passageway. It cuts through a neck of the mountain and comes out into a valley beyond."

"Did you see any of the birds there?"

"None."

"Very well, but be ready for another attack."

They went along the passage, leaving a single man to guard the entrance and to give the owls something to shriek at. Wargallow decided it may be best to abandon the horses for the time being. He anticipated going back, once he had caught Korbillian and his party, and if it was a quick kill, he knew the steeds would wait.

The passage ran on for about two hundred yards through the rock. Beyond it, the valley was silent. Wargallow studied it from cover. There would be little point entering it if it had no way out. The valley seemed to run roughly parallel to the pass they had been climbing, and it rose upward to the high ridges above. In the ridge was one particular dip, like a saddle, and Wargallow pointed to it.

"Djemuta. See if you can reach that place. It will not be the way our prey has taken, but we may yet avoid the owls."

Djemuta knew that he would be placing his life in grave danger, for it would be difficult to resist the owls on his own. Even so he nodded, beginning at once. Wargallow called for a report from the other end of the passage. Apparently the owls had landed, a great flock of them, and were silently watching the cleft in the rock, as though sure that their victims would have to come out eventually, like voles searching for food.

Wargallow was not convinced that the owls had been cheated. Had they known about this passage? Perhaps not. He thought hard on his next move. If Djemuta came back unscathed, he would be none the wiser. Either it was safe to climb up to the ridge, or the owls wanted just that and would fly over the mountain and catch them in the open again. Wargallow watched Djemuta as he picked his way among boulders and drifts, blending well into the terrain. It would have to be at night, but as Djemuta had said, owls usually hunted by night.

Word reached Wargallow that the owls appeared to be asleep out in the snows. More trickery? He would wait and see. If there was a clear moon, they would take the risk. He instructed his men to open their provisions and he placed a guard to watch for Djemuta's return. Moments after eating, he was asleep himself.

RATILLIC SAT APART from his unwelcome guests, and though his eyes were open, he may as well have been asleep. Only Sisipher knew what he was doing.

"He is listening," she whispered to the others. "Somehow he can hear the owls, even though they are out in the snows."

"What of Kirrikree?" asked Korbillian.

"I am not yet used to this strange gift. When he is near, I will know it, but as he flies away, the contact is broken. Perhaps in time I will be able to master this better and sustain contact."

"What of the storm?" asked Guile.

"I don't think it has arrived," she replied.

Ratillic stood up, for a moment himself like a great bird. "It will be tonight," he said. "Wargallow and his rabble are pinned in a mountain cleft. The owls say he can escape, but it will be across a north-easterly ridge and away from the simpler eastern path. It is a route that will take him days away from your proposed route.''

Korbillian had already told him they intended to pass through the mountains by the easiest, quickest route. Reluctantly Ratillic had given them some directions, insisting that since Kirrikree had decided for himself to be their guide, let him show them. Sisipher had had no time to explore her new found relationship with Kirrikree, for he had left at once to harass the Deliverers. She asked Ratillic about the owls, but he had closed himself off, remaining a mystery. Korbillian seemed not to want to discuss his past and the reasons for the animosity between himself and the Lord of the Mountain Owls.

When Kirrikree returned, through some unseen vent in the darkness high above, everyone jerked to attention. The huge white owl dropped beside the girl, and Ratillic stared at it in silent fury, as though it had abandoned him. Sisipher felt her heart thrumming as the bird watched her. She wanted to reach out and touch the power that filled it. There was no voice inside her head, yet she understood Kirrikree's thoughts clearly.

''Do not fear me,'' they said, but the bird already understood that she did not. ''We have trapped the man Wargallow. Later we will lead him away, and into the storm.''

''Kirrikree, why have you chosen me?''

''You chose me. You understand me. You have the gift. Ratillic is afraid. He cannot understand me now. I will not let him.''

''He is angry.''

''Yes, but it is his own fault. He sets a barrier between himself and the man of power.''

''You know Korbillian?''

''Only what is hidden in Ratillic. But what your master fears most, the eastern evil, that I know. I have warned Ratillic of it, but he denies its meaning. He closes himself off from all Omara. He should be a servant to it, as he should have been to Ternannoc. Where he failed once, he has not the courage to succeed now.''

"Failed?"

"In Ternannoc, our world. His power, his understanding of us, and other creatures, could have been better shared. But he is reclusive, jealous. Many men of power were like this. There were those who tried to draw them together."

"Like the Hierarchs?"

"Yes, but they overreached themselves and abused their powers. It was an accident, not an evil act, but the consequences were dire. After it, no one would work together to put matters right. Distrust and suspicion ruled. Ratillic is very bitter."

"Why does he hate Korbillian?"

Ratillic leapt up, his arms flapping wildly. "I know what's happening!" he cried. "Kirrikree, you shame me! Why have you turned against me?"

"You know why," Sisipher heard the bird reply.

"Come with us," Korbillian said suddenly.

Ratillic's face contorted. "I will not!"

"We don't need him," snapped Wolgren.

"For once I agree with you," Ratillic retorted. He stared at Wolgren, but then marched away and out of sight.

Guile turned to Korbillian. "Must we have his maps? We have no idea what lies beyond the mountains."

"Forests," said Sisipher. "We will have to go carefully, though. Kirrikree says there are strange events taking place east of the mountains. Immediately beyond are the forests of the kingdom of Strangarth. He is a bellicose king, and his lands are full of tribes that he can barely control. Any strangers there are liable to be put to the sword."

"And where is the Direkeep?" said Korbillian.

"South of our easterly path. A hundred miles or more," Sisipher went on as Kirrikree supplied the information. "If we travel east and keep to the north of the way we need to go, we should be able to avoid both the main lands of Strangarth, and the Direkeep. After that we will need to turn south east."

"Can we not turn south and pass south of the Direkeep on an easterly course?" asked Korbillian.

"An invading army has come to the lands there, thought

to have landed in ships beyond the great estuaries of the Three Rivers.''

''Does the geography mean anything?'' Korbillian asked Guile.

''I've heard vague reports of the Emperor's ships landing on the eastern continent, but only in isolated instances. I seem to recall word of these Three Rivers. Doubtless they are easily navigable, and some adventuresome captain has gone searching for glory.''

Sisipher was frowning. ''That's odd,'' she said. ''Kirrikree seems to think there are many of these men, and they are equipped for war. And they are from over the sea.''

''From the Chain?'' said Guile, mildly surprised.

''Kirrikree recognizes the name of Quanar Remoon.''

''But why are they here?'' said Guile, looking puzzled.

''Perhaps,'' said Korbillian, and for once there was more than a hint of a smile on his face, ''the mad emperor has at last decided to make war. He has found someone to fight.''

''Yes,'' nodded Sisipher, ''but these men have been here for over a year, steadily growing in number.''

''You read some purpose in that? What does the bird say?'' grinned Guile.

''During your audience with Quanar Remoon, did he not mention these troops to you?'' Sisipher asked him.

Guile snorted. ''He would have absolutely no reason to tell me anything about them. Or any of his other armies. Besides, whatever order he gave that posted them here, you can be sure he has forgotten!''

Korbillian nodded. ''Yet it is interesting that the men still come.''

''Well,'' went on Guile, ''it can have nothing to do with us.''

Sisipher's eyes fixed him in a strange way, and for once Guile did not enjoy them upon him. ''Do you have reason to think it should?'' she asked.

''None at all. We didn't escape from Quanar: we were cast out. If he'd wanted our heads, he could have plucked them from us quite easily.''

"Guile is right," agreed Korbillian. "Even so, I would rather avoid his men."

Sisipher said nothing, but they all knew that she gave the matter deep thought. Whatever powers she had, set her apart from them, even Korbillian, but strangely both Wolgren and Guile found them compelling.

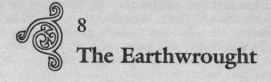

8
The Earthwrought

IT WAS EVENING by the time Brannog had managed to climb any distance up the mountainside, and already he wondered if his actions were really wise. He would have to shelter overnight otherwise he would risk falling off the mountain. He felt a great urgency not to stop, but had to content himself in the knowledge that the Deliverers would also need to rest. He now found that he had mixed feelings about leaving Sundhaven: there were certain regrets, but at the same time he felt again that kind of youthful madness that had spurred him on once before. It was this that lent vigor to him, and although he could not completely dampen his fears for his daughter, he felt an optimism, though for what he was not sure.

When the wind began to reach down from the high passes, bringing with it the whipping flurries of snow, he began to realize that he was in trouble. He would have to shelter quickly. Like a sheep, he struggled to find a place out of the cold. Already the darkness closed in, shutting his world down to nothing. He seemed to be scrambling about for hours, his limbs growing heavier, his ears ringing to the shouts of the angry storm. He found his way between two faces of exposed rock, where snow was already plastering itself in great speckled blotches. The constant freeze and thaw of the frost had made huge incisions in the rock slopes, like the cuts of a massive axe, and Brannog wriggled his way into one of these gashes. Mercifully it seemed to reach far into the rock wall.

He forced his body as far in as he could go, now in near total darkness. The sounds of the storm were muted by a turn in the rock. He could see nothing above, but the snow could not reach him here, although the wind raced through the crevice. He would have to avoid its cutting edge soon, for all his thick clothes. It was not possible to guess how much further he could go inward, but he forced himself on, his back flat to the slippery rock and with the naked face inches before him, now sloping back over his head. Panic glared at him from the darkness.

As he wormed his way inward, he felt the ground beneath him crumble abruptly, his feet kicking for purchase. There was none. His hands slapped at bare rock, but melting snow had lubricated it so that he could not prevent himself slipping downward. The rock face narrowed as he slithered deeper, unable to halt his fall, and something caught his head. He thought he heard a crash of sound, thunder possibly, and the roar of the sea, but then there was nothing but the silent darkness.

The icy drip of water wakened him. It trickled down his face and he shook himself. His hand dabbed at the side of his head, which was tender, and he could feel the stickiness of clotted blood there. He had no idea whether he had been unconscious for minutes or for hours. Slowly he shifted his position to escape the trickle of melt water, and was relieved to find that he had not sustained any bad injuries. He was bruised, but apart from that and his throbbing head, unharmed.

There seemed to be no wind here, and he thought perhaps he had fallen through trapped rubble to the natural bottom of the frost shattering, though there was no light to see by. As he was hungry, he opened his provisions and tried to decide what to do. Rest, or attempt to climb to safety? He assumed it must now be night, and at least he had found suitable shelter. Perhaps daylight would penetrate this place and be his guide. If not, his quest was in danger of having reached its end before it was begun.

He laughed aloud at the thought, mainly to fortify himself, and as he did so, echoes ran away from him into the distance. He knew at once that the crack in the rock extended much further than he had realized. In fact, it sounded as though there could even be a cave beyond. As he was no longer tired, he decided to see if he could investigate, in spite of the darkness. Inactivity would drive him to madness. He knew that he would have to attempt to climb back out of the caves at some time, but until he could see, it would be impossible.

Slowly, with a hand on the rock wall to guide him, he inched deeper into the rocks, now and then whistling or sending sounds ahead of him to point the way. The echoes persisted and seemed to tail off far into the distance. This distance puzzled him as it seemed to him now to open out as if he had stumbled into a huge cavern, although he could not see how that could be possible. How could ice have made such an incision so high up in the mountains?

He listened to the reverberations of his own voice. When silence fell again, he listened to it like a man shouldering a tremendous burden. It would have been easy for him to have slipped into a deeper well of despair then, but there came another sound, not an echo. Possibly the sounds he had made had dislodged something far below, but whatever had made the sound came again, at regular intervals. It did not sound like rockfall. It began to sound more and more to Brannog as if a heavy weight was being dragged along, and that whoever or whatever was pulling it had to pause to gather strength every few yards.

It was impossible to guess how far away it was. There was yet no light and Brannog's eyes ached under the complete darkness. The dragging sound came again, and seemed to be approaching. He decided to go back and his fingers brushed along the wall behind him, only for the precious contact to be broken. He felt a lurch of panic. Where was the wall? He swung his hand anxiously, but could not find it. Only a moment before he had had it close to his back, but now there was nothing. He stepped back, but even now could find no walls; his hands went out before and behind him but he might as well have been standing in the middle of an empty room. He tried stepping in different directions and waving his arms, cursing aloud as he again failed to find a rock wall.

Again the sliding sound reached him, and he felt sure that it had come closer. He tried to look through the wall of darkness in the direction from which the sounds seemed to come and wondered if his eyes had started to deceive him, for there appeared to be a glow there in the distance. Or was it closer? He had no sense of scale.

He kept absolutely still; now he could smell something. It was earthy but unclean, and it confirmed an idea that had been forming in his mind, an idea that he did not want to face, namely that whatever was approaching was alive. The glow seemed to spread, not far away at all, but coming much nearer, a strange green and yellow suffusion. Brannog was transfixed, realizing at that moment that he was shivering with fear. Whatever this thing was, it meant harm. Yet where could he run? The peculiar glow showed him no exits from his predicament. The walls had receded, almost as though pulled aside like curtains.

At last he was able to look properly at the creature and immediately wished he had not been granted so clear a view. Am I dreaming this horror? his shocked mind cried. It was three times the thickness of a man's waist, and had two arm-like appendages at the front of its body which it used to drag itself along in a crippled fashion, for below its waist there were no legs, jut a gradually thinning body like the tapering segments of an enormous worm. Brannog would have considered this incomplete body a distortion of nature in itself, but it was the creature's head that stunned him the most. In a deformed way it could have been considered human, although far too large. It had dish-like, white eyes, which seemed to be blind, for there was no iris, but which were obviously not. The creature suffused its own light, the glow seeping like vapor from the pores of its body. It had no nose that Brannog could see, and a wide, fleshy mouth that reminded him of the mouth of a fish. As it pulled itself laboriously toward him—for he was its definite goal—he shuddered at the sight of its spatulate fingers.

He wanted to run, but had still not decided where to run to. For certain he would back himself inadvertently into a corner, and that may not be to his advantage. How fast was this creature? He guessed not fast at all, judging by its difficult exertions. Already he had slipped his one weapon, a short axe, from his pack, and now he dodged to one side. The head of the creature turned with him and from its slack mouth slipped a tongue, though it seemed no threat in itself.

Brannog moved further away, those vast eyes still moving with him. There was no expression on that huge face, but a kind of oafish resolve. A curled hand reached out for him, but he was quickly away from it. He swung the axe in an arc that made the air whistle. At once the creature hissed, the sound ricochetting around the cavern, and it spat as if annoyed. It moved closer and Brannog zigzagged backward, trying to confuse it. As he did so, the creature gathered itself as if for a rush. Watching carefully, Brannog held his axe in readiness. As he had surmised, the thing launched itself, and although it now proved deceptively fast, he sidestepped it and struck at its arm with the axe. It felt as though he had glanced a blow from a solid pillar of stone, and his arm felt momentarily stunned.

The creature hissed hideously, its mouth working frantically as though the beast was in pain. Before it could move again, Brannog dealt it another savage blow, this time chopping into its flesh. It let out a demented roar that filled the place with sound, and smashed about it with flailing arms. Brannog leapt away. By the poor light, he could see that he had drawn blood, but he was careful not to be reckless. Enraged, the creature swung round and again launched itself, using its lower body as a kind of spring. Brannog barely avoided it as its hand brushed him and sent him stumbling. He rolled over quickly and cut once more with his axe at the hand that groped for him. His weapon chopped between two fingers and as the hand tore away from the agony of that contact, the axe was wrenched from Brannog's grip and sent tumbling away into the dark.

For the next few moments, Brannog and the creature weaved, Brannog trying to keep clear of the hands that would throttle him if they got hold of him, the creature remorseless in its determination to reach its prey. Brannog avoided several lunges by timing his leaps precisely, but his strength and speed couldn't last. Again he was caught a glancing blow, and this time he crashed clumsily to the floor. A hand fastened on his leg, tightening. He could feel his leg going numb as the hand dragged him toward the creature. Looking down he saw blood between the fingers of his assailant's hand where his axe had struck. Quickly he drew back his free leg and kicked ferociously at that injured hand. Something cracked and the grip on his leg relaxed instantly. Again the creature bellowed in pain, now drawing its hand to it and nursing it.

Brannog rolled away and grunted as he landed on the axe. Snatching at it, he watched the wounded creature. He may never get a better chance to finish the battle. Without deliberating further, Brannog rushed in, and let out a shout, almost a scream, that rang back from the rocks. The creature saw his attack far too late to defend itself: Brannog's axe crashed down between its eyes, where he took it to be vulnerable. The effect was immediate—the creature went slack dropping to the ground. Its good hand flung up and knocked Brannog aside, and as he tried to get away, he found himself pinned. Turning, he saw the mouth inches from his body, but there was no movement. Then came a spasm, but that was all. The strange light from the creature dimmed, and he realized he had killed it. He wanted to cry out crazily, but suddenly found himself drained.

It took him a while to pull himself clear and he wrenched at the axe, which resisted him. As he fought to free it, he heard new sounds, and to his fresh dismay knew that they had come not from one direction, but from all around him. He disengaged the axe and whirled, expecting to see more of the creatures. The glow coalesced in a circle and he made out several dozen shapes, though none of them were as large as the creature he had just killed. They seemed to be smaller than he was.

A number of them came forward silently, and Brannog held his axe before him. If he was to die, he would give them a fight. As he marshalled his physical and mental strengths and pushed back the terror that the force confronting him drew out of him, he was undone by a sudden mental image of his daughter. His quest to find and help her was about to disintegrate, and he felt his eyes filling with tears for the things he had lost and the frustration of knowing he could do nothing for her.

An unexpectedly deep voice growled from the shadows before him. "Why do you weep, overman?" Brannog thought he must have imagined it, but again the voice spoke. "You cannot weep at the death of the fleshworm. There is only joy in its death."

Brannog realized now that these new creatures were little taller than children, though extraordinarily broad for their height. One of them was addressing him in a guttural, half-intelligible voice. Brannog wiped at his eyes and partially lowered the axe. Perhaps he would not have to fight them after all. They seemed pleased at the death of the creature beside him.

"Who are you?" he asked.

They pressed in, but cautiously. He could see no weapons, save rough stones that they clutched, ready either to cast them or use them as crude cudgels. Their spokesman straightened and tapped his chest. "I am named Ygromm. We are the Earthwrought." The strange half-man uttered this with distinct pride and as though it would answer all questions, whereas it only served to raise many more in Brannog's mind. A race of beings who lived beneath the mountains? How narrow his view of the world was, he now saw.

Ygromm pointed at the dead fleshworm. "You have slain it," he said with awe. "And thus you are some great power-master. But you will be hunted by its masters for this."

"I don't understand," replied Brannog.

"Are you an enemy? But you must be if you come to slay the Children of the Mound."

"I mean you no harm, as far as I know," said Brannog. "I came here by chance. This creature sought to kill me, for food I suppose, so I defended myself."

"For food?" said Ygromm, taken aback, and his many

companions gasped uniformly, so that a ripple ran back among their ranks, leaving Brannog amazed at the number that must have gathered here. "You know nothing about fleshworms?"

"Nothing until now."

"You came here by chance?"

"A rockfall."

"The fleshworms do not hunt for food. They eat only the flesh that their masters give them, and it is not wise to dwell on such things. Very few overmen have ever come down to the delvings. Those that have were dead before my people found their remains, if not taken away to the Children of the Mound. The fleshworms are collectors. They burrow and search, dragging back what they find."

"This Mound, is it in the east?" said Brannog.

Ygromm hissed. "You know it?"

"I have been told of a great evil there."

"You have been told the very truth. Slowly this evil is eating out the heart of the world, driving the Earthwrought and all others further and further away from their homes, and deeper and deeper into the earth. We are countless delvings away from our home. The Children of the Mound hunt us with a single purpose, to destroy us. They send far worse than the fleshworms against us. Is it not so above ground?"

Brannog was astounded. Korbillian had said that the Mound had no intelligence, but was like a terrible disease. What Ygromm had said seemed to make matters far worse. "Not in my home," said Brannog. "But the Mound is far away, is it not?"

"Yes. But do overmen not know of its dangers, its growth?"

"Some do. And already they are seeking to prepare the world above."

"And you?"

Brannog hesitated. He had no way of knowing whether he could trust these people. To tell them of his quest might not be wise. "I seek to raise men who will oppose the eastern evil. Many will not believe it."

Ygromm seemed pleased with the answer. There was a

good deal of deliberation among the Earthwrought. It seemed that they were extremely impressed with Brannog's slaying of the fleshworm.

Ygromm had come to a decision. "We must take you before the Earthwise. He will know what must be done." Brannog made no objections and instead let the strange beings lead him away from the scene of the fight.

They were descending at once, and by the eerie glow from the Earthwrought, Brannog saw that they were no longer in natural fissures in the rock, but in tunnels that had been excavated in the stone and earth like the workings of vast earthworms. Ygromm made occasional comments, though the journey was evidently a secret one, and one carried out in fear. Ygromm told Brannog that other beings had made these delvings centuries before, but that they had long since died out. The Earthwrought went in silence, their ugly faces deep in concentration, and they listened out constantly for sounds that Brannog could not hear. Time had no proportions in the winding, endless burrows, some of which were narrow and cramped, others of which looked to have been dug by giants. At last they reached a large chamber. At one end there was a raised, flattened area, and beyond it a number of small tunnels that were far too small to admit anyone of Brannog's build. Ygromm called a halt and the Earthwrought arranged themselves expectantly before the raised area.

"I have sent word ahead," Ygromm told Brannog. "The Earthwise will come soon. Do you need food or drink?"

Brannog tapped his pack. "No." He wondered what these beings could possibly find to eat in such a place as this.

"Do these delvings travel under all of Omara?" he asked Ygromm.

"Somewhere in the histories, it will be written down. But you will have to ask the Earthwise. He is our keeper of the Earthlore, and only he of our clan has access to the histories. He will have many questions to ask you, overman. But you are not an enemy, I think."

Brannog smiled, but did not reply. He did not have long

to wait for his audience, for from one of the tunnels above
the raised area came a number of Earthwrought. Unlike
others he had seen, these wore leather harness and were
armed with curled weapons (Brannog thought made of
wood) and with them came a being who was at least half
as tall again as his fellows. He sat down cross-legged and
as he did so, the entire company did likewise, issuing as
they did a salutation. Ygromm motioned Brannog to sit
also, though he towered above those around him. The
Earthwise bowed, then looked straight at Brannog. In spite
of his extraordinary features (no less ugly than the other
members of his race) there was a depth of intelligence to
his gaze.

"Welcome, overman. They tell me you have slain a
fleshworm."

"It sought my life."

"Yet you killed it alone. May I see the weapon that you
used?"

Brannog held up his axe. It was still thick with the blood
of the slain fleshworm. Brannog was aware of the peculiar
reverence that the people around him felt for the axe. It
had almost become to them a holy relic. "I will use it
again on the fleshworms, or any other such monsters that
live in the earth," he said, hoping to meet with favor.

The Earthwise nodded solemnly. "Then we are in your
debt. So far, in this remote region, there are thankfully
very few servants of the Children of the Mound. But to
the east, where we belong, they are like maggots. Unless
they are checked, they will come here, and go beyond.
And one day, overman, they will have to go upward into
the light for their prey. Then your own people will be in
danger. I have heard of cities beyond the Silences, the
great deserts of the east, that have already fallen to the
Children of the Mound."

"I am largely ignorant of these things," Brannog admitted. "Until recently I was a simple fisherman, living
in a small village west of the mountains. Neither I nor my
people had heard of the Mound until a strange man came
to us, a man who claimed to possess power." Brannog
paused to see whether his allusion to power would impress

the Earthwrought, but they were silent, as though he had said nothing unusual. The Earthwise seemed to control their reactions, though, as he waited to hear more. "Since power of the kind he described is not known to Omara, we were not sure how to treat this man. He calls himself Korbillian, and he claims to come not from Omara, but from another world, the world of Ternannoc."

This time the Earthwise reacted, stunned, and there was a growling among his people. "Ternannoc!" he cried. "It is said that the evil of the Mound came from that place."

"Korbillian swears that his purpose is to destroy the Mound, but he must have help, the help of as many of our people as he can muster. Even now he journeys eastward, searching for the Mound."

"He is crossing these mountains?"

"Yes. I am searching for him."

"To join him?"

"Yes."

"Why did you not journey with him initially?"

The perceptive question caught Brannog for a moment but he kept his wits about him. "Other men came to my village after him. They call themselves Deliverers."

"I know of them," nodded the Earthwise.

"Do they serve the Children of the Mound?"

"No. They serve only the Direkeep and its lord, the Preserver."

"They apparently seek to destroy all power, or at least, all belief in it, and belief in all gods. This is strange, as Omarans have no gods."

"The Deliverers are fanatics," said the Earthwise.

"Those who came to my village were led by a man called Wargallow."

Again the Earthwise looked shocked. "Indeed! Is he also above?"

"You know him?"

"Yes, and he knows the Earthwrought. He is responsible for the torture and murder of a number of our people."

"But why?"

"He seeks to learn more of our lore, our homes. But he has not found a way to us. He hates us, as we do accept power, overman. For us, it is real. I will not explain it to you. But when the Preserver learns of gods and power, and his ears are acute on all Omara, he sends his fury against it. He will not allow power. There is a long history attached to this, some of which you must hear, I think, for I see before me the coming of the time that others wiser than I have said must come, that of the sharing. But for now, I would hear you speak.''

Brannog nodded. ''Wargallow seeks Korbillian. Somewhere in the mountains you will find them both. I also seek Korbillian, both to warn him and to strengthen his arm against these Deliverers. They did harm in my village.''

''Did they give blood to the earth?''

Brannog nodded. Still he decided not to reveal that Sisipher was one of Korbillian's party. ''Can you find these people?''

''Possibly. But we are strangers to these mountains, recently arrived. We do not belong here. We have made a few allies under the earth, but overground it is difficult. It takes time to establish allies there. And there is little life in these cold mountains. Our best chance of finding the men you seek would be when they have crossed the range, if indeed they can do that with so hard a winter raging above us.''

''I have to find them, and soon,'' said Brannog. ''Will you help me to the surface?''

The Earthwise considered and spoke again after a long pause. ''We can help you to the surface, and possibly find these men. That in itself would hardly repay you for the death of the fleshworm. I think it is time for greater decisions to be taken. I spoke just now of our histories. We have many, and many legends have grown up beside them in Earthwrought lore. Opinion among the leading lore keepers of our various clans is divided as to the past and as to how we should approach the future as a nation. I am not a great leader among the Earthwise, but I foresee terrible years to come. I see us pursued by the Children of the Mound, deeper into the wildernesses and further underground to where the stone boils. We cannot flee forever. We have to fight. Alone, we would perish, and the Earthwrought would be dust, not even a memory.''

Brannog could feel the grim weight of sadness around him. None of the Earthwrought here disputed the truths that were being aired before them. They had lived with them for too long.

''Now it is not only our nation that is threatened. I believe it is all life on Omara. This man Korbillian who you say comes to call men together, he is right. Overmen must fight beside each other, and beside them must the Earthwrought stand. It is said in some of our very ancient writings that the Earthwrought once lived above ground in cities, but that we were driven under the earth by enemies, invaders from some other world, possibly the Ternannoc you have spoken of. We became the Earthwrought, only to be harassed by the Children of the Mound. Some legends speak of a time of sharing, when we must again rise to the surface and fight for what we once had there. Some believe that our way lies deeper below, while others believe our way lies upward, to the light we once knew. But few overmen know of us, and would sell us to the Deliverers. Yet you have not come to us as an enemy. What then?''

Ygromm stood up unexpectedly. ''Let me go with him, Earthwise! I will fight beside Brannog Wormslayer!''

For a moment there was complete silence, and Brannog thought that the Earthwise might scold Ygromm for his outburst. But he was not the first to speak. Others had leapt up, waving their stones, calling out that they, too, wanted to go with Brannog. To Brannog's amazement, there seemed to be tears in the eyes of the Earthwise. He waved his arms for quiet, and it was a while before the Earthwrought had settled down.

''We should, perhaps seek the advice of a higher counsel,'' said the Earthwise. ''But there is no time. Our enemies beset us and in this man you have called Wormslayer lies fresh hope. If he will accept what you have offered, Ygromm, I will bless the sharing.'' He stood up and came to the edge of the earth platform. In his hands he held something that Brannog could not identify, but he held it out. It seemed to be a stone. "Brannog, whom the Earth-wrought name Wormslayer, will you accept this token of earth power? If you do, then I charge you with the safe keeping of my people, and know that they will protect your life with their own."

Brannog hesitated. The thought of being a kind of champion to them frightened him. What did they expect of him? But he thought of Korbillian, and of his wild determination to bring under his banner any man who would stand against the darkness in the east. Brannog took the stone and felt it pulse like a living organ in his hand. He hid it away in his pelts, and as he did so a great cheer rang around the low hall. Ygromm danced up and down like a child, and the Earthwise did nothing to prevent the celebrations of his people.

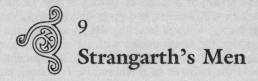

9
Strangarth's Men

THEY SPENT three days in Ratillic's retreat, waiting for the storm to pass. In that time their host withdrew even more into himself and hardly spoke. His resentment never flared into anger or abuse, but it smoldered. Korbillian also became silent, almost sullen, and any attempt by Sisipher to learn something about his past in respect of Ratillic was not ignored, but bore no fruit. Kirrikree had not returned and the storm blotted out everything beyond the walls. Even Guile, usually so loquacious and cheerful, seemed more thoughtful, brooding, although he never allowed his spirits to sag for long and often tried to make the girl laugh. She had casually tried to draw out of him something more of his past, but he had deliberately erected a defence, and she began to imagine that he must have disgraced himself in Goldenisle and genuinely earned himself demotion. It would not be hard to believe. She also knew, intuitively, that he harbored feelings for her, possibly honorable, but as she had no wish to encourage them, she did not press him too hard in conversation.

Wolgren responded warmly to the girl, his worship the one thing she found readable in any face there, but there was little to talk to him about. She had made a point, however, of saying how much she had loathed Ratillic's eyes upon her when he had asked that she be left with him, and knew that her words would be fuel to Wolgren's fire. Ratillic would never get near her while the youth was close by. Sisipher had asked the boy why he had chosen to come with a complete stranger, although by now she had guessed anyway. He had glimpsed another world beyond the prison of Sundhaven (which is how he had seen the place) and Korbillian had given him his opportunity to visit it. Now, although beset by the same fears that beset all the party, the youth pulsed with suppressed excitement and eagerness. It did Sisipher good to feel it, for she could not avoid the twinges of premonition, of shapeless, dark things that crawled out of the future toward her.

When Kirrikree returned to announce that the storm was over, they almost celebrated. Wolgren, with his usual zest, was in favor of immediate withdrawal, and Ratillic encouraged them to go.

"Kirrikree says," Sisipher told them, "that we can be across and on the far, lower slopes before the next bad weather."

Shortly afterward they renewed their journey. Kirrikree flew high overhead, out of sight, but Sisipher heard his voice from time to time.

"Any news of Wargallow?" asked Korbillian as they began the ascent of the highest part of the pass.

"His party has been driven north east by the last storm. None of them died. But they won't get near us now without our knowing," Sisipher added. "Kirrikree has promised to have them watched. By the time we are out of the mountains, there will be far too much land between us for them to catch us. They came on horses, but the owls have driven them back down to the coast. Perhaps the people of the village will keep them."

Kirrikree's prediction about the weather proved accurate. By the time they had found their way through the passes and on to the slopes that led away from them to the east, the sky had darkened once more. Spread out beneath them on the slopes, like an endless black sea, the conifers reached up to them. Beyond them they dimmed into mist, and somewhere above them, far out across the land, the white owl searched.

Wolgren still led the way, though he had long since passed beyond the boundaries of any earlier visits he had made to these mountains. Korbillian was content to walk behind him, warmed by the boy's enthusiasm. Sisipher and Guile brought up the rear, and now that they were descending, it was less tiring to talk. Even so, she began to sense a growing tension in him.

It was the evening of the third day out of Ratillic's retreat when they came into the first of the trees, and at once Wolgren prepared a fire from loose branches and bark. His ability to look after himself in the wilds was quite surprising. Guile, on the other hand, looked for guidance in most things. Not for the first time Sisipher wondered what possible use he could be to Korbillian. He had no skill in anything that she was aware of, although she admitted to herself that his wit did have its value.

"Kirrikree's coming," said Sisipher, knowing that the great owl would arrive so silently that he would frighten them if she hadn't prepared them. Moments later the white shape swooped above them, something clutched in its claws. The bird came again, dropping the small mammal he had killed for them, then settled near them on a fallen trunk. His huge eyes watched them with an expression of amazement, though Sisipher knew it to be an illusion. Wolgren jumped up and thanked him happily, and the great bird merely blinked. The youth cooked the meat, and Guile was glad to help him. Korbillian studied the bird. "He is troubled," he said quietly to Sisipher so that the others, preoccupied with the food, would not hear.

"You can tell?" But she did not wait for an answer. "You are right. He says there are many men abroad in these forests. We will have to go through them carefully. Use as little fire as we need."

"Does Kirrikree know much about the men of these lands?"

"Only a little. King Strangarth holds sway with difficulty, as the tribes are scattered and mostly independent. But there have been many skirmishes with the Emperor's men south of here on the borders. Kirrikree has not been able to learn the purpose of the Emperor's men, but he saw a party of them earlier today, and they seemed to him to be searching for something." She looked at Guile as she spoke, but at that moment he was sharing some private joke with Wolgren.

Korbillian puzzled at her meaning. "Are you certain?"

"It is Kirrikree's feeling, that is all."

"But why? The Emperor was glad to be rid of us. I was a threat to him, or as such his mad eyes saw me. Such enemies as Guile may have had at court would hardly pursue him to a place like this. They would be well rid of him here."

"You know more about him than I do," Sisipher smiled. "Tell me, why did you choose him?"

"He chose me. I am glad to accept those who will follow." He smiled grimly. "I'm not sure that he will be a worthy ally in a fight, yet I have come to value his company."

"Well, he does not seem unduly disturbed by the nearness of the Emperor's men. Yet he is a little edgy. Do you not sense that?"

Korbillian studied her briefly. She was more perceptive than he had first assumed. "You are more alert than I am. I have perhaps taken too much for granted. Even so, I doubt that the Emperor's men would be interested in him. I also doubt that they know he is here."

"They must know you both landed on this coast."

"Yes, but Kirrikree told us these men have been here for a long time. Since before I found my way to Goldenisle. Still, what are your thoughts on Guile?"

"I am not sure that I trust him," she said simply.

"Yet you trust me." It was spoken as a gentle challenge.

She averted her eyes from his gaze. "Yes."

"I will be wary. But I must tell you that I do not think Guile an enemy. He is ambitious, I am aware of that, although he does not know it. He is here with me because he seeks a share in my power. He would never admit such a thing. But he would love nothing more than to raise himself—"

"To what?" she said quickly. "What he once was?"

Korbillian shrugged as if it didn't matter. "Is it important? Most men aspire to power of one kind or another."

"I should like to know his goal," she said. "I think it would surprise us all." She went to join the others at the fire, and Korbillian thought long and hard on her words.

They ate heartily, all of them, glad of the meat that Kirrikree had provided, and as Sisipher was turning to thank the resting owl, it swooped up into the air like a white cloud.

"Something's frightened him!" she said, and at once they were all on their feet. Wolgren and Guile had their weapons ready, and reluctantly Sisipher drew her own heavy blade, though she stood close beside Korbillian. They listened as Kirrikree's wingbeats disappeared, and the evening closed in, hinting at another storm. Then, like distant thunder, a drumming of hooves approached.

"Two riders," Sisipher told them, relaying word from Kirrikree as he glided ghost-like between the great conifers. "They don't know we are here. They are in flight."

"What pursues them?" asked Korbillian.

"Kirrikree cannot tell. But both men are wounded. What shall we do?" They turned to Korbillian, all dwarfed by the trees, with the mist filtering down from the mountains beyond, and with the gloom came the feeling of isolation and exposure.

"Hide yourselves. I will speak to them."

"Are they Empire men?" asked Guile anxiously.

Sisipher shook her head. "No, King Strangarth's."

Quickly they spread out, leaving Korbillian alone by the fire. Guile knelt beside Sisipher in the bracken. "If they're wounded, they won't be seeking a fight."

"And if they do?" she teased him, herself unafraid.

"Will you use that blade?" He chuckled, as if the weapon was ridiculous.

She grinned. "I can hardly lift it."

"Korbillian likely won't want help." Yet as he said it, he looked no less anxious.

Then the riders were upon them and the ground shook to the beat of the hooves. Through the trees they burst, these riders, and as they saw Korbillian like a spectre in the mist, they reared up. Korbillian showed no fear. After a moment, when the two men had studied him, they dismounted, released their steeds, and came to the fire. His great size made them wary.

"Who are you?" one of the men said gruffly. They wore leather harness and light brown tunics, both smeared with mud and sweat. "And what are you about in this place?"

"An Empire spy?" spat the other, whose mind was already made up that he faced an enemy. There was blood on the loose armor of both men. They were dark haired and bearded, close to exhaustion, and looked like men used to being in the saddle, and at war.

"I am not an enemy," said Korbillian.

They could see he had no weapons, but they studied him as though they considered him dangerous. Both had swords, but as yet had not pulled them from their scabbards.

"Don't trust him," snapped the second of the men, but as he stepped forward, he stumbled, then collapsed. His companion's hand went straight to his sword hilt and he watched Korbillian even more intently.

"He needs attention," said Korbillian.

At that moment Kirrikree flew down and sat on a branch high above the two warriors. When the standing man saw him, his face paled. "Who are you?" he said again, and now his sword hissed free.

"A traveler. I wish to pass through your lands. I have no interest in your wars."

"Wars?" The man looked stung.

"I gather you fight the men of Quanar Remoon."

"They trespass."

A groan from the fallen man halted the conversation and Korbillian motioned to him. "You'd better help him. Do you need food?"

The man nodded, dropping on one knee to his companion. Korbillian handed him a flask. "Are you pursued?"

"We've lost the bastards."

"Then you are safe."

The man attended to his companion, whose wounds were not good, but he would live. When he had taken a drink he muttered something and allowed the other to bathe his wounds. The men gave their names as Ilassa and Taroc, the latter the fallen one.

"I will call my companions," Korbillian told them. "Treat none of us as your enemies." Korbillian saw their immediate doubt, as though they felt trapped, but even so he waved the others to him. Wolgren emerged first, his knife in evidence, and Sisipher came to the fire, her own weapon put away. Lastly came Guile, who yet hung back. Korbillian introduced them.

Ilassa managed a grin. "A boy, a girl and a scarecrow. Well, you hardly seem like a war party. Our thanks for the food and drink." He had eaten ravenously. "You must excuse our rough manner. This is no place to expect anything but treachery."

"We intend none. But perhaps you can help us?" said Korbillian.

"Where are you going?" said Taroc, recovering his strength gradually, but in no condition to move far. He was glad of the fire and shifted closer to it.

"To the east," said Korbillian.

"On whose business?" cut in Ilassa.

"My own."

"But who do you serve?"

Korbillian smiled patiently. "I will explain."

Guile interrupted with a rude cough. He pushed forward. "Before you do, I think we should hear something of events hereabouts. Who was chasing you?"

Ilassa and Taroc exchanged glances, but Taroc nodded for his companion to speak. "Along our borders there has been movement by many troops, far to the south. And yet within the last few days, these invaders have been seeping north. There have been skirmishes."

"The Emperor's men?" asked Guile.

"Aye," growled Taroc. "So far the scum have not made their intentions clear. They've been down in the delta lands for a year or more. In the past they've done some foraging, but we've sent them packing. What do you know of them?"

Guile flashed a warning look to Korbillian that clearly said, "Leave this to me." He turned back to the warriors.

"Only what we have heard on our journey. That they landed near the Three Rivers. Are they in great force?"

"So word has it. Up until now they have not shown much interest in Strangarth's lands. They have concentrated on the lands to be found up the rivers, to the east."

"The east," said Korbillian. "Why should they go there? Do they expect to find a land rich in precious metals, or treasures of some kind?"

Ilassa shook his head. "Far from it. The land there grows more barren as it goes eastward. Beyond are the even stranger deserts of the Silences. We hear tales of evil things. Perhaps the men of Empire make war upon them."

"But you clashed with them today," said Guile. "Nearby."

Ilassa nodded. "Aye. A large party of them. There were a score of us. We thought there were no more of them at first and so we challenged them. They declared themselves to mean no harm. On an exercise, they said. Our leader warned them they were in Strangarth's lands, but they insisted they meant no harm. They claimed no quarrel."

"You speak of evil things in the east," said Korbillian. "Can you say more?"

Taroc had dropped into sleep, curled by the fire. Ilassa seemed weary. He sat back, having accepted that these odd travelers would not harm him. "Most of what I know is talk. For years now there have been rumors of strange events in the east. Stranger creatures found in the forests. Refugees crossing the rivers have said their men and women have died of unknown illnesses, or have just disappeared. The earth moves, some have said. And recently, even in these woods, there have been sightings of creatures more beast than man. The skies, too, are sometimes filled with huge flocks of birds, fleeing the east. We thought the men of Empire were here to investigate."

"And what of your fight?" said Guile.

"No quarrel, they said! That was false. They began it, and the battle was cruel, and many men died. A score of them, did I say? Well, there were a hundred more beyond them. They cut us down like grass blades. Taroc and I fled, and must be the only men to have survived."

"And the Empire men?" persisted Guile.

"I doubt that they will seek us now. They have had their exercise, and a pox on them for it!"

Korbillian's frown was deeper than Guile's. Sisipher, too, wondered at the strange tale. She sought Kirrikree and at once his thoughts reached her. "The men they fought have gone," he told her. "North, away from us. We are not in danger of being found. But your master should know—there are other dangers abroad. Be wary."

Ilassa had been examining Taroc, who emitted a groan. "This is worse than I thought," said Ilassa. "The wounds are deep."

Korbillian knelt down and studied the sleeping man, though he was careful not to touch him with his gloved hands. "He many yet be saved. Quickly! Clear a place. Expose the naked earth."

Ilassa stared at him, but anxiety for his friend prompted him to obey. Wolgren was beside him at once, helping to drag away the layers of needles and fallen twigs. They soon had a place cleared and they turned to Korbillian. Sisipher and Guile watched in amazement.

"Loosen the soil," said Korbillian.

Ilassa hesitated. "He is not yet ready for burial."

"He has power," said Guile, nodding toward Korbillian. "Let him use it." Wolgren was nodding, eager to see what would happen. Ilassa thought better of arguing and used the point of his sword to turn the earth. Wolgren used his knife. The work was easy.

"That will suffice. Now place your friend across the soil."

They did it without further question and Wolgren helped Ilassa to position Taroc as asked. The youth's absolute commitment won over Ilassa's doubts. Korbillian next instructed them to heap the earth up against Taroc's sides, and they made a careful wall, leaving his face, chest, and upper legs exposed. Korbillian muttered something in the darkness. Only the firelight lit the watching faces now.

"He will take strength from the pure earth of Omara," promised Korbillian.

Ilassa remained beside his friend, himself now exhausted. He allowed Sisipher to bathe the worst of his wounds and bind them, but insisted that the most he needed now was rest. "You say you are bound for the east?" he quietly asked Korbillian. "You have been merciful to myself and Taroc, and I should have no reason to distrust you, but the east? What do you seek there?"

"The source of the evil that creeps into this land."

Ilassa listened as Korbillian spoke of the city and of the implications of what was beneath it, and although the others already knew the tale, they shuddered in the firelight. Sisipher could feel Kirrikree's fear as he listened from his invisible perch.

"And you are alone?" Ilassa said in amazement. "Against this evil, you are no more than four?"

"I alert whoever I can."

"Then the troops of the distant Emperor waste their time on us. Perhaps my own king, Strangarth, should be thinking of making himself their ally, and warring on this terror from the east. Though he is not a man who would take kindly to such a suggestion."

Korbillian turned to Guile, thinking of Sisipher's words. "What do you make of Quanar's activities here?"

"It surprises me that his men have been here for so long."

"Perhaps," suggested Sisipher, "Quanar does not know his men are here at all."

"Yes, very likely you are right," Guile agreed from his place in the shadows.

Korbillian studied the crackling fire. "Why should his troops be so far north?" He turned deliberately to Sisipher. "Kirrikree told you he thought they searched for something. What?"

His question took her by surprise, as she had thought he had wanted to keep this a secret from Guile. She thought Kirrikree asleep, but it was as though he still listened. He was quick to come to her help. "I speak of rumors and of things half heard by those who traverse the skies of Omara," he told her. "But I would suggest that the real goal of the men of the Emperor is power."

"*Power!*" gasped Sisipher aloud.

Korbillian scowled at her. "What does he say?"

She told him and he looked pained. "So that is it: the power in the east. Already they were aware of it before I set foot in the Chain. Yet Quanar Remoon was oblivious in his madness."

"Others were not," said Sisipher.

"If these Empire men seek to use the power in the east to their own ends," said Korbillian, "they are already doomed."

Ilassa scowled at the exchange. "You have been to the Chain of Goldenisle?" he said with evident suspicion.

"Have no fear," said Guile. "We are no allies to the Emperor."

Wolgren leapt up, not in reaction to the conversation, but to something else. He listened to the woods, but apart from the slowly building wind, the trees were quiet.

"Kirrikree hears nothing," Sisipher told him.

"No, not the sky," said the youth. He knelt down, then lay flat, ear to the ground. But he got up again. "It's gone."

"What was it?" said Guile, who seemed more alert than anyone else.

"Like a distant heartbeat," said Wolgren. "Horses perhaps."

Sisipher looked out to where Ilassa and Taroc's horses must be and though she could not see them, she sensed them. They were relaxed, no doubt used to a rough life.

Korbillian looked once at Taroc, but seemed to dismiss something. Later he was to have cause to remember Wolgren's words. "In the morning," he said, "we will travel on. What will you do?" he asked Ilassa.

"I must report to my king."

"Will you mention us?"

"Would you wish it otherwise?" Ilassa at least seemed prepared to give them a choice.

"No," said Korbillian. "Tell him that I am here to raise men against the east. I need help. I would be happier if you came with us."

Ilassa shook his head. "I have to think of Taroc. I must get him back to his home. He has a family."

"By morning he will have recovered."

"You seem very sure of that."

"If it is so," said Korbillian, "will you both come with us?"

"To what end?"

"You'll probably find out more about what the Empire men are doing here," suggested Sisipher.

"Even so, I have no desire to ride to the east."

"Would Strangarth not listen to reason? Would he send men?" said Korbillian. "I will come with you to him if you think he would."

"To stand against the things we hear of in the east?" Ilassa scoffed. "I think not."

"Then help secure us a safe passage to your borders."

Ilassa grinned. "I will sleep on it." It was not long afterward that he did sleep, curled up beside his wounded companion, who already looked as though he were secure in his grave.

Guile shook his head, speaking softly to Wolgren a little later. "They confuse me. Why did they come this way? Behind us are the mountains. Had they been riding back to their king, they would not have come this way. Who's to say they are not freebooters?"

Wolgren frowned. He had come to like Guile, especially as he often seemed to ask his advice instead of dismissing him as a child, but he was still unsure of himself. "They mean us no harm, I think."

"I wish I could indulge myself in your confidence. Hopefully they will go their own way. If not, watch them, Wolgren. Keep your knife ready. Did you not see how that Ilassa studied Sisipher's fair face?" Guile saw his remark go home and quietly gloated as the boy's hand tightened on the hilt of his blade.

The wind strengthened and the party huddled about the fire, snatching at sleep. From time to time during the night, Wolgren again thought he heard the distant boom, like a heartbeat, possibly below ground, but apart from the wind, the only other sound was the murmur and groan of the man Taroc. Wolgren dismissed as part of a dream the notion that the sound of the distant boom coincided with the groans of the wounded man.

As dawn broke they ate sparingly. Ilassa discovered a few meager supplies in his saddlebags and retrieved them from the patient horses. Taroc came to, and seemed stronger, as Korbillian had said he would. He sat up as Wolgren scooped the earth away from him. While Taroc gazed dazedly about, Ilassa handed him a flask.

"Stir yourself, Taroc. Meet your new companions. We plot an easterly course."

Korbillian frowned. This was not what he had expected. "You go with us?"

"Aye, I've thought hard on it. We'll come so far. Our border is the river Swiftwater. As it leaves our lands, it enters a gorge, and to cross over to the east, you must use the Swiftwater Bridge. Beyond that we will not go, and if you are wise, you will also refrain."

10
Swiftwater Bridge

WARGALLOW LED his Deliverers out of the mountains and down into the upper reaches of the pine forests that stretched for hundreds of miles along the eastern slopes of the range. His men were tired and dispirited, but they did not complain to him. They had lost their horses and were not sure of their ground; the trail of their enemies was far away. After the owls had harried them off their course, the storm had come, forcing them to shelter. Wargallow had wanted to hurry on, but it had been impossible. Something about the storm from the east disturbed him deeply. There was a concentrated viciousness about it, almost akin to hate. When at last it had ceased and they were able to come out into daylight, the owls had gone.

Wargallow thought of his prey, this man named Korbillian. Could he possibly wield power of some kind? It went against the things that Wargallow had been taught, his code of behavior, the Abiding Word. Only the Preserver could wield power. But what if this storm had aided Korbillian to escape? Wargallow shut such thoughts off as Djemuta came to his side.

"Not too many miles to the east, sire, is a river. It runs south and turns to meet the Swiftwater. If our enemies seek passage to the east, they will likely follow this river and try to cross the Swiftwater at the gorge, the only place for miles where there is a bridge."

Wargallow agreed. "Are there villages about?"

"Strangarth's lands lie below us, sire. There should be."

"We need horses. We must reach the bridge first."

Djemuta understood that this was not a request but an order, although there was little he could do about it. He spoke to the men, instructing them to travel more quickly, and he detailed two of them to go on ahead down into the woods to look for signs of people. He expected little in this remote place. The party moved on, keeping above the tree line, where the ground was strewn with boulders but not impassable. They no longer expected to be attacked from the skies.

An hour later they were moving down a narrow ravine cut by one of the many fast-flowing streams. Wargallow, wrapped up in cloak and hood, had said nothing, though Djemuta sensed within him an anger, a strange passion to succeed in this particular hunt. He knew Wargallow to be a relentless man, faithful to the Word, and yet there was an edge to his sharpness now, a chilling dedication, as though this man Korbillian had committed crimes beyond all reason. It made Djemuta the more determined to bring him to earth, as he would earn a favorable report if he did, and could well lead him to promotion. He yearned for the day when he could lead his own party of Deliverers out from the Direkeep and not have to bend to the will of Wargallow. The man frightened him.

Wargallow held up a hand and immediately the entire party stopped. Djemuta was at his elbow in a moment. "Sire?"

"Movement. On the rim."

At once Djemuta barked curt orders to the Deliverers and was pleased to see them position themselves defensively without delay. If he did come to command his own men, they would likely be less effective than these excellent Deliverers. He freed his killing hand and studied the ground. It was not a good place to be attacked, for they were near the stream, down in the throat of the little valley. There now appeared to be movements in the larger of the boulders, but it was not clear what was happening. The ground gave an unusual grumble, as though a stream tumbled far below into a great pool, wearing away a subterranean passageway.

"What do you see?" hissed Wargallow.

"Nothing, sire. Only shadows. But something is there."

As Djemuta spoke, a number of the great boulders before them began to rise from the earth as if forced up by something powerful beneath them. Impossibly the massive stones split to reveal dark, mouth-like openings, and although silent they emitted a foulness of air that made Wargallow and Djemuta reel back. One glance showed them that the entire party was surrounded by these frightful stones, though they no longer moved. Yet, like wolves, they seemed to be waiting their moment to pounce. The earth itself breathed, a mighty beast asleep, but on the edge of wakefulness, and Djemuta felt his gut writhe in terror.

From between the two largest of the boulder-things stepped a new creature. It was short and squat with hideously large eyes and a skin that was encrusted with earth, as if it had just burrowed its way to the sunlight. It hopped forward. "Wargallow," it called in a distorted voice, raising an arm and hand that seemed to be more tree than flesh.

"I hear you," said Wargallow, but his face and fear remained hidden. The Earthwrought he had tortured before now had spoken of such beings under the earth, and he knew that there were others there which even they would not talk about.

"We have not come to kill you," came the croaking voice, implying that it would have been easy to destroy the Deliverers had they chosen. "You seek the man of power."

Djemuta gasped. What could these abominable shapes be? Nowhere on Omara had he heard of such things, although stories were whispered of terrors far to the east, beyond the Silences.

"I seek any man who claims to possess power," said Wargallow. He held up his killing hand. "Any man or being."

The unsightly creature hopped forward and made a

sound that could have been laughter. "Those I serve have no love of the man you wish to find. He is far to the south of you. Without help, you will never catch him."

Wargallow said nothing. There was more to come.

"I can set you on his trail with all haste."

"And who do you serve?"

The laughter came again. "The Children of the Mound. Be not alarmed. They respect the men of the Direkeep. Your cause is theirs. They wish no more than to help you destroy the man of Ternannoc."

"Ternannoc?" said Wargallow, feigning ignorance. "Where is that?"

The creature hopped angrily forward and growled. "You ask too many questions. Accept what is given."

"Which is what, precisely?"

"Go to the river that feeds the Swiftwater. There will be a craft large enough for your men, and a steersman. Let him ferry you to the south. At the mouth of the gorge there will be horses for you and your men. Ride to the Swiftwater Bridge. You will be there before Korbillian."

"And in return?"

Yet again the laughter rang back from the strange rocks. "All that is required is the man's death."

"Why have your masters not attended to it themselves?"

There was silence for a moment, but the creature chuckled for a last time. "You are strong, Wargallow. You have your Deliverers. You will need them all if you are to kill this man. My masters will send help."

Wargallow nodded. "Very well. But tell me, where are your masters? The Preserver will want to know. If you are not prepared to tell me, he will likely wish to send Deliverers to find them."

The creature considered. "I have no answer yet. But when the work is done at the Swiftwater Bridge, we will talk again. For now, find your craft." With this the creature disappeared so quickly that he seemed to have become one of the rocks. Slowly they slipped back into the ground, so that only a fraction of them remained above the surface.

Djemuta broke the ensuing silence with a hoarse whisper. "Dare we trust these things?"

"They seem anxious to dispose of Korbillian, though I wonder at their motives. But as we need to get to the gorge quickly, let us look for the preferred craft."

Silently they went down to the trees, each man guarding his thoughts.

KIRRIKREE FLEW LOW across the tops of the pines, unable to go higher because of the low cloud that restricted his visibility. Satisfied that the path ahead for Korbillian's party was free of danger for many miles, the great owl turned to the north, in search of news of Wargallow's men, and for other information that would help avoid danger of any kind. He spoke to other birds, most of which were terrified of him, fearing he would prey upon them, but who nevertheless told him things that he needed to know. He picked up particles of news from creatures on the land below which were unaware of his passing. No other white owl had come down out of the mountains, that was clear, and it looked as though the Deliverers had been forced to go far to the north.

He was about to turn back with a mind to scout along the way to the Swiftwater, when he picked up word of a party of men riding northward. He could have ignored them and returned to the south, but he decided to give them a cursory inspection. Swooping quickly over the green sea of trees below, he came to an area cleared by another fierce stream from the mountains that was chopping its way to the east. Below him he saw the riders, some two dozen of them. They had stopped to drink at the river and a number of them had taken fish from it, and their laughter came up clearly through the cool air as they cooked them.

Kirrikree chose a high branch as a perch and observed the men without being seen. He recognized the yellow tunics with the twin black border: they were the Emperor's men. Before long it became apparent to him from snatches of conversation that this was part of the party that had attacked Ilassa and Taroc's fellows, and although the owl could not find out what they were doing here, he could see by their casualness that they were not acting with any urgency. They evidently felt quite safe from attack, and as Kirrikree was not aware of any wandering parties of Strangarth's men, the men below him seemed justified in their ease. The owl watched them stripping and washing in the icy stream, laughing like young boys. He had seen enough to know that they would not be a menace to Korbillian's progress, so again took to the skies.

He had not gone far, however, when a flight of pigeons tore past him as if fleeing a fire. Abruptly Kirrikree turned back to see what had alarmed them. He came again to the place where the Emperor's men were, and found complete horror. Most of the men that had been laughing no more than moments ago were stretched out across the rocks and grass, their bodies crushed, covered in blood as though they had been smashed aside by the fist of something gigantic. Those that were alive appeared to be maimed, unable to walk. There was nothing to indicate what had so thoroughly destroyed them. Kirrikree watched for a long time, but the cloud rolled in like a shroud, and nothing moved. The last of the men died with hardly a murmur. Kirrikree heard their minds wink out, but they gave up nothing of the frightful secret of their murder.

Although he searched carefully in all directions for an hour, Kirrikree found nothing. It was as though the men had been cut down in a moment by an invisible foe. The owl flew as quickly as he could to the south. He had not gone far when he picked up the trail of horses and knew that he had found the mounts of the dead men. As one, they tore through the trees below, and he could feel their combined terror coming up to him in a wave. There was one rider, one fortunate survivor, or so he thought until he flew directly above it. It was not a man, but a half-man, a creature the like of which the owl had never seen before, and its thoughts were like the growling of a wild beast at a kill. The evil that permeated the grim being spoke instantly of the east, and all the rumors that seeped from that place. The half-man urged the leading horse on dangerously fast, and the others ran with it, far away from the scene of the terrible killings.

Kirrikree flew away, still unseen. He had no wish to find out what evil was occurring here. It could have no bearing on his own quest. Instead he made his way back over Strangarth's lands. Some time later he realized that other men were coming, and he found a secluded place where he could observe privately. He soon discovered that Wargallow had survived the mountain crossing, for below him, on foot, was the Deliverer, his party almost intact. They were heading directly east and were well away from the path that Korbillian was taking. Moving so slowly, it was not likely that their paths would cross again. Kirrikree waited until they had gone, then flew away, satisfied that the pursuit had been confounded.

ILASSA RODE upon one horse with Taroc before him. The latter seemed tired and sluggish, not properly recovered from his wounds, though in truth only Korbillian had expected him to be so. The others were surprised that his wounds had not worsened and at least made him feverish, and they had to concede that Korbillian had worked something with the unknown power of the earth. Ilassa was the most wary of this, as his people had little time for "power." They had, however, seen strange things in recent times and were prepared to accept things now which once they might have scoffed at. For now, Ilassa was grateful that his companion had survived what should have been his death.

On the second horse rode Guile and Sisipher, though she was not happy to be so close to him. He had not, however, tried to push himself upon her, and she was glad of that, knowing that she would recoil if he did. She would have preferred Wolgren with her, for although his feelings for her were clear, she felt she could control him more easily. However, the youth still led the party, with Korbillian beside him. Kirrikree had gone away to find out what he could about the problems ahead, and although Sisipher found that she could retain contact with him for increasingly greater distances, there were long periods when he was beyond her. She missed his company; somehow it seemed to fill a void in her life, a sense of security that she realized had been missing since she had left her father. She thought of him, and of the pain she must have caused him, with guilt, but even so, she was sure that this journey had to be undertaken.

That first day of travel on the horses it began to drizzle. At first, with the wind dying, it was not so cold as it had been up in the snows (though they had never felt as frozen as they might have) but as the drizzle thickened spitefully, persisting for hour after dreary hour, they could not keep dry and the cold got into them. Even Korbillian seemed diminished by it. He told them, however, that it would at least keep at bay any wandering soldiery, and Ilassa agreed that even Strangarth's men would be loathe to leave cover on such a grim day as this. If there were perils in the endless forest, they too thought better of showing themselves. The travelers spent a restless night under an overhang in the trees, a fire warming them, but not their dreams.

It was the same for the next two days. They were out of the evergreens now and moving through deciduous forest, leafless and skeletal, the drizzle less screened. Wolgren's enthusiasm had waned, and he began to despair of ever coming to the end of the miles of trees. The ground was heavy, in places treacherous, but they moved on, until at last the floor of the forest began to slope steeply away to the south east. Ilassa seemed relieved.

"The river below us feeds the Swiftwater," he said, but he seemed drained by the tedious journey. Taroc, beside him, had hardly spoken at all, as if his mind were tuned to something far away, and they had wondered if he had mended as well as he might have. They began the descent, and the riders soon had to dismount. As Sisipher's feet touched the ground, she shuddered as if she had trodden on the back of a sleeping beast.

Korbillian was beside her at once. "What do you see?"

"The river," she said softly, her words almost inaudible. "It carries blood from the north."

"Whose?"

She shook her head. Moments later she brightened, for she had sensed the return of the great white owl. Sure enough, Kirrikree appeared in the trees above them. He spoke of the things he had seen, confirming that Empire men had died.

"It must have been their blood you saw," Korbillian told the girl. "For we turn south to the gorge."

Kirrikree told the girl of his feelings about the east. He confirmed that something spread outwards from those lands like a plague, waves of evil that made things happen unexpectedly. He had searched the other side of the Swift-water, and although he had found nothing there, he had sensed a deep malice locked into the very stones, as if they were only too ready to welcome intrusion. There had once been a village across the gorge, Kirrikree said, a place where some trade was carried out with the men of Strangarth's lands, but the houses were down, the men long since gone, or dead.

Sisipher agreed that Kirrikree should go on again to keep scouting ahead for them. She kept contact with him, and always he reported that there were no signs of men about. Yet she could feel the clammy grip of something about her, telling herself that it was no premonition, only a blind fear. The party found a path beside the river bank and they made their way along it easily. Still the drizzle came down, obscuring vision, and below them the water foamed and boiled, heavy with rain and melted snows from the far mountains. When they came to the place where it tumbled into the Swiftwater, another valley cut even deeper into the rocks and was thickly treed; they veered south west along the narrowing path.

"Our border," said Ilassa above the noise. "In an hour we will be at the bridge. After that, Taroc and I will leave you."

"What of the lands immediately across the bridge?" asked Korbillian, and Sisipher looked away.

"Hills mostly, thinning out beyond the escarpment to the plains that lead in time to the edge of the Silences. Empty. Used to be villages, but the people moved further south years ago. Keep to the east, along the top of the escarpment and you should be well clear of any Empire patrols. Far below you, you'll see the lands of the Three Rivers. The first of them, the Camonile, will be stretched out below you.''

Kirrikree had returned, bringing with him a freshly killed wild goat, and they paused to cook and eat it. Ilassa had come to accept the extraordinary bird, as he had many things about this unusual party, but he bore them no ill will. If they had not been so determined to cross the bridge and go to lands where only a madman wanted to walk, he might have gone with them, though he was not happy about Taroc. The man had become even more sullen, drowsy. He responded to commands, but showed little emotion, and more than once Ilassa had seen Korbillian looking at him with a shade of suspicion, as if not sure of him.

The gorge deepened, the sound of the Swiftwater's fury coming up from shadowed depths, booming off sheer rock walls, while the pathway led up and around the twists of the great swathe the river had sliced into the escarpment in order to forge through it. Wolgren was the first to see the bridge above them. It was a remarkable piece of architecture, quite out of keeping with the orange rock about it, cut from gray stone, and Korbillian wondered who had put it there. The stones of the bridge must have come from far away, and the knitting of the stones, the fitting of the arched pieces, spoke of great skill. Yet nowhere in the surrounding lands was there evidence of such a degree of civilization.

Ilassa insisted on leading the way, and he now walked, with the two horses barely able to negotiate the narrow path. Both were nervous, eyes rolling at the frothy depths below, out of which the spray came up like steam (though there was no warmth in it). At the bridge Ilassa stopped. It was fifty yards across, but looked as solid and enduring as the walls of the gorge itself. He had to raise his voice to be heard above the noise of the Swiftwater. ''I will speak well of you to Strangarth,'' he said.

Korbillian nodded and stepped out on to the span, and Wolgren was first to follow. His eyes scanned the rocks, the ridges that towered high above them beyond the bridge, for there was much climbing to do yet once they were across the span. The ridges seemed deserted. Sisipher went next, smiling at Ilassa, who bowed. Taroc seemed fixed, waiting for Ilassa to give him his next instruction.

"Is he well?" the girl asked him.

"Better than I had hoped. But it will be a while before he is himself. I will long remember the trick with the earth that saved him. But hurry, girl, your master has already forgotten me." Ilassa chuckled. She was a delight to the eye, he thought, and worth fighting for. But not in the east. No one was worth following there.

Guile stepped after her on to the bridge, and he shuffled with fear, not liking the great height. The bridge was flat and without walls, so that each puff of wind that blew made anyone crossing it fully aware of just how high above a rocky death he walked. Guile trembled, aware that Ilassa could see his fear. But the warrior understood.

"Here," he told Taroc, handing him the reins of the horses. "Hold these." Taroc obeyed wordlessly and stood without moving. The horses scuffed the earth with their hooves, eager to be away from this place. Ilassa strode on to the bridge, but it was slick with the rain, which still fell steadily. He came to Guile and spoke softly. "I see your fear. Let me take you across."

Guile was far too afraid to argue, and he gripped the man's arm thankfully. He let himself be hurried over the span. Korbillian and Wolgren turned to watch, now no more than a few yards from the other side. As they did so, Sisipher screamed, and the sound rose high above the roar from below. Korbillian saw her eyes and whirled. Appearing from nothing, a dozen figures were waiting beyond the ridge, dressed in gray cloaks, exposing hands of steel. Kirrikree, beyond the ridge, seeking danger, heard the scream and turned as quickly as he could back to the bridge.

One of the figures came to the bridge.

"Deliverers," said Korbillian. Wolgren's knife came out as if he would throw it, but Korbillian whispered to him to hold it tightly. Ilassa had seen what was happening and looked back over his shoulder. Beyond Taroc, climbing the path, were more of the cloaked men.

"Taroc!" he yelled. "Leave the horses! Come to me, quickly!"

Taroc was not quick, but he did as he was told. Ilassa pulled out his sword and Taroc did the same. They stood shoulder to shoulder. Guile dropped to his knees, terrified not so much of the Deliverers, but of the dizzy fall. Without Ilassa's hand on his, he was unable to move.

Sisipher had run back to stand with the two warriors, her own sword dangling in her hand, though she could not imagine how she would use it.

"Korbillian!" came a shout from across the span. Wargallow came closer, Djemuta beside him.

"Stand aside," said Korbillian. "We have no business with you."

"I think you do." Wargallow's killing hand gleamed. He was pleased with the events of the last few days. The strange boatman had brought them to the beginning of the Swiftwater gorge, just as promised by the servant of those who called themselves the Children of the Mound, and soon after stepping from the craft, Wargallow had again met the half-man. With him he had brought the promised horses, though they were frightened and had taken a long time to quieten. The time spent waiting for Korbillian's arrival had not been pleasant for the Deliverers, as the eastern lands sat like disease around them, ugly and corroding. Korbillian's coming was a great relief.

He himself did not seem perturbed by the meeting, Wargallow thought. He watched as the man opened his black-gloved hands and spread them, as if to show they were empty. Wargallow stopped at once. He had no idea what the man would do, and he was not prepared to test him. To capture him would be extremely difficult, but he had been planning carefully, guided by the half-man that lurked somewhere beyond him in the rocks. That vile corruption of life would have to be cheated also.

Wolgren pointed. High above them all could be glimpsed humped shapes, devoid of detail, but they were not Deliverers (if they were men at all) and seemed poised and eager to taste the blood of those below them. Ilassa saw the cruel hands of the Deliverers who were approaching him from his side of the bridge. He stepped forward to meet them. "Here, Taroc. Here's a feast for your blade. Let's give the river a few of these vultures." He swung his blade in readiness. Silently the Deliverers came on.

Sisipher felt her mouth drying up. She tried to lift her own blade but it had grown in weight and scraped the ground uselessly. Taroc seemed numb, but at least he shambled forward, like a man half awake. His sword came up, and to her horror, Sisipher saw him aim a blow at Ilassa. It was not slow, but incredibly fast and competent. Ilassa heard it and whirled. His sword came up by reflex and parried the chop, the blades ringing together. But the damage was done, for Ilassa's footing was lost on the rain-slick stone. His free hand shot out to grip the bridge for balance. As he went down, Taroc came to life, though Sisipher knew now that something was frightfully wrong with him. He swung at Ilassa with tremendous strength, and although Ilassa parried the blow again, he was sent tumbling off the bridge. Seconds later the rising spray had swallowed him. Sisipher stood dumbfounded.

Korbillian and Wolgren were also rooted, unable to understand what had happened, but then Korbillian knew. *The earth!* It was his fault, for he had been so wrong about it. Heal? No, it had bled evil into Taroc, and now he obeyed it. No longer was the wounded man slow and dazed. His face had become wild, eyes alive with someone else's hate. He was now a vessel, and had been filled. He turned on the girl and grabbed her by the hair, fingers knotting in it as he dragged her to him. With a great wrench he swung her across the bridge. Her feet left the ground and she rolled over, but the Deliverers had her. They got her to her feet.

Wolgren flung his knife with every ounce of his strength and it flew like an arrow toward Taroc. The warrior had turned to face Guile, about to cut him in half, but Wolgren's blade took him below the chin. It struck with such force that Taroc staggered back, dropping to his knees. Guile wanted to scream, so deep was his terror, but he could see that Taroc might not die. Whatever unhuman force had him in its grip would not let him fall, in spite of the blood that now pulsed down his chest from the wound. Guile scrambled up and swung his sword as though he too were possessed. It was a clumsy, inexpert act, but the flat of the blade cracked into Taroc's temple. The man flopped over the edge of the bridge, leaking blood into the depths below it. There was no further movement from him, and Guile sagged down.

One of the Deliverers drew his hand across Sisipher, slashing at her garment. It parted to reveal white flesh beneath. Against the flesh the Deliverer pressed the flat of his steel, waiting. Guile felt himself go very cold, as did Wolgren. Korbillian turned to Wargallow. Only a moment had passed since the Deliverers had first shown themselves.

"Obey me now, Korbillian," said Wargallow. "Otherwise I will have the girl killed first."

"Spare her."

"Certainly, and your heroic comrades, but obey me."

"Very well."

A figure sprang up from the rocks across the gorge, hopping from one to another dangerously, although it seemed assured of its footing. Squat, almost batrachian, it waved its twisted arms at the leader of the Deliverers. "An excellent trap!" it shrieked. "The Children will be pleased. Now you must finish it, Wargallow. Kill them all. Then the work is done!"

Wargallow turned angrily to the creature that commanded the things that lurked yet on the ridge above. "Not yet. Go back to your masters. I have no further need of their help."

"The price, the price! It was to be Korbillian's life!" screamed the furious figure. "Or shall I bring the stones-that-move down upon you?"

From out of the misty air there now came a swirl of white movement as Kirrikree arrived. He had recognized the vile half-man at once: it had been this creature that had led the horses from the scene of the murder of the Empire men. The bird sensed at once also that it meant harm to Sisipher and the others. Quickly he flew down and his talons snapped shut in the flesh of the half-man, lifting it up into the air and rising with ease. The revolting creature struggled like a fish taken from the sea, but Kirrikree's anger would not permit it to shake loose. Not until he was high over the gorge, and then he did release the creature. It tumbled over and over in the air, through the mist. Wargallow saw it fall and smash like a dropped egg on the rock wall opposite. He smiled grimly, searching the sky for the strange bird, which he could have sworn was more owl than eagle. Well did he remember the white owls of the mountains.

Sisipher spoke to Kirrikree. "Keep away!" she warned him. "There may be a better time to help."

Korbillian had watched in silence, aware that Kirrikree had killed an enemy that could be even more dangerous than Wargallow. "If it is not my life you seek," he called across the bridge, "what then?"

"We must leave here quickly," said Wargallow, indicating the ridge behind him. "Whatever hides up there will not be pleased that the half-man is dead. We must all cross to the other side."

"And then?"

"We will travel to the Direkeep. The Preserver will want to meet you. Your fate will be in his hands, not mine."

Korbillian nodded. "Very well. I am prepared to come. But you must release the girl."

"I will consider it. For now, hurry across."

Wolgren realized, furiously, that Korbillian was not going to use any powers that he possessed to thwart this man. He would have spoken under his breath to him, but as they turned, Korbillian spoke first. "Gently, little warrior. I wish to meet this Preserver. But we will draw Wargallow's sting yet. I must see that Sisipher is safe."

They crossed the bridge, followed at some distance by Wargallow's men. Djemuta brought up the rear, watching for movement behind him, his blood chilled by the possibility of what might pursue them.

Above them all, out of sight, Kirrikree watched. He knew he would have to be patient. He was angry with himself: why hadn't he seen the Deliverers when he had been scouting? And worse, what were these stones-that-moved, which were unseen? Could something like them have slaughtered the Empire men in Strangarth's lands?

Part Three

CONFRONTATIONS

11
Ruan

IF THE JOURNEY to the Swiftwater gorge had been dreary and subdued, the one away from it and along the escarpment rim back toward the west was worse. Korbillian and his companions now sat astride their own horses, those steeds brought from the north where the Empire men had been cut down. Each of them, isolated from the other on instruction from Wargallow, had only his thoughts for company. Korbillian was the only one not tied, for no one had dared touch those sheathed hands. He was silent, his thoughts and mood closed in upon themselves. His concern was for the safety of his companions, but it seemed that the Deliverers would not harm them if he made no move to disobey any of Wargallow's orders. Wargallow's intention clearly was to take them all to the Direkeep, but Korbillian had decided that it would be best for him to confront the Preserver. Yet he wondered if, at some point in the future, at the Keep perhaps, he would be forced to resort to the unleashing of power.

Wolgren, his hands tightly tied, had taken a long time to cool his anger and frustration after being taken by the Deliverers, although he knew he could do nothing about it. His life was in their hands and at any moment they could despatch him. It should have terrified him, but he was far more worried about Sisipher. The Deliverers watched her closely, knowing that through her they controlled Korbillian. They were ready, at a glance from Wargallow, to kill her. Wolgren reflected on the killing of

Taroc. He had never killed before, never seen death, and there had been a disturbing pleasure in seeing his knife sink home. But Taroc had to die, he reasoned, and there must be no remorse. He had become somehow alien, either mad or possessed. Something had taken him, Wolgren thought. Since he had learnt that power did exist, he accepted other apparently supernatural things that his fellows in Sundhaven would have scorned. How narrow their world was! What he could not understand, however, was the fact that Wargallow, a man sworn to destroy belief in power, should have used power—evil power—to bring his enemies to heel.

Guile, no longer trembling with the fear that the dizzy bridge had poured into him, sat on his horse with mixed feelings. Death hovered very close at hand, for these Deliverers did not seem to have minds of their own and operated strictly as instructed by their leader. Why had Korbillian not unleashed his powers to destroy them all? Ratillic had told him that it would be simple enough. Korbillian seemed afraid to use his powers, possibly because of whatever consequences would arise, but he was also, so it seemed, prepared to be taken to the Direkeep. He wanted to meet the Preserver, that must be it. Guile brightened. Even though Korbillian would not allow himself to kill, he would not allow his companions to die. True, he had not been able to save Ilassa, but that had been unexpected. As long as we remain with him, Guile told himself, we are reasonably safe.

Sisipher had felt herself shaking for a long time: It was as though she had been touched by a night creature which had considered drawing her to its black domain. She could still feel the chilling touch of the Deliverer's claw on her flesh, and the rent in her garment allowed the air in to remind her of that frightful moment. Taroc had been terrifying, for he had not been human. She had read something vile in him, animating his body as if moving a dead thing. Whatever Korbillian had tried to do with the power of the earth had turned back on itself. And the evil shapes beyond the rim of the gorge, they had been even more awful. Wargallow's stronghold could not possibly harbor anything as grim, or so she told herself. The future was a dark pool to her, and though she sought to see into it, she could not. Pain swam there, alongside fresh fear, but at least she could not see deep enough down to recognize her death.

Wargallow rode at the head of the party with Djemuta beside him. He had not so much as glanced back at his prisoners since they had been taken. He wanted them, particularly Korbillian, to understand how confident he was that they were secure. Djemuta rode haughtily, a smug grin on his face: his master was quite excellent, he reflected. How cunningly he had used and rejected the Children of the Mound.

"We are not at the Direkeep yet," Wargallow told him quietly.

"Sire?"

"You seem to think our work is over. I doubt that it is."

"You think those creatures will follow?"

"They want Korbillian dead. More than anything."

"And you, sire?"

"I want him alive, for the Preserver. There is something uncanny about him. From another world, they say."

"Ridiculous!" snapped Djemuta, dutifully. I have to be careful, he thought. By law, these people should be dead, but Wargallow is in command.

"It concerns me," said Wargallow. "We have been taught that even such thoughts deserve instant death. The Preserver will not tolerate them, of course. But does Korbillian truly possess power?"

"You cannot believe that, sire? Power does not exist."

"I cannot believe it, no. But those creatures that serve the Mound, what are they? Not allies, for all their help. I cheated them, of course."

"The Preserver will decide."

"Of course. If there is doubt, we must go to him and confess our doubts. If doubting is itself a sin, he has the power to absolve it. That, or we must accept punishment for our doubting. If you can do that, Djemuta, you are a true Deliverer."

This must be a test, thought Djemuta, trying to understand, knowing that he must pass it if he were to gain favor with the Preserver, whom he saw as supreme. "These people are clearly transgressors, sire. Why not kill them now and give their blood to the earth?"

"Because I feel that it is for the Preserver to decide. He may wish to make a supreme example of Korbillian, and by so doing, silence many doubters. He may have many secret followers."

Djemuta accepted this: he had no doubts about Wargallow's loyalty to the cause. Wargallow smiled within his hood, having at last concluded that Djemuta would take the course that best served the Preserver. Whenever he had tested the man, it was clear he was committed to the Preserver and saw in his loyalty advancement. No, he would not be worthy of consideration to that inner circle of Deliverers, chosen by Wargallow to be his own Faithful, most secret of men. Wargallow had another reason for not killing Korbillian, and that was that he doubted his own ability to kill the man from Ternannoc. Ternannoc! he thought. Show me the door to this other world. Can it really exist? Has the Preserver hidden certain truths from us all?

They reached a place on the escarpment where it looked possible to descend to the plain below and where they could see the first of the Three Rivers winding westwards to the sea. Wargallow's plan was to cross the Camonile and follow its southern bank to the east before branching into the rugged foothills that led to the Direkeep. Wargallow thought briefly of the east and the powers there. He would have to take a strong force to investigate in the future, for the threat there could be more dangerous than was realized. He did not want to dwell on what he had seen of it, for it spoke of power, grim power, which could not be ignored.

The descent of the escarpment was difficult but not impossible, and the party managed it without injury. Once beyond the lower slopes, they soon rode into a vast expanse of woodland, leafless and bare, and their passage across the plain was easy enough. The skies brightened and all hint of storm dissipated, with even the eastern horizon free of cloud. Wargallow was making for a small trading post where there was a long bridge across the Camonile. The people at the post would not be troublesome, as they knew of the Deliverers and were careful to abide by the Word. Like many of the inhabitants of Omara, they wanted as little to do with the Deliverers as possible. Wargallow did nothing to dissuade them from their attitudes.

On the journey through the forest, Wargallow called an overnight halt, ensuring that the captives were secured. He still kept them all well apart from each other, knowing it would add to their despondency. None of them had been able to speak to each other since the journey on horseback had begun. Wargallow made himself comfortable some distance from his men, wrapping up in a blanket, and fell asleep quickly.

Djemuta briefly checked to ensure that the prisoners were secured, then sat by the spluttering fire. It was the girl who fascinated him, for her features, especially her eyes, were like no others he had seen. He felt drawn to her, but knew she was a transgressor; to touch that fair skin, the dark flowing silk of her hair, would surely ensnare him. It is only my lust, he thought, and yet another voice warned him that a more subtle force than lust was at work. It would not be easy to give her blood to the earth. For a while he brooded, urging the dawn closer.

Sisipher had closed her eyes, but was not asleep. Many times she had tried to find Kirrikree with her mind, but had failed. There was only the darkness and silence beyond the trees. In the camp she could sense the sluggish thoughts of their captors, like creatures below the ground, not certain of themselves. Perhaps Kirrikree had gone for help, she wondered. Yet where would he find it? The owls of Ratillic? Would any of them have journeyed this far from the mountains?

A sound out in the woods brought every head snapping up. The guards bristled like hounds. There was movement at the edge of vision, and in the shadows all around the camp figures waited. The clink of accoutrements sounded as clearly as a bell, and everyone was alert now. Steel sang, flashing in the fire-glow.

"Who's there?" a Deliverer challenged. They all feared the grim beings of the east. Wargallow was up and at the center of things, studying his men, though all were prepared for conflict if necessary. He was pleased.

A single rider trotted out of the trees, garbed in the tunic of an Empire man. He bowed gently and gazed at the company, a grin that was a little scornful and a little amused on his face. He was young, confident, sure of his strength. "I am Ruan Dubhnor, from the Chain of Goldenisle. With me are a good many soldiers of the Emperor. In fact, your camp is surrounded by them." He looked as though he would chuckle.

"For what reason?" said the hooded Wargallow. "Do you seek a conflict?"

Ruan laughed gently, almost politely. It was a measure of his confidence. "You appear ready for one. Who are you?"

"You are strangers to these lands," said Wargallow. "From the west, I understand. I cannot see that you have any rights here. In fact, it would be well for you to declare your purpose."

Ruan's smile remained. He did not seem prepared to answer Wargallow's challenge. Instead he stared, now arrogantly, about him, noticing for the first time that there were prisoners here. "Well, well. Who are these unfortunates?"

"I owe you no explanations," insisted Wargallow coldly. "Take your men and ride away."

Sisipher stared across at Guile, but he had turned his face away. Did he fear these men more than the Deliverers? Korbillian was also silent, watching with feigned disinterest.

"Well, now," said Ruan, enjoying himself as he trotted his horse slowly around the ring of Deliverers. "You owe me no explanations, you say. I say in reply, that you are mistaken."

Though Wargallow's face was hidden, his anger and malice were not.

"You have no business with us."

Ruan turned on him, leaning forward. "Some days ago

I sent a party of men northward into Strangarth's lands. They have not reported back. You wouldn't have seen them on your journey?''

''It seems that any number of your men ride across these lands at will. Perhaps this party you speak of is one of the those we have seen.''

Ruan nodded. ''You think so? And what happened to them?''

Wargallow did not answer.

''It seems at some point,'' went on Ruan, circling again, and his voice growing less warm, ''that they became separated from their horses.''

Djemuta tensed, ready to kill. One gesture from his leader and he would hamstring Ruan's horse and finish this arrogant rider within moments. Wargallow felt the trap closing, knowing that the horses his men had been riding were those of Ruan's soldiers.

''Why should this concern me?'' he said, continuing the bluff while he prepared his mind for what would have to be a fight. As long as the numbers against them were not too great, they would survive.

''You see,'' smiled Ruan affably, ''we found the horses. Tethered out there in the trees. But not the men.''

''So you are declaring us to be thieves?''

''You are the Deliverers,'' said Ruan. ''I have heard many things about you. How you give blood to the earth.''

''That is so,'' nodded Wargallow. ''There are laws that have to be upheld at any cost, evils that must be cut from the body of the world.''

''And my men? Has their blood fed the earth?'' Ruan's smile had been replaced by a cold stare.

''Not by my hand, nor by the hands of my Deliverers.''

''Then by whose?''

''We found the horses wandering loose, riderless.''

''All of them?''

''Indeed. Not a man with them. I assume Strangarth disposed of them. He is not a king who enjoys trespassers in his lands.''

Ruan snorted derisively. ''Killed the men and released the horses? Good horses such as these?''

"Strangarth breeds better. He is renowned for it, though you seem to know little about him and his country. Otherwise you would not have been so foolish as to send such a small party into his lands. You have no rights there."

Ruan thought about this, certain that the Deliverer was lying about the death of the men.

"Since the horses are yours," Wargallow told him, "you may take them."

Again Ruan laughed. "Rest assured that I will."

"When I have finished with them. For the moment I need them."

Ruan stared in surprise, as though not quite able to comprehend what he had been told.

Wargallow ignored his expression. "I am in haste to return to the Direkeep. Once I am there, I will see that the horses are returned to you."

"And if I demand them now?"

"Why should you? Do you not have enough?"

Ruan looked away, circling again. His horse seemed nervous, as if the smell of so much steel frightened it. Ruan knew that he had the upper hand in this business. He had enough men surrounding the camp to force any issue, no matter how good these Deliverers were (and word had it that they were superb fighting men). Wargallow's coolness worried Ruan. What trick did he hold? Why was he so calm? I must act with care, Ruan told himself. There is no need for blood, and they may not have killed our men. He studied the prisoners, and for the first time noticed them properly. He almost toppled from the horse, but controlled himself at once. *What a blind fool!* he shouted inwardly. *They are here!* Right under my nose. The man of power that I was told to send men to find, and Guile. *Sitting before me.* Now I must step very gently.

He turned back to Wargallow. "I see these people are prisoners. Might I know who they are and why you hold them?"

"The horses you may have, in time," said Wargallow. "But that is all I will give you. My business is the Preserver's only."

"You are testing my patience."

Korbillian, who had been sitting beneath a tree, now stood up. It was impossible to prevent him from speaking. Wargallow knew.

"Who is your master?" Korbillian asked Ruan.

The question fell like an axe, and Ruan stared at him as if he had said something offensive. "Quanar Remoon, Emperor of Goldenisle."

"And who commands you here in the east?"

"Morric Elberon. Why do you ask?"

"Why is he here?"

Ruan laughed, throwing back his head, but the tension in him grew tighter.

Wargallow had come forward. "If your Emperor thinks to conquer this continent, that is his affair. Who rules these lands is immaterial. But the Preserver is not to be disobeyed. The Abiding Word is his law. If you conquer, you must yet accept the Word and be bound by it."

"Keep your wilderness!" Ruan chuckled. "And your laws."

Korbillian frowned. If these men did not want the land for conquest, what did they seek here? Still it was a mystery.

"I say again," said Wargallow, "that the law must be kept."

"And if not?"

Wargallow gently let his killing hand into the firelight. "Those who transgress will forfeit."

Ruan felt a deep instinctive terror, although he masked it well. "I think not," he said, but his voice had dropped, the words hardly formed. Slowly he dismounted and stepped toward Wargallow, though he felt as if he were approaching his own execution. "We must speak privately. I see no reason for blood to be spilled here," he said, so that only Wargallow could hear.

"I agree," nodded Wargallow equally softly, but he had not retracted his killing hand. "Leave us alone. The horses will be returned."

They walked a little way from the others, but the Deliverers watched every move closely. "This man you have with you," said Ruan, his voice now little more than a whisper, "he whose hands are sheathed. Is he your prisoner?"

"It does not concern you."

Ruan fought down his anger at this repeated stubbornness. "I think it does. You see, Morric Elberon has issued orders that we are to search for two men who have fled from the Emperor. You serve the Preserver, while I serve the Emperor. These men have, in some way, defied the Emperor. I have not been told how, but evidently it is in some way that has greatly angered him. Have they also defied the Preserver?"

Wargallow saw now the real reasons for the persistence of the man before him. "I cannot release the man Korbillian to you. He must go before the Preserver in the Direkeep. Should you seek to take him by force, we will not be easily overcome, and each Deliverer will fight to the death."

"I understand that. It is commendable. As a soldier, my actions would be the same. But I have no wish to involve my men in a bloody exchange. I also have no wish to offend the Preserver. Morric Elberon has issued orders that the Abiding Word is not to be abused."

"Then perhaps we understand each other," said Wargallow.

"I must ask you, though, about this other man, Guile. What is he to you?"

Wargallow considered carefully. It seemed as if Ruan was prepared to compromise, even though he must believe Wargallow's men had killed the men whose horses they now rode. Yet unless Ruan was foolish, or lying, surely his prime target would be Korbillian and the secrets that he possessed. What could he want with the other, who appeared to be little more than a buffoon?

"If he means little to you," Ruan went on, "I would be prepared to leave you in peace, if you give him to me. Morric Elberon particularly wants him."

"What has the man done to warrant such interest?"

"As I told you, I have not been informed. But nothing light, I assure you. You can assume that once the Emperor has him, his blood will be spilled. Give him to me, and

I'll report to Morric Elberon that the other is dead. Forget the horses. Keep them.''

"You will tell Morric Elberon that Korbillian is dead?"

"Whatever you prefer."

"Say he has gone to the north, to the ice fastnesses. But not dead."

"Very well."

"Wait here." Wargallow brushed past him and went to his prisoners. Korbillian had been watching with interest, but had heard nothing. Wargallow stopped beside Sisipher and spoke to the Deliverer who was never more than a step away from her side. Slowly the man let his killing hand drop close to the girl's neck. It would have taken an instant only to sever it. Korbillian could read treachery in every move.

Wargallow crossed to Guile, who now looked at him dubiously. He would like to have heard the private discussion he had seen. The Deliverer bent down and in a move so swift that it defied the eye, sliced through Guile's bonds. Guile stood up, massaging his wrists. The steel had not touched his skin.

"I understand you are from the Chain," Wargallow said to him.

"I've been there," Guile said defensively.

"Really? It does not concern me."

Guile looked strangely at Ruan as he remounted his horse. Once astride it, he put one hand on the hilt of his sword. Korbillian came forward, knowing at once that the threat of violence was over. Something had been decided, and there would be no bloodshed.

"What is happening?" he said.

"This man is to go with the Emperor's soldiers," said Wargallow diffidently.

"Why?"

Wargallow had already turned his back. "It does not concern you."

"He travels with me," said Korbillian.

Wargallow pointed with his killing hand at Sisipher. "As long as you desire the girl's safety, you are in no position to make demands."

Korbillian's face clouded, and for one moment it seemed as though he would erupt with fury. He looked up at Ruan, who had brought his horse closer. "Why do you want him?"

Ruan shrugged. "I have my orders."

"From whom?"

"Enough!" snapped Wargallow. "Take him away."

Ruan pulled out his short sword. He gestured to Guile. "Come!"

Guile turned to Korbillian. "They'll kill the girl if you argue."

"Why do they want you?"

"They'll not tell you. These damned troops are loyal to a man. But I cannot believe Quanar Remoon wants me. You know he was glad enough to dismiss both of us. I have enemies at court, but they, too, would be happy to see me as far away from Goldenisle as this dreary place."

"Enough chatter!" snapped Ruan, beginning to sound irritable.

"I dare not use force," Korbillian breathed.

"You must think of the girl," Guile agreed softly. Then he turned to his captor, making a show of putting on a brave face. "Very well, lead on. I'll come without bloodshed, though you'll appreciate I cannot do much harm with these hands." He held them up with a forced grin, but no one smiled. He glanced again at Korbillian. "I'll likely be in better hands with these men of Empire than the Deliverers." As he went, he gave Wolgren a cheery wave, but the youth did not grin back. He imagined Guile was going to his death.

Sisipher wanted to cry out, but the icy blade at her neck kept her rigid. In a moment the night had taken both rider and captive. Guile was gone, and there had been no finger raised to save him.

Korbillian came angrily to Wargallow. "If he dies—"

Wargallow did not answer, nor seem perturbed by the threat.

"Why did they want him?" Korbillian persisted.

"It does not concern me. But it seemed prudent to avoid conflict. Your companion has bought our safe passage, so perhaps you should be grateful. He may survive, but I think the Preserver would have killed him.''

"You hold life cheaply."

"That is not so. We are alive."

"And my other companions? Will the Preserver attempt to kill them?"

"It is not for me to say." Wargallow moved away, soon afterward returning to his bed.

Korbillian would have spoken to the girl, in spite of the steel at her neck, but she had slumped forward, not asleep, but deep in thought. She appeared abjectly miserable. Wolgren, too, seemed to be succumbing to despondency, his youthful zest worn down by the coldness of Wargallow's purpose. The loss of Guile was like a blow to their faith in Korbillian. Korbillian went back to his own place, aware that each move he made was closely watched.

I had little choice, he told himself. I saved the girl, whose gift I need. But what will happen to Guile? I was responsible for him, and I have not served him well in this business. Yet I could not afford a battle. There may yet be a chance to win him back.

Reason told him otherwise.

12
Grenndak

RUAN DID NOT RETURN, nor did other Empire troops harass Wargallow's party after Guile's departure. Sisipher was still unable to contact Kirrikree, and after the events at the Swiftwater Bridge she assumed he was either keeping out of sight and mind or had gone to find help. Korbillian, the girl realized more and more, welcomed the visit to the Preserver's hold. For some reason he wanted to meet the Lord of the Direkeep, and she wondered if he intended to unleash power of some kind against him. Even so, she felt terribly vulnerable, knowing that the Deliverer who kept closer to her than her shadow was always ready with his killing hand. Beyond them, in the south east, where the Direkeep lay, she could detect a scent of blood in the air.

They came out of the forest at last to where the plain was open, low-lying and dotted with marsh and reeds. The beaten path on to the village on the Camonile was safe enough and there did not appear to be any danger if they kept to it. Sisipher felt uneasy, however, for the marshes seemed to her to breathe, as though sheltering things better left unseen. It was a relief to reach the clustered huts of the village. Here the river was half a mile wide, spilling into the marshes on either side, churned to a bright copper, fast-flowing and full of debris from upstream in the east: trees, carcasses and driftwood floated in an endless swirl. The people of the village were inoffensive, prepared to do whatever the Deliverers asked without argument, although Sisipher got the impression that there were far more of them hidden discreetly away. They provided them with food, and some of the bolder men mustered the nerve to ask about the likelihood of trade picking up from the west. Were Strangarth's men likely to come again, they asked, or was there a war brewing? They had been visited by a number of soldiers—the Empire men. Wargallow told them there would be no war, but the strength of the Emperor's forces here puzzled him. Their Commander, Morric Elberon, obviously intended to mount a campaign of some kind. No doubt the Preserver would know more.

That night was spent in the village. Korbillian persuaded his guards to allow him to visit Wargallow. The latter stood beside the flooded river, watching the wide causeway that crossed it as though he expected it to be washed away. Wargallow unexpectedly agreed to speak to Korbillian, and he motioned the two guards away. He still had Sisipher watched, but no longer believed Korbillian would oppose the visit to the Direkeep.

"I must ask you something," said Korbillian.

Wargallow removed his hood, and Korbillian looked at the face for the first time. It was not as cold as he had expected, and the eyes were not deep set as he had imagined, but liquid, wide. There was a fierce will there and a look of constant challenge. Wargallow studied an expression of doubt and uncertainty, the face of a young man that had been lined by, not age, but possibly pain. The man may well have power of some kind (he felt that he could no longer dismiss that) but he bowed to a burden that seemed to reduce not only his will, but his great stature. Wargallow did not fear him, but felt that perhaps he should. He remained guarded at least. "If you wish."

"You are dedicated to the destruction of evil—"

"What is evil? One man's evil is another man's boon, or so it sometimes seems," said Wargallow. "Greed is evil, I think. The desire of one man for something that he has no right to."

"Such as power?"

"A good example, yes. The Abiding Word teaches us that power is corruption."

"And gods?"

"The extreme expression of power."

"And Emperors, kings, Commanders?"

Wargallow smiled. "More subtle. Their rule is more local than that any god would assume. But authority—that, I feel, is important. The law is important. Codes of behavior. For the good of Omara. They are above the whim of any gods."

Korbillian nodded. It would be interesting to question the one who had created the Abiding Word. "Tell me, you will not tolerate power, and yet what of the east? Those beings at the gorge? You allied yourself to them to trap me."

Wargallow nodded thoughtfully. "Yes. My instincts told me to go against them, and I will, in time. There is something in those lands that fills the air with menace."

"Yet you choose to concern yourself with me, rather than with them. Why?"

"You claim to possess power."

Korbillian looked at his gloved hands. "It is no idle claim. I possess terrible power, power that terrifies me." He gently held out his hands and Wargallow felt the nape hairs on his neck stiffen as if touched by an icy draught.

"My law says this is not possible, but I do not doubt you. My law also says you must die."

"I am not from Omara," Korbillian went on, as if he had not heard. "Yet you deny other worlds."

"My law does not permit belief in them."

"I am here to protect your world, to make it secure from its doom. It is what I seek to use my power for."

"What doom?"

"It lies in the east, across the Silences. You heard that creature scream for my death at the gorge."

"Before the bird destroyed it."

"Somehow those creatures know me and what it is I seek to do. What can you tell me of them?"

"Only that they claim to serve others called the Children of the Mound."

Korbillian gasped. "As I had guessed, the Mound."

Wargallow seemed surprised at the man's reaction. "It is important?"

"There must be *life* in that place."

Wargallow had not expected to see Korbillian so troubled. The man was almost gray. "I know nothing of them."

"Sentience?" Korbillian was saying to himself, looking out to the east, up the river as if he could see to its source. "But how?"

Wargallow pulled up his hood. It could be that this man was no more than mad after all. But he felt disturbed by him. "It seems to me that the Preserver knows best. He will give you answers. You are marked because of your claim to power, but the Preserver may see fit to absolve you of your transgressions."

Korbillian finally spoke again as if coming out of a bad dream. "I did not come to Omara to die by his hand."

Wargallow said nothing. He stifled his own confusion and walked away. Korbillian's guards drifted in like ghosts, but they were no more than a gesture now. It occurred to Wargallow that Korbillian should be able to strike them all dead with his power, but it seemed unlikely that he would. Not now.

The following day they rode across the causeway, the weather remaining fair and mild. Again they passed through fields of marsh and reed, and on their south eastern horizon a range of hills rose up; these tiered upward to become mountains, and it was toward these that Wargallow led them. Apart from isolated farms, they saw little sign of human life, although they all sensed that they were watched, by human eyes as much as by the abundant wildlife. For the moment the lands to the east seemed no less tranquil than any others.

Sisipher had almost abandoned hope of seeing the great white owl again, for where his voice sometimes was, was now no more than a void. The further into the foothills the party traveled, the more oppressed she felt, isolated and lonely. Wargallow had insisted on having her every move watched, as though not trusting Korbillian's anger at having lost Guile. Wargallow spoke patiently to the huge man, promising that no harm would come to Sisipher, and though he seemed at times almost reasonable, she yet felt the cold touch of steel in her mind, sure that it must be the true metal of Wargallow's heart. Of all the men she had seen, he was the only one who looked at her without a hint of revealing what emotions she stirred within him. His mind was closed, almost as if it had been locked.

For days they wound through sleeping hills, keeping to the valleys but always rising. This was well known territory to the Deliverers and they were noticeably more relaxed. It was impossible, however, to draw them into conversation. They spoke very little to each other, almost as if talk itself were offensive. Even Djemuta, whom Sisipher sensed wanted to question her, kept his distance, though with an effort. Korbillian had attempted to engage Wargallow in conversation again, but Wargallow would not cooperate anymore and remained stoically silent.

They came around the steepening curve of one of the first mountains and ahead of them had their first view of the unique structure that was the Direkeep. Korbillian nodded to himself as if his view of it had confirmed something. Like a single great tower of rock, the peak on which the fortress had been built rose up from the valley floor, backed by a jagged, forbidding line of peaks. The roots of the tower were like the titanic roots of a tree that had been turned to stone over countless centuries, and as the tower soared up for hundreds of feet, its sides as smooth as glass and utterly unscalable, it narrowed, only to burgeon out in a huge fist of stone at its peak, knuckled and encrusted. It was inside and on top of this extraordinarily gnarled fist that the Direkeep had been built. It almost seemed to Sisipher, gaping in amazement, as though the entire structure, from the Keep to roots, had been drawn up from the molten earth and shaped as though by a potter in one simple working, hardening as it dried. She could sense about it a kind of power, but it was both old and stained. She found that she had to look away.

"How do we enter this soaring building?" Korbillian said aloud, and Sisipher thought for some reason he was amused.

"It is no secret," said Wargallow. "Apart from the Deliverers, no one has ever returned from the Direkeep." He pointed to the sloping mountain whose feet came close to the base of the tower of rock. "We climb. There is a bridge."

Up into the dusty heights they rode, finding the journey deceptively long. The Direkeep was far larger than they had realized. Little vegetation grew here and both Sisipher and Wolgren imagined that something dark and unhealthy spread out invisibly from the Keep, contaminating the land around it. Korbillian noticed the condition of the land, so reminiscent of decay. There was power in this place, he knew well enough, but it was ailing, as if a disease ate into it, weakening it. How could men give themselves to it so freely? It held no fears for him, only a sense of sadness, of waste. He thought of Ratillic, squandering his gifts when he could have used them so well. To the people of Omara, this place must appear terrifying, with its chilling Deliverers and mysterious ruler, and they would not be aware of the decay and dissolution here. To Korbillian it was pathetic, a travesty of true power.

By the time they had reached the place where Wargallow had told them the bridge would be, night had fallen. They were met by men who had apparently been watching their ascent for a long time (everything could be seen from here) and these men, Deliverers, recognized them. As soon as Wargallow spoke, they stiffened to attention and hurried to do his bidding. He turned to Djemuta.

"Remain here with the men. Await my return, or word from me."

Djemuta tried to mask his disappointment. *Wait here?* his mind echoed. After a journey like that, I am not to be permitted to enter the Keep? "But, sire, you cannot mean to cross the bridge alone with the prisoners?"

"No." Wargallow went to the captain of the bridge guard and spoke quietly to him. "I want four of your men. One for the girl, one for the youth and two for the other, as escorts. My own men will remain with you. Do not let them go from here."

The captain issued instructions at once. Simon Wargallow was not a man to argue with. The escort was ready within minutes. Djemuta remained bewildered, but dared not ask why. Had he displeased Wargallow? Had he failed some test? Surely not: he had done his duty well, and during the fight with the owls had shown no fear. When the party was ready to move, Wargallow spoke again to Djemuta.

"When I return, there will be many men at my back. I will ask the Preserver to allow me to retain you as my immediate deputy. I am pleased with you, Djemuta." He said no more, but turned his horse away, leaving Djemuta no less baffled. And yet, if there were to be many men riding out, could this be war? An attack on the arrogant men of Empire?

Wolgren saw the twilight pierced by a long sliver of moving rock which emerged from somewhere across the drop to the Direkeep tower. The bridge met this side of the mountain, dust swirling as it settled, and through the shadows the youth saw the narrow but high opening across the span in the sheer side of the tower. Wargallow had given final instructions and they rode slowly across the bridge. It was narrow, the drop frightening, but the horses kept their heads well. There was no breeze and the air was silent, the stone fortress hushed but almost expectant as if the Preserver's eyes saw them through the layers of stone.

Wargallow was well pleased with his decision to leave the party of his Deliverers behind. Fortunately the captain on duty was known to him, not one of his chosen Faithful (though a potential candidate) and would do precisely as told. Djemuta was faithful to the Preserver, and Wargallow had reached the conclusion that he might even betray Wargallow if it promised a reward. He would not be given the opportunity. Already Wargallow had laid his plans.

As they rode under the arch that led into the tower, they came into torchlight hung with smoke. They were aware of men on either side, toiling at the wheels and devices that operated the bridge of stone. Wolgren felt horribly trapped, as if he had entered a region of terror, a prison fashioned as nothing less than a place of execution. The only way he was able to cling to his sanity was by seeing Korbillian's calm, as though he saw no threat to their safety here. Sisipher's heart thundered in her breast. So much pain clung to the naked rock, and she could hear the echoes of long dead screams.

After they had dismounted, Wargallow spoke to yet more Deliverers in the tunnelled passageways. Some of them started to lead Sisipher and Wolgren away, but Korbillian spoke up at once. "I insist that we are kept together."

Wargallow tensed. "In the Direkeep, you insist on nothing."

"I have promised to obey you. Let them come with me."

Wargallow spoke softly to him. "Many ears are listening." He turned abruptly. "Take them away!" he snapped, and to Korbillian, loudly, "If you wish them unharmed, let them go."

"What do you intend with them?"

"I have no quarrel with them. It is you who are responsible for them, and their actions."

Korbillian was surprised. "You accept that?"

"I do. And will say as much to the Preserver. Whatever he decides for you will apply equally to them."

"Then they are quite safe."

"Quite safe. Unless, of course, you decide not to cooperate."

Korbillian looked at the girl and youth, and they seemed here no more than children, but he nodded. "Very well."

As they were led away, Wargallow breathed words so quietly that only Korbillian heard him. "I have my position to think of. I dare not be seen to accede to your demands, or accept your claim to power. But they are safe."

As Sisipher and Wolgren were led away, the youth at last managed to speak to her. "He protects us," he said. "Remember that."

"We will not die here," she whispered back, the certainty of her statement like a torch before her. They were taken up endless flights of stone stairs that made their legs ache, until eventually they reached a door that led into a simple room. There was water and surprisingly, fresh fruit. The guards left them, locking them in.

Wolgren went straight to the open window, but immediately pulled back from it when he saw the sheer drop beyond. They were so high up that the ground was invisible. Sisipher collapsed, sobbing with exhaustion, suddenly unable to resist the need to give in to it. At once Wolgren knelt beside her and put his arm about her, embarrassed and unsure of himself. But she was glad of the comfort and hugged him out of sheer relief. Within moments she was asleep. Wolgren felt himself on the brink of tears. How desperately he wanted to caress the girl. He told himself repeatedly that Korbillian would not let them down.

Wargallow led Korbillian up a broader, more gently curling stairway than that taken by Sisipher and Wolgren. Although he felt secure in the fastness of the Direkeep, he found himself becoming even more reconciled to Korbillian's claims. The latter was unawed by the Keep, as though there was nothing here, not even the Preserver, that held any terrors for him. And if he was not afraid of the Preserver, did he believe his powers to be greater? If they were, Wargallow would have to plan accordingly.

Korbillian felt as though he had entered the body of a giant that was riddled with disease. He calculated that they had reached the upper heights of the Keep as they had been climbing for so long. He had noticed that everyone they had passed (less of them higher up) had acknowledged Wargallow, and he had come to the conclusion that he must be as important as anyone else here, saving the Preserver. That was good: it meant he would be dealing with the real power behind the Direkeep.

They reached a wide hall with a spectacularly vaulted ceiling, and along one side it was open onto a fountained courtyard, a square beyond which the last towers poked up at the night sky.

"I am taking you to the Preserver now," said Wargallow, the first words he had spoken since the climb began. "I am sure you would prefer to meet him without delay. Assuming he will see us, of course."

Korbillian nodded. "Indeed."

Wargallow again noted the anticipation. In spite of the

lined face, the seeming anguish, he did not appear disturbed. Wargallow had to know, quickly, what it was that drove him.

They came to guarded doors that would well have graced Quanar Remoon's opulent palace, and as Wargallow spoke to the men there, they stood aside to open a smaller door set into the large one. Wargallow stepped through and Korbillian followed. He was surprised to find himself in a large hall, but one that was completely bare of everything but the basic requirements of any household. There was a small fountain, a few simple wooden seats, vases filled with scented plants (the only real luxury here) but no magnificent tapestries, carpets or paintings, no treasures, no works of art. Somehow he had expected all these things. Possibly this could be abstinence, part of the image the Preserver had created for himself.

Wargallow motioned him to sit on one of the featureless seats, and as he did so a white robed figure appeared. It was the first woman Korbillian had seen here. She spoke quietly to Wargallow, then left them. Wargallow threw back his hood. The scent from the plants was almost overwhelming, thick as perfume, even by the night lights.

"He is asleep," said Wargallow. "But he will be woken."

So you have that much influence? thought Korbillian, interested. And it seemed odd that the Preserver was not aware of their coming. Presently another door opened and four bearers entered, carrying a litter with white silk hangings. They placed it down opposite the seat on which Korbillian sat. For a while there was silence, broken at last by a harsh cough from within. The hangings parted, and Korbillian's amazement was chalked across his features. The man within was incredibly old, wrinkled and haggard.

"So my favorite warrior has returned," said the man in a voice that choked off in a spasm of coughing.

Wargallow stepped before him. "I have, sir, and wasted no time in presenting myself." He seemed perfectly at ease here, confident, almost arrogant. He waited for the old man to cease coughing, and with a dismissive flick of the wrist sent the bearers away. When the Preserver had ceased coughing, his face turned to Korbillian, who received yet another shock, for the man was blind.

"You are not alone," said the Preserver, whose other senses at least were not impaired. "This must be someone you think most important."

Wargallow took another seat and a servant, a girl in a short white tunic, appeared and offered what looked like wine. He shook his head and waved her away gently. "I am convinced of it, sir."

"A transgressor?"

"Of the first order," agreed Wargallow, smiling at Korbillian, almost as if sharing a private joke with him. What deadly game was the man playing?

"Yet you have not given his blood to the earth, but have brought him before me. For this I would normally chastise any Deliverer, for the Abiding Word is very clear on these matters." He was speaking to Korbillian now. If there was a threat in the words, it was directed at him, and not at Wargallow. "I will not tolerate transgression. Omara must be kept pure."

Korbillian said nothing, letting Wargallow speak for him, hoping that he might reveal his true motives.

The Preserver was speaking again to the Deliverer. "However, you do my work better than any other, Simon. Since you have brought this man here, you must have good cause."

"I believe I do, sir. But, of course, I am open to your judgment. You may yet feel that I have failed you in allowing this man to live, in which case I will submit to your decision."

Korbillian frowned. So easily, so willingly? Wargallow could surely not be so dedicated to the Preserver's law.

"Tell me about him," the Preserver said, sitting back in his pillows as comfortably as he could, closing his lids as if asleep, but in fact listening acutely to everything.

Wargallow nodded to Korbillian. "You have made many claims. I have told you that my duty should have been to give your blood to the earth. Now you must explain yourself in full. My master will act according to his judgment, and in the best interest of Omara, which he serves.''

A sudden flame burst into being a few feet from Korbillian's eyes, forming itself into a white hot ball. It fizzed, emitting sparks. Wargallow drew back, not afraid, but uneasy. This, Korbillian saw, was the sort of spontaneous expression of power that had kept him at his master's heel. No doubt there had been many other such bursts of energy from the ailing Preserver. In the fire, there was far more power than Korbillian would have expected.

''I hope,'' he said wryly, ''that he is a better servant to Omara than he was to Ternannoc.''

The Preserver went rigid, as though a poison snake had raised his head inches from his neck and he could see it poised to strike him. His mouth hung open, saliva dribbling from it. The fireball danced at Korbillian, but a gloved hand moved, bursting it effortlessly. Wargallow leapt up, horrified by the entire incident.

''Don't let him near me,'' gasped the old man to Wargallow, shaking his head pitifully. Wargallow whirled round, his killing hand raised instinctively.

Korbillian shook his head. ''Put your weapon away, Wargallow. It will be useless.''

Wargallow did not obey, but guessed that Korbillian spoke the truth. In the first play, the Preserver had been rebuffed.

Korbillian had not moved from his seat. ''Stand aside. I will not touch him.''

''His hands,'' said the Preserver. ''Sheathed?''

Wargallow felt the same iciness at the back of his neck that he had felt at the Camonile river. ''Aye,'' he said, fending off dread.

''When I saw this tower,'' said Korbillian, ''and how it had been sucked up from the stone lands around it, sculpted by forces only a Hierarch could control, I wondered. But when I saw you, Grenndak, I did not recognize you at first.''

''What do you mean?'' said Wargallow. If he had ever been in a position of advantage, and as the minutes ticked by, he began to doubt that he ever had, it was lost now.

He had never manipulated this stranger, even with the girl, for how easily he had snuffed out the fire! Wargallow had seen what that flame could do, how it could seek out life a hundred miles from this place and burn it away in a moment. Yet the Preserver was terrified, *terrified!* For all his power, all his mastery, he had been reduced to this. And Korbillian spoke of Ternannoc, as if the Preserver knew of it!

"This man you call the Preserver is Grenndak, and he and I have met, long, long ago. He is scarcely able to preserve himself against the onset of time."

Grenndak's reaction amazed Wargallow. "Don't kill me," he said, tears in his eyes. "Leave me in peace, Korbillian. After all this time, let me be. Forget me."

"Strike him down at once, sir," said Wargallow, but he was merely playing a part. His master was helpless, already beaten.

"You could not have known, Simon, but you have brought me my death."

"Surely not."

Korbillian stood up, knowing that a part of Wargallow had been hoping for this, as if he resented serving his master. "There are things you must be told, Wargallow. If you truly wish to serve Omara faithfully, you had better hear me out. Call all the guards you wish, but they will not prevail. I did not know that it was Grenndak I would find here, though I should have guessed it would be someone like him. So you must be told."

"The east?"

"Exactly. The death of Omara waits there, as it did in my world, in his world."

Wargallow turned to Grenndak. "Who is he?" he said softly.

From the pillows came what sounded like the last croak of a man who has given up the will to fight an illness that is killing him. "He is the executioner."

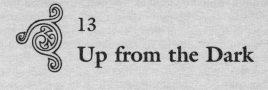

13

Up from the Dark

BRANNOG NOW HAD a full company of some fifty Earth-wrought to accompany him on his search for Korbillian and his daughter. They led him through a remarkable system of burrows and caves, Ygromm explaining that many of these were the work of creatures long extinct, others were made by beings who had migrated far to the west and gone below the sea. At times it was impossible for Brannog to negotiate the narrow workings and detours had to be made, while at others the delvings were almost like caves. They came to one place where a vertical shaft about a hundred feet across sank down into what must be the very bowels of the earth. There were tunnels that they rushed past for fear of something unpleasant emerging, and others where the Earthwrought spoke with sadness of friends who had strayed and never returned. Ygromm insisted that it was yet safer to keep below ground until word came to them from above. Brannog was not certain how far-seeing the Earthwrought could be down here, but they had allies, it seemed, and had their own special communication with creatures of earth and sky. He had no reason to doubt them, but knew that they held the surface in great fear, having been mistreated there whenever they dared emerge. Yet now they were working their way nearer to the surface with every step, and Brannog could see far more complex and larger root systems about him. He was supplied with food from time to time, mostly a peculiar fungus-like growth, although he dared not eat too much of it as it seemed to put strange visions in his head. On the move, he felt at times as if he were gliding through the ground, and had to shake himself to escape the mild hallucinations. Any sleep he snatched down here was full of dancing light and abstract shapes, so that whenever he felt himself on the edge of real sleep he dragged himself back, panic lapping at him.

At last Ygromm came to him, somewhat breathlessly, after he had sent scouts upward through a narrow funnel of earth to possible daylight. "They have been sighted!" he said. "The scouts have spoken to the horned folk, who saw them, and the skywatchers say that they are in the gorge of the river Swiftwater. But there is great danger." Ygromm answered Brannog's rapid questions, and the latter learned that it was Korbillian and the others in the gorge, with two men he knew nothing about.

"One of these men is evil," said Ygromm with a shudder. "I have heard this from other sources beneath the land. This man was put into the earth."

"Buried?"

"Not dead, no. He was put there to heal him of wounds he had received. The man Korbillian knows the old rituals and sought to draw strength from the earth. Yet something got the scent of the wounded man and instead of succouring him, the earth poured darkness into him, the darkness that the evil from the east controls. Now he rides with Korbillian, and from what I hear, none of them understand what it is that sits with them. Also above the gorge there is terrible evil. The stones-that-move." Ygromm described them and Brannog shuddered.

"How soon can we get to the gorge?"

"By evening at the earliest, with every speed. There is a cave system not far from us that will take us to the bottom of the gorge far more quickly than a surface journey."

Brannog wondered if this were the truth, knowing Ygromm's fears. At night they would be far happier on the surface. He nodded, however, and encouraged the little figures around him to make all speed. "What are these stones-that-move?" he asked Ygromm as they sped along.

"The eastern power can pour life into them like blood into veins. The power of this black blood gives a kind of life to the stones. I have never seen them, only heard of them and tales about them are probably distorted. But I am afraid that even the worst tales about the east, even the most exaggerated, may be less than the real truth, for the east is truly a bad place. Have you seen madness?" he added.

Brannog thought carefully. "Once, in a village dog."

"There is no reason in such a thing. The east seems to be invested with such a madness, and yet with a purpose. I cannot say why."

"Korbillian does not realize this," said Brannog. "To him the east is like the mad village dog, wild and without purpose. Mindless. It is vital that he be told the truth."

They made all haste, but Brannog feared they would get to the others too late to prevent their impending clash with whatever lurked across the Swiftwater. Even though they were now in well-worn passageways that made progress easier, Brannog and the Earthwrought knew that evening had come and that Korbillian had been in the gorge many hours before. Much depended on where they would stop for the night. Ygromm was hoping to have word from the surface, from the deer he called the horned folk, or from other wild creatures, but the land above was devoid of such. The skies were also empty. Something had long since frightened them all away from the gorge, leaving a residue of terror clinging to it.

"Can you hear?" Ygromm asked Brannog at last, and the latter nodded. It was the roar of the river, surging through the bottom of the deep gorge. It sounded some distance away, but as they rounded a curve in the tunnel, they found they were very close.

The noise rose in volume and they had to shout to make themselves heard. "They will have crossed the bridge, high above us," said Ygromm. "When we learn if they have gone over, we can follow. Best for us to go beneath the river."

They emerged now from the earth, and Brannog blinked. Daylight was fading and hardly reached down to this great gash in the rock. He stood on a broken slab that jutted over the foaming water, watching in fascination the mad plunge, the boiling foam. The sides of the gorge seemed to rise up forever, their tops lost way overhead. "Is there no word?" he asked.

"Scouts are searching," replied Ygromm, scowling at the river. "But there is no life here. Only the river, and it has nothing to say to us."

"And the stones-that-move?"

"Gone, I think. Eastward."

"In pursuit?"

Ygromm shrugged. They waited, deafened by the waters, until the various scouts came back. Some had scaled the rock walls, nimble as spiders, some had gone under the river to tunnels there, but all reported the same thing, that there was no life. Ygromm said they must go up to the Swiftwater Bridge. Only there could they know for sure that Korbillian had passed by.

Brannog stared up into the darkening fastness above. "Can I climb this gorge? You have skills that I do not possess, Ygromm."

Ygromm pointed down the gorge. "There is a way that it easier." As he did not elaborate, Brannog assumed that he referred to a path of some kind. Possibly wild goats lived here and had made a path up, just as the wild sheep of the mountains behind Sundhaven did. If not, the climb would be bad enough by day, but at night, not one he wanted to contemplate. His role as champion of these little people was a fragile one, he knew.

A few hundred yards down the gorge they stopped. Another scout was coming toward them from downriver, his scowling face anxious. "Here!" he barked. "I've found one!"

Brannog's heart pumped and his body froze. At once he went over the rocks, moving dangerously quickly, for there was always the threat of a fall, a smashed limb, and yet his feet were surprisingly sure. Which one had been found? Dead? There was no time to talk. High above them they could just discern the span of the Swiftwater Bridge, but there was no movement.

The scout pointed to a place among the rocks where

sand and shingle had built up over the centuries, forming a basin, a miniature beach trapped in walls of rounded rock. Brannog had his axe ready, for he trusted nothing in this ominous landscape. There was a body there. His heart pounded. It was a man. With Ygromm beside him, he went to it, scrambling down the slippery rocks to jump into the shingle. Carefully he turned the body to see the face, but it was that of a stranger.

"A man of Strangarth's kingdom," Ygromm said, and explained. "He was with Korbillian, one of the two strangers."

"The evil one?"

But Ygromm shook his head. Brannog started to examine the body. He found bruises, but no wounds. "He must have fallen from the bridge," he said, peering up again at the span high above. "A fight?"

Ygromm had stiffened, his head bent upward like that of a scenting wolf. "Blood!" he hissed. "On the bridge."

Brannog felt caged, trapped down here without knowing what had happened. Were they all dead? Prisoners? "We must get up there as fast as we can."

Ygromm scowled down at the body. He bent to it, putting his ear to it, then gasped, and the sound came clearly to Brannog in spite of the roar of the waters so close to them. "He lives!"

"It's not possible."

"It may not be for long." Ygromm gave a great shout and the Earthwrought scampered toward them from where they had been keeping watch. Ygromm hissed instructions and at once as many of them as could gathered around the body of the fallen man. Brannog could not see clearly, but they all appeared to put their hands on the man. Ygromm began a deep rumble, which was quickly joined, and the Earthwrought worked together. Brannog shook his head. Here was another aspect of power, magic, whatever it was, that he had been taught did not exist in Omara. But he knew now, could feel in his own bones, that it was very real.

Long moments passed, until eventually Ygromm drew back. There was a unified sigh from the Earthwrought

which Brannog felt like a ripple through his body. The
little men relaxed, slumping back on to the rocks, breathing heavily as if they had all been running for many miles.
Ygromm beckoned Brannog to him.

"Can you save him?"

"We have read things," said Ygromm. "There was a
fight on the bridge. Swords." He was able to tell Brannog
everything that had happened up to the moment that Ilassa
had fallen from the span. Beyond that Ygromm could not
say. "I think," he ventured, "that Korbillian and the others must be prisoners, not of the east, but of Simon Wargallow. Unless he has already given their blood to the
earth. But I doubt that. We would know."

"Whose is the blood on the bridge?" said Brannog.

"It is a man's. It may be the blood of the man Taroc,
the evil one, who sent Ilassa over the edge, or it may be
the blood of a Deliverer spilled in the fight. We must climb
to find out. There will be a trail to follow."

"To the east?"

"The stones-that-move are not commanded by Wargallow, and yet—"

"You fear an alliance?"

Ygromm grimaced. "We will know when we reach the
bridge."

Brannog looked down at Ilassa. The man was white,
one side of his face badly bruised, swollen and blackened.
"We should bury him, or is it dangerous?"

"We will carry him. He still lives, but it will need many
more workings to save him."

"Then he can be restored? Is that possible?"

"I cannot promise it."

"Then you must try."

Ygromm nodded. Soon afterward he called to his fellows and they took up the burden without a hint of complaint. Ygromm told them sternly that this was to be an
important test for them, to see if the new sharing with the
overmen was to be approved by whatever powers watched
over them all. "Do well with this fallen one," he said,
"and it will bring great favor with the Wormslayer." If

circumstances had been different, Brannog would have smiled at the little man.

They began the long climb, and although it was tortuous and hazardous for Brannog, he surprised himself, drawing on strength he had not been aware of previously. The land held no terrors for him, and the Earthwrought made light work of the climb, even with their burden. They reached a place where they could join the path that led along to the Swiftwater Bridge. Once on this path they moved quickly, surrounded by darkness. There was no moon, and a thick screen of cloud to hide any peering stars. Brannog found he could see better than he would have expected. *What is happening to me?* his mind whispered.

As they came to the span, Ygromm held him back. "Someone is there," he said.

Brannog's lips drew back in a silent snarl. "If it is an enemy," he breathed, but did not finish.

They went forward cautiously, but saw no one. The bridge was deserted. Ygromm sniffed at the air in each direction. He whispered to Brannog. "The stones-that-move have gone, back to the east. I sense them, but far beyond the rim."

"Then who is here?"

"I cannot say. But it is evil. A solitary watcher. A guard set by the east. But alone."

"The bridge, then."

Keeping together, the party moved on, watching every shadow. They came to the ancient stonework. Ygromm insisted on going to the bridge alone, saying he would be safe enough from attack there, although Brannog was not so sure. He watched the stooped figure cross the bridge, pause, then return. The roar of the river came up from below, but nothing moved to suggest an attack. Ygromm trotted back, keeping hunched over, making himself a tiny, difficult target. Again he stopped on the bridge before returning.

"The blood is the man Taroc's. There is no other. And I have more heartening news."

Brannog gripped his shoulder. "Yes?"

"Korbillian and the others did not cross to the east. The

trail will be confused here, with so many comings and
goings. But I feel sure that Wargallow took them away.
He would have sacrificed them here if he had been going
to. They must be alive. Korbillian and three others, one a
girl.''

Brannog jerked upright. "She is well," he breathed.

"She is a gifted one," said Ygromm. "And special to
you?''

Brannog nodded. "Yes, she is. But where would they
go?''

Ygromm's face twisted into a deep scowl. "It can only
be to the Direkeep.''

"Surely we can catch up with them now?''

"We can try. But it will be more difficult. They have
horses.''

As they moved away, Brannog felt tiredness gnawing at
his bones. The party would have to rest. Surely the Earthwrought were tired too. But if Wargallow had horses, how
could they make up time on them? Only by night when
the Deliverer would rest. Ygromm confirmed that the
Direkeep would be many days' ride away, so there was yet
a chance of overhauling them. Brannog knew that if they
did not catch them before they got to Direkeep, there
would be little hope of getting into the place.

They did rest briefly, but long before dawn were on their
way again, picking up the trail of Wargallow's party easily.
Ygromm had decided that it would now be quicker for the
Earthwrought to travel overland, although they were
frightened of the unfamiliar daylight and could not see
well in it. Ygromm told his men that it was something
they would have to get used to. "One day," he said, "your
children will live by light and not under the ground. Remember, we are the forerunners." Although they had
made a rough stretcher for Ilassa, they were still able to
move much more quickly than Brannog would have expected, and he was relieved when Ygromm told him that
Wargallow's horses were obviously not being ridden hard
and were travelling at a gentler pace in general. Brannog
ate more of the Earthwrought food and his own strength
pulsed, renewed.

At their midday rest, Ygromm drew Brannog aside. "Ilassa grows stronger and will survive. There is a river to be crossed, the Camonile. Better if you take Ilassa to the villagers at the trading post and leave him there. We can do little more for him. It is best if the Earthwrought go under the river, rather than over the causeway. The villagers may well attack us, or delay us at least. It is the way of most overmen, you understand?"

Brannog nodded.

"There is some bad news. We are followed. Whatever was watching us at the Swiftwater Bridge. An emissary of the east."

"The solitary guardian?"

"Yes. I have had scouts circle back, but they have not found it."

They moved on, passing out of the slopes of the escarpment, following Wargallow's route down to the forest. They decided to stop for a longer rest that evening, gathering together in a camp. Ilassa, remarkably, had murmured in his sleep, and Brannog saw that the bruising on his face had subsided. He was still pale, but not the ghastly white he had been when they had dragged him from the edge of the river. It still seemed miraculous that he had not died, and again Brannog wondered at the power of the Earthwrought.

Some of Ygromm's people had been in favor of camping under the earth, but Ygromm told them they must learn to accustom themselves to living on it. Even so, they never made a camp without first inspecting the surrounding terrain for potential tunnels into the earth—old animals lairs, or landslips, ancient delvings, anything that would give them an easy access to whatever workings would be found below (for there were inevitably some). Near this camp they had found the abandoned lair of a bear.

After they had eaten, one of their scouts came bursting into the camp. "To earth! To earth!" he growled anxiously. "Soldiers!"

"Whose soldiers?" called Brannog as they all made hasty preparations to flee. But the scout could not tell. They were not Strangarth's men, and they were not Deliverers was all he could say. Quickly Ygromm got his men ready for the flight to the old lair, but as they reached the place they drew back in consternation, knowing at once that something was there before them.

"The creature that has been following us," said Ygromm. "It has gone inside!" He had no sooner spoken than a figure came shambling to the overgrown portal. It was a man, or had been, for its face was misshapen, bestial, the eyes yellowed, the mouth feral. A look somewhere between savagery and cunning twisted the features in the way that no human could have, and its clothes were caked with earth, torn and rotting as if it had clambered up from its own grave. Ygromm pointed to its throat where something gleamed.

Brannog felt himself weakening. It was the hilt of a knife, and the point was lodged in the creature's throat. The darkness on its shirt front was dried blood. How could this thing be alive? It stepped forward and gave a sudden horrific howl which seemed to fill the very world. And it waited.

"Stay clear!" hissed Ygromm. "One touch from that thing is death."

Brannog was appalled. This was the power of the east, far worse than he had imagined.

"It is the man I spoke of," nodded Ygromm. "Taroc. The power that fills the stones-that-move has filled him. We dare not go near it."

Behind them came the drumming of hooves. There was no escaping them, and Brannog got the Earthwrought to form a tight circle. They wanted to break and flee, but he would not let them. He held his axe at the ready and they took what strength they could from it. As the horsemen arrived, the creature that Taroc had become withdrew into the lair, as if it had fulfilled its purpose in trapping the Earthwrought. In a moment they were ringed. A score of soldiers rode around them, and they wore yellow tunics with the edges trimmed in a double bar of black. Ygromm whispered to Brannog that he did not know them.

Horses snorted, dust flew. "What have we here?" called one of the soldiers. He pointed with a short sword at Brannog. "What are you, wild man? And what in the name of the Empire are these creatures?"

"None that will harm you. They are the Earthwrought. I am Brannog of Sundhaven, in the west."

"Is that a wounded man I see there?"

There was no denying Ilassa's presence. "Aye. And who are you? You speak of the Empire. Surely you cannot mean that of Goldenisle?"

"The same. Servants of Quanar Remoon to the last," laughed the man, with a mock bow, and each of his soldiers laughed with him. Brannog was even sure that one of them spat.

"You're a long way from home," he told them.

"So, it seems, are you. Sundhaven, you say. Where's that? Not in Strangarth's lands?" As he was speaking, other horses were coming up from beyond the trees. This must be a larger party than Brannog had realized. But what were men of the Empire doing here in the east? He tried to recall the things that Guile had told him, but that now seemed so long ago. One of the soldiers beside the spokesman leaned over to speak quietly to him and he seemed annoyed by what the man had said.

"Your wounded man—where is he from?"

Brannog said nothing, trying to think for a moment. "I have no idea," he said at last. "We found him in the woods."

"One of Strangarth's rabble?" said the man, coming closer. "Better to let him die, if he is." He was about to give orders to his men, but was forestalled by the arrival of the new party from which a single rider detached itself. This rider was cloaked and wore a hood to mask itself, for it was not cold in spite of the coming of night.

"What have you found, Ruan?" it asked the leader of the first party mildly.

"Something that has crawled from the earth I think, sire. Here! Bring torches!" Ruan bellowed, and at once brands were brought forward. The cloaked man rode very slowly up to Brannog's company of Earthwrought. Brannog could feel their fear. Silence fell, and none of the soldiers seemed prepared to break it. Their respect for the cloaked man was quite plain.

"I have done no harm," said Brannog. "Neither have my companions."

The cloaked man gasped audibly. "I know that voice!"

And I know yours, thought Brannog, trying to place it. The man threw back his hood and grinned, leaping down from the horse. "I did not recognize you, Brannog!" He clapped the latter on the back before the big man had moved. "It is you!"

Brannog's confusion deepened. "Guile!"

Guile turned to Ruan who also looked baffled. How was it that this earthy, dishevelled man of the woods could be greeted with such joy by Guile?

"Go back to the camp," Guile said. "Prepare food, whatever is needed. These are no enemies. They have my protection, is that clear?" He turned back to Brannog, who watched in further amazement as Ruan did as he was told, shouting orders to his men.

"You command these men?" said Brannog.

Guile laughed. "I have some explanations to give you. I told you that my only gift is my tongue. But I must have news. What are you doing so far from Sundhaven? Where have you been? You have changed so. And these people—"

"They are the Earthwrought," Brannog told him with pride, and he introduced Ygromm and his followers. Ygromm bowed, hiding the trembling fears in his chest.

"Sisipher," said Brannog. "Is she safe?"

"So you followed us?"

"It's a long tale. But, my daughter—I must know."

"Safe as yet. But a prisoner. We both have much to explain."

Ygromm's ears picked up. So the girl was the Wormslayer's own child. Why had he not said so?

"What do you know of the Deliverers?" asked Guile.

Brannog told him as much as he could, speaking quickly, talking of the pursuit and of the creature in the lair. Guile scowled at that, at once suggesting they get to his camp. He gave men orders to flush out and destroy Taroc, and they readied torches for the grisly work. The

camp was less than a mile away and Brannog was able to
persuade Ygromm and his people that they were in the
hands of friends, overmen who would be only too glad to
join their own cause. Ygromm expressed anxiety about
Ilassa, as the man Ruan had seemed keen to have him
dead.

Guile suddenly realized who it was they have saved.
"Ilassa! Alive? How is that possible?"

Again Brannog explained. They reached the Empire en-
campment, which was unexpectedly huge, boasting well
over a hundred tents. There was an army here, Brannog
realized. But why?

"Korbillian may be in danger," said Guile, when at last
he was able to sit with Brannog in the privacy of a long
tent. Ygromm and his people were now treated with def-
erence by the soldiers, for Guile's orders had gone around
the camp quickly. There was no mistaking his position;
he was respected here. Brannog wanted to question him
on that, but knew it would have to wait.

"You are speaking of Wargallow?" Brannog said.

"Yes, Simon Wargallow. An icy customer, Brannog.
What he seeks is beyond me. But he has your daughter,
and the youth Wolgren (and there's a lad who deserves
honors) and Korbillian. Wargallow declined to make sac-
rifices, blood to the earth. He is taking them to the Preserver, and Korbillian seems to welcome the meeting. He
has no fear of the meeting, and thus I feel your girl is safe.
Korbillian has faith in his own power, and we have both
seen something of it."

Brannog nodded. He had not forgotten the wave at Sundhaven.

"But the Direkeep is a stronghold and infested with
Deliverers. Even so, I have a mind to put that place to the
test."

"With this army?"

Guile laughed. "Why not?"

Brannog remained perplexed, yet he managed a smile.
"Why not? And we are no longer alone. Let me tell you
more about Ygromm's wonderful people. They are more
than ready to lend their powers to this conflict."

The flap of the tent was abruptly flung back and into the tent walked a tall, muscled warrior, dressed in light armor and with eyes that would have shrivelled a less stout heart than Brannog's. He gazed at the latter and then at Ygromm, finally chuckling to himself, privately amused.

"Ah, Morric," said Guile calmly. He turned to Brannog. "I must introduce you. This is Morric Elberon, Supreme Commander of the armies."

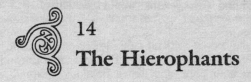

14
The Hierophants

WARGALLOW HAD NEVER FELT quite so vulnerable in his life before, and yet he had anticipated this shift in power. It was as if he had been dismissed by the two men of Ternannoc, commanded to removed himself from the debate that was to follow. But he had already made his mind up not to accept that. The Preserver's fear, something he had only dared hope might exist, was going to unhinge him, and if it did, Wargallow would not be caught up in the fall. Yet he still had certain motions to go through.

"Remember the girl," he told Korbillian. "My instructions to my men were very explicit."

Korbillian's expression did not change. "You see me as an enemy, one who has come to destroy you. I hope to show you otherwise. Grenndak, how much of your past have you told Wargallow and your servants?"

"Very little," said the Preserver softly. "But if you have not come to destroy me—"

"Then it is time to reveal the history of what happened to our world." Korbillian sat down again, apparently at ease. He was expecting no attack, no rush of guards. "Well, Wargallow, you hold Sisipher's life in your hands. I have no wish to see her die. But will you listen to the story of Ternannoc?"

This was what Wargallow wanted to learn above all else, but he turned to Grenndak. Suddenly the old man's eyes widened and a wild gleam came into them. He sat up, pointing. Fire flared around his hand. "No!" he hissed.

"Silence him, if you can. He speaks against the Abiding Word."

Wargallow turned with caution. Which of them would prove the stronger? He had to know. "The girl dies if you harm us."

"If she dies, I will raze this tower and all in it," said Korbillian acidly, "and every Deliverer that draws breath will die before the next dawn breaks." Wargallow was surprised by the venom in a man who had until now seemed far too mild to make such a threat.

Grenndak's mouth worked almost imbecilically. "Is this the man who stood before us and preached peace?"

"Your master," Korbillian told Wargallow, "is from my own world, Ternannoc. Unlike Omara, Ternannoc was a world where everyone had power. The high and the low. Everyone. Even the animals and the growing things. Is that not so, Grenndak?"

Grenndak did not answer and so Wargallow gently prompted him. If this was true, a whole world!

"Yes," admitted the Preserver at last. "All had power."

"Most powerful of all were the Hierarchs," went on Korbillian, and he explained something of their great powers and of their workings. "There were no gods on Ternannoc, and no rules in the usual sense, although countries had their leaders and their councils. The Hierarchs and their powers were available to everyone, in spite of their independence. It was their first law, to help those in difficulty. They considered themselves above the rest of the world, and there were those of Ternannoc who whispered that the Hierarchs had assumed the role of gods. So although they were invaluable, the Hierarchs were not completely popular. There were also people who had developed certain other powers, not so complete as those of the Hierarchs, and who worked closely with the earth powers and with the creatures of the earth, and they were the Hierophants. They taught the only real religion of the world, if I may use the word for convenience, and they held that the world was alive, a single being, with everything a corporate part of it. All life was its blood."

"So it is held in Omara," said Wargallow.

"I will come to that. The Hierophants, like the Hierarchs, shared their powers, healing the wounds of the world, although there were some who went their own way, hiding themselves and ignoring their responsibilities. This was the tragedy of Ternannoc, that those with the greatest powers did not always share or consult with the greater numbers, those that did not have them." Korbillian spoke then of the working that had led to the opening of the world-gates and of how it had brought ruin upon the world. "The Hierarchs consulted no one but themselves before deciding to undertake the working."

Wargallow listened in disguised amazement. He could see merely by glancing at Grenndak that everything Korbillian said was truth, and he felt the foundations of his own beliefs, that had been driven into him since boyhood, shifting.

"After the disaster, there were two schools of thought. The Hierarchs, who had already caused such terrible destruction, held that Ternannoc could be saved if everyone was prepared to sacrifice their powers to do it. No matter how small the power, if it could all be pooled and poured into a counter-working, Ternannoc could be saved and the evil undone. The world-gates would have been sealed quickly.

"But the other school of thought, that adhered to by the Hierophants, who had now banded themselves into their own Council, refuted the claim of the Hierarchs. They said that the Hierarchs were responsible and had to be broken. Ternannoc could not be saved, for too much damage had been done. To sacrifice anymore power, said the Hierophants, would not only have seen the end of Ternannoc, but the end of the entire race. No one would survive, they said. There were dire arguments, and when the masses of Ternannoc saw the terrible indecision, they grew afraid and more confused. They began the exodus, and they used the gates to escape into other worlds, thinking soon that Ternannoc would be no more.

"When the Hierarchs realized that their efforts were going to fail and that the great communal sacrifice was not going to be possible, the majority of them reached another decision. They did not want their own powers scattered across a dozen worlds. The strength of their power was in its combining. Their only hope rested in that belief. Even though they had wrought havoc, it had not been deliberate. They had in mind only to do beneficial things. They had lost a great deal of power, power that had been drained by the working, and power that had been burned up in an effort to reverse the working. And power that had gone out from them to be twisted into a mindless destructive force on other worlds. Now they sought to keep all their remaining power together. But how?''

''They had no right!'' snapped Grenndak, again coming to life. As Korbillian had been speaking, Grenndak had been staring sightlessly ahead, as if seeing everything again before him. ''We each had our own power, our own control of it. To take it from us was a foolish plan. Only I can control my power. In another's hands it would be dangerous.''

''Then what Korbillian says is true?'' asked Wargallow. ''You were one of these Hierarchs?'' At last! he thought. The truth about his power.

Korbillian answered for him. ''Not all of them agreed with this plan. Those that did not fled before the final decision was made. Grenndak was one of them. He must have fled here to Omara, for its world-gate was open.''

''But no longer!'' Grenndak said quickly.

''No, not anymore. All the world-gates are now closed. Many worlds have died, or been spoiled. But nothing else will escape Ternannoc now. And you, Grenndak, came here and set yourself up as the Preserver. You brought with you your own law, a law for this world, the Abiding Word.''

Grenndak nodded. ''Yes, I could not allow the same unforgivable thing to happen to Omara. Power had caused it. Therefore I vowed to ensure that never again was power to be allowed to have its sway. In Omara there was no power, except for that handed down by the refugees from Ternannoc. I created the Deliverers to sniff it out. Many of the descendants of those ancient flights are in complete ignorance of their ancestry, but even so, we are finding them.''

''And giving their blood to the earth,'' said Wargallow. ''Because, to use your very words, the law says that Omara is alive, a single being, with everything a corporate part of it. We cleanse transgressors of their sins by releasing whatever powers they have, even if it is only thoughts of power, or gods, and let their blood soak into the purifying body of the earth.''

''So all teachings of religion, such as it is in Omara, originated with you Grenndak. The teachings of Ternannoc, except that this insane shedding of blood was never done. The people of Ternannoc did not take life, they gave it. What you have taught here has another name. Murder.''

Wargallow frowned. ''If the Abiding Word teaches us to rid Omara of power, by acts of what you call murder, it is because power is evil. Better to have no power at all and thus remove the risk of its misuse. That is the Preserver's law.''

''You see,'' said Grenndak softly. ''The simplicity. Wargallow is my greatest disciple. He understands. I could not let power get out of hand again, Korbillian. Such a sin, to waste a world. There is no murder when the blood goes back to the earth. Omara lives and her blood does not die.''

Korbillian shook his head. ''The Hierarchs never willingly took life. They gave it. As with the Hierophants.''

''What happened to them?'' said Wargallow.

''For the most part they agreed to leave Ternannoc and go their own ways, leaving the Hierarchs to their fate. They took a vow before the Hierarchs that they would always oppose them, even war with them if they crossed paths again, which was a foolish thing. The Hierarchs, weakened by all that had happened, knew that their only hope was in unity. They would concentrate their power. They would give it to one custodian. But who could they choose for such an onerous commitment? It had to be someone who was so radically opposed to the use of power that he would never consider using it if it were put into his charge. It had to be someone who had been opposed to the working and who had wanted to see all power sacrificed to save Ternannoc. It had to be someone who could be relied upon to sacrifice himself if necessary to make whatever amends he could for what had happened. And most difficult of all, it could not be a Hierarch, for none could be trusted.

"Thus there was great argument, while Ternannoc was dying. Some Hierarchs, like Grenndak, fled, taking with them their powers and so lessening what was left. The remainder made their choice. It was one that could not be fought against. They enforced it." Korbillian held out his sheathed hands.

Wargallow stared in fear and wonder. "You? You have their power?"

Grenndak shuddered. "Let him go on. Let him tell you how they ordered him to hunt us down, to take back into him our powers."

Korbillian's anguished face seemed even more agonized now that he had reached the truth. "I was a Hierophant. A master of the elements. I was the only one who disagreed with the other Hierophants. I wanted to see everyone sacrifice their power to save Ternannoc. It would have worked! We would have had a world without power, without our harmony with the things around us, but why not! It would have been better than a dead world. But no, there was too much greed. Power is a great breeder of avarice."

"So where are the Hierarchs now?" asked Wargallow.

"Finished, just as Ternannoc is finished."

"You and Grenndak are *all* that remain?"

"Possibly a few Hierarchs are elsewhere, on remote worlds. And there are Hierophants alive, some here. And the descendants of the common people of Ternannoc. The people you are trying to wipe away. That must stop, Wargallow."

"I heard they had chosen you," said Grenndak. "The only Hierophant who was not jealous, who did not hate us for our blunder. The only one of them who agreed to the sacrifice of all power."

"I never sought this burden," said Korbillian quietly.

"Which is why they gave it to you. Anyone else would have used it to become a god, a ruler of world after world."

Korbillian shook his head. "There is a purpose for it. I have tried to use it in other worlds, sealing gates, trying to save those worlds that the working polluted. But I have not saved one yet. I cannot do it alone. But now I must use the power up, all of it, to save Omara. I don't know if there is enough."

"The east?" said Wargallow.

"Yes, the last great poison from the Hierarch's working. Lodged here like a plague, spreading, already killing. It will pollute all of Omara if it is not cut out. Surely, Grenndak, you knew of this?"

"The east? Desert, waste land. Little else."

Korbillian looked appalled. "Are you insensitive to it? Have your own dreams of ridding Omara of power closed your mind to it?"

Grenndak shook his head. "There have been a few reports, but rumors, no more."

Korbillian looked at Wargallow. "Well?"

"I have seen something of it, as you know. Had I known of its existence, I would have had Deliverers deployed there to find out more. But there is much I don't understand. These scattered powers—"

"I need them!" said Korbillian, and it was almost a cry of pain. "Even with what I have here, I need every last particle. You are killing the very people who can save you. I go to the east, and to destroy that evil, I need power, Wargallow. As much as there is. That, or Omara and everything in it will perish."

"So you want mine!" laughed Grenndak. "You did not come here to destroy me, but to seek my help."

"What do you know of this eastern power?" Wargallow asked Korbillian.

"Not enough. I thought it no more than a disease, a mindless thing, spreading randomly. But I am no longer sure. On other worlds where I have seen it, it was so. Voracious but without real purpose. But there is a frightening difference about it here. What are these Children of the Mound?''

Wargallow described his meeting with the stones-that-move and all the creatures that controlled them. "Be sure of this, Korbillian, they wanted your death. I see why now.''

Korbillian nodded. ''It seems worse than I thought. There must be an intelligence of some kind dwelling in or near the Mound. Unless beings have found a way of using that power. When I first came ashore at the village of Sundhaven, I wondered at the storms. The fury in them, and the way they changed, as though seeking me out. They came from the east.''

''But what can lie in the Mound?''

Korbillian shook his head. ''I know nothing of the history of Omara, not of this continent. Even in the Chain it is unknown. But nothing could possibly control that power. I cannot believe that.''

Grenndak broke his thoughtful concentration. ''The Silences are said to be the oldest part of this world. They were old even when I first came here. They hold histories from beyond time. No one alive could possibly tell you the secrets of Omara's lost past. The Silences themselves are dead. Once they were seas.''

''And the land beyond, where the Mound lies?''

''A plateau that once rose up from the seas. Dead, like all the rest.''

''Dormant,'' said Korbillian. ''But not dead.''

WHEN SISIPHER FELL ASLEEP in Wolgren's arms, she slipped into a dream almost at once. She felt as though she were soaring high over a dark, troubled landscape. The images blurred, as did the sensation of flight. She fell into false wakefulness. Figures coalesced before her and she heard them speaking. She saw again the hall of Ratillic's mountain retreat and he was there, the great, bird-like man, sitting at his table, brooding and downcast. Opposite him, claws locked on to a chair back was Kirrikree.

''You remain adamant?'' said the bird, and in her dream, Sisipher heard the bird speak.

Ratillic seemed to be struggling to suppress the same fury she had seen when he had confronted Korbillian. "This is the old argument, Kirrikree! Of all the Hierophants, only one, *one* insisted on the madness of sacrificing everything in an attempt to save Ternannoc. Save it! When it was already doomed by the lunacy of the Hierarchs! We should have united ourselves, oh yes, and destroyed them! While they were weak."

"I accept that Ternannoc would probably have perished even if all power had been gathered together," said the owl.

"You do? And yet now, when the same man demands that power is gathered here, in Omara, you fly straight to him!"

"I have seen the enemy," said Kirrikree. "You have not. This is not our world, Ratillic. Our people have served each other well, and we have shared our gifts. But you do not have the right to control our gifts."

"But Korbillian does?"

"No. We choose what path we will follow. Omara is in great peril. It may fall just as Ternannoc fell, and we may not be able to save it. But the gates are closed, Ratillic. *Closed.* No power can open them again. There is nowhere else for us."

Ratillic closed his eyes, apparently drained. In a moment he looked again at the unblinking eyes. "You see this war as inevitable?" He looked ghastly in the strained light.

"The people of Omara need help. They are unaware of what reaches for them, and they war among themselves. These Deliverers kill the men and women of their own world. They have taken Korbillian to the Direkeep."

Ratillic scoffed. "He will not fall to them."

"No, but the girl is in danger. She is from Ternannoc stock, Ratillic. How else did she have the gift? And how many others are there here from our world, sharing our blood? Why must you deny them your help? Is it pride? Refusal to admit you were wrong?"

Ratillic gathered himself for a last argument. "Power," he said, "belongs to everyone. It should be used by them all. It should not be gathered and put into the hands of a few, and not one man. You understand what Korbillian has? What he *is*? Absolute power.''

''No. He does not have all power.''

''But you would give it to him.''

''I would see every creature of this world bending their power, no matter how small, to defy that evil in the east. It will take an army, and Korbillian is not an army.''

''And after this evil has been purged? What will Korbillian do with his power then?''

''If there is any left,'' said Kirrikree, ''it will be a miracle.''

Ratillic held his head in his hands, staring down at the table top. ''Another war. More death, scattering.''

''It is wrong for one to hold power,'' Kirrikree echoed him. ''And is that not what you do, Ratillic, shut away here in the snows? Hierophant, communer with all living things? And do you share this gift, and teach other men how to speak to the owls, or the fish, or the voles? Have you opened their minds to what is around them?''

Ratillic looked up at him. ''So that they could use you? Mistreat you?''

''Some may. But you should not sit in judgment. You said once that there was no reason in sacrificing all power to save Ternannoc if it meant a world without power, without the harmony it had. Yet in Omara you have allowed a world without power to exist. You have even done nothing to prevent the destruction of power, the giving of blood.''

''You have said enough!''

''I never believed you evil,'' said Kirrikree. ''You have meant well and have served my people well. But I will take them from this place. My duty is plain. I am sorry that it ends here.'' He spread his magnificent wings. ''There is little time.''

''Will you leave me nothing?''

Kirrikree flew up toward the hidden exit, preparing to call his owls together for the long flight. ''You have your maps,'' he called.

Ratillic sank back, and for a long time stared fixedly at

a point in the darkness before him. The darkness grew and swirled, and Sisipher's dream ended, though her sleep did not.

WARGALLOW SAT in a room that, like his master's, was furnished with the bare minimum. There was a wooden trestle table, scarred by his killing hand where he had traced patterns on it a hundred times, letting his mind run over and over again the plots and counter-plots that were ever there, never still. He looked at his steel hand now and smiled at it wryly. So all the giving of blood had been wrong? It must stop? Yet how were the Deliverers to be told? If the Preserver was to be deposed, and his law annulled, what use would the Deliverers be? It was one of the many problems Wargallow thought about. His gaze went from the candle on the table to the fire that crackled in his hearth, and in the flames the images of past days taunted him. Korbillian had been given a room for the night. It had been locked and guards put on its door, but somehow Wargallow did not think such things would deter him from getting out of the room if he wanted to. Korbillian's last words still rang in his ears, although they had been spoken quietly enough.

"I will give you the night to think. In the morning I must prepare for the journey to the east. There is little time to waste." He had said this with every confidence, suggesting that whatever the Preserver had in mind, it would not be allowed to interfere with his own plans.

Wargallow was stretched by doubts. Grenndak had hidden so many truths. And Ternannoc! A world where every man, every creature, had power! It seemed impossible to believe, and yet Grenndak had not denied it. Not even after Wargallow had secured Korbillian and gone back to the Preserver. For the first time he had seemed like nothing more than an old man, not far from his death. In the past, Grenndak's appearance had meant nothing; he seemed weak and ailing, but Wargallow knew that power beyond understanding—beyond question—suffused those old but deceptive bones.

"He is a danger to us all!" the Preserver had told Wargallow. "He will drag us all to ruin, just as he sought to in Ternannoc. Had he got his way there, everything would have died. I have heard nothing from him now to make me repent. I chose what I thought best. The Abiding Word is still my law."

"You did not think Ternannoc could be saved?"

"No! Impossible. The effects of the accidents were too far-reaching. Which is precisely why I have given Omara the Abiding Word, to prevent such an accident occuring again. All this talk from Korbillian is foolish. Now he seeks to drag us all together and do here what he could not do in Ternannoc. He must be stopped."

"How?" It was the one question that burned within Wargallow, for if there was no answer, it would change everything for him.

"He is mortal, just as we all are. He has terrible power, but one swift stroke of your killing hand would finish him."

"And the power he holds?"

"It would dissipate. Go back into the earth. Strengthen it. Why, it would likely work against the evil powers he babbles of."

"You doubt their reality?"

"He speaks of controlled evil. It is an obsession with him. The power in the east has been there for centuries, millennia perhaps. It is not sentient! What we released was volcanic, mindless energy."

"I have seen those who worship it."

"I do not doubt that," snapped Grenndak testily. "But I will not concern myself with it here. For now, we must dispose of Korbillian. Where is he?"

"In the Eagle Tower, as far from the earth as I could put him."

"I doubt that he will sleep easily. He may suspect treachery from me, and if he does, he will be listening to the door, not the window. Pick your man carefully, Simon. He will have to scale the Eagle Tower, climb upon its roof and then drop down to the window."

"I have several men who can do this."

"Is there a bowman amongst them? A man who can see

in the dark, Simon, a man who can use a single arrow to good purpose?''

''I am sure of it.''

''Use poison.''

''And the others? The girl and the youth?''

''Tomorrow we will give their blood. I will perform the giving myself.''

Wargallow studied the flames, imagining the assassin crawling across the sloping roof of the Eagle Tower. Was it to be so easy? Power, he thought. More power than I had dreamed of. And with Korbillian dead, there would be only Grenndak. And the east. I am not so sure that its power is weak. If Grenndak dies and I succeed him only to be faced with this eastern menace and with no power of my own to go against it, what have I gained? Yet if Korbillian defeats this power in the east and loses his own power—or if he should die in the conflict—there would be only Grenndak. Unless he were disposed of first.

Wargallow watched the fire reflect from his hand. Grenndak to die now? As I have planned for so long. But what is to become of my killers? How to rally them all to me, those who are not of my chosen Faithful, those who are spread wide across Omara. I could turn them all upon the powers in the east. Blood enough there, Korbillian says.

Yet Korbillian has not come here to kill Grenndak, not if the Preserver is prepared to ally himself to his cause. If Korbillian knew that my master plotted his death, perhaps he would act as the Hierarchs charged him and take his power into himself. Perhaps, perhaps, it is all perhaps. How to swing this to my advantage?

Wargallow spent another hour considering the possibilities. At last he reached a decision. Having done so, he left his room and went in search of the picked men he knew would suit his purpose perfectly, and who would obey him above anyone else, even the Preserver.

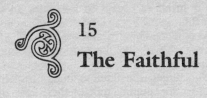

15
The Faithful

SISIPHER AWOKE in darkness. She thought she heard the beat of wings, but it must have been the breeze outside, or else the echo of her dreams. The conversation between Ratillic and Kirrikree puzzled her. There were still mysteries surrounding Korbillian that had to be clarified. Gently she moved, finding that she was slumped against Wolgren. He was fast asleep, his arms locked protectively about her, and very slowly she tried to move them. He was awake at once.

"What is it?" he whispered, expecting danger.

"Nothing," she whispered back. "I woke. Are you all right?" It seemed a stupid question, but he stretched in the dark.

"We've been left here for the night."

"I'm sorry about earlier," she said, remembering the tears. She got up, going cautiously to the window.

"You were tired," he said in the shadows, but she could feel his eyes on her. "Do you think Korbillian is all right? This place is full of confused—" He tried to find a word to suit him, but all eluded him.

"I think if he were dead, I would know it," she told him. She tried to see out into the night, but the towers of the Direkeep were a shadow landscape. "I dreamed about Kirrikree. He was talking to Ratillic. It was strange. Ratillic said Korbillian was absolute power."

Wolgren was silent, considering her words. "Can you find the bird with your mind?"

Sisipher closed her eyes and faced the night. It was as though she had been slapped in the face. Wolgren must have seen her lurch and leapt to her side, an arm automatically going around her. She did not object, but stared at the darkness outside. "He's near!" she whispered. "I didn't realize."

"Keep silent," came Kirrikree's voice from the void. "You are all in danger. Better that no one knows I am here yet. But I am close. Watch for me."

Sisipher whispered the words of the white owl to Wolgren and he grinned. He took his arm self-consciously from the girl, but the darkness hid his embarrassment. He had not meant to take liberties with her. He would do anything to protect her, to serve her, but he would presume nothing. Instead he concentrated on the night.

Their eyes grew accustomed to it, and soon they were able to make out a few details of the towers and roofs. Nothing moved, and there was silence, until Sisipher pointed at what appeared to be the highest of all the towers. It was to the left of them, fifty feet above them. Something moved on its pointed roof; they discerned a figure there, lowering itself gently and silently by rope to the very lip of the roof. Slowly it negotiated the narrow gutter and began to drop like a spider on a thread, feet brushing the stone in silence. There was a window below it, its likely goal.

"This is strange," said Wolgren. "Who can it be?"

"Rescue?" said Sisipher. "Someone in that tower?"

"Could it be Korbillian?" said Wolgren, craning his neck out of the narrow window. As they watched, the figure reached the window and peered in, using the wall to hide itself. It braced itself on the wall, the rope securely tied to its waist, and unstrapped from its back a bow. In a moment its purpose became clear, but neither Wolgren nor Sisipher found their voices to break the spell that seemed to hold them. The man was an assassin, and was drawing back an arrow that could have but a single purpose.

"Korbillian!" gasped Sisipher.

A sudden bolt of white light shot down out of the skies.

The archer was on the point of releasing his arrow when the thunderbolt crashed into him. Claws tore at his face and he lost his footing. His bow and arrow dropped down into the well of darkness below, and the man swung from his rope, banging up against the wall of the tower. It was Kirrikree who had thwarted him and now the huge owl swooped down upon him again, the claws ripping not into flesh but into the rope. Strands parted and the man cried out.

There was a face at the window, and although Sisipher could not be sure, she thought it was Korbillian's. Kirrikree had taken to the sky. His voice did not come, and in a moment the dark had claimed him. The man in the window had seen the figure below him, which was trying to pull itself up the rope. The face withdrew. Then an extraordinary thing happened. The dangling man suddenly stiffened, loosing his grip. His feet spasmed horribly.

"He's been killed!" whispered Wolgren. "Something has killed him." The rope had obviously been badly frayed by the talons of the owl and now it snapped, plummeting the dead man down into the night.

"How do you know?" said Sisipher.

"I heard the whistle of an arrow. Another bowman."

"Why?"

Wolgren shook his head. "Perhaps Kirrikree can unravel this. I don't understand. But I'm sure it was Korbillian in that room."

While he was speaking, Wargallow was rushing from another tower room, where he had been watching from its window. Things had gone far better than he had hoped. That owl! Surely it was the great bird that had killed the half-man of the east in Swiftwater gorge. Protecting Korbillian? It must be. He was a Ternannoc Hierophant and could control such creatures. Pity the bird had not severed the rope in its first swoop. It would have saved an arrow. But the second archer could be attended to later. By now he would be well hidden by Wargallow's Faithful.

Wargallow raced up the stairs to Korbillian's room, high in the Eagle Tower. There were guards there, and they were alert. They saluted Wargallow and unlocked the door at once. Wargallow knocked loudly upon it.

"Korbillian," he shouted. He heard nothing, but flung the door open anyway. A candle burned within. Korbillian was by the window, searching the courtyard far below. "Korbillian?"

The latter turned, his face puzzled. "What is happening?"

"You are alive," said Wargallow, putting as much relief into his voice as he could. He shut the door behind him and locked it, which puzzled Korbillian further, just as Wargallow had hoped it would.

"Well?"

"Come away from that window, man! One of the Preserver's assassins has just tried to kill you."

"Grenndak?" Korbillian moved from the window. There were interior shutters to it and Wargallow slammed them shut, turning on Korbillian with a look of consternation on his face.

"He does not want you to live. His killer came from above you."

"You saw?"

"Aye. Some of it. A guard alerted me. By the time I got to a window, it was over. A bird, a great white bird, attacked the assassin. I have seen that loyal bird before."

"Yes."

"I have sent men to retrieve the body. If the man is alive, which I doubt, his body will be hidden. Otherwise Grenndak's spies will have others sent."

"You defy him?"

"He did not trust me with the task of killing you. Besides, I refused. For the first time in my life I refused to do the will of the Preserver."

"Why?" Korbillian studied the man closely. He was aware of just how cunning he must be, how easily he could play the political game. He was no pawn, no dog to obey obediently and without question.

"I am not sure that you are to be so easily dismissed. If I had been, you would have died long before now."

Korbillian nodded thoughtfully. "Grenndak does not

matter to me. His power does. I need it. He will not re-linquish it, nor share it.''

Wargallow looked at his sheathed hands and spoke qui-etly. ''Then you must take it.''

Korbillian scowled. ''You would change masters so easily?''

Wargallow chuckled. ''I am my own master. But this is an unequal contest between you and Grenndak. I can see that. If he were the stronger, he would have destroyed you the moment he knew who you were. But to send an assas-sin, crawling across the roof to you, that was pathetic. Is it how you would better him?''

''So what will you do now?''

''It is plain to me that the Direkeep has been built on lies. It cannot remain as it is, with Grenndak in power.''

''The Abiding Word and all its laws are to be revoked,'' said Korbillian. ''I will no longer tolerate the giving of blood to Omara.''

''Then you had better kill Grenndak quickly.''

''If he dies, what of you and the Deliverers? How many of them are there?''

''Here? Several thousand. Across Omara, I cannot say. More than I know about. They can be recalled, but it would take a year at least.''

''If Grenndak dies, who rules them?''

Wargallow chose his words carefully. ''Since you are revoking the Abiding Word, they will need to see a dem-onstration of your power. No doubt they would follow your lead then.''

''They will have it, in the east.''

''Fear rules them, Korbillian. Fear that the Preserver can strike any one of them dead, even for thinking ill of him. Will you hold that threat over them?''

''It is no way to command.''

''It is the most effective.''

''Still it is not my way.''

''But you would have the Deliverers with you in the war,'' Wargallow persisted.

Korbillian nodded slowly. ''If they could accept me.''

Wargallow smiled. "They will obey me."

"Is that what you desire? To rule them?"

"They need a ruler. Otherwise they will never be organized. They will go on blindly spreading the Abiding Word, sacrificing. I may be able to control them. I will lead them with you to the east, to meet this power. They will have a purpose, that of shedding its blood. When it is done, they can put aside these." He held up his killing steel. "They have to have a reason to do that."

Korbillian saw the logic in this. The Deliverers needed something to justify themselves, their grim task. The blood of the east would absolve their own transgressions.

"But first," went on Wargallow, moving carefully towards his goal, "Grenndak must die. If I am to desert him and control his people, he must die. Otherwise he will destroy me."

Korbillian looked grieved. "More death. Is there no other way? If I draw his power into me, he will perish."

"Let me have him killed. He still trusts me. Let me go to him now. I will tell him you are dead at the hands of his assassin. While he relaxes, I will strike myself."

Korbillian thought of this for long moments, but at last shook his head. "No. It is for me to deal with. I cannot sanction his murder."

Wargallow cursed inwardly. The plan had failed; Korbillian had assumed Grenndak had sent the assassin, but it had not been enough to force him to retaliate. "Very well. Wait here. I will send an escort to collect you. Let me return to my rooms. I will pretend I have slept through all this. Grenndak will still think me loyal. I will see that you get an audience with him." He unlocked the door and was gone.

Korbillian heard the door lock again. How was he to deal with this? Take Grenndak's power? He recalled all too vividly the high command of the Hierarchs who had forced his grim burden upon him. "If you find renegade Hierarchs, show them no mercy! Take their power from them and combine it with ours. Anything less than absolute power will fail you."

* * *

WARGALLOW DID NOT HASTEN back to his rooms. He went instead to the chamber of the Preserver. Evidently Korbillian would not kill him unless he was more strongly provoked. How, then? Perhaps if the youth and the girl were killed by Grenndak? Wargallow's mind played with the possibility. He was committed now to Grenndak's death. Korbillian was the stronger, the man with the real power. Grenndak had to die.

The Preserver was wide awake, waiting for word of Korbillian's death. Wargallow came to him, seeing the old man's face agitated by fear. He looked even more pathetic and despicable, this tyrant who had held every Deliverer in his hands for years. It was well that they had at last found the weakness in his armor to bring him down.

"The assassin failed. Now Korbillian will come to you in anger. Yet even now he would rather not kill you. He abhors death."

A faint hope gleamed in Grenndak's blind eyes. "Then what?"

"A trick. You must offer him everything, and when he takes the bait, strike."

"How?"

Wargallow leaned as close as he could and began to whisper the instructions that he had been formulating. When he had finished, Grenndak seemed pleased. "I will leave now," said Wargallow. "If I am here, he will certainly suspect me." Quickly he left. Moments later he was speaking to his chosen guards, men of the Faithful who wanted nothing more than to see the Preserver dead.

Korbillian had opened his window again and tried to see if the great owl was about, but could not. One thing he would insist upon now was that he was reunited with Sisipher and Wolgren. He had allowed himself to be separated from them earlier as he knew they needed rest. They had been exhausted, but if Kirrikree was here, he must have the girl speak to him.

As Wargallow had promised, the guards arrived, six of them, and they politely escorted Korbillian down to the levels where the chambers of the Preserver were to be found. Korbillian came to Grenndak, who was alone, but on entering, the six Deliverers stood behind him, watching in silence.

"You tried to have me killed," he said bluntly.

Grenndak was in his bed, head propped upon his pillows. He looked as if he were about to die himself, ageing rapidly, dissolute and haggard beyond belief. He lifted a limp hand that was pitifully thin. "Yes, it is so, Korbillian," he croaked. "I have been ailing for a long time, but I seem to have little strength left with which to fight. What power I have is not worth having."

"If this is more deceit, it is despicable. To see a Hierarch of Ternannoc like this is sickening! You behave like a child." Korbillian watched him carefully, as he would have watched a venomous snake. He drew closer.

"Say what you will. I am dying."

"I do not believe it."

Grenndak coughed. Korbillian was on the point of wondering if any of this act could be true, when the old man shot bolt upright, energy pouring into him like water racing through an open sluice. Both gnarled hands shot out and Grenndak howled like a wolf at a kill. Korbillian felt the raw power snap shut like iron about his biceps, banding his arms above the gloves in a grip that he could not loosen quickly. Grenndak poured every ounce of his power into holding that grip and Korbillian struggled in desperation to summon up his own power. He had not expected such a colossal surge from Grenndak: he had been preparing carefully. It would take time for Korbillian to tear free, time to prepare his own power.

Grenndak howled at the six guards. "Now! Now! His hands! Take your steel to his hands! Quickly!"

Korbillian felt a freezing wave of terror burst over him as the six guards stirred themselves. They had been prepared for this! They ran forward and Korbillian heard the swish of metal behind him as they freed their killing hands. He tried to break free of Grenndak's grip, but it was too soon. He could not be ready in time. The six guards were around him, steel flashing.

But they ran on, swift as light. As one their six curved hands chopped down, not at Korbillian, but at the Preserver. The power that locked Korbillian lessened and in a moment he had freed himself as if bursting out of manacles. He rushed to the bed. The Deliverers drew back, their cloaks stained scarlet, the sheets also. Grenndak's mouth opened and shut like that of a fish dragged from a lake. His hands reached up weakly. Korbillian grabbed them with his own sheathed hands and felt another great kick of power. Grenndak could not speak, and as his power surged into Korbillian, his tiny body shrivelled.

When it was over, Korbillian staggered back in sheer horror. The Deliverers had already withdrawn into shadow, wiping their bloody hands and removing their garments. Their faces were devoid of emotion. For a long time Korbillian stood there, aghast, locked in stone. The power was gone, stored within him, part of the other. But the awful sight of the killing steel descending remained.

When the doors burst open to admit Wargallow, Korbillian still looked numbed. Wargallow smiled grimly, but then his face assumed a deep scowl. He turned to the six guards, who had already bundled up their cloaks.

"The Preserver sought to kill Korbillian, sire, just as you warned us he might. We were forced to defend him."

"You have done well," said Wargallow. "Go and clean yourselves." He gave them all a brief, private look, and as the last of them left, he whispered softly, "It was as I said?"

"The Preserver took your bait," was the reply.

Wargallow approached Korbillian. "It is done, then."

"The fool," hissed Korbillian. "He could have killed me, though. If his guards—"

"I chose them carefully. I did not trust him."

"There was far more power in him than I realized."

"And now you have it?"

Korbillian turned to him coldly. "You knew this would happen. Is that why you had your own men bring me here?"

"He was adamant that you die."

Korbillian turned away. "Once before I tried to persuade him and others like him to what I thought was a good cause. They, too, hated me for it."

Wargallow pulled the sheets over Grenndak's body, hiding the sense of triumph that ran through him like wine. "What are your plans now?"

Korbillian grimaced. This man Wargallow was full of poison, of treachery, he was sure. He had already dismissed the Preserver, a man he had served loyally for years, as nothing more than a carcass. How loyal had he really been? "Bury him in the earth. And bring me the girl and the youth."

"They are asleep."

"Then wake them and find me another room. This one must be scrubbed."

"Of course." Wargallow led him away.

Sisipher and Wolgren had not been able to get back to sleep, and had hardly tried. The girl kept shuddering, smelling blood in the air. She had sought to find Kirrikree again, but he was gone. They watched from the window, but there was no further sound or movement, except for the muffled voices from far below when they assumed the body of the assassin was being removed.

When their door was unlocked, they drew back. Wolgren stood in front of Sisipher. A torch was raised and it was Wargallow himself who stood there.

"Awake? Good. Korbillian wishes to see you. You will find much has changed this night. You are in no danger, I assure you. The Preserver is no more."

Wargallow led them down into the keep, letting their imaginations play with the few words he had given them. When they reached the open hall where Korbillian was waiting, they remained confused by the events of the night. Sisipher saw at once that Korbillian was both distressed and agitated.

He came quickly to her. "Can you find Kirrikree? He is somewhere near us."

Sisipher looked at Wargallow, who watched patiently with that familiar, teasing smile on his face. Korbillian made a gesture that suggested she should ignore him as well as the other Deliverers who stood like sentinels around the hall.

"I will try," she said. "But what has happened? Is the Preserver really dead?"

"Yes." He seemed prepared to say nothing else for now, and so she closed her eyes and tried to contact the great white owl. And found him. Very close, as he had promised.

"It is safe," she told him. "Apparently the Preserver is dead."

"It is never safe," was the soft reply. "But I will come to you."

Korbillian went to the wide terrace that overlooked an outside square and watched the skies. In response to Sisipher, the great owl soon came winging down, alighting on a balustrade, flexing his wings proudly.

Wargallow watched the huge bird, impressed. "A magnificent creature," he said. "And dangerous. I have seen these owls fight."

Kirrikree spoke in Sisipher's mind. "His men bear the scars of my claws. This is the most deadly of them all. Korbillian must know this."

Korbillian stepped forward. "Tell the owl," he said gently to the girl, "that Wargallow has pronounced himself an ally."

Sisipher and Wolgren both looked stupefied.

Wargallow laughed. "It is true. I served the Preserver on pain of death. But when he sought to overcome Korbillian, he met his match."

Korbillian ignored Wargallow's glib explanation. "Ask Kirrikree what he saw on the roof of the tower."

Wargallow's composure wavered. *Ask* the bird? How was that possible?

Kirrikree responded to Sisipher's question. "A Deliverer, bent on killing Korbillian with an arrow dipped in poison."

"Who killed the assassin?" said Wolgren loudly.

Korbillian frowned. "What do you mean, boy?" he asked gently.

"Kirrikree attacked him, but there was another archer. His arrow killed the man. He died before he hit the courtyard."

Korbillian turned suspiciously upon Wargallow. "What do you know of this?"

"The youth must be mistaken," said the latter in consternation. "Are you sure, boy?"

"I heard the arrow, and I saw the man stiffen suddenly," said Wolgren.

"Sisipher?" asked Korbillian.

"I didn't hear anything, but Wolgren told me at the time."

"What did Kirrikree see?" asked Korbillian.

The great owl could confirm no more than that he had severed the rope, intending to attack it twice, but one slash of his talons had done the work. He had not seen nor heard another archer.

Wargallow, masking his shock at realizing the girl could communicate with the owl, went on with his deception. "We have recovered the body. Falling from such a height it has been badly damaged. But there was no arrow I assure you."

"Perhaps I ought to see the body myself," said Korbillian.

"It has been disposed of."

"Convenient," whispered Kirrikree's voice to Sisipher.

"I do not see what this implies," Wargallow went on, his face seemingly innocent. "Who would have wanted to kill the assassin?"

"Not the Preserver," said Korbillian. "Since the assassin was his. Someone who obviously wanted me to survive the assassination attempt. They would not have known that Kirrikree was watching."

"But I found no evidence that the assassin had been killed by an arrow!" Wargallow protested. "The boy has a strong imagination."

Korbillian considered for a while. Best, he thought, not to pursue this now. But Wargallow has used me. I am sure that it is through him that Grenndak was trapped, and murdered. That would have suited Wargallow. He turned to Sisipher and Wolgren and explained briefly the events of the night. He said nothing about having been manipulated. "Grenndak made two attempts on my life, and both times was thwarted. Wargallow could have lent his own strength to Grenndak's and very likely have achieved my death, but he did not. Therefore, I am in his debt." Let him feel that, and that I feel I can trust him. "The guards that took me before Grenndak were loyal to Wargallow and had not Grenndak been blind they would have cut my arms from me. After that, my death would have followed."

"I think not," whispered Kirrikree to the girl, who shivered.

"Wargallow has turned from his master," said Korbillian. "He is prepared to help me in my quest in an attempt to destroy what lies in the east. Well, Wargallow, perhaps you would be good enough to tell us why it is that you are prepared to help."

Wargallow smiled. "You imply that I have a choice."

"You do."

"By destroying the Preserver, you have left the Deliverers without a ruler, although word of his death remains a secret. Let us keep it so. So far I have allowed it to be shared only with those few who are loyal to me. I would welcome the leadership of the Deliverers. I will not deny that. But if the Abiding Word is to be refuted, the laws of a score of lifetimes removed, I will be seriously questioned. My choice is to be to find a new way of life for my people, as you, Korbillian, will not tolerate the old one. This teaching that the destruction of all power is crucial to the well-being of Omara is widely believed. I cannot change that in a night. But the chosen Deliverers will follow me to the east and war on the evil powers there." He turned to the girl and the youth. "I do not expect you to feel anything but distrust, scorn, for me and my men, but I can only apologize for the discomfort you have suffered at my hands. Remember, though, that by the codes I followed, I should have given the blood of you both to the earth when I found you. I did not, and that judgment has proved sound."

Both were too surprised to reply. Wargallow turned back to Korbillian. "So what is your intention?"

"How many men can you muster?"

"Give me a day and you can have a thousand. There will be more each day, but I will have much work to do to prepare them. We must cross the Silences, and that will not be lightly done. We must equip ourselves with great care."

One of his guards detached itself from the shadows and Wargallow excused himself to speak privately with the man.

Wolgren drew close to Korbillian. "Can he truly wish to ride with us? As an ally?"

"He has his reasons. And he is curious about the eastern power."

"I will never trust him," whispered Sisipher.

Wargallow came to them again, having issued brief instructions to his guard. "Interesting news. I have been wondering about the Emperor of Goldenisle and his intentions."

"Quanar Remoon?" said Korbillian.

"Not in person. But, as you know, he has many troops in the lands of the Three Rivers. It seems the Direkeep is to be honored by a visit. Apparently an army approaches, and my scouts tell me it is well prepared for a siege."

Part Four

THE SILENCES

in the Black Gate threatened to overrun. I want no
Ygromm. I know nothing of your people, but Guile has
told us that we are to share...

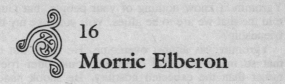

16
Morric Elberon

MORRIC ELBERON STRIPPED off his armor and put aside
his sword. He helped himself to a ladleful of water from
a wide pitcher and having drunk, splashed some uncere-
moniously over himself. He was a tall, large man, muscles
visibly hardened by exercise, and he looked capable of
rebuffing any potential attack. He moved surprisingly
lightly on his feet, but there was something dangerous
about him. His face was rounded, his eyes clear, and his
expression was that which spoke of a man born to command, a man others would respect. He had noticed
Ygromm with Brannog, but he had not reacted visibly. He
was not a man prone to outburst and whatever his thoughts,
they remained closed.

"News?" said Guile, as if he were expecting some.

"Little. But Wargallow's party has crossed the Camonile and must be near the Direkeep by now. Ruan was a
damn fool to let them go."

"I don't think so," said Guile. "Korbillian can look
after himself, and his own." He smiled reassuringly at
Brannog. "I say again, I am sure your daughter will be
safe." He turned back to Elberon. "We have a number of
guests. This is Brannog, from the village of Sundhaven,
and he is the father of Sisipher. He has been following us.
On his journey he met Ygromm, who is of the Earthwrought race." Guile said something about the little man.

Elberon came forward with a friendly nod and offered
his hand to Brannog. "We will do all that we can to pro-

tect the girl,'' he said seriously, and Brannog read honesty
in the man's gaze. Elberon bent to Ygromm. "Welcome,
Ygromm. I know nothing of your people, but Guile has
told me that we are to be allies. Will you take my hand in
friendship?''

Ygromm was almost overcome. He could not believe
that so many powerful overmen would offer friendship
rather than the expected hostility. He shook hands solemnly, his hand swallowed up in Elberon's immense fist,
but there was gentleness in the big man's grip.

"The Earthwrought are indeed anxious to form an alliance,'' said Guile. "And I am equally anxious to extend
good relations between us. In these matters we have the
perfect ambassador in Brannog.''

"Do they know why we are here?''

"Not yet, but now that you have returned, I must explain. Since you, Brannog and Ygromm, have been good
enough to furnish me with details of how you came to be
here, I must return the compliment. I have to confess that
the story I told in Sundhaven was incomplete. I hope,
when I have expanded it, you will understand my reasons
for subterfuge.''

Brannog nodded. "It is clear from your familiarity with
this army that your meeting with it was no chance one.''

Elberon chuckled. "But he has been more than a little
lucky.''

Guile also grinned. "You recall I spoke of flight from
the Emperor?''

"As I recall," said Brannog, "it was banishment.''

"I did not lie about that. But it was how I tricked Quanar
Remoon. In fact I was fleeing. I was not able to leave
Goldenisle of my own volition, so I had to find a way of
confusing the Emperor so that he would send me away. It
was his Administrators that I had to trick, for they rule the
Empire.'' He then recounted a little of the story of his
leaving Goldenisle for Ygromm's benefit. "What Korbillian did not know, and what I have not divulged, is that
there is a move afoot to overthrow Quanar Remoon. As
an Emperor he is hopeless, though an ideal puppet for his
Administrators. The poor man really is quite insane,

through no fault of his own, and is not capable of ruling the Empire. His Administrators are a poor lot, greedy and grasping, and between them they will carve up and ruin the Empire before many more years pass. Fortunately there are sensible men alive who understand this, men like Morric here, who is, or was until his defection, Supreme Commander of the Twenty Armies. Actually there were three armies, but Quanar insisted that he knew of twenty at least, hence the extravagant title.'' He grinned again at Elberon, who nodded patiently. "Most of Quanar's relatives are dead. Never a very strong family, with far too many hereditary flaws, and a number of them have disappeared, somewhat mysteriously—''

"The Administrators?" said Brannog.

"I am sure of it. But there is a cousin, whose birthright would be hotly disputed. Ottemar Remoon, who could prove his claim conclusively given the right circumstances."

Elberon guffawed at this. "Aye, at the point of a sword.''

Guile ignored him. "Ottemar knew that Morric would support him, and so the first plans were hatched. Ottemar was secretly snatched from his place of imprisonment and now waits at a place known to only a few loyal supporters. Morric had word put out that he himself had been vanquished in one of the remote but imaginary 'wars' that the Emperor was so fond of. Morric came here, where Empire men had not been previously. After all, no one was interested in what was thought to be a dreary continent. Gradually Morric arranged for more and more men to defect, until he built up an entire army. With ships he was able to pirate other Empire vessels, and often the crews were more than happy to join Morric. Well, the army is now almost ready to move against the Emperor.''

"And what is your place?" asked Brannog.

"I am one of Ottemar's most trusted spies. The Administrators were suspicious of everyone, and I doubt if I could have escaped them but for the affair with Korbillian. Even the Administrators have to obey Quanar.''

"And Korbillian knows nothing of this?"

"Indeed not! I gave strict orders that my identity should be kept secret. Morric and his troops knew I would be coming, hence the search."

"As well we were searching," grunted Elberon. "Since you fell foul of Wargallow's killers."

"Yes, an unnerving experience. I'm afraid that Wargallow, Korbillian and the others were all led to believe that I had been captured by men anxious to punish me for some unmentioned 'crime' against the Emperor. Ruan deceived them very well. I'm sure he was wise to avoid battle, though Morric here would likely have gone in breathing fire."

Elberon snorted. "You are not the only man in Ottemar's camp capable of stealth."

"But what of Korbillian's cause?" said Brannog. "I have sworn to enjoin this war on the east, as has Ygromm. The Earthwrought will follow us. Where does Ottemar stand in this?"

Guile nodded understandingly. "It is a difficult situation. I have not been permitted to go before Ottemar, but I have sent a full report. He has fortunately agreed that the matter should be pursued. Firstly, I am anxious to be reunited with Korbillian. And with Sisipher and Wolgren. Their safety means much to me."

"And Wargallow?" said Brannog.

"We shall see. I have Ottemar's permission to ride upon his Direkeep. It may even be necessary to besiege it."

For once Morric Elberon was not laughing, his brows clouded. "Damn waste of time! The place is well fortified. We would lose many men."

"If you should rescue my daughter," said Brannog, "and release Korbillian and Wolgren, what then?"

"Ah, that is a real question. I will need to go before Ottemar, if I can persuade a certain bull-headed Commander that it is necessary! But for now it is better to get some rest and begin afresh tomorrow. Your people are comfortable, Ygromm? If there is anything they need, please let me know."

Ygromm bowed, not sure how to behave in front of this overman who evidently had great rank among his own people. "You have been most generous," he nodded. The Earthwrought had been provided with a place of their own in the camp, a hollow protected from the prying eyes of inquisitive soldiery. Ruan had been told to see that nobody disturbed them, and had provided them with water, which was all they had seemed to want.

"We will talk at length shortly after daybreak," Guile told Brannog.

"Very well, but you will understand my anxiety to go on to the Direkeep with all haste."

Guile nodded. "We leave promptly, I promise."

As Brannog and Ygromm left the tent, Elberon was frowning. "You speak again of the Direkeep. Why must we concern ourselves with it?"

Guile helped himself to wine. After his journey, it tasted like nectar. "It is Korbillian that concerns me, Morric. It must be very difficult for you to comprehend what he is, and what he has. Have you ever encountered power?"

"Sorcery?"

"If you like. Power to control the elements, to raise or subdue a storm? Such things are not believed possible in Omara."

"No. Wargallow's people kill those who accept such things."

"Indeed they do. But Korbillian has power, believe me. What it is that he carries in his hands is beyond me." He sipped thoughtfully at his wine. "But I am sure of this, it can withstand anything the Direkeep throws against it."

"Then why consider wasting men to rescue him if he does not need you!"

"For two reasons. On the one hand, I have seen other powers, an evil in the east that could be, as Korbillian believes, a threat to us all. Greater by far than Quanar's regime. Korbillian's power will go against it, but he needs help. Secondly there is our cause. If I am seen to attempt to aid Korbillian, even though he needs no aid to free himself from the keep, he will remember it well. If we had him with us when we sail upon Quanar, Morric! I have seen him control the very sea! He would ensure our success, I swear it. That is why I have tied myself to him for so long.''

''He knows nothing of your part in the rebellion?''

''Nor of the rebellion. But I will explain it all to him.''

''And if he refuses to help?''

''How can he, if we help him in the east?''

Morric's frown deepened. ''The *east*? You would take men there?''

''I will need several hundred of your best men.''

Elberon looked amazed. ''Oh, is that all?''

''Not quite. I want you to lead them.''

Elberon groaned. ''This is madness. We have spent a long time preparing this army—''

''And is it ready to sail?''

''Not yet. But in less than a year—''

''That's all that's needed for this affair in the east. Less. I feel sure that Ottemar will grant me permission.''

Elberon chuckled. ''Yes, I'm sure he will.''

''We have potential allies in Ygromm's folk.''

Elberon scoffed. ''Half-men? They are like children.''

''I am not prepared to dismiss them so easily. This continent is full of strange things.'' He finished his wine. ''I had forgotten how truly wonderful this wine can be. Now I will sleep. You'd better begin preparing troops for the ride to the Direkeep. We'll test the Preserver's strength.''

Ygromm's people were relieved to see him again, for they were uneasy in the camp of the overmen, surrounded as they were by them. Ruan had ensured that the soldiers kept away, telling the men that it seemed likely they would be on the move soon. Many of them were restless, bored by the inactivity and eager to ride to war, or at least to the Direkeep, for rumor had quickly spread that the place was to be attacked. Several men had asked Ruan about Ottemar's spy, but Ruan said little about it, enjoying the secrecy and his part in it.

Ygromm also enjoyed being able to walk proudly among his men, whispering to them that he had been accepted as an equal. The overmen, he told them, were good, and would not, as some of them seemed to think, devour Earthwrought flesh when it suited them. Yet Ygromm spoke gravely to Brannog. "My people are not used to being above ground, Brannog Wormslayer. This is all happening a little suddenly for them."

"In the morning we leave for the Direkeep. On our own if we have to."

"And these warriors?"

"Can we go under the earth?"

"Of course. We are Earthwrought."

"I will suggest this to Guile."

"He seems prepared to besiege the keep."

"I wonder why," Brannog mused.

"You do not trust him?"

"I am not sure. Why has he followed Korbillian? What course will he follow when we have finished with the Direkeep?"

"You think these warriors will ride upon the eastern powers?"

"They are Ottemar's men. Why should they?"

A shout from a nearby tent drew Brannog's attention. It was the only tent the Earthwrought had wanted, the place where the injured Ilassa had been resting. One of his Earthwrought guards had called to Ygromm. Quickly he and Brannog went to see what had happened. Ilassa had come round for the first time. The Earthwrought had worked their powers on him several times and his health seemed to be mending miraculously. The Earthwrought were delighted with their success, seeing in Ilassa's recovery an exceptional omen.

"Who are you?" Ilassa gasped, for the sight of the crowding Earthwrought, lit by their own eerie body-glow, unnerved him.

Brannog gently pushed through them. "I am Brannog, father of the girl, Sisipher." He began to explain.

"You must excuse me," Ilassa said dazedly, shaking his head. He insisted on getting up to sit on the side of the bed. "Where are we?"

"In the camp of Morric Elberon, the Emperor's warlord."

Ilassa sat upright, gasping. "Empire! Then we are prisoners!"

"No," smiled Brannog. "You fought with Korbillian and Guile against the Deliverers?"

"Why, yes—"

Brannog sketched out the details of what had happened, and at the end of it, Ilassa gaped.

"Then these soldiers are not really enemies of Strangarth? They do not covet our lands at all."

"On the contrary, we have a common enemy in the east. You saw them?"

"Barely. But there is Wargallow—"

"Korbillian will be with him now. We will follow, as will Guile."

"Guile the spy," whispered Ilassa. "It seems incredible. He was the weakest."

"Don't be misled. He has a quick brain."

"And Taroc? Did you find his body?"

Brannog's face clouded. He had not mentioned him. "No," he said at last. "We saw nothing of him."

Ilassa nodded sullenly. "No. Dead, I would think."

After an awkward silence, Brannog said, "So what are your plans?"

"What do you suggest?"

"You must alert Strangarth to events here. Tell him of the east, and of the men who are rising against it. Tell him of the Earthwrought and of Korbillian. And that the soldiers of Morric Elberon—"

There was a discreet cough at the tent flap, and Ruan appeared, followed by Guile.

"I heard that Ilassa was awake," said the latter.

Ilassa stool unsteadily. "It is good to see you safe."

Guile came to him and gripped him warmly. "And you are alive! It is amazing! I owe you my life, for you kept me alive on the Swiftwater Bridge. My dread of high places made a fool of me there."

"I have seen stranger fears in men."

"I can hardly believe you recovered. I saw you fall from the span, and yet Brannog tells me the Earthwrought have pulled you back from death."

"It is true."

"Well, I will not tire you tonight. But I must say this:

we are not at war with Strangarth. Morric Elberon has given strict orders to his men not to incite quarrels of any kind with your king. They are not here to steal his land."

Brannog told Guile what he had suggested. "I was about to say he should tell Strangarth that the men of Empire are allies."

"Good," nodded Guile. "I agree that Ilassa should ride to his king. Could you persuade Strangarth to send men, Ilassa?"

"To war on the Deliverers?"

Guile shook his head, grinning. "No need. But I think we must all go eastward soon. Morric is grumbling like an old woman. After all, he has prepared to attack Quanar for some time. But leave him to me."

"Then we are united," said Brannog.

"I never doubted Korbillian," said Guile. "It is wise to share his fears. But are you fit enough to ride, Ilassa?"

"By morning he will be," said Ygromm.

Guile called to Ruan, who stepped closer. "I want you to go with him, Ruan. It is important that Strangarth knows the truth."

Ruan pleaded. "Will the Commander—"

"Permit it? I think he will see the reasoning."

Ilassa smiled. "You have my word you'll be safe." He turned to Guile. "If I can persuade Strangarth to send men, and it will not be easy, where are they to come?"

"To the Direkeep. We may not have pierced its walls, but until Korbillian is free, we will be camped beside it."

Soon afterward, Guile and Ruan left, and Ilassa sank back, tired yet, but hungry. The Earthwrought provided him with their own strange food, which he wolfed, then fell asleep.

"Later we will work gently again," said Ygromm. "He is young and healthy, and lucky not to be tainted. By morning he will be strong."

Brannog sat down, himself exhausted. "A long day," he sighed. "Who would have expected so many paths to cross each other?"

Ygromm nodded. He seemed to want to speak, but hesitated. However, he finally gave voice to his thoughts. "It is your daughter you seek?"

Brannog nodded. "I did not say so, for fear of losing your support, Ygromm. I did not want you to think my quest a selfish one. Her safety means much to me—"

"Of course."

"But there are other matters now—"

"None of them more important than the girl's safety," said Ygromm at once. His wrinkled face stared into Brannog's quite openly sincere, and Brannog could have hugged the little man.

"I think, Ygromm, there will be a storm."

"If this man Guile can draw men to him, then the east will have cause to tremble."

"Just so," Brannog yawned. But his suspicions remained. Why should Guile turn aside from his true purpose to go on Korbillian's perilous trek? The thought still nagged at him as he fell asleep.

In the morning the camp was humming with activity. Brannog found Ygromm's folk ready to travel at once. He met Guile, who was himself ready to ride, and who seemed to have been up since before dawn. He looked a little tired, while beside him, terrifying in his war gear, Morric Elberon looked fresh.

"We will find our own way," said Brannog. "We meet there."

"Very well. And Ilassa?"

"Eating heartily," Brannog chuckled. "He is greatly restored."

Guile smiled at Ygromm, whose features looked exceptionally fierce in the morning light. "It still seems a wonder that he lives at all."

Ygromm bowed, and Guile pondered the strange powers of the little folk. But he was businesslike at once, turning to Elberon. "See that they are escorted from the camp and set on their way. Find horses—"

"No need," said Brannog. "We travel below the earth."

Guile nodded, but he wondered at Brannog. How changed he was, even in so short a time. It seemed like months since they had first met. Brannog had cut an impressive figure at Sundhaven, a man that the entire village had looked up to, but now he seemed to be imbued with something even stronger. The Earthwrought again? What had they done to him? Even Morric had been impressed with him and it took a good deal in a man to impress the huge warlord.

"As you prefer," said Guile.

Brannog held out his hand and Guile shook it warmly, at once sensing the strength flowing in the man's veins. "Will you wait if you are there before me?"

"I will," Brannog agreed.

"And I for you, if need be," said Guile.

Soon afterward, Brannog and the Earthwrought were gone as if they had never been, and the soldiers buzzed with chatter about them.

Elberon was grinning. "This continent breeds strange children. I will be glad to go home," he laughed. It had taken Guile a long time that night to persuade him that pursuit of Korbillian was the best course.

"Is Ruan ready for his ride?"

Again Elberon laughed. "Aye! Shaking at the knees. He thinks this is a cruel way to repay him for saving you from the Deliverers."

Guile himself laughed. "Not so. He is an excellent man. And I think Ilassa will not let us down. Strangarth may be difficult, though. He has lost men to us."

"You think he can be persuaded to our cause?"

"To Korbillian's first. You see, again Korbillian is the key."

Ilassa was already checking the horse he had been given, and had pronounced himself well satisfied with it to Ruan. Guile noticed that the two men seemed to respect each other. Elberon, however, had told Ruan that the Earthwrought had worked their magic on Ilassa, and Ruan was now wary of him.

Guile spoke quietly to the soldier. "I would not send you with him, Ruan, if I did not feel certain that he is an ally. He spoke well of Korbillian, and you must be our ambassador in Strangarth's kingdom. Try and bring us men from there.''

"There is to be war?"

"On the eastern powers, first."

"And Wargallow?"

"Less important. When Strangarth understands that we are opposed to the eastern powers, he may well join us."

"I will do my utmost."

"Then meet us at the Direkeep." Guile went then to Ilassa and shook hands for the last time. "There will be strife," he told him. "Strangarth cannot stay out of this quarrel now. He must know that it won't be long before the Children of the Mound seek to cross the Swiftwater into his lands in force. We must take the battle to them."

"If ever I weaken in my resolve," said Ilassa dourly, "I have only to think of Taroc and what was done to him. Strangarth thought kindly of him."

"You know about Taroc?"

"Ygromm told me."

Guile nodded. "I have not forgotten. Good luck."

Ruan and Ilassa mounted and were gone, thundering back to the north, the trees swallowing them. Guile clapped Elberon on the shoulder. "Eastward, then, Morric! And where is your good humor?"

Elberon stared eastward. "East! We should be riding to our hidden fleet, and sailing west."

"When we do, my friend, there will be such a strength in our arm that we will sweep all before us. You may yet become Supreme Commander of the Twenty Armies! Why not? I must use my influence with Ottemar Remoon to win you that honor."

Elberon chuckled, snapping down his visor. "If Ottemar grants me such a distinction, I would seriously consider it time to depose him. Perhaps a military emperor, a new line, would be called for." They rode out to the troops, laughing like children.

NOT LONG AFTER the guards on the bridge to the Direkeep had signalled to that soaring tower that they had seen what looked like an army approaching, a single rider came

across the bridge to where Djemuta waited anxiously. Djemuta did not recognize the man as he rode up to them,
not knowing him for one of Wargallow's Faithful. To Djemuta's chagrin, the man came not to him, but to the captain of the bridge, and he could not hear what was said.

"You are loyal to Wargallow?" the Deliverer asked the
captain, his whisper like steel in darkness.

Everything depended on his answer, the captain knew. He
felt sure that there was rebellion, led by Wargallow. His answer meant survival, promotion possibly, or death. "I am."

"If necessary, first?"

"Yes." He had said it, cast his life into the balance.

"Good. Has the man Djemuta spoken to you about Korbillian, whom he brought here?"

The captain's heart raced. He had answered as desired!
There was no retreat now. "He has. He questioned Wargallow's actions in not giving the blood of all the prisoners."

"Do you accept Wargallow's action?"

"Yes." But he wondered.

The Deliverer turned away and raised his voice for all
to hear. "You are all to return to the safety of the keep at
once." He stood his horse aside to allow the guards to
pass. As Djemuta came abreast of him, he checked him.

"Wargallow has asked me to escort you and your men
to special quarters. If you would follow me." Like many
of the Deliverers, the man was cold, his expression un-
readable. He did not elaborate on his orders, merely waited
for the captain and his guards to go on ahead, then followed them. Djemuta mounted his horse and called his
own men together. For a second he fought an impulse to
flee. He knew better than to ask more of the guide, but
wondered if he was to be rewarded or punished. But why
should Wargallow punish him? However, it was wise to
go into the keep, for there were many soldiers coming, far
too many to oppose in the open.

Once inside the keep, the guide led Djemuta and his
men downward, a fact which further disturbed Djemuta.
The better quarters were higher up in the keep. There were
other Deliverers waiting for them and they soundlessly di-

rected Djemuta's men to rooms which looked comfortable enough. Djemuta himself was taken to a room of his own. There were no windows, but a fire burned and the table was set out with enough food for three men.

"Why this treatment?" he said at last.

The Deliverer's face remained set. "Wargallow was anxious to see you and your men adequately provided for. Everything you need is here. Later, when you require one, there will be a woman for you. You only need call."

"*Call*? Is this a cell?" gasped Djemuta.

"No. But you must wait until fetched."

"What of the prisoners, do you know?"

The Deliverer stood by the door, hand on its external knob. "Which prisoners do you mean?"

Surely this man knew about the prisoners, Korbillian and the others, Djemuta's mind cried. The entire keep should be alert to the news. But before he could ask more, the door closed and Djemuta knew he had been locked in.

"Wait!" he yelled, his left hand thumping on the thick wooden door. "I must speak to the Preserver! Do you hear me? It is imperative. He may be in great danger."

There was no reply. Djemuta cursed. Was that it? Betrayal? Had Wargallow hidden the prisoners and not informed the Preserver? That so-called power of Korbillian's, had it corrupted Wargallow? To what end? Certainly he had made no attempt to give Korbillian's blood to the earth, and had even allowed the Empire soldiery to take away the man Guile to ensure Korbillian's survival. Why, Djemuta had remarked upon that to the captain of the bridge. As he thought it, he went cold, feeling the trap closing. A test of my loyalty? How can I let the Preserver know what has happened?

Later, when the girl came, painted and perfumed for the arts of love, Djemuta had thought of a way, using the girl. But he had been away for many weeks and the girl was chosen for her extreme skill. He slipped into oblivion naked in her arms, unaware that his whispered orders would never be carried out, just as he was unaware that she had poisoned him.

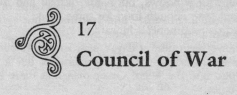

17
Council of War

MORRIC ELBERON RAISED HIS HAND, halting the long line of troops behind him. Guile sat astride his horse beside the warlord, gazing up at the mystery of the Direkeep. It had been a fast, trouble-free journey, but the climb to their present high vantage point had been strenuous. As had been expected, the Deliverers had shut themselves away in their fortress, though Elberon had made no attempt to disguise his coming. Many eyes would be studying his men, he knew. He looked at the sheer walls across the chasm, but could see no feasible way into the tower, no hint of weakness in its mocking impregnability.

He turned to Guile with a typical chuckle. "So here we are. And how do you plan to enter? Can you put forth wings? I fancy Quanar Remoon would attempt such a ploy."

Guile, though perplexed, also grinned. "A remarkable fortress." He had not been expecting such a place as this.

"If you wish to starve them out," said Elberon, still grinning hugely, "I should remind you that we have enough food of our own for about a week without going back."

Guile laughed, about to retort, but his attention was snagged by something behind them. "Ah—up on the higher slopes. Someone has arrived too late to scuttle for cover."

Elberon's smile faded, his manner at once efficient, prepared. "It is Brannog and his strange companion, Ygromm."

Guile waved and at once the two figures came down the slope to meet them, dusty and begrimed, but apparently no more worn out by their journey.

"We have been here a day," said Brannog, but it was not meant as a boast. "There is a bridge, but it can be drawn back into the keep. Other than that there are two ways to enter."

"We have discussed the first," grinned Elberon, pointing to the birds that circled high overhead above the mountains.

"Aye," Brannog agreed. "But there are also the roots of the tower. Ygromm says that it may be possible for the Earthwrought to get inside and climb. He is willing to lead them."

"How many?" said Elberon, at once the warrior, seeking every possible opening in his opponent's armor.

"Word has spread in the delvings. As many as several hundred Earthwrought could be mustered. They would be happy to see this Direkeep torn down."

Elberon nodded thoughtfully. "Weapons?"

Brannog seemed disturbed. He shook his head. "I cannot ask them to go against the Deliverers. They are small, and all they have are crude implements and stones."

"Can my men follow them in?"

"They can try, but you must understand," Brannog went on with some embarrassment, "they have certain skills. The ability to pass through places where a man could not go."

"Yet you travel with them."

Guile interrupted. "That is because Brannog enjoys something of their power."

"You understand?"

"I am beginning to," nodded Guile. "There is far more power in Omara than I ever realized. I no longer question that."

Elberon shrugged. "I'll not argue. But if we cannot follow the little folk into the keep—"

Ygromm's shout cut him off. They looked and saw the

stone wall across the chasm move. They studied it as one and within moments saw the bridge of stone being worked across the drop toward them. Their horses shied as the dust rose, but they controlled them as the bridge dropped into place.

"To arms!" shouted Elberon and swords flashed out in the sunlight. Elberon smiled. These men he had trained well, and those who came against them in battle would rue it. He watched the opening across the bridge, expecting a company of Deliverer cavalry, probably out to frighten the invader into quick submission or flight. His own sword gleamed. "Find cover," he told Guile and the others. "This is the work I do best."

They now saw, however, a single figure riding slowly across the bridge. It was cloaked and hooded in the garb of the Deliverers, but it was huge.

"Be wary," said Guile. "This is Wargallow's ground."

When the figure reached them, it did not remove its hood, but Guile saw the face. "Korbillian!" he gasped.

Although his face was as lined and weary as always, the big man smiled. "Guile," he said simply.

"Why the unfamiliar clothes?" said Guile.

"Secrecy. Many eyes watch. But I am as surprised to see you as you are me. You are not a prisoner." Korbillian suddenly realized that it was Brannog standing so close by, and his expression changed to one of shock. "Brannog!"

Brannog nodded. "Is my daughter safe?" he said at once.

"Yes, quite safe. And Wolgren."

"What of Wargallow?" said Guile.

"There have been many changes. He may no longer be our enemy."

Guile's face hardened. "You jest. Do we befriend wolves?"

"You will learn everything. Bring your men, all of them."

Elberon's humor had vanished. There was no trace of it in his voice now. "To the killing ground? I understand you to be a friend of Guile's,'' he said bluntly to Korbillian. ''But think what you ask.''

''I have called a Council of War,'' said Korbillian.

''War with whom?'' said Elberon.

''The east,'' said Guile, answering for the huge man.

''No harm will come to anyone who attends,'' said Korbillian. ''That is my promise.''

''Well?'' Elberon looked hard at Guile. Brannog and Ygromm were already prepared to cross the bridge.

Guile nodded. ''We came here to get inside.''

''I suggest the men wait here,'' said Elberon.

''Very well,'' agreed Guile. ''But I want you with me. There are things I want you to hear. Things that you will have to repeat to Ottemar.''

Elberon grunted agreement. He turned and spoke to his immediate subordinates, and the men put away their swords (not without disappointment). Korbillian then led his small party across the bridge to the keep. Beside Brannog, Ygromm's mind was in turmoil. He knew as soon as he had seen Korbillian that he was in the presence of a terrifying power, and the little man's eyes kept stealing glances at those gloved hands as if they were on fire. Would the Earthwise believe this? And now he was going to enter the very Direkeep itself! As he did so, Ygromm felt the pain of the stone, urged up from the earth by sorcery, fused unnaturally into this pile. The Deliverers had never been friends of the Earthwrought, and yet Korbillian, friend to the Wormslayer, had declared Wargallow to be an enemy no longer. Ygromm's faith was to be tested, he knew, but as the stone closed over him, he sensed that far below there were recently killed men, and they had been Deliverers.

Korbillian, still wrapped up in his cloak and hood, led the party high up into the keep, following the precise route taken by Wargallow when he had brought him here. A few Deliverers stood silently on stairways, or at junctions where there were numerous corridors, but no one opposed the party. Elberon felt like an animal being led to a slaughterhouse, but Guile had insisted that Korbillian was to be trusted. Did he have such power over the Preserver, about whom so many ghastly tales had been told?

When they reached the inner hall that had been the Preserver's private audience chamber, they saw, seated at a large table, a number of people. Brannog's eyes went straight to his daughter, and as she recognized him, her heart leapt. She rushed into his arms and he swung her off her feet as easily as he would have a puppy. Ygromm was greatly moved by the open love between father and daughter and at once made a vow with himself that he would protect Sisipher's life with his own. And the girl had power! He knew at once; it was the gift of seeing!

Wolgren had also come to Brannog and the big man clasped the youth to him in a great hug. "You are a boy no longer!" Brannog laughed. "Though it has been such a short time. But tell me, is all well with you both? Have you been harmed?"

"No," said Wolgren softly. "Korbillian protects us," he whispered.

Brannog had seen the Deliverer at the table, and guessed at once that this was Simon Wargallow. Brannog thought then of Eorna, whom he had not loved, but whose blood had been spilled through the instructions of this man.

Wargallow had not moved. He was content to permit these reunions. He wanted no hostility, no mistrust, if his own plans were to come to fruition. Guile glanced at him, trying to read something in those liquid eyes, but could not. Elberon's stare was more obvious. He noted not only Wargallow, but the dozen Deliverers standing not far away, discreet enough not to be obviously noticeable, but there to protect if need be. Wargallow measured Elberon calmly, guessing him to be high in the ranks. But this man Guile was a mystery. Where did he stand? Ruan Dubhnor had said he was hunted by the Emperor, and due for punishment, and yet he was no prisoner. There was intrigue here, and Wargallow warmed to it.

When the reunions had cooled, Korbillian, who had thrown off his cloak and hood, called them to order, and they took their places at the long table. Sisipher sat be-

tween her father and Wolgren, her hands clasping her father's as if afraid that he would disappear.

"Many things need to be explained," said Korbillian.
"For our own reasons, each of us carries his secrets. It
may be that we must share them now. Firstly you should
know that the Preserver is dead." He nodded to Wargallow, who stood up at once and smiled enigmatically.

"The death of the Preserver is at the moment private
knowledge. Only my most loyal Deliverers know of his
death. Otherwise it is still believed that he rules the Direkeep. For now it is convenient that the change in control
is known only to those who would not oppose it. Hence
the need for Korbillian's disguise. I knew that he would
be the only man capable of persuading you to enter the
keep, and if all those who were watching had known it
was him, there may have been certain problems."

"What is the change of control of which you speak?"
asked Elberon.

Wargallow's smile did not flicker. "The details will follow. I think, however, we should fully introduce ourselves, and say what we present."

Korbillian nodded. He spoke then of his own history,
telling the company the things that he had told Wargallow
and Grenndak. He spoke of his powers, given to him by
the Hierarchs, and of what he intended to do with them.
And he spoke of the passing of Grenndak. Each of those
present looked at the gloved hands, and Ygromm's face
became even more amazed.

Wargallow spoke next, fluent and convincing. "Naturally the things that Korbillian told me came as a great
shock. When I saw how Grenndak reacted, when he failed
to deny a single charge, I found myself in confusion. There
are many Deliverers spread across Omara, and the Abiding Word has been our law for centuries. Some of us, I
will say, have wondered about its strictures. Now I am
told that to destroy power, to deny it, may mean that we
open the way for a greater evil, that of the east. I have to
let this truth out slowly, for I cannot change the teachings
of a lifetime, a score of lifetimes, in a night."

"And now you rule the Deliverers?" asked Elberon. "You have become the new Preserver?"

"I assume neither the name nor the role. But I command them, yes."

Brannog took his turn and introduced Ygromm. He recounted his leaving of Sundhaven and what had happened to him, and he spoke in detail of the Earthwrought and of their full knowledge of the east. Ygromm spoke up nervously and expanded this. Wargallow seemed fascinated by the little man, and his gaze made Ygromm waver. It was not possible to forget how this man had sought a way into the Earthwrought delvings, intent on persecution.

"More truths to shake the foundations of the Abiding Word," said Wargallow after Ygromm had again sat down. "You all have good reason to hate me. And what of Guile?" he said with a bland grin. "I am surprised to see that you have not been put to the sword by your slighted Emperor. Or is that particular execution merely pending?"

Guile equalled the smile, explaining to those who did not understand, how he had tricked Wargallow with Ruan's help. "I am not the Emperor's man of course. My real mission is to give support to his cousin, Ottemar Remoon, whom I would place on his throne."

Korbillian seemed puzzled. "Why did you not tell me all this?"

"Because you have been a mystery. I had to protect the interests of the heir. You spoke of, and demonstrated, great power. It has been my hope that when the time came, you would lend this power to my mission, and help Morric Elberon's army depose Quanar Remoon. I still entertain that hope."

Korbillian accepted this, not sadly, though he seemed disappointed. "I understand. Power is ever the attraction."

Guile indicated Elberon. "Morric commands the defected army. It is made up of crack troops, trained and primed for war at any time."

"Formidable, undoubtedly," said Wargallow. "A kind

of power that I understand. And loyal to the next Emperor.''

Elberon laughed. ''First and last, I serve Ottemar.''

''You appear to follow Guile's instructions,'' said Wargallow.

Guile grinned. ''He is advised by me, when it suits him.''

Korbillian spoke for Sisipher and Wolgren, though Wargallow was not satisfied that he had said everything about them. Why should the girl be with him? Not as a lover, he felt certain.

''Our company would seem to be complete,'' said Korbillian.

Wargallow looked thoughtful, as though, like a man at the gaming table, he was preparing to make a useful throw. ''I think not. Aren't you forgetting that remarkable bird?'' He directed his level gaze at Sisipher. The bird, he knew, was her concern, and perhaps this was her part in this strangest of companies.

''You must explain everything,'' Korbillian said to her, knowing that it was better not to keep anything back and thus sow distrust.

Sisipher gathered herself, encouraged by a look from her father, and began, telling how her relationship with the great owl had developed. Ygromm was nodding to himself, understanding only too well how the girl could communicate with the owl. It made him even more determined to protect her, and he began to look upon her as he would have a goddess. The Earthwise would be overjoyed for here was proof that a sharing with the overmen was the right course of action.

''And where is the bird now?'' said Wargallow.

''He has brought his own people to the peaks beyond us. And he has rallied other birds of the mountains, although many of them have already fled to the far west,'' Sisipher told them.

Guile saw Elberon's amazement. ''You see, Morric? Power. It is wherever you look! Ygromm's people have it, it is with the very birds of the air. And what do you say to this, Wargallow?''

Wargallow inclined his head. "How can I persist in denying it? It came from Korbillian's world, Ternannoc, is that so?"

"Yes," agreed Korbillian. "And it must be used against the power of the Mound. You must all see that. You must put aside your differences, your private wars. You must!"

As he said this, Sisipher closed her eyes and sat back, listening intently. Everyone turned to her. Brannog had been particularly amazed by her tale of the owl, but here, he knew, was another of the gifts given to her by her mother.

"Kirrikree!" said the girl. "He is above, and he brings news from the lands of Strangarth. It's about Ilassa." She opened her eyes wide and stared at Korbillian in disbelief. "But—he died."

"I must explain," said Brannog.

"Perhaps," said Wargallow, "you would wish the owl to join us?"

Korbillian nodded and Wargallow spoke at once to his men. While he did so, Brannog, with Ygromm's help, told the company how Ilassa had been rescued from the very brink of death. As he finished, light streamed in from a window high up in the vaulted ceiling. Moments later the huge white shape of Kirrikree swooped down. He found a place to perch and studied the gathering with his great shocked eyes.

Ygromm's eyes were no less astonished, but a silent word from Kirrikree reassured him. Sisipher knew at once that Ygromm could hear the bird as she could. It gave her a sharp pang of pleasure to know it. Later, when there was time, she must talk to Ygromm, for there must be so much to learn from him. For now she relayed Kirrikree's news to the company.

"Kirrikree says that many birds and creatures of the land have been stirred by the strange happenings in the lands about us. When the stones-that-move and those other grim powers rose up against us, many more creatures abandoned the land and went to the west and north. Kirrikree has spoken to other birds that have come to these mountains and has pieced together an odd tale. It seems that

Ilassa and Ruan rode north, but were followed by some evil creature.'' She paused, confused, as if the owl had told her something unthinkable. She shook her head.

"What is it?'' said her father, putting an arm around her at once.

"Taroc?'' she gasped.

Ygromm was nodding. "It is what Kirrikree says.''

"But he died!'' Sisipher gasped. "Wolgren killed him.''

"My knife took him at the throat,'' said the youth. He glanced at Korbillian and Wargallow. "You saw?''

Wargallow agreed. "An excellent strike. The man Taroc could not have survived.''

Brannog shuddered and Sisipher felt the thick arm tremble. "Yet he did survive.'' Brannog described the grim pursuit by what Taroc had become and how he had hidden himself in the old lair of the bear. "But surely you sent men to destroy him,'' he said to Guile.

Elberon answered. "I had word of that. My men used fire, but they found nothing. This creature Taroc had fled into the night.''

"Then he lived,'' said Sisipher. "And remorselessly pursued Ilassa and Ruan. He came upon them by night when they rested briefly in the borderlands of Strangarth's kingdom, and with Taroc were other creatures that Kirrikree cannot describe. They attacked Ilassa and Ruan and would have killed them but for the wolves.''

"Wolves?'' said Korbillian.

"There was a pack of them, huge beasts, and wild dogs, too. They fought with Taroc's vile followers and beat them off. And they caught Taroc. Several of them died, but they—'' She broke off, shaking as if she could see the ghastly spectacle before her.

Ygromm stood up. "They tore him limb from limb!'' he said. "And scattered the enemy. Kirrikree says it was a man who led them and whom they obeyed. He saved Ilassa and Ruan, who are well.''

"A man?'' said Wargallow.

"Who commands wolves?'' said Guile. "Then we do befriend them!''

Sisipher had recovered. "It was Ratillic,'' she said.

Korbillian closed his eyes, as if in prayer. "Then he has come out of his mountains."

"Who is he?" asked Wargallow as patiently as he could. Was this to be yet another source of power?

"A reclusive Hierophant," said Korbillian. "One who once would have been glad to have seen me dead, but perhaps no longer."

"No," said Sisipher. "There is more to this yet. Ratillic went with Ilassa and Ruan before Strangarth himself. There they learned that the king's eastern borders had suffered raids by half-beasts and fiends from the wastes there, more evidence of the eastern powers. Ilassa spoke well of our attempts to gather strength against it, and Strangarth was impressed by Ratillic. It was his eloquence that won the heart of the wily king."

Korbillian's eyes flashed open. "Won him? His support?"

"Yes. When he learned of the death of Taroc, and how Ygromm's folk had saved Ilassa, he prepared a hundred of his best men. Ilassa commands them. The king would have sent more, but he needs men to patrol his eastern borders against more attacks. Ilassa and Ruan are on their way."

"This is better news than we could have hoped for," said Korbillian. "And Ratillic?"

Sisipher smiled. "He rides with them, and with him are the wolves. Kirrikree has not spoken to him, but he believes he has finally chosen to join the war against the east. I sense that something has passed between them, though, for in my dreams I heard them arguing."

Korbillian nodded. There was a long pause in which they all weighed their thoughts. None of them was more fascinated by the various revelations than Wargallow. He looked at last to Korbillian. "Well, then, what is it to be? What action do you intend to take?"

Korbillian sat back with a sigh. "I can see nothing but war. We must pool what we have and carry our power across the great Silences to the Mound. I want every man who will come."

Ygromm bowed. "I will see that the word is spread

quickly to all the Earthwise. From every delving the Earthwrought will come.''

''And I ride with my father,'' said Sisipher, ''with Kirrikree's people overhead.''

''Guile?'' said Korbillian.

''Oh yes, I ride with you, as before. Morric's best soldiers are camped on the mountain.''

Elberon cleared his throat noisily. ''It strikes me, as a military man, that this is a rash journey. What preparations have been made? Supplies, camps, routes? How are so many, forgive me, formerly opposed forces to be expected to work alongside each other?''

''It must be done,'' said Korbillian. ''Speed serves us best. If we delay, there is more risk. The east is awake and preparing.''

Wargallow nodded. ''You can be sure of that.''

''What help will you provide?'' Elberon challenged him.

Wargallow gestured magnanimously. ''Whatever is required. In the name of the Preserver. No one will question his commands. I myself have already thwarted the east, when I failed to oblige their creatures at the gorge. Possibly I am marked by them. Since Omara appears to be in dire peril, however, I will place my men at Korbillian's disposal. I am prepared to bow to his command.''

Lying through his smile, thought Guile. ''And the price?''

Wargallow's smile never wavered. ''The freedom of Omara. You, of course, have a price of your own in mind.''

''Omara's safety is enough,'' Guile grinned. ''We understand each other at least.''

They were interrupted by the arrival of one of Wargallow's guards. He spoke to Wargallow, who addressed the company at once. ''Your man Ruan has been sighted. In an hour he will be at the bridge.''

''Already!'' said Korbillian.

''I will have them brought here safely,'' said Wargallow.

''I'd better see that there is no trouble between my men and Strangarth's,'' suggested Elberon. ''Not too long ago they were cutting each other to pieces.''

Sisipher answered. "Kirrikree says Ruan has already spoken to Ilassa's men. They will not cause trouble."

Elberon chuckled. "No, but I would be more at peace reminding my men to steady themselves."

"Excellent," said Guile. "And you'd better get word to Ottemar."

Elberon nodded and excused himself. None of Wargallow's men interfered. Their own instructions were very clear. The Faithful would not dispute his decisions, and he had told them to make it clear to any other Deliverer that the Preserver was holding a number of audiences with men from outside and that there was to be no disobedience. When Elberon led the next party of men up into the keep, there were many secret glances, much puzzlement, but no one impeded them.

Ruan and Ilassa entered the audience chamber side by side and Brannog was pleased to see them both in good health. Korbillian was also relieved, but a shadow clouded his face as he confronted Ilassa. "I am deeply sorry for what happened to Taroc. I sought to use the earth to save him."

"Aye," nodded Ilassa. "Yet it was the power of the earth that saved me." He beamed at Ygromm, whose own face had lit up with delight.

Ruan eyed Wargallow dubiously once the reunion was complete. "I trust my little deceit is forgiven, under the circumstances?"

Wargallow laughed gently. "You acted commendably. I have to applaud you for your presence of mind."

Into the hall now came Ratillic, his expression mournful, his eyes avoiding Kirrikree as if his own guilt stood before him. No one ran to him, or called out cheerfully, though Korbillian went quietly before him.

"I hope that the enmity between us is ended?" he said.

"If Omara is truly in peril, I cannot stand by. I will go with you, and add what power I have to your own," Ratillic said bluntly, though his deep resentment could not be completely hidden. He was far more subdued now, but Korbillian sensed his resoluteness. He had made a decision, and one that pained him, but he was committed.

Korbillian looked around him. "I had begun to think that our quest would be hopeless, but now I am not so sure."

"Success is not guaranteed," said Ratillic.

"Perhaps not," Korbillian addressed them all. "Then you are willing to be led by me?"

No one demurred.

"I can promise that men will die."

Ratillic ignored this and brought forth from his robes a number of rolled parchments. He placed them on the table. "These are the maps you asked for," he said, looking now straight at Kirrikree. "They mark clearly the way to the edge of the great Silences, and across them. But beyond that, as you will see, the paper is blank."

Wargallow seemed startled. He came forward and watched eagerly as Korbillian unrolled the first of the intricate maps. The inkwork was meticulous, the detail beautifully worked, and more than one breath was drawn in at sight of such beauty.

"I am indebted," said Korbillian. "To all of you." But can I weld them together? he wondered. There is so much hatred here. How can they trust me? Even Ratillic, my fellow Hierophant, has wished me dead before now. Is it truly possible that they will follow me to a place where death waits?

Wargallow gave further instructions to his men, who left at once to obey him. "I suggest we seal this remarkable gathering in a toast. We pride ourselves on the quality of the wine in our keep. Will you take a little?"

When it arrived, Ygromm was first to sample it, and he pronounced it good (implying somehow that he meant it was not poisoned) but Wargallow was amused by the expressions on the faces of his guests. He insisted on drinking first. "To us all," he said, as goblets were raised. "And to success in the east."

The company echoed him.

"And also," added Wargallow, "to the fall of the mad Emperor of Goldenisle, Quanar Remoon."

This time there was hesitation. Wargallow smiled at Ruan and Guile. It was time to move another piece on the board of his game. "And of course, success to the Emperor's cousin and his cause. I hope it will not be too long before you take your rightful place upon the throne, Ottemar."

Guile's face gave nothing away, but before he could reply, Wargallow spoke quickly to Ruan. "You did very well to steal him away from me, but that was before I realized who I had in my grasp," he chuckled.

Ruan's eyes sparkled as he lowered his goblet to the table. "I guessed you did not know, and so my risk was a calculated one. The life of the heir—" But now he stopped, frozen both by the look of triumph on Wargallow's face and by that of shock on Guile's and Elberon's.

"Hold your tongue!" snapped the warlord, and it seemed that he must surely bring out his sword.

Guile's hand clamped on his arm, and his anger was well concealed. "He's tricked you," he told Ruan, but without malice.

"Come, come," said Wargallow. "We have already agreed that now is a time for honesty! Since we are to pool our fortunes, let us see what it is each of us risks."

"Then you are Quanar's cousin," Korbillian said to Guile. "How much that simple fact explains."

Guile bowed. "You can hardly blame me for wanting to maintain secrecy."

"There is no need for others to know," Korbillian said, with a pointed look at Wargallow.

"Quite so," said Elberon, with an equally sharp look at the Deliverer, "just as the death of the Preserver should be a secret."

Wargallow inclined his head. This was politics that he understood. "I am content to agree." He looked across at the crestfallen Ruan. "I would say that matters between us are equal."

No one but Wargallow smiled, and Ruan's goblet slipped over, spilling red wine across Ratillic's map. A ribbon of scarlet ran across the map to the east, collecting in a pool where their destination would be found, and as it did so there was a crushing silence.

18
The Storm

THEY EMERGED from the mountain passes a week later, Ratillic's maps having proved accurate, and they camped that evening on the lower slopes of the range facing east. Clouds obscured that view, but they knew that they were within a few days of the desert's edge. Korbillian had been relieved at the way the mixed company had conducted itself on the journey. Strangarth's men, most of whom he had now spoken to quietly, had been rowdy and cheerful, but Ilassa (who controlled them well) put this down to their nervousness. They had never been this far from their homelands and were not at all sure of the other men around them. Elberon's troops were a different breed; orderly, disciplined, they were careful not to breach their military codes, and they were much more prepared to accept the others. Elberon had said that once any fighting began, new friendships would be forged. The Deliverers (and Wargallow had kept his word and assembled many of them) moved on with their usual silence, none of them appearing to question their orders. There was, however, something of an atmosphere hovering over the army, and the tensions that flowed through it ran deep.

Brannog detached himself from the company a number of times, going with Ygromm to rally the Earthwrought, who preferred to travel their own separate ways to the east, though their presence near at hand was somehow always felt, and it brought an unexpected comfort to the travellers. In those small folk pulsed an excitement, a hunger almost, to be beyond the desert, to confront what waited there. Kirrikree and his people were not often seen, for the owls were wary of so many men, but their presence was also felt. And there were hawks and ravens, eagles and falcons which swooped above, often in groups, all moving eastward.

Ratillic was rarely with the company and wandered to the far flanks of the march, and when he was seen, it was in the company of wolves and other creatures, but he was no less purposeful than the others.

Evening fell on the slopes, a brief twilight as the mountains swallowed the sun. Korbillian sat with Wolgren, who rarely left his side, Guile, Sisipher and Ilassa. Elberon, as he always did at this time of day, was visiting his men, looking for signs of unrest or drop in morale. He had not yet found either, although he knew that his men were unsure of the cloaked Deliverers, sharing no conversation with them as yet.

Wargallow walked up to the knoll, to where Korbillian and the others sat, knowing that he would never be accepted as part of this company in the same way as they were. Yet it suited him. He felt sure that he was not trusted, in spite of his reassurances that he had come to terms with the need to work together against the common evil.

"The desert is not far," he said. "We have been fortunate to come so far without incident. Is there news from the others?"

Korbillian shook his head. "Kirrikree and his birds scour the land on all sides. Everything is quiet. Unexpectedly so."

"And beneath us?"

"I am expecting Ygromm's report at any time. What of your men? Are they ready for the crossing?"

"We will need fresh water soon."

"Ygromm will tell us where it is safe to draw it. Kirrikree says it will take us at least seven days to cross the Silences. There will be no water in the desert."

"And on the other side? Will the water be safe there?"

"It can be purified."

"Then we will all be in your debt," Wargallow smiled.

"As I am in yours."

Brannog arrived soon afterward. "The word from the Earthwrought is promising. There is a clear lake between us and the desert and we should have all we need for the crossing. Ygromm has met not only his own Earthwise, but three from other tribes, and all have sent men. But we reach the place where it is impossible for them to travel below the ground. They will cross the desert with us, and there will be many hundreds of them."

"It will give confidence to the men," said Wargallow. "Mine are no less uneasy than any of the others. They are uncertain."

"Are you?" said Guile.

"Of course," nodded Wargallow. "But I have made my decision."

"I don't foresee an attack," said Korbillian. "The Silences will be no place for conflict. The east will be ready, though. We must expect that."

Sisipher stared straight ahead of her, face white. "It is like a hound scenting the wind. I see through the jungle there, and beyond."

"Use your gift," urged Brannog. "What do you see, Sisipher?"

She studied an unseen future terrain, searching it for tangibles, then her eyes seemed to find something. Shock stabbed at her and she recoiled, only her hands preventing a scream. Wolgren and Guile moved closer at once, and Brannog held her.

"What is it?" said Wargallow. "What does she see?"

But the girl had withdrawn into herself, shaking her head.

"Will she not speak?" Wargallow persisted.

Brannog waved him away. Holding down his annoyance, Wargallow turned to Korbillian. "What do you know of this?"

"I have said that the east is diseased. We cannot expect to find anything but terror there. Sisipher should not try to look for it."

"But what use is her gift?" said Guile.

"It can still help us," said Korbillian. "There will be pitfalls in the Silences as there were in the snowfields above Sundhaven."

That night, though they were not attacked, they felt a change in the air, as though something had billowed from the east like a cloud, and in their fevered sleep they saw the plateau beyond the desert and each of their imaginations depicted it crawling with all manner of evil. Even Ratillic, who remained aloof, higher above them in the rocks with his wolves at his feet, felt the onset of this invisible cloud. It had eyes, he thought, and was sure that messages sped back to the east moment by moment. It was becoming very difficult to keep the birds from westward flight, and only the wolves remained with him of the other creatures.

No sooner had the first pale rays of dawn filtered through the eastern mists than the army marched. It was orderly, efficient, and there was little delay as the various columns threaded their way through the foothills and down to the forests below. These were much greener and fuller than the forests of the Three Rivers to the north west, although oddly silent. Word came from Ygromm's folk that all of the creatures that had lived here had long since migrated, and overhead there were no birds, their usual incessant song sadly missed. The only creatures that Ygromm's folk found were dead, with nothing to show why, or how long they had been dead. Yet their corpses had been somehow preserved for the army to stumble across.

Elberon came to Guile as they rode through the grave-like silence. "How much more of this deathly forest? There are soldiers here like dead men. I would rouse them with a marching song, but something within me will not respond. The place seems devoid of life, and yet we fear to make a sound."

"It is empty," returned Guile. "Ygromm reported an hour ago. Under the earth are many bones. But the evil has retreated, too. Soon we meet the Earthwrought at the lake. After that they will remain on the surface with us. This is truly a grim place. And yet we have not even reached the Silences. It may have been a mistake to attempt this crusade.''

Elberon glanced sharply at him. ''But if this power is spreading, it is well that Korbillian has forged this army. It may have been better to have brought every last man.''

Guile's brows raised. ''Oh, you sing a different song?''

Elberon showed no sign of amusement. ''How could we know what was here, and what lies beyond? Evil such as this must be destroyed.''

Wargallow, riding at the head of the long column of Deliverers over to the left of Elberon's troops, was thinking very much the same thing. No king or ruler could feel safe in his capital with powers like this abroad. Every man here would need his wits about him day and night from now on.

A few days later they reached the lake, but it did little to raise spirits. Although the water seemed clear and unpolluted, a mist clung to it, wraith-like and full of elusive movement. No one drank from the waters until Korbillian gave the word. When Ygromm appeared at the edge of the dreary forest at last, it was to confirm this as the last safe water they would find. Each man filled his containers, and spare horses were loaded with water carriers. As they left the lake and went on through the forest they found the way dropping downward and they could feel the heat of the lands below rising up to meet them like the hot breath of some awesome beast, with nothing at all wholesome in it. The trees thinned and became scrub-like copses, scattered about like the remnants of a fire, and the vegetation was withered and thin. The earth looked scorched, burned up by a freakish heat, the grass seared. Already the transition from forest to barren moor and wasteland seemed too dramatic, too unnatural. Geographical changes that normally took hundreds of miles had been shrivelled into a mere score, conditions warped and fused.

Another day passed and there were no trees. The ground was hard and dry, boulder-strewn, the stones cracked and blistered. No one could doubt that each step eastward brought them to a land already dead. The Earthwrought traveled with them now, none of them prepared to find a way below ground for fear of the effect that it would have on them, for Ygromm pointed out that they could see and feel more suffering in the very soil than they would have believed possible.

Wolgren thought of the snows and the blasts of winter back in Sundhaven (was it yet winter?) and it seemed unreal to be in such heat so quickly. The sun here blazed more fiercely than any summer sun in his village home, and he felt faint as it reached its midday zenith. Korbillian alone seemed unaffected, his thoughts and emotions, as so often, completely clouded.

When they came to the cliffs that marked the upper edge of the Silences, they rested. Beyond them now was a drop of several thousand feet, the sheerness broken by the great slopes of scree and collapsed rubble from the cliff walls. Once the sea had battered these majestic ramparts, even overlapped them, but now there was nothing beyond but an endless ocean of dust, without a rock to break its monotony. Korbillian called together the leaders of the columns, and they all studied the spreading panorama before them. There should be no desert here, they all knew. It should be water, with islands, forests, abundant life. The sun should not be so cruel, but the real heat came up from the sand, up from beneath it, as if a furnace blazed there, fueled by the unthinkable forces beyond this desert. Each of them was aware of the immense depth of power that could twist a season, make a desert of a sea.

"There is no way to reach the Mound," said Korbillian, "except by crossing this dead ocean." Close behind him, clinging to a rock, was Kirrikree, who was dusty and less imposing than before. "The owl has found the safest way down for us, and his birds will show us a possible route to follow. There is great evil in this place below. What lies buried here is a mystery beyond time, but the power of the east has sent out its workings through these sands. We cannot know what effects they have had on anything there. If there is life, the east may use it to attack us."

"But you are ready to defend us?" said Wargallow.

Korbillian nodded. "One thing is evident. The east is expecting us."

There was little further discussion, and the group quickly broke up. Korbillian walked along the rim, and Ratillic appeared at his elbow. "Do you expect any of these people to survive?" he said quietly.

Korbillian did not look at him, but watched the dust clouds sweeping across the desert far below. "It is their choice to come. I need them."

"As a shield?"

"You know what awaits us, Ratillic. We have to attempt its destruction. It will be over, then. All that has gone before will be wiped away."

"Blood to the earth return," murmured the tall figure. "And the Hierarchs?"

"They will sleep more easily in their graves."

Ratillic glanced at the sheathed hands and said no more.

Brannog sat with his daughter, aware of the effect the land was having on her, and he tried to cheer her. Guile joined them, also attempting to amuse the girl and her father.

"It's no place for a girl," he told them. "Look, many of the horses will have to be sent back. Only the hardiest can try and cross these wastes. Let me arrange for Sisipher to have an escort back to my camp near the Camonile. I would travel more happily knowing she was safe."

"My thanks," said Sisipher before her father could reply. "But no, I have already seen myself on the other side of the Silences."

"What else have you seen?" said Guile.

She shook her head. "If I told you, no one would go there." She closed her eyes and Brannog put his arms about her. Guile moved away, and as he did so, Wolgren watched him closely. He had noted the way this man who would be Emperor looked at Sisipher, and the anger flared in him. Would Sisipher not favor a man who would rule all of the Chain? She might, if Guile survived this trek.

During the night many of the company were woken by strange sounds, a dirge almost, that led them at first to believe strange forces were amongst them, preparing to attack, but by the light of their torches and a waxing, bloated moon, they discovered the Earthwrought locked in a ritual chant. It was for the good of the company, but those who heard it were not easily charmed back to sleep. Morning came as a relief, and no one complained at the immediate start.

Ratillic guided them to the most passable slope downward and the long descent began. Already the air was still, and the silence from the desert far below closed in, suffocating them. The dry heat came in waves, and for each yard they slid down those crumbling slopes it became worse, so that it was an effort not to drink constantly. Elberon and Wargallow were strict with their men, and Ilassa pointed to Elberon's soldiers as an example to his own men. Only by constantly railling at them had he managed to keep Strangarth's warriors from abandoning the journey. None of the horses found it easy, not being used to this terrain. Only the Earthwrought seemed agile and capable, though their fears for what might be around them were visible.

As they wound downward through great gashes in the collapsing cliffs, they sent small rockfalls ahead of them, raising a dust cloud that curled high over the Silences like a beacon. In the vault of the sky, which seemed to be white in the dazzling sunlight, the faint dots that were Kirrikree's people could occasionally be seen. Nothing else flew there, and there were no sinister carrion-eaters circling in hope of food.

By late afternoon they were on the dead sea bottom, though there was nothing here now to suggest that water had ever been here. The air was a wall of heat, even in shadow, and the sand was white and fine, almost a powder. Korbillian began singling out horses that he thought could be risked on the crossing. The remainder were to be taken back to the higher lands by a handful of men. Once this had been done, the army traveled out into the sands, still dropping downward, for the world tilted away, the horizon submerged under thick clouds of dust. Masks had to be worn, for the particles of sand began to find their irritating way into every pore.

"Better to rest by day," Ygromm told Brannog. "Travel at night. Easier to breathe."

Brannog passed this on to Korbillian, who saw the good sense in the suggestion. No one argued, but Elberon spoke roughly to Guile. "We cannot survive many days of this. If we do, we'll not be fit for war. This is ill-planned. Korbillian and the bird-man have their own powers. We have not. Even the little folk are gifted. What are we, fodder for the enemy? Necessary but expendable?"

Guile was already exhausted, and not fit to argue. "Can't stop now, Morric."

They journeyed far into the night, the air much colder, but they could take that, and although the going seemed easier, nothing changed around them. The sand was flat and featureless, like a pond on an airless afternoon. When they made camp, all parties gathered together, and with the desert as a shared foe, there was no complaint about who stood by who. It was here, in this arid wilderness with its absolute scorn for anything living, that the disjointed army at last became a unit. The common bond of suffering fused it, and Korbillian sensed it, just as his commanders did. Barely shielded from the rising sun, they closed ranks in silence, and though they spoke to each other, every sound seemed to be sucked into the void, as if the silence imposed itself, intolerant of the slightest whisper.

Some of the remaining horses succumbed and were buried, though Ygromm feared any disturbing of the sands. By night they moved on, and after three days came to another long escarpment, far less steep than the first, that dropped them a few hundred feet to another level. The moon turned the sand into a white carpet, and the men longed for a rock or a dune to break the crushing monotony. When dawn came, and they closed together again to camp, Kirrikree swooped down and told Sisipher that they had made good time and were halfway across.

"Ask him what news of beyond," Korbillian told Sisipher.

"The owls won't go close enough to land there to see," she answered. "But there's a jungle there."

"Beside the desert?"

"Such is the power under the earth," was all she would add.

During the day, when most of the men were asleep (it came far more easily to them now) the Earthwrought began to feel restless, and anyone watching them would have noticed that none of them slept. They watched the sand suspiciously. Ygromm came to Korbillian, his face even more fierce than usual.

"Bad things," he said.

Korbillian looked uneasily at Brannog. "What is it?"

"This is the deepest part of the Silences. Under us, the sand is shallower than elsewhere and leads to firm rock. But the Earthwrought can feel movement. It is rhythmic."

Ygromm hissed, pointing into the shimmering distance. "See!"

Korbillian shielded his eyes and studied the northern horizon. There seemed to be dunes there, the only feature visible for scores of miles.

"They were not there an hour ago," said Ygromm.

Other Earthwrought guards paced the perimeter of the camp, and no one now questioned their doing it. Even the silent Deliverers noted them with relief, knowing that their alertness was something unique and not to be decried. One of the Earthwrought came before Ygromm, and the two of them rushed off to study the southern horizon. Before long Ygromm reported dunes on every horizon. There was a stirring in the camp, and already there were very few left asleep.

"Closing in," said Brannog. By now the word had spread and the army roused itself, looking anxiously to its leaders for instructions.

"What can it be?" said Guile.

"The enemy," said Korbillian. He watched each horizon, but any movement was too subtle to see, though there was no denying it. "Very well," he muttered. At once he issued commands.

Ratillic stared at him fearfully. "What do you intend?"

"Whatever this is, it will not be easily defied. And not with steel. It will take a storm."

"Here!" gasped Ratillic. "Where is the army to shelter?"

"I will protect it. See to the animals."

"This is suicide," Ratillic snapped, but he could do no more than protest. Korbillian made his way to the center of the army and had it arrange itself in concentric rings around him.

"Face away from me, out into the desert," he told them. There was very little dissent. The Earthwrought formed the inner ring, the warriors and soldiers the outer, with the horses between the two rings. Ratillic took charge of them, keeping his wolves close at heel, and the Earthwrought helped to get the horses to the ground, talking to them and soothing them. Even Wargallow's men accepted Korbillian's promise that there was to be a storm.

Korbillian now stood alone, raising his arms to the sun. The world seemed frozen. Out in the desert the dunes seemed to be motionless, but there were spiralling dust clouds drifting about them. These rose up, thickening, so that it seemed as if clouds had come gently streaming across the sky, darkening it. Already the sun had lost its glare, its fierce rays barely filtering through this curtain. Half an hour passed and now the daylight had altogether faded, as if Korbillian had brought down a false evening on the world. He had not moved. Those who dared to look at him saw him still with arms raised high, his eyes closed, his lips moving.

Through swirls of dust which now eddied up along the desert floor, the watchers could see the movement of the dunes much more clearly. Still they advanced, and now it was apparent that they were huge. The force that moved them must be abnormally powerful, and great ripples of fear ran through the army. Panic strained at its leash. Overhead there was a crackle of lightning, and the dust clouds had merged with other clouds, the air swollen with the threat of rain.

More lightning threaded the sky and it seemed to rise up from Korbillian and not strike him from above. Guile watched him, and saw the black gloves glow as if they were molten. Had the storm come from within them? How else could Korbillian have dragged the elements into a storm? Now the winds came, a fierce breeze at first, quickly building into a slicing gale. They spread outwards from the heart of the circles, and every man dropped to the sand, whipped up and driven outwards like huge ripples away from a stone tossed into a lake.

The dunes towered now, threatening to engulf everything like great waves. From their highest ridges the sand streamed in plumes like surf scattering. A great bolt of lightning tore down into one front and seemed to explode, sand gushing upward in a fountain, dispersed in seconds by the howling wind. Its force increased, and no longer was the desert silent. It screamed as the fury of the wind tore at it like a maddened beast. While the men crouched down, almost blinded by the tremendous sand blasts, the dunes writhed, the sand stripped from them.

Ygromm and his Earthwrought would not look at the dunes, but closed their eyes and minds to whatever it was that surged within them. Sisipher and her father and Wolgren gripped each other, and the youth knew that whatever horrors were out there were partially known to the girl and her father. They shared power with the Earthwrought and there were times when it brought more suffering than joy. As the wind contrived to rise and the noise became atrocious, the army dug itself in, curling up like a single beast, trying to shut out the madness surrounding it. No one could see Korbillian now, enshrouded as he was within a blanket of screaming power.

Wargallow's mind roared, almost bursting with the sheer amazement of realizing that Korbillian had done this, had launched this storm out of nothing. It shattered the ears with its lightning, and Wargallow bent still further into the sand. One of the towering dunes collapsed in on itself as if it were hollow, and it rolled backward as if it had met a wall of rock and, like the sea, been rebuffed. The sands rushed back. As the wind tore from its central point, each line of dunes burst or collapsed and was driven back by power too immense to resist. If anything lived within the dunes, it was not seen, and it either slid deeper into the sand or fled quickly away.

Although the thunder ceased, the roaring of the wind went on until no one could even guess how long they had been there. Sand raced away from them, the very ground beneath them draining like water through a sieve. Men clung together, and the Earthwrought had difficulty in keeping the horses from tearing loose and being smashed away by the colossal forces at work. Slowly the roar died down and the wind eased, becoming no more than a strong breeze again. Those who had the strength looked up to see a changed landscape. Great swathes had been cut out of the sand, and so deep were some of these that bare rock showed through like the bones of an immense corpse.

Wargallow made himself peer at Korbillian, around whom the dust had settled. He stood on a great slab of stone that had been exposed by the storm, his arms lowered. Still he watched the desert as the wind died and a deep silence came again. The sand was heaped and hummocked on all sides, churned up like a miniature range of hills, peppered with rocks. The entire sea bottom had been reformed.

"Now can you doubt his power?" Guile whispered to Elberon, who merely shook his head in stupefaction. If anyone here had needed a demonstration, no longer could they doubt. As if in answer to Elberon's thoughts, an abrupt cheer went up, and scores of swords were raised in a tribute to Korbillian. It was echoed by others, until the entire army shouted its approval. Its belief in Korbillian was complete. Now, he thought, they could go on with better heart.

Brannog saw that Ygromm was very still, staring down a canyon of stone that had been sculpted out of the sand by the wind. It led to a deeper level of desert, a level that had been buried for centuries. Ygromm's wonder was so real it could be touched.

"What do you see?" Brannog asked him. "There is evil there?"

"I think not. But there are secret things waiting." His people seemed wholly aware of the narrow canyon now, and held back from it.

Korbillian was pointing to it. His voice came very

clearly across the stilled air. ''The way to the east lies through that pathway. Let us go at once.''

Brannog studied the rocks, and it was then that he saw the floor of the exposed canyon, noticing for the first time the stairs that had been carved there.

19
The Whispering City

As THE ARMY FILED through the narrow canyon that sloped yet further downward, there was now very little sand beneath its feet; this floor was bare rock. Almost at once the men found themselves on the first of the stairs that had been chopped into this rock countless millennia before, and as the Earthwrought stood upon the naked stone, they gasped, their eyes closing as if they had been touched deep within themselves by something invisible, something distant in time. Sisipher and Brannog also felt an inner stirring, a dim awareness of the incredible vista of time that spread backward to infinity, filled with shadows and shapes, like a darkened landscape that cried out for light. The further the army moved down the stairway, the wider it became, and for another mile it went down into a great basin in the rock strata, a hollow where, to everyone's bewilderment, a city had once stood. Sand had buried it, but the storm had raked it over with gigantic claws, heaping the sand up and shovelling it aside to reveal rectilinear streets, uncovering buildings which were yet clogged. Broken statues gaped up blindly at the sky and fallen archways and columns littered the roads. Over all the wilderness of ruins presided the silence, made more terrible by the ruins themselves, as if it were alien to this place, which should be alive, thriving.

Korbillian led the descent, but found that it was Ygromm who now stood at his side, the little man watching the dead city as if he were wide awake in one of his own dreams, or racial memories. Korbillian was aware of the murmuring of the Earthwrought, as though they were offering up prayers to some special guardian of this place, or performing a protective working to shelter themselves from it. Yet there was no hint of evil here. Whatever had lurked in the moving dunes had departed, and Korbillian sensed that it could not touch this city. Only time could do that, but slowly.

"You know this place?" he asked Ygromm.

"The legends of the Earthwrought speak of a time when we lived in cities above the ground. This is one of those ancient cities. The memories sleep, deeper than the sand that buried it. I would that our lore master, the Earthwise, were with us. I would that all the tribes could see this place."

"We will rest here for the remainder of the day and travel on by night."

Ygromm nodded. "There will be water here, perhaps deep below, but my people will find it."

As they descended, they began to appreciate the true proportions of the city. What had seemed large ruins from the top of the long stairway were now seen to be immense, their spires and domes reaching high up from the valley floor. Many of the towers had fallen, or were in a dangerous state of decay, and most of the domes were cracked like eggshells, with gaping holes spoiling their symmetry. Some of the statues were vast, and by the strangeness of the figures they represented, they suggested some long lost pantheon of gods. The glaring sun reached down to the streets, but many were in shadow, like miniature gorges from which the sand had been blasted away. It had not failed to impress the company just how powerful a storm Korbillian had released, and every man of the company looked upon him now with a new respect. Sisipher alone did not fear him.

Wargallow sensed the anxiety in his men, and some of them asked him discreetly if this were the place where the evil powers were to be confronted, but he told them it was not, in so doing acting by instinct. He felt drawn to the place, sensing that something was indeed buried here, and that part of him that had closed itself to all belief in power and which had been eroding for years, awoke properly. He burned, and he hungered. He had traveled Omara with his eyes and mind closed, shuttered by Grenndak's laws. Here was truth, worth crossing a dozen Silences to find. And share.

Just as Wargallow pondered the secrets of this place, so did Guile. My instinct, he told himself, was right! Korbillian does not hold all power. Omara holds power deep within her own bosom, like a mother protecting her infants from wolves. What fountain is this city? Who lived here and what did they achieve? Where did they go? His mind cried out for answers, and beside him Elberon sensed his excitement. He was more guarded. This place seemed long dead, but even so, his sword was ready, and he quietly readied his warriors for sudden action. If there was anything here worth finding, it would likely be protected.

The great stairway led to one of the main thoroughfares, cleaned by the wind and easily accessible. The horses were far less nervous on its surface, as if the city alerted no sense of danger in them. But the Earthwrought were like hunting hounds, taut on their leashes. To them the air seemed full, the city teeming with visions.

Korbillian looked for Ratillic, who kept himself apart. With his wolves he moved along the edge of the grand boulevard, lost in thought. Since the storm, the air had become still, with not even a suggestion of a breeze. It remained so now, dry and heavy, but the silence was broken by a faint whisper. Many heads snapped up at the same moment, so it was no illusion. Ratillic's wolves howled, but he silenced them with a word and they dropped to their bellies. Ygromm listened, nodding as if someone spoke to him. The whisper came again; there were no words and there was no meaning. It came and went, with no pattern to its susurration, an invisible tide ebbing and flowing around the streets. Ygromm pointed.

"Through there." He indicated another street that led away into the shadows.

"What will we find?" said Korbillian.

Ygromm shrugged. "Only by searching will we know.

But this may be the city which our legends call the place where time died." There was a murmur among the Earth-wrought. "No evil," said Ygromm, but there seemed about him a great weight of sadness.

They moved on, following the route he had suggested, and came at length to a great square. It was partially awash with sand, its surface whorled and patterned by the eddy of the wind, and once there had been vast flagstones paving it. The army assembled. Beyond the square was a building that was, like many others, domed, but which appeared to be, largely intact. None of its mighty pillars had fallen, its stairs were not broken, and the dome itself offered no immediate evidence of cracks. As the men looked at this timeless marvel, the whispering flooded around them, elusive as a dream, voiceless but yet like voices, as if the city itself sought to speak to them all and impart some lost truth.

Korbillian looked down at Ygromm and saw to his amazement that the little figure had dropped to its knees, its mouth agape. "What is it?" said Korbillian, concerned at once.

"It is here," gasped the Earthwrought. "The Forbidden."

"Within the dome?"

Ygromm nodded. "Can you not hear its voice?"

Brannog had come to stand beside them and he touched Ygromm with great tenderness. "No evil," he told him softly. "Unless truth is evil."

"What does he fear?" said Korbillian.

"It is not fear," said Brannog gently. "But reverence. The city speaks to us. We are the first to hear it since it died."

Korbillian did not want to break the spell that held them all, waiting, knowing there was more, an answer. Finally Brannog walked forward. "Who will enter?" he called.

Ygromm stood up. "Since we are enjoined in making war on our enemy, let us go together." Behind him the Earthwrought murmured their agreement.

They approached the huge building, seeing now that it had after all suffered at the hands of time. The stonework

had been etched and gouged, and at the top of the stairway, the doors (probably once made of wood, Korbillian
assumed) were gone, leaving a gaping black rectangle,
ninety feet high. He stood in the portal, peering into the
building. After a moment he could see more clearly, for
light slanted in from a dozen concealed openings in the
huge dome. Sand was heaped against everything, but the
pillars had survived. The building was a magnificent feat
of architectural engineering, the work of a major civilization. Yet there were no artifacts to be seen, and on the
circular walls, no paintings, or none that had survived.
Korbillian and Ygromm went on together, and behind them
came the army, like pilgrims to a shrine.

Again the whispering came, and tiny clouds of sand
puffed up from the center of the building as if there was a
grille there leading down to a source of power. Ygromm
stopped, eyes widening as he saw the truth. There were
two enormous slabs placed side by side, resting in a circle
of smaller stones, which had been placed in the precise
center of the edifice. At first Korbillian thought perhaps
the slabs had crashed down from above, but then realized
how exactly they had been positioned, like the equal halves
of a book, sculpted in the great stone. That image of a
book grew in his mind.

Brannog's mind was also racing, flooded with images.
Inside his shirt, burning against his breast, was the stone
that had been given to him by the Earthwise. He pulled it
out and it almost burned his fingers. For the first time he
saw the rune that had been subtly chipped into its veins,
or perhaps the rune had never been quite so evident before. As he looked at it, the whispering amplified.
Ygromm saw what he was holding, his eyes widening. He
spoke a single word and Brannog knew by instinct that it
was the uttering of the one rune.

At once the whispering focussed on the great slabs, as
if they spoke to each other. Every eye in the building was
turned to those slabs. As many men as possible had
crowded in, craning their necks, and as many more were
outside, eager to learn what was happening. Those that
could see now noticed the faint lines that had appeared

down the sides of the stones, lines which came and went, then thickened. They were runes. Brannog went to the stones, which were twice as tall as he was. He touched the stone that he held to the great slabs and at once felt the heat surge along his arm. Then he put his stone away and turned to the men.

"It is as Ygromm says. The stones speak. To all of us. Whatever secrets this city guards are here. It will not deny us those secrets."

"A revealing," said Ygromm, his voice carried to the doors by the acoustics of the building, and word was passed to those outside. "It is how the ancients are said to have shared knowledge."

Ygromm now went forward, apparently having appointed himself as the one who would conduct the ritual, and no one raised a voice against him. As Brannog stood back to let the little man press his hands against the stone, Sisipher stood by his side.

"How do you know these things, father?"

He smiled. "They are in all of us, hidden just as the city was."

Ygromm arranged now for each of the leaders to come forward and place his hand upon the stone, saying that what they heard, their men would hear, just as though a single voice spoke to each man present. Korbillian motioned Guile forward, but Elberon held back, not eager to touch the stone, hand yet on his sword hilt. Ruan stood beside him, but Ilassa went to the stone. Wolgren also went, as did Ratillic, though on his face was a look of such anguish that it brought to Sisipher's mind the dreams she had once had of Korbillian. The girl went with her father to the stone. Wargallow also came forward, his mouth a grim line of doubt. If truths were to come out of this, they may not all be welcome ones.

"There is one other," said Ygromm.

As he said it, there came a beating of wings, and looking up, the watchers saw Kirrikree, who had alighted on top of the stone.

"Those I have brought with me," he told Sisipher, "are gathered on the dome. I am ready."

"Then we begin," nodded Ygromm, and as one they touched the stone. The whispering began at once, increasing in volume, stretching, swirling, until it changed pitch, then dropped very low. Outside, where the press of bodies was greatest, they could hear the voices focussing, until they had become a single voice, melodic, gentle. It was neither that of a boy nor girl, man nor woman, but a blend of all four. And the history of the dead city began to unfold in every mind.

"I speak of the Fall of Cyrene, and of the Sundering of Men, and of the Descent," said the voice of the stone. "Cyrene was the proudest of man's cities, the cradle of men, and all men of Omara looked to her in awe. She rested beside the wide ocean, where ships from across all the world came to lavish upon Cyrene the Beautiful the gifts of their journeying. It was said in those days that a man had not lived a complete life until he had visited Cyrene, from whence all men had come.

"I speak also of another city, child of Cyrene, of secret Xennidhum in the east, rising up on the high plateau, watching the world hungrily, jealous of the majesty of Cyrene. And the men of Xennidhum were as the men of Cyrene, but they were ruled by a long line of Sorcerer-Kings. These had turned their eyes not outward to the bright world of Omara, but inward to other worlds, and the secrets of their own keeping. Xennidhum was the keeper of power, the guardian of the Openings."

Korbillian felt the hairs on his neck stiffen at this. He tried to see Ratillic's reaction, but the Hierophant was bent forward like a huge black crow, his hair covering his face, masking him from view. How far back did this history go?

"It was known in Xennidhum, but shielded from common knowledge, that once the Sorcerer-Kings had been omnipotent. They had searched greedily for forbidden knowledge, for dark powers beyond the understanding of the men of Omara. In their great folly, they had found the Openings, the gates to other places. They learned the secrets of the Aspects, that Omara is not one world, but many worlds, each of its many Aspects separated by a portal, an Opening. Once they had discovered this primary law of sorcery, they sought to open the way to the nearest Aspect.''

Korbillian felt himself flooding with cold fear. This was too familiar, and yet, within this mystery was another elusive key. He shied from it, but had to grasp it. Ratillic, too, would be frightened by what was unfolding.

"In time the Sorcerer-Kings succeeded, and they found a way into another Aspect of Omara. Yet it was a darker one, an Aspect where such grim powers thrived that the Sorcerer-Kings withdrew quickly. In other Aspects they found more such terrors, and though they sealed up the Openings leading to such things, yet they could not prevent something of this evil seeping into Omara itself. Although sealed, the Openings were weakened. In their private writings, the Sorcerer-Kings recorded that they had caused great evil to thrive not only in its own Aspect, but in several. Even so, they had great power, enough to chain the evil.

"Over the centuries the line of Sorcerer-Kings waned, their powers dwindling. Yet their great working, their Chaining, remained, fixed upon itself, holding Omara in safety from the powers of its other Aspects. Xennidhum became as other cities, and from it went the shadow of its former rulers. Only the very citadel of the Sorcerer-Kings was shunned, and the power therein went on working, unhindered, protecting the world.

"Yet there came a time of chaos. Something stirred in one of the other Aspects and broke free, and its power met with the chaining power just as two perfectly matched warriors meet in battle. None was the stronger, none the weaker. It was the beginning of the great destruction, the scourge of Omara.''

Korbillian's head felt as though it would explode. He had the key, the answer, but he could not find the lock. Ratillic? But he was like a dead man, slumped against the stone, motionless.

"Xennidhum felt the worst of the power, as if many storms and many explosions had ripped out her heart. Deep in the earth beneath her, powers writhed, powers from across the Aspects, partially freed from their chains, but now racked by the chance collision of powers unleashed by whatever had freed itself from the first Aspect. The men of Xennidhum were driven out of the city. Nothing could survive as the earth heaved and threw up such changes.

"The men of Cyrene were full of fury and bitterness. They did not show mercy, but made war upon their fellows, blaming the refugees of Xennidhum for what had happened. For many years this war raged. Cyrene, flower of Omara, became a divided city, her buildings damaged, her inhabitants more depraved. From the plateau of Xennidhum there seeped twisted power, shaping the land, corrupting. Like a curse, the power fell upon the two nations and the men of both cities began to change. In time no other cities would traffic with them. Cyrene's war ended, but the race that had emerged was alone, cut off and despised by the rest of Omara.

"The terrible upheavals in Xennidhum went on, for one of the great Openings to the Aspects had been ruptured by events there. There had been a similar disaster and chaos within other Aspects, for through the broken Opening there now came men of one of these Aspects, themselves refugees from the horrors that had been unleashed. They bled into Omara until the Opening was again sealed during further upheavals, but it was feared that other ruptures in the very fabric of the Aspect had caused temporary Openings to allow flight into Omara.

"Down into the great plain these refugees spilled. They were not bellicose, seeking only safety, freedom from destruction that had torn their own world to pieces. Yet the men of Cyrene set upon them at once, seeing in them the cause of their own fall. Those who came had simple powers. But they were no mages, no great bearers of power. Even so, there was a war, and so desperate were the refugees that they turned upon the men of Cyrene. The conflict that followed was far worse than that which had gone before. In time the men of Cyrene were driven out of the city, and they found themselves ruthlessly hunted by both the refugees and by other men of Omara.

"Thus they took to the earth, hiding themselves lest

they be destroyed utterly, and they called themselves the Earthwrought.''

Ygromm nodded solemnly, as if the voice spoke only to him and his kind, and Brannog could feel the weight of guilt and sorrow upon his own shoulders.

"Though the refugees took Cyrene and made it theirs, many of them went out across Omara. In time all the portals to their Aspect closed. From the black ruins of Xennidhum the power came in waves, now strong, now less so. It caused many upheavals, the worst of these being the one that reshaped the very ocean. Just as water will cleanse a wound, so the ocean rushed up and swallowed Cyrene. The new inhabitants fled before the inundation, many of them escaping, but thousands were lost as the sea bed rose up. Water stood above the city for many years, and at the bottom of the ocean the silt covered it.

"From Xennidhum the evil power continued to seep outwards, like an ever-bleeding wound on the skin of the world. It dried up the land around it, using up its goodness, and gradually turned the ocean into a desert, the great Silences that ring the plateau. Over all Omara the refugees fled, mingling with other men to form a new race, while the men who had once been masters of the world, now the Earthwrought, burrowed deeper into the earth, hiding from light and from the killing vengeance of the men above them, whom they called the overmen. And on all Omara was power held in contempt, and there were those who punished its acceptance with death.

"This was the Fall of Cyrene, the Sundering of Men, and the Descent."

Silence rushed in like the ocean that had flooded the city so many millennia before. No one broke it, each man there alone with his private thoughts. Korbillian saw that Ratillic appeared to be unconscious, leaning against the stone. He went to him and touched him gently.

"Ratillic," he whispered.

Slowly the head came up and through the lank hair the haggard face looked up at Korbillian. Its torment was shocking. "They were wrong," he said softly. Ratillic drew in a great breath and sighed. "The Hierarchs, don't you see? They sought to perform a working that would open gates to other worlds. *Other* worlds, Korbillian. For all their power and wisdom, they had not discovered the Aspects. Ternannoc is not another world.''

Korbillian began to see the veils lifting. ''It is the first Aspect of Omara.''

''Why did the Hierarchs seek to open the gates? Was it because one of these Sorcerer-Kings blundered into Ternannoc and then withdrew, leaving no more than a hint of what was possible? Little wonder the Hierarchs were so determined to search. Their working went awry, founded as it was on a fundamental mistake. When they undertook their working, the power clashed with the power here, and as the voice told us, two perfectly matched warriors fought out a stalemate, while around them the worlds collapsed. It was from Ternannoc, this ruin. The Sorcerer-Kings had the intelligence to use their power to bind the evil they had unleashed, but the Hierarchs blundered through the Opening and damaged the Chaining.''

''And the refugees were from Ternannoc.''

Ratillic nodded. ''Our view of Omara has been clouded.'' He nodded to Ygromm and his people. ''There are the true men of Omara. The rest are the mixed peoples of both worlds. A little ironic, is it not?''

Wargallow had heard this and had come forward, a strange expression on his face. ''Is this true?''

Korbillian frowned. ''The working on Ternannoc did cause other portals to open here. I came through the last of them myself and I sealed it. Other refugees came through these portals before me. But the inhabitants of the two cities, Cyrene and Xennidhum, were not the only people here when the tragedy began. Some of those Omarans had spread, as the voice told us.''

''A few scattered cities,'' said Ygromm beside him. ''The world was centerd on the two cities.''

''How are you sure of this?'' said Wargallow.

Ygromm shook his head. ''The stone has opened many closed rooms. I understand much more than I heard. It may be so with us all.''

''So you're telling us,'' Wargallow went on, ''that when

the invaders came, there were only a few men here to deter them? That Omara belongs to the little men, and that my people, and those of the Chain of Goldenisle and of King Strangarth are the sons of the invaders!" He swung on Korbillian before he could answer. "And it would follow, would it not, that, as with our ancestors, the people of Ternannoc, whose blood runs in us all you say, each of us has power?"

Korbillian thought at that moment that Wargallow looked as dangerous as he had ever done. His words, however, could not be denied.

Wargallow suddenly laughed. "Oh, but Grenndak should have lived! Yes, he should have journeyed with us. This would have opened his mind. He wanted to rid Omara of all power, yet had he known!"

"So you see," said Korbillian, when the mocking laughter had died down, "the giving of blood is like the killing of one's own family."

Wargallow's eyes blazed as if Korbillian had struck a nerve. "Family! Aye, that's well chosen! Grenndak would have appreciated that, too! How many infants died at his command?"

Brannog shifted closer to him, uneasy at this outburst.

Wargallow's calmness had deserted him, his face changed dramatically by the sudden mood. "Grenndak may have thought himself above the simple people of Omara, and he may have behaved like a god, but he was no more a man than you or I. And no less!"

Korbillian glanced at Sisipher, noticing that Wolgren was very close to her side, an unwavering guardian. "You speak in half-truths."

"Grenndak took women, as any man would. Sometimes they bore fruit. He could not permit that, could not permit his seed to live, not when it would inherit his power. So they were destroyed, just as the women who carried them were." He gazed furiously outwards, seeing nothing but the bloody past and some private murder that he would not reveal. The air was charged with waiting violence.

Guile, who had been forgotten, broke the spell. "Then

Grenndak was no less insane than my own cousin, Emperor Quanar Remoon.''

"And his Abiding Word,'' said Ratillic, directing his voice out to the gathered Deliverers, ''is as evil as the power that seeps down from the east.''

Wargallow spun round to search the faces of his men. There were almost a thousand of them, he knew, all loyal to him, but still he looked for dissent. He could not see them all, but he heard nothing but the silence. Not a man among the Deliverers would have spoken for Grenndak. Wargallow raised his killing steel. ''I will have blood!'' he shouted, and at once he was answered, so suddenly that Korbillian and the others felt themselves shudder at the speed of the reaction. Wargallow swung his arm down, and whether by accident or intention, the steel caught the stone behind him and a flurry of sparks arced from the metal. Wargallow howled and leapt away. His steel hand glowed blue, and his eyes fixed upon it. Before his men could react again, he raised his hand.

''The stone has answered!'' he called.

Morric Elberon's fingers tightened on the sword hilt at his side. What direction would this fanatic take? But Wargallow seemed calmer now as he lowered his steel. He grinned at Korbillian. ''Since we all have power, let us use it.''

''On the Mound of Xennidhum.''

''Just so.''

After that they went out of the dome and used the great square to make their camp. As Ygromm had promised, water was found in wells below the city and it was pure enough to drink. But the army, once refreshed, split itself, with the Earthwrought alone. Brannog sat with them, talking to them quietly, saying that it was even more important now for them to persuade every other Earthwrought tribe to come from the earth and begin the rebuilding. But it was agreed by all that it would not be here in Cyrene.

Korbillian and Ratillic sat apart. ''The Sorcerer-Kings eclipsed the Hierarchs,'' said Ratillic.

''Yes. Isn't that why the Hierarchs were so eager to find them again?''

"As you say. Their greed disgusted me. But it is in my mind now, Korbillian, that what lies in the east may not be so easily contained. What plans do you have?"

"The Chaining power was damaged. We must repair that damage. Bind once more the powers that these Sorcerer-Kings awoke. Success lies in the hands of Omara. The power has been scattered, and so Omara must act as a body."

Ratillic nodded, his hostility toward Korbillian now directed elsewhere. A poetic solution, he thought, but as he looked at the army around him, and felt its tensions, its guilt and its aggression, he wondered how realistic Korbillian's dream was.

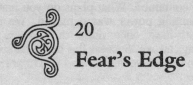

20
Fear's Edge

KORBILLIAN ADDRESSED the army from the steps of the domed building, while above him the owls and other birds watched. He faced the sun setting in the west beyond the rusting sands and watched the shadows pushing into the square. The whispering of the city had ceased, as though in confessing some great sin before its god it had unburdened itself and was at peace. Only the silence remained. Korbillian told the gathering he had given deep thought to the campaign. Essentially, he said, they were to be a spearhead, and although he intended to destroy the evil in Xennidhum, law would have to be enforced thereafter, and to that end others would have to follow from the west. Cyrene, he suggested, should be a base, so that those coming here from the west in future could break their journey. He called now for representatives from each section of the army to go back with an explanation of this, so that as many reinforcements as possible could be sent. At first, no one was eager to make the crossing back, fearing the dunes and what had transpired there, but the leaders went among the men, choosing from them those they considered worthy of Korbillian's charge.

Morric Elberon called upon Ruan and Guile chuckled at the young man's disappointment. "The task you are being given," he told him, "is not an easy one, nor a light one. It is only now that our illustrious warlord here has realized just what confronts us, and not only us. I have to put aside my own cause, Ruan. If I do not, if I lead you back now to war with the Emperor, how safe would I be on his throne? How long before this sickness creeps across the continent to the western sea, and then on to Goldenisle? No. We have to fight, with all we have. When we triumph, think of the strength of our alliance here in the east. Better to make an ally of Wargallow than an enemy, eh?''

"Must the Emperor be told?''

Elberon laughed. "No, boy! His Administrators would be glad to see us swallowed. They'd likely support the east!'' But his humor had a brittle edge to it here in the twilight. "Bring every last man who is loyal to Guile. They'll come.''

Ilassa chose his men, though he later confided in Korbillian that he could not be sure how Strangarth would react to a request for more men. He had been amicable enough about sending his contingent (with Ratillic and his wolves standing by) but now he might prove more typically irascible.

Wargallow was content to send men back. He wanted his deputies at the Direkeep to know how matters were developing. He would have to exercise caution for a while yet, he knew, for it would be all too easy for jealousies to arise there, and for some hitherto unknown rival to seek his position in his absence. He had no desire to return to find himself deposed before he had taken his place of power. Grenndak's death would not be a secret for long.

Lastly it was agreed to leave a number of men in the city to make a base of it, with Earthwrought to exploit the water supplies. Once all the men had been chosen and those selected for the return had departed, the army moved eastward into the night, while hovering over them like a ghostly cloud were Kirrikree's own forces. Some of these flew far ahead, searching the dark sands by starlight. Kirrikree was able to report no immediate dangers. Ratillic, who could again hear what passed between Sisipher and the white owl (the latter saw no reason to embitter Ratillic now that he had capitulated) studied his maps. He had traced a path to the plateau, but there was nothing beyond it on his parchments, no detail. Only the dark stain where

Ruan's spilled wine had run marked the empty space. Ratillic's wolves trotted beside him, obedient as dogs, but restless, hating the desert, so that he had to calm them with soft commands.

Brannog glanced at his daughter from time to time, wishing that he had never allowed her to come. Surely Korbillian did not need her? How much would he use them all? No sacrifice would be too great, that's what he believes, Brannog was thinking. We may all perish yet. But he shook such thoughts from him. Ygromm, who had been persuaded to ride one of the hardy ponies that Ilassa's men had brought in reserve, had felt Sisipher's mind brush his, for the girl had yet to realize the full extent of her gift. Some things she had not been told, but too much power too soon could damage her. Ygromm was far too polite to impose himself, but he directed waves of calmness her way, smoothing down the restless anxiety he could feel in her.

Ygromm was always aware of the youth, Wolgren. He was afraid, but it seemed to Ygromm that the boy would follow the girl wherever it was necessary. The cause meant little to him, except as a means to riding beside and protecting Sisipher, and Ygromm had seen the way the youth had secretly watched Guile, whose eyes always rested longer on Sisipher than they needed to. Guile's desire for the girl, Ygromm estimated, came second to his other desire, which was for power. It was what had lured Wargallow here, the man with the killing hand. He was the most terrible of all, and would bow to no one, whatever his promises. Ygromm was certain of that. Even the Preserver had not tamed him.

Although the army was aware of vague movement on the horizons, the dunes did not return. Three days out from the city, again travelling across nothing but sand, they began to rise up an interminable slope, and Ratillic directed them through a narrowing sand valley that rose up to the first rocky outcrops they had seen since leaving the dead city. These poked through the sand like broken hulks from the sea, lifeless and bare. From a vantage point high on this crumbling ridge, Korbillian looked eastward to the pre-dawn skies. The sand rose up in motionless swells, and beyond them he could see at last the huge plateau. It was like an immense block, several thousand feet high and its walls stretched away and back like the shores of a continent thrust out into an ocean of sand. It was dark and blotched and from here it was impossible to see any detail. Above it was a layer of cloud, or steam, as if volcanic fires burned there, but Korbillian knew this was an image, no more. The unnaturalness of it, the wrongness, impressed itself upon the mind like a shout.

Kirrikree came to him, alighting nearby. Korbillian nodded to the owl as if it had spoken directly to him. "I can feel its power from here, Kirrikree. Like a beast watching an approaching hunter." As he watched, the sun rose up behind the plateau, splashing it with vivid pink light, and while the sky turned to blood behind it, the silhouette seemed to darken, stark, massive, immovable as a world. Sisipher had climbed beside Korbillian, and as she watched the dawn spreading from its wound in the skies, she swayed dangerously at her first sight of the plateau.

"So much death," she whispered.

Korbillian caught her words. "You foresee our doom?"

She shook her head. "So many have died there. Everything is so confused. It is as though time has been riven, knotted upon itself. Too many possible ends are interwoven. I cannot look without—" She turned away, overcome by nausea. It was Wolgren who steadied her.

Korbillian gave instructions for the army to rest for a few hours only. No one argued: they were all too eager to move on, in spite of the growing heat, now that the plateau was in sight. When they began again at mid-morning, they found the sand less shifting, with rocks exposed in places. The slope rose more gradually, affording them frequent views of the plateau, and although not a man among them was not glad to be coming to the end of the desert, they all felt the power of that huge mass. It soared up, higher by the mile, malignant and intensely oppressive, scowling down like an angry god. The horses shied often and had to be coaxed and calmed by the Earthwrought. Ratillic's wolves stopped more than once, crawling forward on their bellies.

Ratillic watched them closely and spoke to Korbillian. "They smell that place from here, just as they would decay."

Korbillian ignored him. He needed no reminding.

When they came to the edge of the sands, right under the brow of a final escarpment, it was close to sunset. The walls rose up sharply before them and the dying sun picked out no pathway up, just sheer rock. The plateau was hidden, and Korbillian was glad that it was so, knowing how unsettling its imposing dominance affected everyone. He arranged that the army camp under the cliffs, and the men did so, most of them collapsing.

None of the Earthwrought seemed to have slept for days, not since the desert crossing had begun, and now they sat and gazed out at the sands, drowsy but always aware. Wargallow came before Korbillian once he had settled his Deliverers down.

"How are we to scale these cliffs?"

"I have asked Ygromm to find a way, if one exists," said Korbillian.

Later, when Ygromm returned, Wargallow again came out of the night to hear his words.

"There is a path under the cliffs which will bring us up beyond them and under the great walls. There is water," Ygromm told them.

"Clean?" said Korbillian.

Ygromm shook his head. "Better to use what we have. This comes down from the plateau."

"Is there anything we can eat?" said Guile, who had also joined them, eager for news.

"Kirrikree has found fruit, but although his people can eat it, it may harm us," said Ygromm. "I have sent men to study the land beneath the plateau. There will be ruins, I think, unless Xennidhum was built higher up. It is hard to say where the tides once reached."

Wargallow's face had clouded. "Is it safe to travel beneath the ground? Surely we can find a way up this cliff face?"

Korbillian shook his head. "No path is safe. We are in the very jaws of the old powers. Have every man readied at first light. Ratillic, let your wolves lead us along Ygromm's path."

"Let me go with them," said Brannog. "I have travelled far under the earth with Ygromm. I understand the dangers."

"So be it," nodded Korbillian.

They broke up after that, their spirits weighted down by the task ahead. Elberon confronted Guile anxiously. "We need a good killing," he said softly. "Something to lift morale. The men are tired, nervous, unsure of what we'll find. Nothing will restore their confidence better than a blow against this evil."

"I'm sure they'll have their killing," said Guile. "Soon."

That night the desert ignored them, maintaining its silence and utter lack of movement. By the time dawn came, the men were eager to move on into the passage under the cliffs. Ratillic and his wolves, with Brannog beside them, followed Ygromm to the place where the passage had been found. Once it had been the course of a stream, but now it was dry, the mouth choked with dust and sand. The wolves sniffed at it, then snarled as if something awaited them within. Brannog raised his axe and spoke to them softly, and Ratillic seemed surprised. How well he hones his own gifts, he thought.

They entered. Enough of the Earthwrought pressed close behind Brannog and Ratillic to afford the strange body-luminescence that threw the low passage into relief. The floor sloped upward, the walls curved and pitted, sound dulled so that only the taut breathing of the company could be heard. Brannog coaxed the wolves on, and their teeth seemed to gleam, mouths open as though about to fasten on some unseen foe. For a long time they went onward and upward, and gradually the tunnel widened until its ceiling was some fifteen feet above them. Ratillic pointed out the webwork of roots that suggested life somewhere overhead, but Ygromm warned the men not to touch them. Eventually the roots thickened, but they were a ghastly white, splotched with a fungal growth that looked to have leeched away all goodness. If there were trees of any size above, they must surely be dead. One of the roots that ran alongside the widening tunnel had become extraordinarily thick, twice as wide as an oak's trunk, and Ygromm paused to listen, as if he could hear the sap running through it. Abruptly the wolves faced it, fangs barred, howling. In the confined space the sound was horrifying. Brannog heard the shifting of earth first, and Ratillic's eyes confirmed it. In another moment a great tremor ran through the root, dust and earth falling in gentle cascades from it.

"It moves!" Brannog said, and his words were taken up at once, threatening to spread panic down through the ranks. Brannog watched in horror as a ripple ran along the great root. Korbillian had joined him, watching equally horrified. Ygromm groaned, as though something in the immense root stirred a terrible fear in him.

"It reaches up to the very plateau!" said the Earth-wrought.

"Quickly!" snapped Korbillian. "Move everyone through."

Ratillic and Brannog exchanged glances, but Ratillic spoke to the wolves. They loped up the passage with several of the Earthwrought. The procession moved on, all eyes turned to the quivering root. Korbillian watched closely, and as Wargallow arrived, motioned him on.

"What is it?" said the Deliverer.

Korbillian shook his head. "I dare not disturb it. The roof might collapse." Then the root heaved and there was a rumble above as rock shifted and earth tumbled. Suddenly the root seemed to pull itself, dragged quickly from its bed, thinning out as it passed, tapering down until a fall of soil completely blocked the place where it had been. Wargallow shouted at his men to keep moving, and though they did so, their killing steel was out. Elberon's men were no less prepared, but the great root did not return. Although the army passed now without harm, not one man felt safe. The image of the moving root remained with all who had seen it and word of it was passed back. By the time Ratillic and Brannog had reached daylight, the entire army was eager to be free of the earth. It was as though they had emerged from a living being.

Brannog stared around him in amazement. They had come out into a semi-circular depression, half a mile wide, partially ringed by low walls of rock, and there were several pools here. But it was the vegetation that shocked the eye. Trees, shrubs and spreading vines were uniformly gray. Trunks and boughs were blotched and gnarled like arthritic hands, and all leaves were the same dull gray color. There was a thick film of dust over the pools, and reeds thrusting up in clumps near the edges, also gray and drab. The vines were both tiny and large, the thickest like great snakes, digging into the collapsing rock walls. It seemed that everything here was transmuting into desert sand.

"Is any of this alive?" Brannog asked.

"All of it," said Ratillic. "Be warned."

While the men emerged into daylight, Korbillian looked up to study the towering mass of the plateau beyond them which seemed to reach the sky. Grayness mottled its immense walls, but there was a sickly green foliage there, too, rampant and suffocating the stone. It seemed to have spilled over from the top of the plateau like a creeping flood, sending down roots like enormous cables to the sands far below.

"How do we get up there?" said Guile. "There can be no path."

A shout drew his attention, and he turned to see some of his men jerking away from one of the vines. One of them had hacked at it with his sword, and it had writhed like a man in pain. An entire wall of the sickly vines convulsed, but became mercifully still again.

"Touch nothing!" called Korbillian. "You transmit messages to the plateau as if you speak to it."

Ygromm pointed to the rocks. "We must go along that ridge. There was once a way up to the the plateau. Xennidhum is above, I am sure now."

By midday, after another difficult march, they had found no way up to the plateau. Its walls leaned over them, unscalable. Even if it had been possible to climb, there was the unsightly vegetation to consider. It was a variety of hues, and grew in the most unlikely of shapes, eerie and mocking. No one dared touch it, as if it were poison. While the men rested, eating into their supplies, now running dangerously low, Ygromm's scouts came scampering into the camp.

Ygromm reported breathlessly to Korbillian. "They have found old ruins, possibly a place where there was once a harbor. But it is overgrown with—well, you must come."

Korbillian mounted up and as he rode across the gray sand, he found Wargallow and Guile beside him, their faces mirroring the strain on his own. In silence they crested a rise and looked down upon an unexpected sight, for all Ygromm's preparing them. What ruins there were here had fallen, almost completely rotted by the heat, columns and walls eaten and cracked, tumbled this way and that like the discarded toys of children. What had displaced them seemed to be huge domes, pink and striated, like vast mushrooms. As the men watched, they pulsed like living organs, their bases apparently dug into the earth as if they fed on the corpse of whatever city had been here.

"Their roots," said Ygromm from nearby, "are like the one we saw in the passage. They run very deep."

"Are they dangerous?" said Wargallow.

"No," said Ygromm. "They feel, as we do. But they are not hostile. No more than the plants we know of in the west. But there is more power in them than we—" He stopped, his mouth slack. Wargallow drew back. One of the huge, ovoid growths had puffed itself out to twice its size, about fifty feet across, and had wrenched itself free of the ground. It lifted up, floating like a great spore, dangling fibers and roots beneath it. In a moment it had sailed high up, finding a thermal in the sky and it used this to spiral still higher. Where it had been was a shallow crater, and the men could see thick roots there.

"A single plant," commented Ratillic, who had been studying it. "When its seeds are ready, they break free and drift with the wind."

Something occurred to Korbillian, who was still watching the great oval floating away upward. "They are going up to the plateau. They must be—the desert would kill them."

Ratillic nodded. "It is their only hope of survival. But the chances of their growing successfully up there are little better than in the desert."

"Tell me, can they support men?"

Ratillic stared at him, considering the possibilities. "Perhaps. But there is an army here!"

Korbillian pointed. "We need men up there. To see what lies beyond. To provide us with information. Possibly even to find the way up for the army."

Ratillic's face creased in a rare smile. "I will investigate." He rode along the rim of the uncanny valley, watching the great domes as they gently pulsed, and beyond a cluster of them saw what he was looking for. It was vast, a giant of a dome, and the veins stood out vividly like thick scars. Ratillic dismounted and approached the plant. From the low ridge, Ygromm and a number of his people watched.

"No harm," said Ygromm. "The wise one understands them." He had shown particular awe of Ratillic, and the Earthwrought thought of him as being even more powerful than Korbillian, in spite of the storm, for Ratillic communed far more deeply with living things.

Ratillic closed his eyes and stood before the towering dome. He could hear the gases escaping its curved sides and feel the movement of its complex root system connected to the main tap root which threaded like a mighty artery beneath all the domes. He opened his mind and images tumbled in like flood waters, almost knocking him to his knees. But like a ship ploughing through heavy seas, he kept his course and slowly mastered the confusion. After a while he was able to allow his own thoughts and questions to penetrate the thought patterns of the plant. What he learned both surprised and pleased him.

When he rode back to Korbillian, he seemed relieved, but tired. "I have found an ally where I did not expect one. These plants wage their own kind of war upon the plateau and its life forms. They are descended from other kinds of life, these domes, possibly human, and their sentience, their reason, lifts them above the madness that surrounds them. As you suggested, Korbillian, we can go up to the plateau. But you must select a party. The entire army cannot go up on the domes. Only a few can be spared, and only a few are ready for flight. But they are willing to help. They know why we are here. There is an alternative to the domes, but it will be difficult. Yet we came for war, so we must fight.''

''What alternative?''

''There is a canyon that cuts into the plateau and leads up to the city of Xennidhum. This was the dock area of the city. The canyon is choked and overgrown, barely visible, but there is a road within it. Many of the plants that block this road now are dangerous, deadly poisonous. And hostile. So hostile that they are at war with themselves, preying on each other to survive. And they, too, know we are here. They have been told.''

Korbillian nodded as though it was no more than he had expected.

''Another thing,'' said Ratillic. ''We can eat the flesh of the domes. It is permitted. Think what that means,'' he added. Another sacrifice, he thought.

Korbillian rode back to the main body of the army, organizing the men at once, preparing a group to go up to the plateau. He spoke again to Ratillic. ''One of us must go up to establish a foothold. The other must lead the army against whatever blocks the road.''

''I will be happy to lead the men into battle. It will be a long struggle, but we will have help. These plants have developed certain powers of their own. However, you are the commander. Might it not be wiser for you to lead the army? The men would respect a commander who stood in the van.'' He knows this, Ratillic thought. What is he thinking? What have I missed? To contemplate not leading the army now is insane, unless he has an excellent reason for going on ahead.

Korbillian considered his words. ''You are right. Then you must go up to the plateau. Find the surest route to the Mound. It may yet be days away. I will bring the army.''

"Who am I to take?"

Korbillian chose all of his main followers to accompany Ratillic, not wanting to risk any of them in a conflict. Again, this puzzled Ratillic, who saw something behind this that he could not quite fathom.

When the men were told, Wargallow demurred at once. "There may well be grim risks at the plateau summit, but my Deliverers would likely scorn me if I deserted them and let them fight without me. No, I will stay with them and take my chances in battle."

Korbillian reluctantly agreed.

"Similarly," said Ygromm, "I must lead the Earthwrought."

Elberon spoke up next and at once Korbillian had a rebellion on his hands. "We are an army now," Elberon chuckled. "Empire troops, Deliverers, Earthwrought, Strangarth's warriors, everyone! Let us fight as a unit. You are lucky we have held together for so long."

Wargallow smiled. "You are a man of peace," he told Korbillian. "That is admirable. But you are faced with the inevitable. Let those better versed in blood guide you. Morric Elberon, like myself, is a man of experience."

Korbillian could not smile with them, but nodded. "Then I will select another party. Sisipher, I insist that you keep from the fighting. Ratillic, you will go up, and Wolgren."

Elberon's grin widened. "May I suggest Ottemar. I am not sure that I want to return to Goldenisle and attempt to place a corpse upon the throne."

Guile chuckled. "It is no secret that I am inept with the sword. I'll go with Wolgren."

"Brannog?" said Korbillian.

"I will take a small company of Earthwrought," he said, as much to Ygromm as Korbillian. Both agreed.

"Find the city," said Korbillian.

Ratillic bowed. "We will have the help of the dome-plants. What lies up there is a bitter enemy to them. I will commune with them again." As he rode off, this time with Ygromm and a number of the Earthwrought, Korbillian prepared those who would go with them, and shortly after the march began once more. The men were apprehensive about this bizarre terrain, and those intimidating cliffs always seemed about to come down like fists. Yet the men knew that the conflict would begin soon and in that understanding there was a measure of relief. They watched the skies, seeing the wheeling of the birds far above them. Kirrikree and his folk, however, kept well aloft, and it disturbed Sisipher that she could not speak to him.

She had communicated with the great owl a number of times before he took to the far skies, and it had become clear to her that all his efforts were spent controlling the birds, most of which would rather have winged away to the west and safety. Kirrikree had little opportunity to scout across the plateau, and what glimpses of it he had seen were fleeting, the land being a deep tangle of vegetation, every growth indistinguishable from the next. That there was other life there, the owl was certain, but it could not be contacted, shrinking from his mind like paper from a fire, and all that he felt in return was a rhythmic malice; the very earth was alive with it.

Ratillic had returned to the huge domed plant, and when Korbillian arrived, Ratillic told him that he was ready for the flight up to the plateau. Like passengers embarking on a strange ship, those chosen for this perilous flight followed Ratillic, and they found it surprisingly easy to clamber across the surface of the dome to its flattish top. The Earthwrought who were with Brannog immediately sensed the life force within the plant, heartened by its empathy with them, and Brannog also knew that here was the first haven in this blighted land. Once the party had assembled, Ratillic, now in the role of steersman, seemed to speak privately to the plant. It trembled, drawing itself in as if taking a preparatory breath, then broke free of the earth. Wargallow (and many another observer) gasped as the great dome soared above the cluster of smaller domes, trailing countless scores of tendrils like anchors. It gained height quickly, and its human passengers were lost to sight. As it went, a dozen smaller domes left their own moorings and accompanied it like moons circling a planet.

Korbillian pointed ahead to the base of the cliffs. "Ratillic has told me where the canyon begins. There is a road cut into the rock.''

Wargallow drew out his killing steel and beside him Elberon raised his sword. ''Let us begin,'' they said together, and at their side Ilassa had his own blade ready.

Korbillian glanced at the heights. There is something here, he told himself, that reaches into all of us and tries to twist what is there, looking for the darkness, conspiring with it to make us evil. That is our true foe, that darkness within us. He called upon the power within him, shut far down in some mental sea, and like a remote surge he felt its molten shape surfacing. Up on the heights it was echoed by the similar awakening of power, as though a leviathan of the deeps had turned to face the challenge. Korbillian felt its glee, its faith in its invulnerability, and tried not to let his own faith shudder.

PART FIVE

THE MOUND

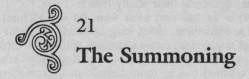

21
The Summoning

KORBILLIAN'S ARMY FOUND THE PLACE where the ancient road led up into the canyon, and as they rode toward it, the vegetation shivered like a single being preparing to attack. Several thick roots protruded like cables from the rock and dug into the earth, and now they heaved like the stirring limbs of a god. Ygromm pointed to one and Korbillian followed the instructions he had been given by Ratillic, who seemed to understand these things best. Korbillian dismounted and walked to the nearest root, watched by the entire army. It was five times as thick around as he was. Quickly he placed both gloved hands upon the sickly flesh of the root and called upon the powers within him. They answered, eagerly, thirsting for release. The root convulsed and almost flung Korbillian backward. He went to it again and this time it burst into flame, the fire streaking back along the root toward the cliffs. In moments a great sheet of fire roared upward, and the vegetation that was not immediately scorched by it curled back in waves.

Ygromm shouted out to the Earthwrought above the din of the conflagration. "Close your minds! All of you!" His warning came barely in time, for the screaming agony of the burnt plants would have torn into the Earthwrought like steel. They shut it out at once. Korbillian had remounted, hardly able to calm his frightened horse, and in a moment had ridden ahead to where the road began. Scorched stone pillars and dead, blackened vines marked the way as he rode upward. Behind him the army came on, but the plants had hardly been touched; they hung in festoons, unfurling their sticky fronds.

As soon as the first men were on the incline, these snaked toward them. Steel sang and flashed. From out of the tangled greenery came scuttling, spider-like creatures, many-legged and fast, and they were difficult to kill. Korbillian reached out to more thick vines, gnarled trunks, overhanging branches, and all burst into flame, which roared back into the deeper growths. Like a molten river, the fire torched up the inclined road. Clouds billowed up toward the top of the cliffs.

Ilassa fought off one of the dreadful pink-hued spider creatures, slashing through the strands of gossamer it had tried to net him with. He saw the first of the dome-plants breaking free of the mother root and lifting upward. They drifted above the scene of the battle and the first of them burst, showering a cloud of thick brown dust down onto the plants below. As it struck it caused the vegetation to shrivel, withering away as the poison took instant hold. Ilassa grinned at this unexpected help, but his grin turned to a wince of pain as something deep within him constricted and he felt his bones bruising as though this place worked its havoc within him.

The things that rushed from the vegetation were cut to pieces by Elberon's swordsmen as they found their weaknesses. Elberon himself was in the thick of the fighting, striking about him, face grim beneath his visor. Wargallow was no less active, his own men a deadly force. After an hour the denizens of the plateau had drawn back, as though like a single warrior they had received a terrible wound and sought a respite. Korbillian watched the fires he had unleashed burn themselves out some way above. There was still a long climb ahead, but the vegetation slithered away from him, faster and more sentient than any other plant life he had ever imagined. It seemed to know that he wielded its doom. Beside him, Ygromm watched, his ugly face set.

"This is nothing," he said. "A trial of strength. What waits above us is far deadlier. This is no test at all."

"Neither am I tested," grinned Korbillian. He watched another wave of dome-plants drift past and burst over the verdure, destroying it as effectively as he had been doing. The army rested, congratulating itself, but Korbillian was content to let the men think they had won a victory. He looked for casualties, and mercifully there had been few. It would be a long day, and a tiring one. He began again.

Far above, Ratillic had seen the smoke clouds drifting upward to where the dome-plant spiralled gently on the wind, and he knew that Korbillian had begun the work. He told his companions and Sisipher shuddered. Guile was sitting in the middle of the rising plant, hugging himself and trying not to move, terrified by the dizzy drop beneath them.

Brannog studied the plateau. They were above its brow, where huge, tubular roots clung like sculptured architecture to the stone, ivy a thousand times thicker than anything he had seen before. He was certain he could feel the liquid sap running within it like a stream, thick with poison, feeding the terrible growths below on the cliff face, being rushed there by an invisible, all-embracing commander. Wherever the road came up, it was not visible, for not only had the jungle smothered everything, feeding on itself in places, but mist billowed over it all. The green carpet spread away on all sides, shrouded and deep. The city of Xennidhum could not be seen, nor the terrible Mound that had thrust its way up into its heart.

Ratillic was able to direct the plant, but could see nowhere that looked suitable to land until a bare outcrop of rock pushed up from the mist. The plant hovered above it and then floated down, deflating as it did so. Its roots sought a hold on the stone, but found no purchase, and Ratillic feared that it would die here. Once the party had alighted, Ratillic allowed the plant to rise once more, and it drifted with the thermals.

Again they tried to see the landscape around them. Unlike the Silences, this green wilderness was full of sound, the screeching of low-flying birds, the scream of unseen beasts hidden by the thick screen of vegetation, the rhythmic thumping of something unknown out in the mist. But there was nothing to see other than the matted greenery, and this bare rock seemed isolated, some geomorphic exception. When the clouds lifted, it should be possible to see far across the plateau.

Sisipher was staring directly to the east and Ratillic knew instinctively that she was facing what they had come to find. "Do you see it?" he asked.

Her face was white, streaked with fear, as she nodded. "Beyond the jungle. The city. And at its heart, the Mound." She turned away. Ratillic frightened her: she thought of their first meeting in his cave, where he had stared at her and asked her to be left for him. She drew closer to her father for comfort. If she told him, he would break Ratillic's back.

Brannog was studying the strange growths that lapped at the lower slopes of this outcrop. "What can we achieve here? We'll not find the road. Everywhere is overgrown."

Ratillic was pointing. "I can feel the road. We would achieve nothing by trying to cut our way to it. But there is a way to attack the plants that cover it. Korbillian should already have had help." Ratillic nodded at the small cloud of floating dome-plants. They had circled the plant that had brought them up here, and Brannog noticed that they had kept to a particular formation.

"They are sentient," he said.

"All life is part of the same stream," said Ratillic, and beside him the Earthwrought escort were nodding solemnly. "It is possible to share oneself with all living matter. Have you not begun to discover this, through the little folk?"

Brannog nodded. "Aye. And you are fully attuned, by your arts."

"It is my gift."

Sisipher jerked at the word. For a moment the world around them shrank and everyone's attention focussed on her as if she had shouted. Wolgren sat beside her, in his hand a sword that Elberon's men had given him. They had teased him, enjoying the sternness of this youth, but he had come to take a special place in their hearts. They knew of his worship for the girl.

"My gift," muttered Sisipher, as though from a dream.
"I have to use it now."

"To see ahead?" said Brannog.

"Something moves beyond my sight."

Guile scowled. What does she mean? The mist? Or her
inner eye? If she can foresee things, we must be guided.
It is her purpose. Let her speak!

Sisipher rose up and stood with her hands by her side.
She became like a statue. The Earthwrought formed a ring
around her, all squatting down and gazing out across the
jungle. Brannog, Wolgren and Guile were all sitting now,
but Ratillic had gone down the hill a little way, trying to
learn more from the land about him. Why did Korbillian
send us here? he was asking himself. Why must he veil so
much from us?

Sisipher found herself sinking into a silence that was
even deeper and more final than that of the open desert.
The light above her faded and the totality of the vacuum
had never been so powerful. She was unable to stop or
control it. Whatever came now used her as a vessel, willing or otherwise, and it could not be avoided. Her body
went rigid and Wolgren fought with himself not to wrap
his arms around her and howl his denial at whatever disturbed her. But he watched. A word from her lips and he
would gladly kill for her. Sisipher saw the world sliding
away, but her eyes rose to meet an inner panorama. There
was a world of shade, gray and drab, but at its boundary
rose up the distinct shape of a huge hill, the Mound. Black,
featureless, it seemed to be alive and writhing, impreg-
nated with a malign power that suggested pain and destruction, livid evil. There was no direction or purpose to
it that Sisipher's vision would reveal. Behind the Mound
the pale orb of the sun rose as if leeched of brilliance.
Sisipher found herself swooping toward the Mound like an
eagle diving for prey and as she rushed on, she saw the
silhouettes upon the brow of the hill. There were ten of
them, and although they were pitch black and blurred like
frozen menhirs, she recognized Korbillian and his leading
followers, though she could not tell one from another.
Above them another shadow floated, spreading wings as

it glided to land between them. The Mound seemed to focus its evil upon them all, and in horror she watched as five of the figures began to slide into the earth, as if sucked down into a morass. Then she had shot by and into the blinding light. It exploded, making her reel, and when she came to, Wolgren and her father were holding her upright.

"What did you see?" Brannog asked her. Guile leaned closer, eager to hear.

She shook her head to clear it, then held out her hands, examining them as if they were alien to her. She flexed her fingers. "Ten," she said. Her right hand dropped to her side like something dead, and she stared now at her left hand. "But which five?" She had swooned, and they let her down gently, the Earthwrought murmuring quietly over her, tending her with extreme care.

Ratillic was standing beyond them, watching. "She will be well. She is exhausted, but not harmed. It is a rare gift, the gift of telling. But it is not always wise to look ahead. You do not always see what you wish." There is more to this girl's gift, he told himself. What is it? How can I wrest it from her with every blade ready to defend her at the first hint of trouble. "It may be she has other talents."

"She needs to rest," said Wolgren, his tone implying that he would stand against anyone who disagreed.

"What did she mean?" said Guile. "Ten and five?"

Brannog shook his head. "The fingers and thumbs of both hands, as she held them out. Ten. She took away her right hand to leave five."

"Wargallow's hand?" said Guile.

Ratillic was shaking his head, trying to read the mystery. "The hands of power, Korbillian's, perhaps."

"He will lose one, is that it?" said Guile.

"She said, 'Which five?'" answered Ratillic. "Not 'Which one?'"

Brannog was muttering names under his breath, and suddenly he stiffened. "There are ten us of," he gasped, and went on to name Korbillian, Ratillic, Guile, Elberon, himself, Sisipher, Wolgren, Ygromm, Ilassa and Wargallow. But then he gazed at the sky. "Kirrikree!" he said.

"That's eleven," said Guile. "But what were you thinking of?"

Ratillic's shadow fell across them. "An interesting theory. Possibly accurate. It may yet fit. If Korbillian is the body, then perhaps we are the ten fingers of his hands, focal points of the power he seeks to unleash. He has told her how essential we are to his working."

"Go on," said Guile.

"You heard the girl. 'Which five?' "

"Which five will perish," said Brannog, and around him the Earthwrought sighed as if he had made a true prediction.

Guile stared at Sisipher, but she had not recovered. "We must question her further! Can we not revive her—"

Wolgren's sword hovered close to Guile. He felt the anger in him begin to flow, felt something writhe and give, as if it was right to feel this joy, this thirst for hatred. "Touch her and you will be the first of the five," he hissed.

Guile drew back as if stung, trying to laugh. "My, my. Such teeth, Wolgren. I've no reason to harm the girl."

"Hold your sword up!" snapped Brannog testily. "There'll be no killing among ourselves." Wolgren's eyes narrowed, but then he seemed to come to his senses and he muttered an apology.

Ratillic stepped between them. "We should not pay too much heed to one possible view of the future. Likely this evil place sends these things to torment the girl. We should make no decisions on them."

Sisipher groaned and sat up. Once she had shaken her head, she appeared to be herself. She forced a weak grin and stood up. "I must have fainted. I had a strange dream, but I hardly remember it."

"It was not important," said Ratillic, and he looked pointedly at Guile, who shrugged. "Do not be misled by it." Sisipher was glancing at her hands, puzzled, but Ratillic drew her attention away. "Korbillian and the army will ascend the road, but they will need help. There is power here, mostly dark and infected, but I sense that there may be more help of the kind the dome-plants have given us. Your gift, Sisipher, not of the telling, but of the communion, does it tell you anything?''

"What do you mean?''

"Does it sense anything here other than hostility?''

Sisipher made herself put aside her loathing of Ratillic. "I was not aware—''

"I will try to lend my own understanding of the life here. The Earthwrought must do so also. Concentrate. Search.''

"For what?''

"We are surrounded by hostility. Somewhere here there is anger against what has been done to this land. I can feel it, but cannot reach it. Between us we may find it.''

Sisipher would have veered from the thought of sharing any kind of mental exercise with Ratillic, but something in his words had struck a chord of recognition within her. She nodded. She took her place on the highest point of the outcrop, ringed by the Earthwrought, with Ratillic inside the ring. Brannog, Wolgren and Guile sat outside it and watched as the search began. Very slowly Sisipher was turning in a circle, letting her open eyes scan the land below. The Earthwrought were murmuring, their deep voices becoming a chant, a concentration of energy.

Guile could not rid himself of her previous vision. He glanced at Wolgren, but all the youth's attention was on the girl. He sees me as a rival, Guile thought. How jealous he is! Yet he cannot be her lover. Far too young for her. But I must be wary. There was blood in his eyes for a moment. He meant what he said about killing me. Without the soldiers, I would be easy for him, young as he is. Weapons are simply not my skill. Yes, I must watch the boy. In the heat of battle, it would be easy for him to slip his steel into me. Perhaps I should act first. Damn this place! It twists the mind.

Sisipher had stopped her slow circle of movement. She faced the edge of the plateau and the open desert beyond. Ratillic, aware that something within the girl had locked into place, sent his own mind reaching out across the edge of the plateau. Almost at once he felt it tugged. The Earthwrought leapt up uniformly and ran to the edge of the rocks to shout unintelligibly.

"What is it?" said Guile.

Brannog shifted uneasily. "I feel something. Under the sand."

"Feel it? How?" said Guile impatiently. He felt nothing.

"I don't know."

Before Guile could ask more, the Earthwrought began leaping about like children. Sisipher had not moved, but Ratillic pointed to the desert. Clouds of dust rose up from a number of points there and there were far more cracks spreading across the flat rock outcrops. Ratillic shrank back, clutching his head as if smitten by agony. He stumbled back, dropping to his knees. As the others watched, they could see that the cracks in the desert were fresh, as if there was an abrupt disintegration in progress. It occurred to Guile that as the desert floor was so far away, these fissures must be huge, miniature canyons. An entire section of the desert abruptly folded in on itself and disappeared. While the clouds of dust gathered into a huge single cloud and rose up and outward, the Earthwrought fell to the ground, their heads pressed to the stone.

Sisipher spoke something over and over again. "Naar-Iarnoc, Naar-Iarnoc."

Up from the crumbling desert floor there now came a sight fit to shake the reason of all of them. Even Ratillic, a man of power, gaped in disbelief at the awesome size of the organism that had risen up like something born again from its deep grave. The whirling dust obscured much of the detail but outlines were visible. It seemed to be part plant, part vessel, as though somehow an artefact had been not only constructed from materials, but also grown. It drifted like a gigantic version of the dome plants, and yet it had sail-like structures above it, spread like plumes. From its curved sides protruded spines which widened into fibrous leaves, and as these moved forwards and backwards in oar-like fashion, they propelled the superstructure through the air. Hanging beneath it were cabled roots and trailing vines, as if a hundred anchors had been carelessly left suspended there. The body or hull of the super-structure was studded with smaller growths, parasitic plants that appeared to be feeding on the monstrous body.

"Am I seeing this?" said Guile, eyes agog.

Wolgren stood beside him, his face pale. "It lives! The power in the land has created this."

"In a way," said Ratillic, breaking his concentration. "I tried to commune with it, but there is too much power there, too much screaming anger at what has been done to it. But it is not evil. The power here is corrupt, distorted. It has warped that being terribly. What you see is Naar-Iarnoc, the last of the Sorcerer-Kings. Its pain is only transcended by its anger."

The organism slowly rose up, sand pouring from its curved back, and its freed cables uncoiled beneath it.

"But what will it do?" gasped Brannog.

Sisipher turned to him, and he was stunned to see a smile on her face. "He will open the way."

"How can you know that?" cried Guile.

"He knows we are here," she said, her words indisputable. "He has been waiting for Korbillian. The weight of the years has filled him with a dreadful purpose. You will see!"

Brannog could hardly believe the sudden change in the girl. She seemed feverish, obsessed by the sudden need to throw everything into Korbillian's cause. He, too, felt the rightness of opposing this eastern madness, and yet it was as though his daughter had become another person. The land here worked upon them all. Guile was more surly, more introverted, without his humor of earlier, and Ratillic had changed from the insular, cool pariah to the curt, almost arrogant commander, sure of himself and what must be done. All of them were ready to unleash violence on this land, as though the stored emotions of their lives had balled into a hard knot to be wielded brutally. It would have to be controlled, Brannog knew, otherwise he could see the outcome, a backlash of mindless power, like that which saturated this place. And yet, something was using it, shaping it. The Children of the Mound. They still had not shown themselves or their real purpose.

When the gigantic organism had burst up from the desert, Korbillian and the army had again taken their attack to the growths on the ancient roadway, sending tongues of fire into the heart of the hostile plants there. They were forced to stop and watch the incredible spectacle as the organism raised itself into the air, impossibly light for its size.

Wargallow felt his reason wrenched by the vision, for no amount of compromising belief in powers he had long scorned could have prepared him for this. He, and many of his Deliverers, staggered back, fearing that the desert had sent its worst disciple to crush Korbillian's challenge to its might. Korbillian could feel the horror of the men around him, for Elberon and his troops also looked appalled, and he was quick to cry out that here was aid. The Earthwrought, led by Ygromm, had fallen to the ground, but they began a chant by way of praising the immense sky-creature, and their attitude brought home to the men around them the potential truth in Korbillian's words.

They waited. Slowly the organism drifted toward the plateau, a mass that darkened the sky, a mile long and half as wide. As it came, the dome-plants that were already in the air floated up toward it, and at the foot of the plateau other plants broke loose and floated up in a blanket, filling the air like countless seeds, acolytes flocking to their god. As they drifted higher, they brought the extraordinary size of the organism into perspective. It made belief and comprehension even more difficult.

"Sisipher has summoned this," Ygromm told Korbillian. "As she speaks to Kirrikree, so she speaks to this. But neither I nor the Earthwrought have the power to do this. We only know that it is not harmful to us. It thrives on its hatred of the plateau and the evil that floods from it. It is Naar-Iarnoc, the last of the Sorcerer-Kings."

Korbillian's mind shuddered to the impact of Ygromm's words. So this was her true gift! To wake this being, this monster. Had she known? She could not have.

"Now comes the reckoning!" cried Ygromm, shattering his thoughts.

As he spoke, the huge organism approached the plateau

and discharged a sudden cloud of vapor. It sank down over the summit of the plateau and spilled downward, absorbed by the verdure before it could reach Korbillian and the army. While this cloud began its terrible work, charring and poisoning whatever it touched, the great plant dropped lower, and from it now there came what seemed to be bolts of fire that crackled on the air. In the verdure there was instant turmoil, and roots and tendrils of enormous thickness flailed up at the sky, the ends reaching for and curling around the trailing growths beneath the aerial plant. These groping horrors were attacked by the dome-plants, but within moments there was a locking of the two forces. The walls of the plateau shook and fire scorched downward in a rain.

Another great cloud discharged from the organism, scorching the roots that held it, but they held on, others rising up, blotched and gray, out of the havoc below. The dome-plants were scythed from the air by the great sweeps some of these roots were making, bursting in showers of brown gas. The organism surged on over the plateau lip, wrenching scores of giant roots from the earth as it passed, while scores of others rose up to attack it. A titanic struggle ensued, with the great plant being dragged slowly downward. At last it sank under the sheer weight of tendrils that had wrapped around it and it ploughed into the canyon in a bizarre tangle of verdure. The shudder of the impact knocked many of Korbillian's army to the ground, and they felt the ground thundering.

A pillar of fire rose up into the sky, thick black smoke erupting from it, and there came several deafening explosions. Great fragments of rock burst from the plateau, tearing with them huge chunks of vegetation. Korbillian could feel the effects of these explosions like mighty spells being cast far below ground, causing fire to spread in all directions. Like an earthquake, the explosions rocked the entire plateau rim.

Ygromm, pressed close to Korbillian, looked horrified. "It cannot live through this."

"But Naar-Iarnoc has opened the way," said Korbillian. When the clouds began to disperse and the frantic conflict above had eased, it was possible to see that the landscape had changed. Instead of a sheer wall of vegetation, there was a deep cleft, scorched bare. The road went on up into this great ravine which opened up deep into the heart of the plateau. Of the massed jungle, there was little obstructing the way now, and fire continued to ravage the slopes of the canyon, far up into it. Of Naar-Iarnoc, nothing could be seen, nor of the dome-plants.

The first sacrifice has been made, thought Korbillian.

Ratillic had watched the final scenes of the staggering conflict, his mind closing off the tremendous psychic detonations. He felt the ground convulse as Naar-Iarnoc tore into the canyon with the force of a meteor. As the smoke boiled away it revealed a thick rift that had opened along the plateau to the east, as far as the eye could see. Much of the vegetation around the exposed rock was either dead or quiescent, and below them now the jungle seemed stripped of nerves, crippled. It would be safe to leave the outcrop and search for the road now, and Ratillic said as much to his companions. The Earthwrought readily agreed, but Guile glanced uncertainly at the terrain.

"You mean us to walk?"

"It will be safe. The repercussions of that struggle were far-reaching. Naar-Iarnoc unleashed terrible energies." Ratillic had already started to descend.

Guile drew his sword uneasily, keeping close to Brannog as he followed. They reached the first of the wasted trees, and although they were strangely hued and packed closely together, it was possible to pass through them. In their shadowy avenues, the air was still and cool, rich with the smell of charred wood and smoke. The Earthwrought guarded the others closely, watching the trees, using their noses like hounds, though nothing stirred.

Sisipher, who had barely recovered from the shock of realizing that she had woken Naar-Iarnoc with some hidden power that she had not known about, only to hear his death cry ring out like thunder across the plateau, suddenly remembered Kirrikree and the birds, but there was no trace of them anywhere. She could, however, feel the hostility in the damaged growths about them, but sensed no movement in them. The crash of the colossal plant had spread a paralyzing poison throughout this part of the plateau, but it could not last. Sisipher called for stillness, knowing that shapes were emerging form the trees. Three of them came slinking forward, but Ratillic held up his hand.

"The wolves," he said, and a moment later the three great brutes came to him and he stroked them. They fell into place, growling deep in their throats, but no one spoke about them.

A while later the group broke through the trees and found itself in a badly burnt area where everything had been turned into black ash. Before them the canyon opened. To their right it dropped away to expose the floor of the Silences. To their left it swept up through the plateau, its sides either smoldering or bare of growth, as if it had been cut by a blade still hot from the furnace. Ratillic seemed to be trying to find something with his senses, and eventually pointed to the abrupt slope beyond them.

They climbed down carefully, up to their calves in places in warm ash, until they were on a bare rock slope. Beneath them they could see the wide road cut into the side of the canyon, unveiled by the great conflagration that had so quickly ravaged the plant life. Coming up the road from below them, tiny figures on its blackened surface, they could see Korbillian and the army. Guile could see Wargallow, Elberon and Ygromm, and wondered for a moment if Ilassa had fallen, but moments later noticed him. He rode on a horse behind someone else, and seemed to be clinging on as if he were wounded.

22
The Road

THE SUN HOVERED in the west, about to set. Circling high over the jungle, Kirrikree picked out from a great height the figures moving down the ash-streaked terrace toward the road below. He sent a gentle probe, anxious not to alert enemies, but in seconds realized Sisipher was down there. He dropped down and could now see Ratillic leading the party. As he swooped, he saw down the highway where the army advanced, and he flew on and over Korbillian and the leaders, sending word to Ygromm beside him that the others would soon meet them. He also gave a report to Ygromm, who passed it on to Korbillian.

"Everywhere has gone silent," said Ygromm. "Kirrikree says to be most wary. The way to Xennidhum is open, but it is a trap. The city seems to be empty, but the Children of the Mound are far below, and their many servants will rise up to attack when they are ready. Already the owls have been attacked, but there are few aerial servants of the Children, and those that were not ripped from the sky fled back into their holes below ground." Ygromm made no bones about the unpleasantness of the conflict.

Twilight had begun its brief vigil of the pleateau when Ratillic led his party to the road, a matter of minutes before Korbillian reached him. The two Hierophants conferred privately, watched by the hungry eyes of Ratillic's wolves. Ratillic could see that something disturbed Korbillian, as if he had received grim news.

"Ilassa," said the huge man softly. "I fear that the

power of the Earthwrought that healed him is being re-
versed in this place. I sought to get him back to Cyrene,
but he has said that he has to go on or Strangarth's men
will insist on remaining with him. I cannot blame them
for their loyalty."

"Then you won't relinquish them?" Ratillic said coldly.

Korbillian frowned in anger. "You think I want anyone
sacrificed?"

"Why did you bring the girl? Oh, I know of her gift
with the bird, and with the little folk, and the telling. But
it was not that."

"But the telling—"

"She sees many paths. All contain fears, terrors even.
Better not to look along them and be dismayed. Do they
guide us?"

"Perhaps."

Ratillic considered for a moment. He had to probe Korbillian's motives. There were still so many doubts. "On
the summit, she saw the Mound." He told Korbillian about
the vision of the hands, the five that were to be lost. "Is
that not how you would interpret this? Five of us."

The news had unsettled Korbillian. "If our old friend,
Nadorn were here, he would unravel it. But it is foolish
of us to do the work better suited to a Hierophant versed
in prescience."

"I agree. Hence I wonder about the profit in bringing
this girl. At least, I did, until it became clear that she has
other powers. You knew she could summon?"

"*Summon*? Then Ygromm was right. No, I had no fore-
knowledge."

Ratillic snorted. "Deceived. The Hierarchs are behind
this!"

"I did not know that Naar-Iarnoc was beneath the sand.
Just like the power placed within me, it rose when it was
needed."

Ratillic shook his head. "This entire expedition is
founded on a base of sand."

"What do you mean?"

"Consider: Guile seeks an empire and cares little for
your cause, seeking no more than a share of your power.

Elberon certainly has no wish to be here. Wargallow is little better. The youth, Wolgren, is here because of the girl.''

"And you suspect me?"

"Of what should I suspect you?"

"Some ulterior motive? Greed for power? You think I wanted this curse?"

"Probably not. I just wonder to what extent you have been cursed, as you put it. But you understand what faces us. Have you made it clear to these people? That they have little chance of surviving?"

Korbillian controlled his anger. "I accept responsibility for them, but this is their world. What are you saying, that I am using them?"

"Send them back," said Ratillic. "Let you and I go on alone. Let Kirrikree guide us."

"Send them back!" repeated Korbillian. "Throw aside their combined power?"

"What is it compared to the raising of storms, the searing of the jungle, the sealing of the Opening?"

"But you saw what the girl can do—"

"So you think the others have powers that have been hidden from you?"

"I don't understand."

"Perhaps you are being used," said Ratillic, and at that moment his eyes were as penetrating as the eyes of his restless wolves. "How much of the Hierarch's power do you understand? How much are you depending on instinct? Are you master of your borrowed power, Korbillian, or are you its instrument?"

Ratillic's words filled Korbillian with fear. He looked up at the rapidly darkening road ahead as if it were filled with fresh horrors. "You think that?" he said quietly.

Ratillic's gaze softened. "I know you for an honest man. I know you are not moved by greed. But you should beware."

Korbillian's anger had gone. Ratillic meant to be fair, no more.

"Are we to camp here, or move on?" said the latter, and the conversation was at an end.

The army traveled on, and the men were glad to move as far up the canyon as they could. The road remained broad, testament to the one time greatness of the city beyond. The walls of the canyon narrowed, but became less towering, less oppressive. On their rims the treelines were broken now. Nothing moved, but the feeling of being observed intensified. They felt as though they were crawling across the body of some mythological monster rather than the earth of their world. It was agreed to camp under the walls of the canyon and climb the stairway that Kirrikree had described as being cut from the end of the canyon, at first light. Not far from the great stair, the army gathered itself in and waited.

Sisipher was concerned for Ilassa, watching him with Ygromm. The Earthwrought studied the man's pain as though he were responsible for it.

Ilassa, shivering in the half-light, managed a smile at the girl. "Poor Taroc fell a victim to the earth power," he said. "In this grim place it seems it turns within me."

"We must begin a fresh working," said Ygromm, but in his heart he knew that the creeping darkness would not release the man. There was no power here that would give him surcease.

"No, my friend," said Ilassa. "Save your strength for the city."

"You should go back," Sisipher told him, scowling up at the shadowed stairway cut from the end of the canyon.

Ilassa shook his head. "Back? No. Get me to the city, girl, and my men will follow. I have a score to settle up there. For Taroc, eh?" He subsided, and already his bones were weakening, softening, so that in the darkness he seemed twisted, crippled, as he would have been by his fall from Swiftwater Bridge.

Sisipher left him, afraid she would weep for him if she remained and that perhaps it would shame him. She wanted to be alone for a moment, but it was far too dangerous here. Kirrikree fluttered near her, and she wondered why she should deserve his protection.

"There is a place beside the road," he said. "You will be safe. We watch over you."

Sisipher passed through the broken stone balustrade of the road and went down the gentle slope beyond, sitting in a pool of moonlight. She could not see, but sensed the owls not far from her. On the road, guards walked quietly up and down, but in the motionless forest below her there was nothing, no hint of life. Naar-Iarnoc had given his life to ensure the destruction of an awesome part of the plateau's power.

"You are no longer alone," Kirrikree's voice whispered and she turned to face the intruder on her privacy. It was Guile.

"Your pardon," he said as she rose. "I did not mean to disturb your thoughts." She did not reply, so he went on quickly. "I was concerned for Ilassa."

"Is he worse?" she said, showing her fear.

"I only know that he is ill. What has happened?"

"A wound, perhaps," she said guardedly, and went to pass him.

He caught her arm gently. "I think not," he said. As he had moved, Kirrikree swept low overhead. Guile ducked instinctively, watching the darkness, but he did not let the girl go.

"What do you want?" she hissed impatiently.

"The truth. Is he dying?"

After a while she nodded. "I think so."

"And who else is to die with him?" he whispered.

Kirrikree again flew overhead, and Guile had to duck as the claws came dangerously close to his scalp.

"What are you saying?" she gasped.

"The five! You saw five die—"

Something gripped Guile's shoulder and he was swung round so that he lost his balance. As he looked up, Wolgren came from the shadows, a knife raised. Guile stumbled away, but Wolgren was after him.

"Wolgren, no!" Sisipher called, but still she kept her voice low. There was no need for conflict between them; there would be enough problems in Xennidhum.

"I should finish him here," the youth snorted, his knife poised.

Guile was on one knee, fumbling for his sword. He

thought of shouting for Elberon's men, but if he did he would be charged with molesting the girl. Surely this could be settled quickly and sensibly. Kirrikree swept down and this time his claws brushed Wolgren's arm. The youth was taken by surprise and inadvertently leapt forward into Guile, and the two of them tumbled to the ground, rolling down the steepening slope.

Sisipher rushed to its edge, shocked by the ludicrous turn of events. The two figures had toppled further toward the trees. She could hear them grunting and knew they must be grappling with each other like children. "Stop!" she hissed at them. As she scrambled down the slope, she was aware of other shapes emerging from the darkness, drawn by the scuffle. For a moment terror rushed at her until she realized that it was Ygromm's folk.

When she was able to see the two figures below, only one of them stirred. Guile was extricating himself from Wolgren's twisted frame, and in his hand was his sword.

"What has happened?" Sisipher cried hesitantly, coming closer.

"The fool!" Guile snarled. "He attacked me—" He stopped, noticing that Wolgren had not moved. "Wolgren!" he gasped, bending to him, but keeping his sword point poised to strike. Suddenly the Earthwrought rushed in. They pulled Guile to the ground, pinning him and wrenching the sword from him. Sisipher stood over Wolgren, then shook him. She touched his chest and her hands came away bloody.

"Wolgren!"

Kirrikree, confused by what had happened, flew down beside her, alighting on the ground. "I thought he meant to kill Guile. There was a kind of madness on him."

"He's dead," said Sisipher. Already two of the Earthwrought were listening for the youth's heartbeat, but they sat back grimly, affirming the girl's words. There came a rush of movement above them on the slope. Morric Elberon and several of his guards stood there.

"What's happening?" Elberon growled.

"Morric!" called Guile, still gripped hard. "Get them off me!"

Elberon came down the slope cautiously.

One of the Earthwrought turned to Sisipher, and the moonlight traced a gleam of tears down each of her cheeks. This could not have happened! It must be a mistake, a dream.

"An accident!" cried Guile. "You can't let them kill me. Tell them to free me at once!"

Elberon made to climb down, but Sisipher stopped him with a gesture. "One move," she said. "One step further, and your precious heir to the throne dies."

Elberon kept absolutely still. "But why?"

Sisipher turned back to Guile. "You killed him," she said, venomously. She felt again his hand upon her and it goaded her anger. "You say by accident, but that's a lie! You wanted him dead."

He shook his head wildly. "Spare me! What do you want, girl? Haven't we shared enough on this accursed journey?"

Sisipher felt the seething anger within herself, trying to check it, but could not. Like a fire, it fed on something combustible in the atmosphere of this haunted place. "Shared? With you?"

Kirrikree's voice pierced her fury. "The boy had a knife. Guile had to defend himself."

"Listen!" gasped Guile sure that he was going to die. "What do you gain by killing me? There is so much you can have if you spare me. Think of it, Sisipher. I am to be Emperor. Emperor! And you could sit beside me, girl. Think of that."

Elberon stiffened, appalled by Guile's lack of nerve. Sisipher let Guile go on speaking.

"Spare me! It was an accident. Come back to the Chain when this is over and sit with me. Bring Brannog—I will make him a commander."

Elberon felt his fists balling. This was absurd! What was the man trying to do? Had he murdered the boy out of jealousy? Elberon knew that Guile had been looking hungrily at the girl; it was not something a man could easily disguise. They both knew that Wolgren worshipped her, but Elberon could not credit that Guile would kill him as a rival.

Sisipher was walking toward Guile. Still the Earthwrought waited, quite prepared to kill. The girl looked up at Elberon. "Well?" she said to him, and the word was like a directed blade.

He did not move, but his eyes were cold.

"Release him," said Sisipher to the Earthwrought. They obeyed at once. Guile struggled to his feet indignantly and made to approach Sisipher, but the look on her face deterred him.

"Keep your kingdom," she said. "I want nothing from you." She turned away and pointed to Wolgren's body. The Earthwrought gathered round it.

Guile made his way up to Elberon, who stared past him at the hidden trees below. His gaze would not met Guile's and the latter was forced to walk past him and on up to the road.

In a moment Korbillian appeared at Elberon's shoulder. "This is an evil place," he said.

"You saw?" said Elberon bitterly.

"At the end. That was not Guile speaking."

But Elberon shook his head. "Make no excuses. I knew he was no fighting man. I accepted him as an administrator, capable of righting his cousin's ailing empire. But this—"

"The evil here twists like a knife in us all. And it will turn us upon each other if we allow it to."

"Then let us hasten to dispatch it," grunted the warlord, and he turned away.

Korbillian cursed under his breath. The change in Elberon was most marked. If his men saw it, it would damage morale. He went down to Sisipher, seeing the tears in her eyes. "He is dead?" he said.

She nodded. "Too late to save him. And here, it could not be done."

"I have further ill news."

She whirled on him, but his terrible face kept her silent.

"Ilassa," he breathed.

"What must we do? We cannot place either of them in this earth."

He shook his head, thinking of Taroc. "A pyre. Only fire can purify them." He left her to her sorrow and climbed the hill. Brannog and Wargallow stood there, grim as menhirs.

"An accident," Korbillian told them both. "The boy is dead. Guile is not to be blamed."

Brannog groaned as though a blade had been put into his own flesh. "Ah, not the boy! Not the boy." He went down to his daughter at once. Wargallow watched him descend.

"We cannot remain here," he told Korbillian. "The air chokes us with its evil. I fear mayhem. No one will sleep."

"You are right," agreed Korbillian. "We should begin the ascent of the stairs at once. First, let me attend to the pyres."

"I'll ready the men."

Brannog gently folded his daughter in his arms, and he felt the transmission of her sorrow. "You loved the boy?" he asked gently.

"He was not my lover, father. But I knew he wanted my love. He was too young, and yet, you yourself said he was a boy no longer."

"Was this an accident?"

"They fought. Wolgren drew his knife, it is true. Already he had threatened Guile."

Kirrikree's voice interrupted her. "I meant only to ward the knife away when I swooped," he said. "I feared that he would use it. There was a strange fury in him. If I had not interfered, this might not have happened."

"You were not to blame!" Sisipher was quick to insist.

When she repeated the exchange to her father, he nodded. "Guile was defending himself."

"Wolgren had dropped his knife," Sisipher protested.

"In the darkness, Guile would not have seen. You must not blame him."

"He should not have accosted me! How dare he demand explanations of me when I have none."

"He was wrong, I grant you. But we must travel on

with great care. The death has shamed Guile, but let that
be enough. The evil in this place would be glad to see us
riven. What disputes there are between us, we must put
aside."

She looked at the Earthwrought as they began preparing
the pyres, only now fully realizing that Ilassa had also
succumbed. "This should never have been."

Brannog held her as she wept. He thought then of Eorna,
who had died at Wargallow's instruction. The village expected him to avenge her, but he had used her as an excuse
to leave Sundhaven. Should he avenge her and kill Wargallow? He had thought of this many times, prepared to
wait for the proper moment. But the assault on the Mound
was far more important. Wargallow's motives were
clouded, yet he seemed to accept that the old ways of the
Deliverers had been wrong. Perhaps later, on the return
journey, he would answer his own questions, Brannog
thought.

Ratillic stood with his wolves near the broken balustrade
some time later. He watched the flames dance then roar
as the pyres caught. The orange glow gleamed in the eyes
of the wolves. "You were not to blame," Ratillic whispered for Kirrikree's ears. "The boy wanted Guile's
death."

"He loved Sisipher deeply."

"Aye. It could be felt as keenly as the heat from those
flames. And does Guile love her?"

"What he feels is not love," said Kirrikree.

"But you prevented Wolgren from killing him."

"If the boy had done so, neither Sisipher nor Brannog
would have praised him. He would never have won her
love."

"Then you interfered—"

"Not to see him die! I did not expect Guile to use his
blade. But it is done, and I carry the shame, just as Guile
does. Perhaps Wolgren has won the girl now. And Guile
can never do so."

"You are glad!" said Ratillic.

"It pleases me that Sisipher refused his offer. He is not
worthy of her."

Ratillic said no more, watching the final consummation of the two bodies. Behind him the army was already preparing to march. Although there had been no sign of attack, no hint of movement from the slopes of the canyon, there was now an acute awareness of malice among the men, a feeling that the dark had drawn itself together to strike.

"Do you feel it?" Wargallow asked Korbillian.

He nodded, sensing also the current of pleasure in that coiled evil, as though the deaths had been a triumph.

"Is the business below finished?" Wargallow asked. "The men are eager to be gone."

"The darkness is within us all. Guard your back."

Wargallow wondered at the remark, but already Korbillian was gone. The ascent got under way. Negotiating the great stairway would not have been easy in daylight but by the splashed moonlight it was treacherous. Many of the ancient stairs had been eroded so badly that the climb meant that men had to hoist each other upward. Somewhere above, great statues gazed down at them arrogantly, but always there was that feeling that living eyes also feasted.

The night wore on as the army climbed Ygromm and his folk, numbed by the death of Wolgren and Ilassa and the depth of Sisipher's grief, could sense the unrest under the earth, feeling the powers like waves of energy preparing to unleash themselves. Tempers were on tight leashes, nerves frayed. Brannog kept Sisipher close to him, afraid that she might see yet more spectres from the future.

They arrived at the flat top of the stairway just before midnight. There had been a proud wall around the city of Xennidhum once, but it had wasted away, now eaten by the plants that clustered about its bones, splotched with moonlight. Two huge idols had survived, carved from blood-red stone, not a sign of erosion upon them. Their faces studied the sky as if earthly matters were of no interest to them. Between them was the entrance to fallen Xennidhum, and in the streets beyond, nothing grew. Korbillian knew by instinct that not a single seed that had fallen upon those stones would ever have taken. Mists swirled about the crumbling ruins. There was no ancient splendour, no suggestion of far-gone majesty. Many buildings had survived, fed by something unknown far below, but the air undulated with a feeling of decay. As the army marched past those indifferent idols, a new wave of unease lapped at it, a cold breeze from the dead wastes of memory, more dreadful than the jungles below.

It was not possible to see beyond the clustered buildings of the city, dead and wasting as they were, but Korbillian knew that the great Mound was not many miles distant. He did not pause for reflection now. The army was ready, every available weapon prepared to strike. The place was to silent, too vulnerable. They felt that death must surely sweep in suddenly, yet it did not come.

Kirrikree's folk swooped to and fro, alighting on roofs like ghostly inhabitants, but the great owl reported nothing yet. The city appeared deserted. Yet its spell worked on the men, inflicting silence upon them. Each man stood close upon his neighbor. No one strayed from the main street, no one sought to look into the houses. No one whispered. For an hour they marched and saw nothing other than rubble and dust. The silence smothered everything.

Korbillian felt as though he were crossing a gigantic corpse. He knew that within it the maggots writhed, and they would rise. Where were the Children of the Mound? Why did they not strike? He stopped. Ahead of him the nature of the city was changing. He knew why at once. It was the Mound. They were coming to it at last. Once it had been no more than a slope in the city, but slowly it had pushed itself upward until now it had become a huge hill, its sides steep and treacherous. It had pushed out the houses upon it so that they leaned at bizarre angles, thrust sideways by the acuteness of the angle of the slope; some had toppled, sending whole chain reactions of collapse down the sides of the Mound. Darkness hid the upper reaches of the great hill. At its foot, many of the buildings were so heaped that they had become a formless wall, as if to ward away intruders.

"This is the place," said Korbillian, raising his hands.

"Prepare! Once we begin the climb, we will be attacked. They have drained Xennidhum and all the land around it to fortify this place of evil. They have allowed us to come unopposed, but no longer."

There were murmurs amongst the men, but no one desired to turn back. They thirsted for activity, for relief. Korbillian stepped over the wall, his leaders with him. He could see beyond that the Mound was ruptured in numerous places, and the holes that gaped went deeper than his mind dared fathom. He felt the rising of evil, and as he climbed, the first real onslaught began.

On his left a score of figures poured from some hidden opening, wrapped in dark robes and wielding long weapons that must have required great strength. With single-minded purpose these inhuman creatures raced upon Korbillian. The first of them smote at him, but he allowed the barbed weapon to meet his gloved forearm. It exploded, and in the blazing light of the explosion, the assailant burst into flames, staggering away. Wargallow, Elberon and Brannog each cut into the enemy, and within minutes other men had come forward to support them. Between them they dispatched the rabble from below quickly. Cheers went up from the men of the army.

Korbillian was quick to shout to them. "This was nothing! There will be many more. You will need all your strength to deal with the numbers. I cannot remain here to help you as I have to find the heart of the Mound. It is a place where no other may go. While I begin the working, you must protect me. I need my power for the destruction. I can spare no more of it for the vermin below. The slaughter of the spawn of this evil I leave to you."

Again the army cheered, vowing to do as asked. Ratillic said nothing, but his doubts assailed him. Is this why you brought them? he asked. To *protect* you, who carry the power of the Hierarchs! You told them you wanted their combined power, to fortify your own, and that your own would not be enough. Yet now you seek to use them as fodder for the weapons of the enemy. Or is there some other reason? One that you are not aware of, one that they never told you of, just as they did not tell you of Naar-Iarnoc, who waited so long for the girl.

Ratillic felt suddenly very cold and exposed as he climbed. The air was redolent with treachery. What lives, and what has truly died in the past of this world and its Aspects? he asked himself. Korbillian, he was sure now, did not know the answers.

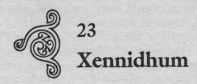

23
Xennidhum

JUST AS KORBILLIAN HAD PREDICTED, the forces of the enemy now began to swarm from their hiding places in the Mound. Down in the city, too, there was movement and the men at the back of the army saw entire columns of cloaked figures racing toward them, spreading out around the base of the Mound, out of sight where it curved away. Within moments the fighting had begun, and it was fierce and unrelenting. Steel sang and the air whined. Shoulder to shoulder Deliverer fought with Empire warrior, and beside them yet fought the Earthwrought. Initially the waves of opposition that came at the army were made up of the cloaked beings of Xennidhum. They had no visible features within their hoods and seemed so insubstantial that it was almost as though they were no more than an illusion, but they fought with swords and with pikes and with other weapons not seen before and as these scored, they were as deadly as the men they fought. Although they were no less fierce than the men they sought to bring down, they lacked the excellent discipline and training of Korbillian's army, and for every man they slew, a dozen of them were felled. Above them all, the moonlight seemed to blaze like the eye of a god hungry for sight of the carnage.

Elberon led the vanguard up the Mound, hewing with his weapon, a grim battle smile on his face. Korbillian refrained from using his own power now to keep back this rabble, but he was well enough protected by the warriors about him. Out of the deep earth came the crawling things, huge, misshapen creatures, hardly recognizable as worm, or toad, or serpent, and their tongues flicked hungrily at the advance. Even so, the army dealt with them, cutting them back. Ratillic felt the mindless power emanating from them, as if wild dogs had been released. Many of these terrible creatures were so crazed as to turn upon each other, sinking fangs into the flesh of their neighbors and rolling aside down the slopes of the Mound. The battle raged, the noise growing as men swore and steel grated, and the press of bodies grew tighter. Higher up the Mound the army advanced, struggling for footing.

The slope was bare of grass and there were no longer any buildings. Like an empty expanse of moorland it rose up to its flattish top, and there the mist shredded away to reveal nothing but wasteland. Korbillian reached the highest part of the slope, and he could see from here that it was only the rear of the army that was under attack, but it could not be prevented from climbing.

"Keep well back from the center of the Mound!" he called, and the order was passed to everyone. "Form a circle around the perimeter." Slowly the army fanned out, and as with the incident in the desert when Korbillian had summoned the storm, the men occupied the top of the Mound, encircling him at a distance of some fifty yards. They yet beat back columns of the attacking army, but there were no fresh surges of beings from below the Mound. Their numbers had been severely depleted by Korbillian's army, but in the city below it was evident that thousands had gathered. The entire base of the Mound was circled by the servants of the Children of the Mound, and the sound of their murmuring rose up to the watchers like the sound of a dark sea.

"There's ill in this," said Elberon. "We did well to win this hill, but it was far too easy. See how we are outnumbered! They have surrendered to us the best position, but we are trapped here, unless we can fight our way out again. How many of them are down there!"

As he spoke, there was movement beyond the outer line of the army's defense. Up from the earth came the blunt noses of the stones-that-move. Slowly they rose until scores of them had raised themselves, great monoliths that ringed the army in like colossal teeth. Men drew back from them, sensing in them a power more bestial, more purposeful than that of the rabble down in the city. These were not mad dogs, no battle fodder. These were evil, rich in black power, and had stood for centuries, patient as night and just as enduring. They were far worse, thought Wargallow, than the stones he had seen.

"The stones-that-move!" cried Sisipher, and Wargallow nodded. As they watched, they saw dark openings in the stones, fathomless mouths from which the waves of hunger pulsed.

Ygromm's people pushed their way to the front ranks of the army, insisting that it was for them to deal with this threat. At once they set up a quiet incantation, but the great ranks of stones gave an impression of immovability, as though nothing could weather them, nothing shatter their terrible presence.

Ratillic went to Korbillian. "Destroy them," he hissed. "You have the power. The army cannot fight these things. They are fueled by the very evil we have come here to destroy."

"I must begin the working," said Korbillian, in a strange, dream-like voice, the perspiration standing out on his brow in great beads. "I must open the Mound. The stones will not attack."

"How do you know that?" snapped Ratillic.

Korbillian shook his head and the droplets flew off. "I don't know. But I am sure of it."

"Do you understand what is happening?" Ratillic went on. "What's wrong with you? You have planned this carefully. Now you are here, you seem at a loss! Think, Korbillian! Concentrate. You have brought an army here. You are responsible for them. What must they do? Think for yourself, and not as the Hierarchs have commanded you. Obey your own instincts."

"I must go below. I must not be stopped. Protect my back," he said, but still he seemed a little dazed. Ratillic scowled out at the army. Was Korbillian in control? The dread feeling that he was being used came to Ratillic over and over again. I must watch him. I must be careful, otherwise everything will go wrong here. There are powers at work here I can neither control nor understand, and I am not certain that Korbillian can either. The stones have ringed us, keeping us here for some reason. These people are in frightful danger.

Out among the black monoliths, figures had appeared. Half the size of men, like skinny versions of the Earthwrought, they capered and leapt like children in a frenzy. Their skin was translucent and strange organs pulsed within as they moved, their faces contorted as they shrieked. Some of them danced forward, teasing the front ranks of the Earthwrought, trying to break the strength of the chant against evil, until at length groups of them came to attack. Fights broke out and warriors joined the fray, cutting these new assailants to pieces easily, but the danger was in the Earthwrought breaking ranks. Their chant had power. Wargallow called to his own men to stand their ground, but a division of them was forced to draw back as another great stone thrust up from below in an effort to break the Earthwrought power. Men dropped back, a number of them falling to the ground and screaming as if they had been gripped by something invisible and powerful there. Wargallow went to the scene, his weapons gleaming. The monolith seemed to tower over him, several Deliverers at its feet.

"Keep well back!" he snarled, and his men had already obeyed. The ground beneath him seemed to shiver and he went down on one knee. It was as though he was being sucked into the very earth and he brought his killing hand down on to the soil, furrowing it. The monolith moved over him, almost as if it would fall and crush him. There was a flurry of movement as a dozen Earthwrought broke from their chant and rushed to his aid. Ygromm led them, shouting instructions. Wargallow watched through tears of pain as the tiny figures ran to the stone and pressed their hands against it. Something foul escaped from its black maw, and the figures were flung back. They scrambled up and again put their hands on the stone. A great cry went up from all the Earthwrought ranks and Wargallow knew that they were discharging power of some kind into this thing, and the effect on the stone was devastating.

Wargallow could only move his legs now, as if pulling them from a steel trap. He started to drag himself away. Again the Earthwrought were repulsed by the stone. A dozen of them were sprawled on the ground, either dead or in agony. Those that could went to the stone again. Wargallow wanted to shout out against this madness, but could find no voice. Ygromm ran at the stone, bawling in a voice that rang back at the watching army. He thrust his fists at the black stone and they seemed to be swallowed by it. Great cracks appeared in the monolith, and as Wargallow managed to scramble clear of the power that had sought to drag him to his doom, the stone fell. Ygromm was unable to move away, and the great weight bore him to the earth, crushing him.

Brannog had seen the tragedy and was about to rush forward, but it was Wargallow who prevented him. "Hold! Keep away from the stone."

"Ygromm!" cried Brannog, but the stone was sinking back into the earth like a corpse being absorbed, and of the fallen Ygromm there was no sign. Brannog turned on Wargallow, eyes smoldering with fury. "How did this happen?"

Wargallow shook his head. "He gave his life for me," he said, amazed that it should be so. "Why? My people have persecuted the Earthwrought, hunted them."

"Blood to the earth," said Brannog. "Will there be enough blood shed here to satisfy you?" A vision of Eorna sprang up before him now, and all the bitterness her murder had instilled in him wept like a fresh wound.

Wargallow looked at him coldly, as if he would use his killing steel to silence any further insults, but he shook his head. "This place makes killers of us all. Brannog, I have been responsible for the taking of Omaran blood. No more."

It was Sisipher who restrained her father's anger, her eyes filled with tears for the death of Ygromm and the other Earthwrought who had fallen. "Ygromm died to absolve you," she told Wargallow. "He carried the burden of guilt for his people."

"Guilt!" protested Brannog.

"For Xennidhum and what it has become, and for the Fall of Cyrene. I think Ygromm had made up his mind to give his life as an atonement."

"The guilt," said Wargallow, "belongs to them." He indicated the two figures that were just visible on higher ground within the protective circle of the army.

"Let them purge the earth," said Sisipher. "And let us not quarrel. We have more work to do yet."

The Earthwrought had already renewed their joining of power and had set up a fresh incantation. The others watched the monoliths. For a time they remained motionless, but the fear that others would burst up among the ranks of the army remained, and there was a slow withdrawal toward the center of the Mound. The sadness of the Earthwrought at not having been able to recover the body of Ygromm was a sharp ache in Sisipher's breast.

Guile stood beside Elberon, but the warlord had said little to him since the death of Wolgren. "Five would die, the girl predicted. You should have let me question her further. She sees the future. Why do we not demand to hear it?"

Elberon did not look at him. "Your insistence on questioning the girl brought about the death of a fine boy. Yet still you make demands."

Guile felt the intensity of Elberon's contempt. "But Morric, I meant no harm. I thought he would kill me. Only the bird saved me."

"I promised you a throne, Ottemar. We have been friends. But when I saw you pleading, I saw something I had not expected of you. I saw the fall of your dignity. It diminished me. We may all die here, and so I will tell you this. How am I to respect you now? You tossed the throne at the feet of the girl, a girl who means little to you. A throne that possibly thousands of men will die for. Am I to watch while you do this? Am I to risk my own life for such acts of rashness?"

Guile laughed, but could not hide his uneasiness.

"There was no meaning in my words. I thought they would kill me. What else could I say? You must know I don't want the girl. She is nothing."

"You would sacrifice her if need be? To be sure of the throne?"

"Of course!" he laughed again.

"And these others? All of them?"

"You know me well enough, Morric. If need be, so be it. Korbillian's cause is noble enough, but when it is done, our cause remains the same."

Elberon nodded, as if it was what he had expected. Still he did not turn to Guile. "So you would give your word, but break it to suit yourself, and spend the lives of the men who would make you an Emperor. And my life? Is that to be thrown aside when it suits you?"

"This is fool's talk! It was not easy for me to persuade you to come on this venture. You were eager enough to abandon these people to it once."

"So I was. I was concerned about my friends in the Chain who are depending on us. But you convinced me that these people were worthy of support. That the safety of Omara precludes that of the Chain. And besides, there are codes."

Guile did not like what he read in the warlord's face. "Of course," he agreed. "And loyalty. Remember who I am."

"I will not forget it," Elberon nodded, but his mind had moved away. Guile knew at that moment that he had lost him.

Presently there was a great shout and the clash of steel. From beyond the monoliths another wave of the enemy had surged forward, and once more a bloody battle ensued.

Ratillic heard the noise and turned to Korbillian. "Go and help them," said the latter. "I must begin my work." Korbillian stood at the very apex of the Mound, and there were small stones here, ringing it, though there did not seem to be any life in them. Ratillic watched as Korbillian reached down and pushed his hands into the earth. In a moment there was a distant roar, as if a storm raged not above in the heavens, but deep below the earth. Ratillic withdrew, joining the ranks of the fighting men.

Korbillian felt the power within him surging up at his call. What had been fused into him by the Hierarchs responded now and he exulted in it. Beneath him, immersed by the Mound, was the lost citadel of the Sorcerer-Kings of Xennidhum. And within it, somewhere, was the sealed Opening to Ternannoc, as well as the Openings to the other Aspects where the source of the evil lay. Korbillian felt the earth move, and saw the hole appear. Like a window on the stars, it spread, a pool of darkness above which he felt himself floating. Power streamed from his arms down into the pit, and below him he saw nothing yet heard a roaring like the sound of falling mountains. Gently he began to drift down into that abyss.

WHILE HE WAS PERFORMING HIS WORKING, the army fought to hold back the enemy, for now it seemed that the Children of the Mound sensed that they were under real attack from Korbillian and pushed their forces forward. Time and again they were repulsed by the heroic efforts of the defenders. Man by man, the warriors and the Earthwrought were cut down, but they continued to die dearly. The enemy slain were piled high, making it impossible for the battle to be fought properly. The defenders had to give ground, but they continually changed their front ranks, bringing in fresh men from the rear. Elberon and Wargallow were both superb organizers when it came to battle tactics, and they were everywhere around the defensive circle, ensuring that men rested and that no ground was given without maximum defense.

In a brief respite, Wargallow came upon Elberon. "Ill in this indeed," Wargallow commented, recalling Elberon's words. "Are we to stand here and die? Where is this sharing of power?"

Elberon wiped blood from his cut arm. "I am a fighting man. The only power I have ever known is here, in this. But unless Korbillian can release another of his storms, we are dead men."

The battle began again and they separated. Elberon

launched himself into the fore of the attack, a splendid example to all around him, seemingly indefatigable. Yet he was deeply troubled. This place ate into him just as a disease would have done (as Korbillian had once explained it would) and the despondency threatened to engulf him. He tried to reason that Guile had acted from an instinctive self-defense, but somehow the bond that had existed between them had been severed. It's this place, Elberon told himself. Guile is Guile and no worse than he should be. I am unreasonable. Elberon fought for concentration. He flung himself into the fray with new abandon, and it was this schism of concentration that undid him. Somehow he found himself separated from his men, surrounded by the grim fighting spectres from the dead city. Their smell choked him and they pressed in, careless of their own lives, packed like rats in a sewer.

"Elberon!" someone roared above the battle din. He swung his blade in a bloody arc, but could not save himself from the upward thrust of a barbed pike. It tore into his underbelly and caught there. He slashed down at the hands that held it, severing them, but the cruel weapon was deep in him. He dropped to his knees and in a moment the enemy swarmed over him, absorbing him. Mercifully he died quickly.

When word came to Guile, he sagged back, safe for the moment from attack. Ratillic found him at the back of the army, where a number of wounded were being tended.

"What is it?" said Ratillic.

"Elberon. The fourth victim in the girl's vision."

Ratillic scowled. "We are not beaten! Pick up your sword, man. Your warriors need you." He turned to the skies and called out to them in words that Guile did not understand. At once there was a flurry of wings and Kirrikree swooped down. "It has to be now, great owl!" said Ratillic. "Korbillian has begun. We are hard pressed. Bring your birds down upon the enemy."

Kirrikree swooped away and soon afterward Guile saw him lead a great cloud of birds as they dived upon the ranks of the enemy. They tore with their claws, attacking the front ranks of the cloaked men, and in the skies there

were other winged creatures now, unlike anything the men
had seen before, undoubtedly the spawn of the Mound.
These attacked the owls and the hawks and the eagles, but
Kirrikree's folk were faster, more sure of their flight and
the aerial battle was an uneven one.

Ratillic had noted how clumsy the attack of the enemy
was all round them. It was only partially organized, and
every one of the enemy was expendable, as if their lives
meant nothing. Yet some power had organized a defense
of the Mound. The power within it should be mindless,
without purpose, and yet it was not. It sought to defeat
Korbillian, to prevent him from carrying out his working.
Who were the Children of the Mound? Ratillic studied the
army as it fought, supported by the diving birds. It was
holding its ground, still superbly drilled even though Elberon was lost. Wargallow seemed to be in command, and
he was no less capable than the warlord had been. Elberon's warriors took his command for granted, which was
good. Ratillic slipped away, going up to the forbidden
ground once more.

He found the gaping pit that had been opened by Korbillian. It offered only darkness, like a window on to the
deeps of space between worlds, but he could hear the thun-
derings of powers far below. Cautiously he walked to its
edge, then allowed himself to drift down. He must follow
Korbillian. He had to know what he would do, what powers were really at work.

Korbillian was far below, as though he had entered another world. His dream-like fall into the pit had ended
when he found himself standing within another circle, this
time of sand. His hands blazed with white heat, garishly
lighting the surroundings, and he could see that he was in
a circular chamber, hewn from solid rock. Miniature
monoliths stood at its edges, and upon them were the runes
of a lost epoch. Beyond them were a dozen corridors,
leading like the spokes of a wheel away into the Mound.
One of them led to the inner citadel, the place where the
Opening would be found. But there were guardians and
they stepped forward now into the ring of white light.

These, he knew by instinct, were the Children of the

Mound. Like the priest of a temple's holy of holies, they confronted him. They held high their sigil-woven staffs, rich in earth powers that Korbillian did not understand. Their heads were not visible, hooded in white, their bodies draped in folds of thick material, but somehow their shape did not seem human. As one they directed their staffs at Korbillian's head, and he lifted his arms in response. Powers locked, but there was no explosion, no incandescence. Instead he heard words, just as he imagined Sisipher heard the words of the great owl. The voices blended, but were clear, seductive, winning.

"We are the Children of the Mound," they told him. "You trespass, Korbillian. Omara is not your world. You are a blasphemy upon it. Take your power and go back. Do this, and your people will be saved."

"I will not go back," he said aloud, his words racing away down the corridors.

"Then you will die with them."

"No." He shrugged off their grip as easily as he would have shrugged aside a child, and they could not disguise their fear. He felt it writhing in his mind.

"You mean to repair the broken Chaining of the Sorcerer-Kings. If you do that, you condemn every Aspect where the old powers lie."

"What do you mean?"

"You understand nothing of the powers within the Mound."

"Only that I have come to destroy them."

"You do not have the power. Listen to us. Hear the truths that have been kept from you by your foolish masters. We are the servants of the Mound. Long ago the masters of Xennidhum stumbled across the mysteries of the Aspects, the many phases of the world. Through their interference, the Sorcerer-Kings discovered many of the old powers, whose minds drifted freely between the Aspects. In attempting to chain these old powers, the Sorcerer-Kings were only partially successful. They were able to lock them into a limbo between Aspects. Omara was free of them. They called this their great Chaining, and it ensured that none of the old powers could materialize in any one Aspect. This Chaining would have lasted, but for the Hierarchs of your Aspect, Ternannoc. Jealous of the knowledge of the Sorcerer-Kings of Omara, who had visited them and foolishly boasted of their powers, the Hierarchs agreed to perform a working of their own to find the secret Openings between Aspects. Armed with insufficient knowledge, the Hierarchs did this.''

"They had not been told about the Aspects," said Korbillian, recalling the words he had heard in Cyrene.

"Quite so. Thus they caused havoc. They damaged the Chaining. The old powers seeped out into many Aspects, destroying some blindly.''

"Why? Why this blind will to destroy?''

"The old powers are still chained. Only certain of their powers seep like dreams into the Aspects. As you are aware, these broken powers are like a disease. The old powers cannot control it.''

"And here in Omara?''

"The Mound is a manifestation of the old powers. They seek to heal themselves. To this end they have shaped us. We seek to heal the Mound, to bend its power to our will, the will of the old powers.''

"To do what?''

"To free the old powers from the Chaining.''

Korbillian looked appalled. "And then?''

"The old powers that were wronged can be returned to their true Aspects. The seeping of powers will cease, the blind evil that threatens to engulf Omara and that has already destroyed so many other worlds. Had this Chaining not been performed, such release of evil would never have occurred.''

"You wish me to use my power to *destroy* the Chaining, to release into Omara the old power? What will it do?''

"Restore order.''

It was a reasoned argument, but Korbillian thought back over the things he had known in Omara: the creature that had shrieked for his death at the Swiftwater Bridge; the frenzied efforts of the powers around Xennidhum to kill him; the death of Ilassa, Taroc, Wolgren and all the others. He could envisage the kind of order that the old powers would impose. Ordered evil, a thousand times more appalling than the corrupt power of Grenndak's Abiding Word. The Sorcerer-Kings had recognized the terrible nature of these old powers and had known they were a threat to all the Aspects. If they were set free, a new kind of world would emerge, one given over to darkness and pain. Man would cease to be. Korbillian shook his head.

"Stand aside," he said softly, knowing that the Children of the Mound were fashioned out of the power of the forces that he had come to destroy. They knew him for their bitter enemy and would not submit.

Realizing he would not be swung from his purpose, they closed in, and he let the power given to him blaze up. It was far too potent for the Children of the Mound and they were hurled back, smashing into the walls of the chamber. Korbillian heard the rushing of feet and there were suddenly many creatures and half-men choking one of the main corridors. It was a token gesture of defiance; he used his power mercilessly, directing a bolt of white fire at them, charring and smoldering them, cutting a swathe through them and passing on up the corridor without glancing at them. They could not touch him.

Into his mind came a last mocking howl from the Children of the Mound. "Pass on, Korbillian! But you shall never have what you desire."

He ignored the voices, insisting to himself that they lied and sought only to cause him pain.

The corridor went on for half a mile, like the drained artery of a dead god. At its end he came out into an enormous chamber, the walls and ceiling of which were lost in shadowed distance. Its vastness hung over him like a world, and within it were ancient ruins, the heart of the original city of Xennidhum, the very citadel of its lost Sorcerer-Kings. Across what he took to be a plaza that had perhaps once opened on the sky, he saw, rising up like pillars that would support a world, twin columns that dwarfed everything. Into each of them had been inscribed the forgotten histories and pictographs of the city, work for a hundred historians. Korbillian had no desire to ponder that epoch-spanning detail. The burden that had been

placed upon his shoulders would be heaviest here, for between these mighty pillars was a darkness that spoke ir-
refutably of the portal, the sealed entry to the other Aspects
of Omara. Beyond here would also be the chained old
powers, the god-like beings who had been locked into
limbo for so long.

While Korbillian stood before this most terrible of al-
tars, Ratillic had come down from above to the floor of
the pit. He rose to his knees and saw the figures gathered
around him. They held him locked in that position of near-
supplication with their staffs.

"The Children of the Mound," he muttered, then heard
their voices inside his head.

"You come too late to prevent the betrayal," they told
him, allowing him to stand.

"What betrayal?"

"He will open the gate," said the voices. "You trusted
him, you fool. He serves the old powers. The Hierarchs
will not destroy them, for they serve them. Now they will
free themselves." The laughter hammered at him and he
also fell again to his knees, but it was a trick, more deceit,
his mind cried out. He sensed the desperation of these
creatures, the nearness of their despair. He forced their
laughter from his head.

He ran from the chamber, and they did not stop him.
He saw the corridor, the ruin of bodies there that marked
the terrible passing of Korbillian. Lies! his mind told him.
The Hierarchs sought to destroy the old powers. They
would submit to no other power but their own. They would
rather perish than see their power eclipsed. Yet the doubts
trickled in. He stopped, breathless, at the mouth of the
huge cavern, peering into its monumental shadows. There
he saw the huge pillars that framed the Opening. It was
closed, but a pool of light betrayed Korbillian. Like a tiny
statue he stood before the pillars, his hands aglow, his
preparations almost complete.

Ratillic made to rush forward, but an abrupt movement
from Korbillian froze him into immobility. He had stripped
off the sheathing gloves, revealing white light that threatened to burn away the sight of all who looked upon it.

Ratillic averted his eyes and he felt the deadening of his nerves as the paralysis took hold of him. Korbillian spoke to the black Opening and far away there was an answering boom of thunder, like the roar of a forgotten god waking from the sleep of eternities.

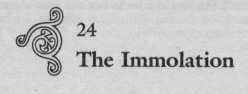

24
The Immolation

KORBILLIAN DREW from within himself the powers that had been put there, powers that seemed eager now to be released, and he wondered if they would remain under his control and allow him to do what he knew must be done or if they would struggle to shape their own futures. Before him the darkness between the pillars misted, shifting like vapors over a pool. He held his blazing hands outstretched toward it and white light stretched forward like twin streaks of lightning, absorbed by the darkness in silence. But there was movement in the dark. Gradually colors formed, writhing into a shape, a great face with an open mouth, but there was no sound. The face seemed to expand, rushing forward until it seemed that it would swallow everything before it, but instead it dispersed around the Opening, leaving yet another well of darkness beyond as though Korbillian and the place about him were sinking into the body of a god. Darkness became light, with featureless shapes humping up, almost like dunes in a desert of storms. Instead of sand, there were other substances, and Korbillian could not tell whether he looked upon some primeval swamp, some mud-flat or pre-dawn soup of life. He seemed to be looking into different worlds, remote, dreary places where the earliest forms of life were stirring in their first beds. The Aspects of Omara, his instincts told him, as they had been in the beginning. Part of his mind drew upon the powers he had been given and from them came insights, glimpses of truths. What he was seeing through this window on time and space was the genesis of Omara, Ternannoc and all the other Aspects. Deep in this primordial mire he saw the great shapes, obscure, huge, moving restlessly like predators in a heaving sea. The old powers, forces that had been there before time had truly begun. And they were not of Omara, but were from outside it, like great parasites feeding on the blood of a host. The vision sharpened and Korbillian found himself dropping down to share the worlds of these old powers.

Like thought given form, the great shapes toiled, spreading waves around them that turned into life, creating landscapes, molding their worlds, pouring power into them. Down into the undulating creations Korbillian sank, and as he did so, he felt the shock of the power there, the extremity of evil, for the Aspects of Omara had their own creative energies which resisted the workings of the intruders. At first the activities of the great beings were random, life spewing from their movements like the capricious thoughts of children, but slowly an orderliness came to the workings. Even so, it was chaotic. There seemed to be no purpose, no goal, except for the amusement of the old powers. They created and controlled at whim, like men asleep, and there was no room in their scheme of things for reason or compassion.

Time had no meaning here, but Korbillian knew that if he had to study this turmoil for long, his own mind would topple into it and be absorbed by it. He used his powers to wrench away, to find a way out of the trap. He saw then that so much had been spawned by the great shapes, that some of it learned to protect itself from them and develop itself, drawing on the life forces of Omara for sustenance and survival. This was how the Aspects had raised themselves out of the storm. The old powers slept on, while in Ternannoc the powers shaped themselves, realizing themselves in the Hierarchs. And in Omara the Sorcerer-Kings grew in strength. Through the Opening, Korbillian watched the procession of time, ordered now, and he saw the Hierarchs become the great force they had been on Ternannoc, and he saw the rise of the mighty Xennidhum.

They were separated then by their own worlds, each un-aware that the other existed, and the old powers were for-gotten, like something buried far, far down in the psyche of the inhabitants of the various Aspects. In the end, the old powers were forgotten as though they no longer ex-isted, and in both Omara and Ternannoc the masters of power no longer knew of them. It was thus for many cen-turies.

New powers were being tested. The Sorcerer-Kings were the first to discover the Openings to the Aspects. Korbil-lian saw now the disputes that raged among the Sorcerer-Kings, for many feared to unlock the gates, not knowing if it would be the undoing of their world, but curiosity and hunger for greater powers and knowledge urged them on and a few of them made the transition. By chance, one of them entered Ternannoc. In secret he met certain of the Hierarchs, but they did not trust him and were jealous of him; they killed him because he would not reveal to them the secrets that he carried. The Hierarchs never learned the truth about the Aspects, though they knew now that there were gates to other places, if they could find them. They set about urging their fellows to pursue the matter, thus paving the way for the great disasters that were to follow.

In Omara the Sorcerer-Kings had undertaken the work-ings that revealed the Openings, but so advanced were their powers that they stumbled across the deep truths, realizing that the old powers existed, slumbering like gods somewhere in the very fabric of every Aspect. They had never been truly awake, but such power existed outside of them now that they could be woken, the Sorcerer-Kings realized. If they woke, the consequences would be beyond imagining. The Sorcerer-Kings withdrew at once and sealed the Aspects, working the great Chaining that would ensure that the old powers slept on, gradually decaying, passing out of existence altogether. Time would secure the safety of all the Aspects.

It had been a mistake for the Hierarchs to kill the Sorcerer-King who found them, just as it had been a mis-take for him not to have confided in them. Korbillian saw, for the first time in detail, the raging disputes among the Hierarchs that led eventually to the decision to search out the other world where the Sorcerer-King had come from. They did not know that Ternannoc was an Aspect of Omara. Korbillian watched the horror unfold as the great working of the Hierarchs exploded in their faces. The reverberations of that explosion cracked the shell of many Aspects, and worse, it cracked the links of the Chaining. Here in Omara, the old powers seeped out into Xennidhum and beyond it, a slow tide that would in time engulf the entire world.

Korbillian saw now what was buried at the heart, not only of Omara, but of his own world. Yet in Ternannoc the old powers slept on. Ternannoc had been ravaged by the effects of the working that had gone wrong, the powers that clashed blasting the world, but the ancient evils there did not seep out, threatening to engulf the world. Korbillian sought to unveil more of this mystery, but he found now that it was closing to him, as though he was being deliberately shut out from it. At once he fought this darkness. The void before him rippled and then convulsed, and Korbillian found himself locked in conflict with the very powers that had been given to him. They seemed to have decided that he had seen enough, but he knew there was more. The time of deceiving was over. He set his mind to prising out the last of the revelations.

It was an inner struggle that brought him to his knees, the sweat standing out on his brow. Ratillic, dazed by the light, half watched from beyond, thinking that Korbillian must be in agony, but Ratillic could not move to help him, held rigid by the awful powers that yet blazed from the unsheathed hands.

Korbillian asserted himself over the great powers that had been poured into him, drawing on every fiber of memory that went back to the dawn of his own forebears. The Hierarchs had allowed him the discretion to use his power, to wield it, and so they had let him command it. Slowly he forced their will to bend and he began dragging from them the knowledge that he sought. Again the Opening writhed, flinging up visions like storms. The truth! Kor-

billian's mind howled along with the silent fury beyond
him. And it came. He saw now the last refuge of the Hierarchs on their crumbling world, recognizing the chamber
where they had gathered to make what plans they could to
save their world, the same grim place where they had finally taken him and poured their power into him against
their will. He saw their lined faces, their anger, their sorrow, their collapsing unity. And he heard them.

Too late they had discovered the truth about the Aspects. Too late they had discovered that Omara was facing
a desperate fate, even worse than that of Ternannoc. "It
is true," said Kurdetto, one of their leaders. "I have been
there, to the place of the Sorcerer-Kings. What sleeps under Ternannoc is yet chained, for all the havoc we released
here. But in Omara, the Chaining is damaged. Black power
seeps out and will destroy the world. One day it may seep
through the very Openings. It has to be stopped. The sealing has to be made good. Once this is achieved, the Aspects will again be safe."

"Will the Sorcerer-Kings help us?" another of them
asked.

"Only one has survived the disaster. Naar-Iarnoc, and
already the terrible forces at work have changed him, almost killing him. But he will help us. He has been trapped
by the powers that seep from Xennidhum, but if we can
release him, he will open a way to the city. Beyond that
he can do nothing. He fears that if there is life in Xennidhum it will be warped to the darkness."

Again Korbillian felt a surge of power within him as the
strength of the Hierarchs sought to withdraw from him
these visions of the past. There were yet truths that they
did not want him to learn. He beat back the onslaught and
held firm the visions beyond the Opening. Kurdetto's face
loomed large once more and he forced its lips to speak.

"It will be a long time before we dare to set our powers
against what seeps from Xennidhum, for now they are
stronger. The balance will change, and only when it moves
to us can we act. Naar-Iarnoc is chained beneath the sands
of the Silences, just as the old powers are chained, but we
will have him woken. That which stirs in Xennidhum will

expect Korbillian, wielder of our powers, to do this, but there is a way to preserve our powers intact within Korbillian and also deceive Xennidhum. We will use the common people of Omara, those who will be the descendants of our own refugees. They are not without power, and some of them may have power enough for the waking of Naar-Iarnoc.'' Korbillian saw then how the threads had been woven, how the people of Omara had been manipulated, how he himself had been used. The Hierarchs had placed the gift of summoning in an unsuspecting girl, and she had gone into Omara with other refugees. And through her line the gift had passed, disguised until Korbillian had arrived, unsuspecting also.

He felt his anger rise. The gift of telling! No more than a veil for the gift of summoning, passed down to Sisipher, who had woken Naar-Iarnoc without Korbillian's power. If she had known what it was that she carried, she would never have used the power, so the Hierarchs had argued. And the girl's mother, as with all the mothers before her, had died, once she had passed the power on to her child. An in-built death that the power carried. Korbillian thought of the girl above him on the Mound. Had that death been built into her also? Before he could drag an answer from the stored power, other truths came spurting from the wounds he had made in their defenses.

''Korbillian will find the girl,'' said Kurdetto. ''It will be part of the conditioning we give him, though he will not realize it. And she will follow him dutifully, not knowing why.''

It had been done, just as Korbillian had been forced to accept the power of the Hierarchs, believing when he did that he would be the instrument of doom to the old powers, the terrors that threatened not only Omara, but all the other worlds. But he had not known the true nature of the old powers. He had seen them as random, mindless. Now he began to see further down into the purpose of the Hierarchs. The time had come to act, to destroy what was here in Omara. The Chaining had to be repaired. Power had to be poured back into that damaged working. Korbillian readied for the task, for no matter how he had been used,

he recognized that this had to be done, or everything would
be lost.

He let fresh waves of power rise in him, seeking ways
in which to channel them. The fabric of the Opening suddenly burst as if a huge stone had plunged into a pool,
sending up great gobbets of foam. He saw again the restless dreaming of the old powers, but now there was a
difference. One of the great shapes was spread there, a
heaving mass with a thousand poisonous thoughts, and
like an assembly of nightmares they rushed up at him as
if they would engulf him where he stood. The old powers
were defending themselves. They had sensed the threat to
their existence, had felt through their sleep the instrument
of power about to make its incision.

As the wave of power rose up for him, visions flashed
on Korbillian's inner eye. Instructions—the means by
which he must seal the Chaining. It must be by sacrifice.
The Hierarchs had finally seen that they had to sacrifice
all their powers, but it needed more than that to repair the
damage in Omara that would spare Ternannoc. It would
take the sacrifice of still more power, the power inherent
in the people of Omara, people that only one such as Korbillian could have mustered and persuaded to come forward against the evil in Xennidhum. Above him now there
were hundreds of them, fighting to keep back the countless
hordes of the servants of the Mound. They had been
brought here to die! Korbillian's mind shouted. He heard
Kurdetto's voice far away in the darkness. "Power from
outside the old powers, power from Omara itself. Power
from its life force, the power of blood. Blood from the
earth that would seal the Chaining, just as it had done for
the Sorcerer-Kings."

No! Korbillian's mind screamed at the combined powers
within him. *I will not betray them.* He saw the frightful
powers of the sleeping one come rushing up through the
Opening, knowing that they would tear through it and
claim him. If they did, Omara was doomed, and all her
people, and after that, none of the Aspects would be safe.

There is another way. Time split down into the merest
particle of a second, cramming thoughts and alternatives

into his mind before that wave of madness could claim him. *I can open the gate to Ternannoc.* He had been tricked into believing Ternannoc had been utterly destroyed. It had not been. There was no power there, but it was not the black cinder he had been led to believe it was. He could open the portal and let this wave of darkness break there, let out all the diseased power in Omara, let it crash and thunder like a sea on poor Ternannoc. And then seal it in and make good the Chaining. His mind reeled at the thought, in so doing prying still deeper truths from the Hierarch power. He learned now that it was impossible for two of the old powers to occupy the same Aspect. They canceled each other out, but in such a way that the Aspect would be annihilated. It was the final answer that he needed.

He did not hear the screams of the Children of the Mound as they tried to rush forward from their hiding places. This was what they had feared most, that Korbillian would uncover this last truth. In vain they had tried to trick him into releasing the old powers from their chains, freeing them to reach dark perfection in their own Aspect. But the Children of the Mound could not cross the great plaza to Korbillian. As the light struck them, they blazed like torches, and Ratillic averted his eyes as they were incinerated.

Korbillian yet saw the power of the great shape beyond coming for him, almost suspended in time. He stretched out his hands and let forth the powers. They fought him as if every Hierarch had returned from his grave to defy his act of ultimate blasphemy to their cause, but he was beyond their control, he was all-powerful, and he was a match for the old powers. Shattering bolts of light now tore outwards into the Opening and there came a crescendo that smashed apart the two huge pillars at its side.

Korbillian watched as another huge orifice appeared beyond the Opening, like a mirror of it, but as it rushed forward, consuming the first and its rising horrors, he saw through its window to the world he had known. Ternannoc. It dominated everything, and his breath rushed out of him as if he had been punched by a giant. This must be Ternannoc as it had once been, his reason told him, but the powers that writhed about him told him otherwise. This was Ternannoc as it was now. All he had to do to step into it was cross the threshold of the Opening. He would be home. In the present.

Ratillic saw his world, too, through tears of pain. He cried out, but was not heard, for the land was fresh, the trees and plains flourishing. There was no debris, no cracked land, no fallen mountains. The grim destruction of the Hierarch working was long over and the world was repairing itself. A few birds wheeled in its sky and Rattilic could feel the presence of animals in the undergrowth, watching him as if they knew their destiny stared back at them.

Time came down upon Korbillian like a hammer. He had to act quickly. What had been a simple choice had now become an agonizing decision. He could do precisely as the Hierarchs had wanted from the outset, save Ternannoc, even though it had been at their expense, and damn Omara's faithful above, or save the world he had promised to deliver from the darkness that beset it. He thought then of all the misery that the Hierarchs had unleashed, and of all the other Aspects he had visited and had not been able to save from chaos.

He felt himself a traitor now, and this was a far greater burden than anything he had yet had to bear. But he went on with his working, opening wider the gate to his world. Up from the deeps of Omara came the livid anger of the old power, smashing through the Chaining, but it did not fall upon Korbillian, nor did it surge out into Omara. Instead it gushed like poison into Ternannoc. The chamber shook as if battered by the fists of the gods, and dust poured down from above as though the ceiling up there beyond vision must surely fall.

Ratillic's eyes wept in the brilliant light as he strained to watch Korbillian holding to his task, realizing what was happening. He was leeching the old power, directing the flow of its energy into Ternannoc, where it would destroy utterly a world that had not died, but which was ripe for rebirth, pure, free of darkness. Shrieking, Ratillic burst

free of the spell that held him, and tore across to where
Korbillian stood. Like a madman he clawed at him. But
as soon as his hands touched him, he was tossed back like
a straw doll across the chamber. He fell among the ashes
of the Children of the Mound, who had not survived to
see the passing of their god into a cyclone of destruction.

Through the Opening, Ternannoc's skies began to turn
violet. The earth there heaved and then boiled as the great
forces sent into it began to take effect. Whatever had been
dormant below Ternannoc, chained, was not asleep anymore. As the shudders of the impact of Omara's released
power hit it, it woke. Abruptly the portal closed, and there
were more tremendous booms, as though thunder fumed
right here in the very chamber. The Opening had gone
dark. Korbillian performed the working spell to seal it.
Ratillic crawled to a sitting position, his hands burned, his
clothes ripped.

Silence gradually asserted itself, and the dust began to
settle. Korbillian noticed the solitary figure. Ratillic was
trying to get to his knees. He dragged himself closer.
"What have you done?" he gasped.

Chest heaving, Korbillian drew himself up. The light in
his hands had subsided, but the glow remained. "Omara
is safe. The old power is gone. There is nothing here to
Chain." He pointed to the remains of the Children of the
Mound. "All we need to do now is clear away the rabble
from the streets and put Xennidhum to the torch."

Ratillic's tears still ran. *"What have you done?"* he
repeated.

Korbillian stared at him as he lurched to his feet as if
drunk. He knew that Ratillic had seen the final act. "I
elected to save Omara," he said. "As I swore to its people
that I would."

Ratillic staggered closer, blinking away the tears. "You
have destroyed Ternannoc. I saw it. Not dead."

"And would you have welcomed it, a place without
power, the very Ternannoc that you did not want, you and
all the other Hierophants?" Korbillian snapped. "You refused to sacrifice all power to save Ternannoc. A world
with no power, you said, would not be acceptable."

Ratillic had no strength to argue, and stood, bemused.

At that moment the Opening behind them burst, showering out light and great chunks of earth and stone. They were flattened, but Korbillian was quick to turn to see what had happened.

"The old powers," he murmured. They were clashing, annihilating each other in a storm that dwarfed every storm in the history of time. Winds tore through the ruptured Opening, but Korbillian forced himself to rise and walk to the lip of the Opening. He tried to summon up what was left of the Hierarchs' power, and although there was little remaining to him, even that was fading away, dried up by the enormous releases of energy in the working. Even so, he sought to reseal the portal, to ensure that the havoc in Ternannoc did not extend to Omara.

Ratillic felt as if his bones had been squeezed to pulp within him, but he overcame his agony to lurch to his feet. They used him! But he should have seen it, should have known they would want only their way. He had let the power rule him. What was he doing with it now? What remained of it? A sudden terrible thought came to Ratillic. *The Hierarchs.* They had deceived Korbillian from the outset. Were they still? Was he now releasing the last of their power for—

He rushed toward Korbillian. "Wait!" he howled above the wind.

"I must seal the gate!" Korbillian shouted back, but his words were torn from him.

"They must die!" Ratillic cried, but Korbillian could not hear. Ratillic looked around him desperately. Beside the ashes of one of the Children of the Mound he saw its fallen pike. He rushed to it and snatched it up. The Hierarchs are not dead! *He means to let them back in to Ternannoc.* His mind was howling in unison with the winds. Quickly he ran forward.

Korbillian could feel the gate being forced shut as the last of the power began to drain out of him. A final effort would do it. Ratillic came up behind him as he focused his concentration, and drove the point of the pike as fiercely as his anger-fueled strength would allow. It seemed to surge eagerly through Korbillian's body, ripping from his chest, grating through his rib cage. Korbillian was flung forward into the darkness. It swarmed forward, enveloping him, and his last conscious thought was that he had succeeded. Within seconds the great hole had closed up behind him, shutting off the wind like a closing door. Silence closed in and the noise died.

Ratillic stood before the dark wall. The gate was sealed, and he knew that it could never be reopened. But Korbillian would not survive nor would the powers he carried. Neither, Ratillic knew, would Ternannoc. It would scatter like the wind. The first surge of guilt struck him then. Korbillian had not been trying to release the Hierarchs at all! He had been sealing the gate. He had tricked them, of course he had. Cheated them when he sacrificed Ternannoc. But I wanted my revenge, Ratillic confessed to himself. For being wrong. For my jealousy, my anger, I have murdered him.

He stared at the dark gate. From above it came a trickle of sand, and he realized as he watched that the walls of the chamber were under a great strain now that the twin pillars had fallen to the ground. They had cracked so badly where they had fallen that already parts of them had turned to dust. The history inscribed upon them was disjointed, faded, never to be read again. With the passing of Korbillian, the last of the Hierarchs' power had gone. And so it seemed had that of the Sorcerer-Kings. Naar-Iarnoc had been the last of them. And I? thought Ratillic. Am I the last of the Hierophants?

A huge chunk of masonry crashed down not far from him. Quickly he turned and ran down the corridor to the place where he had first arrived beneath the Mound. Darkness rushed in like a tide filling a cave. There were a number of creatures about, the mindless servants of the Children of the Mound, but they were staggering around as if bereft of all reason. Some groped at Ratillic, but he brushed them off easily. He stepped to the center of the circular chamber and gazed up. Far overhead the moonlight streamed down and he felt himself lifting up toward it.

High over the chasm, Kirrikree circled, watching the flickers of the angry power like the fires of a volcano far below. He saw the Mound shuddering like a frightened beast and heard the thunder deep below it where it seemed the very gods made war upon each other. Around the top of the Mound the battle was now raging, the forces of the Mound trying to push back the defenders to the lip of the opening. Kirrikree's bird army had ripped from the skies the awful things that flew there, and now concentrated on swooping down upon the grim defenders of the city. As Kirrikree watched the chasm, he saw the single figure drift up from it, almost an illusion. Moments later the gaping hole was gone, and on the dust where it had been stood Ratillic.

"It is over," he told the owl as it dropped down beside him. "Omara is safe."

"And Korbillian?"

Ratillic shook his head. "He sacrificed himself and the power he carried to save Omara."

"Is the power Chained?"

Ratillic drew a deep breath and nodded. "Better than that. It is no more. Destroyed. The creatures that attack us have no masters to serve. The citadel below us will collapse upon itself." As he said it, the ground shook, and the first crack appeared in the ground.

"Then we must get the army away!" cried Kirrikree, taking to the air. "The Mound is going to collapse. I can feel it. The powers that raised it are gone. It will return to what it was."

While Ratillic moved away from the center of the Mound, shadowed as he did so by the three forms that abruptly materialized from the very earth, Wargallow was rallying the army. Exhausted yet determined, he spurred his Deliverers on, and gave fresh heart to the commanders of Guile's warriors and Strangarth's survivors. They had no difficulty in outfighting their opponents, but sheer weight of numbers pressed them back. Wargallow had realized that there were concussions going on far under the Mound, but he forced himself to concentrate on the defense of the ground he had been told to hold. At last he saw the forces surrounding the army pulling back, regrouping as if for a new attack. But the skies were alive with seething cloud, and the ground heaved gently like a ship in a swell. What powers had Korbillian stirred below them?

"They're pulling back!" Guile cried to one of the soldiers beside him, scarcely able to repress a note of hysteria.

"Hold your position!" Wargallow yelled, and the cry was taken up. "If we give chase now, they'll drive wedges into us and cut us to pieces. Hold, I say!"

Ratillic had found him at last. "We have to flee the Mound," he gasped. "It will fall in on itself. Look, they're already breaking ranks." As he pointed, the enemy did exactly as he said. Whatever controlled them had lost its grip. Like herds of wild steeds, they swarmed down off the flanks of the Mound, back into the city, as though they sensed that the earth was about to open.

Wargallow looked at Ratillic, saw his hands that were bound, the exhaustion. "This power that Korbillian seeks to take from us—"

But Ratillic was shaking his head. "He had been deceived, Wargallow. The Hierarchs were using him. But he cheated them. Omara is safe. There's an irony in it, too. The Hierarchs wanted us all sacrificed to make good the Chaining. Our blood would have ensured success."

Wargallow gasped. "The giving of blood—"

"But Korbillian gave his own, and that of the Hierarchs to destroy the evil powers."

"Then we were not needed."

"I think we were. But let us discuss it when we are free."

Wargallow nodded. "We must avoid panic. Our escape to the city must be orderly. I will form columns." He was gone at once, already shouting out his orders.

Brannog and Sisipher were beside Ratillic at once. "What has happened?" said Brannog.

Ratillic looked at Sisipher, trying to mask the stab of fear he felt for her safety. He had seen the vision that Korbillian had forced from the Hierarch memory, and knew that she carried her own death within her. Perhaps, he thought, she may be safe if she does not bear a child. But there was no time to think of that now.

"He's dead," said the girl.

"I think he knew it was inevitable," said Ratillic. "But Omara is safe." He had come to cling to those words, he realized. Omara is safe, as if they abjured his own sins.

The ground rocked and another split appeared. Several men were trapped by it and disappeared beneath the earth.

"Hurry!" Ratillic bawled, and in a moment the entire army was on the move. It was a further tribute to Wargallow's skill that there was no panic, no wild flight. Keeping together, they trotted as one down toward the city below them, which had already absorbed the fleeing enemy.

25

Flight

"HOW MANY HAVE WE LOST?" Brannog asked Wargallow.

"A third." He studied the men behind him, leaning up on his horse to see that there were no stragglers. Beside him, Ratillic sat silent and thoughtful as they came to the first of the buildings. "Tell me something," Wargallow asked him. "You say we were not needed for the sharing of power. Korbillian had been deceived. Then there is no power in us?"

Ratillic stiffened. "There is. We may yet need it."

"But the old powers are destroyed?" Wargallow was looking back at the Mound. Already the top of it had crumbled, sending out jagged cracks down its sides like questing serpents.

"Yes. When Korbillian found out how the Hierarchs had sought to trick him, he sacrificed himself and their powers."

"Then they were not dead?" gasped Brannog.

"I think not," Ratillic lied.

Guile had nudged his horse up beside them. He looked even more dishevelled than the Hierophant, his eyes wild. "It seems cruel that he should die for us."

Ratillic nodded. "I misjudged him. It seemed to me that he was prepared to sacrifice everything but himself for his cause. I was wrong." And now his death sits upon my conscience. I cannot tell them! It is better that they don't know that he sacrificed Ternannoc for their world. It would sadden them to know it, and there will be sorrow enough when they count their dead. "You played your parts," he told them. "Korbillian needed you at his back while he undertook the working. This has been no wasted journey."

"We may have saved Omara," said Wargallow wryly, "but we ourselves are far from safe. Look." His arm swept in a curve around the buildings. They knew then that they would have to fight their way out of Xennidhum. Up from below the last of the servants of the Mound had come, disturbed by the colossal upheavals of the Mound's collapse.

"Their leaders are dead," said Ratillic. "They are like beasts with no mind of their own. If they attack, we shall beat them off."

Wargallow shook his head. "Perhaps. But I want to take no chances." He rode back along the ranks, speaking to the men, conferring with those who now controlled Elberon's troops. Within moments the army had prepared itself for defense. The Earthwrought were alert, their senses turned to what was waiting in the city. They heard the roar of falling earth, and the Mound heaved, further cracks appearing as it folded, swallowing buildings and rubble. Great clouds of dust rose up, swirling down upon the army below, covering it and masking it.

Shielding their eyes from the dust, coughing, the army waited, and the inevitable attack came. Thousands of the denizens of the city came rushing forward in a wave, intent on pushing the army back to the brink of the huge pit that had opened behind them. Steel rang on steel and shrieks rose up dreadfully. As Wargallow fought, he realized at once that this was organized. He cut down his enemies like wheat, then at last found himself facing a white robed figure whose strange eyes blazed with anger and terrible purpose. This being fought with a staff, and as Wargallow smote it, sparks flew from it.

"So a few of the Children have survived," said Ratillic beside him.

"You'll never live to boast of your victory!" snarled the robed one. "The Mound may have fallen, and many of the Children with it, but there are enough of us left to marshal the armies of Xennidhum. When we have wiped out your vermin, we will cross the deserts.''

Wargallow thrust the figure back, ready for a fresh on-slaught.

"There are no restrictions upon us now," the figure laughed. "We are our own masters, and we make our own plans.''

Before Wargallow could press his attack, three shapes bolted forward. Ratillic's wolves tore into the figure and within moments had ripped the life from it. Other crea-tures took its place and Wargallow found himself shoulder to shoulder with Brannog, whose axe took a deadly toll of the enemy.

"We have to survive this," Wargallow called to him. "These hordes are not without leaders. They mean to break free of this black city and ride to war. Without prep-aration, the continent will fall.''

"The streets are choked with them," Brannog called back. "Our men are drained. Unless we rest soon, it will be a matter of time before we are completely over-whelmed.''

They fought on, well beyond the dawn, until it became impossible, for the slain were piled high on every side. But the army had not given ground. It had moved yard by yard into the city. As the sun rose, the enemy withdrew, and the army took fresh hope.

While the army rested, eating what was now seen to be the last of its food, the leaders came together. Guile, who had thrown himself into the fighting with more energy than anyone would have expected of him, dabbed at a bloody gash on his scalp.

"Take heart!" he laughed. "I keep thinking of Sisi-pher's vision.''

Brannog scowled at him as if to warn him to silence.

"Five from the ten," Guile went on, no longer caring if Brannog or the others shouted him down. "And we have lost five.''

Wargallow's face sharpened with anger. "Five? You speak of five? Are you blind? Can you not count the dead around us?''

Guile inclined his head. "Of course. I mean no disrespect to them. But if five of our leaders are to survive this, why then, so must hundreds of others. Do you see?"

Wargallow studied him, his strange expression, but thought better of argument and turned away.

Ratillic frowned at him. "You have placed your own interpretation on Sisipher's vision. Only four have died."

"Korbillian—" Guile began.

"Did we not agree that in the analogy, he was the body, not the hands?"

"Stop it!" cried Sisipher. "You cannot act on what I saw. Even I do not understand it."

"But you can show us the future," said Guile. "Use your gift and point us toward safety."

Her eyes smoldered with anger. "My gift! It is a curse! I have been conditioned, just as Korbillian was. I served my purpose when I summoned Naar-Iarnoc. This petty gift of seeing tomorrow is a trick. I will not use it again."

One of the Earthwrought, Ogrond, now their leader since the death of Ygromm, looked at her sadly. "Your gift of sharing, mistress," he said. "That is no curse."

At once she touched him, but she could not speak.

Ratillic felt sorrow well up in his own breast, knowing that the girl was indeed cursed, and that if another one of them was to die, it could be her. Be childless, he thought. It is your only hope. He heard the ground below them rumbling, but shut it out. He wanted to think of life beyond this terrible place.

Ogrond's face was creased with anxiety. One of his men came to him. After a few words, Ogrond turned to the others. Wargallow listened, seeing in the eyes of the little man the face of Ygromm.

"Bad," said Ogrond. "We have tried to find a way down through the earth. The Fall of the Mound has opened great splits below, but there are such things living there! And the earth itself seethes with power that will poison. This place is ill, masters. It is well that we have rid it of its rulers, but nothing will live here for generations. What can ever cleanse this ground?"

"The Silences will contain them," said Wargallow.

"When we return to our countries, we must see that the Silences are watched. Korbillian said we were the spearhead. The war has merely begun. We will have to attend to the placing of a circle of towers, a watch."

"Aye," Ratillic nodded. "And Kirrikree's folk will—" He looked up, suddenly realizing that the great owl was nowhere around. "Sisipher?"

"The owl? His folk have flown. I think he is trying to rally them, but the collapse of the Mound terrified them. But he will return."

Wargallow watched the skies. "There may still be powers here. But none that can be met in the field. We must prepare Omara."

"If we get out," said Guile.

They heard then the renewed roars of the enemy, and as one got to their feet, knowing that the respite was over and that the next wave was coming. But as they took up stations, they saw that they were not yet under attack. Out in the city, where the dreadful commotion had begun, they could see great clouds of thick brown dust rising skyward. Through the clouds floated dozens of dome-plants, and it was these that were responsible for the discharging of the clouds. Moments later Kirrikree swept overheard, and it was a while before he had confirmed for Sisipher that the dome-plants had come over the city in force. He had brought them and now scores of them were attacking the enemy ranks, driving them underground, choking them with their poison.

The wind was not strong, but it blew the poison away from where the army waited, and at last, by the afternoon, Sisipher said that it was safe to ride into the city. Jubilant, the army began the march, and above them the dome-plants drifted, eddying and patrolling like wolves of the sky. Ratillic knew that many of them had taken to the air prematurely and were not ready to seed, but they understood, through the great owl, what it was that the army sought to achieve. They sacrificed themselves willingly to bring about the confounding of the creatures of Xennidhum.

By nightfall the army had reached the twin idols that

guarded the great stair. The men had not been attacked for some time. The last of the dome-plants had drifted out across the jungle beyond the city, slipping down into darkness, and Ratillic feared that it was to their silent deaths. Kirrikree dropped down beside him.

"The city rouses itself," said the owl. "In an hour you will be faced by even greater numbers. There are things below you that will test the strength of mind of your men."

"Listen to me, Kirrikree," Ratillic told the great bird. "You must take as many of your birds as are left and flee this place. Xennidhum is not dead, and we have not the power to destroy it, not today. But other armies will come here to finish our work. I fear that we are doomed. Word must go back across the desert. You must spread it to all of Omara. You must find ways. There must be men and women of power out there, even if they hide this power from themselves. You heard the words of the stones in Cyrene. What Korbillian has started, you must finish. He gave his life for this world—"

"I understand that," whispered the bird. "And I understand what it was he sacrificed."

Ratillic felt himself go icy under the wide-eyed stare. "You know?"

"He was right. I would have chosen as he did."

"Then you know also that I killed him."

Kirrikree stretched his wings. "I know that he died ensuring that the powers of the Hierarchs ended." He took to the air as though no more was to be said. "I am reluctant to leave you here, but what you have told me to do is urgent. I will take the birds at once."

Sisipher felt his mind then, wondering why he had shielded his words with Ratillic. She understood now what the bird had to do. "Goodbye," she called to him.

"Endure," he called back to her. "For my sake, Sisipher, endure." Then he was gone and this time the vacuum left in her mind seemed more total, more final. There was a flutter of wings as the last of the birds joined Kirrikree and they were a brief cloud against the darkness of the night, disappearing westwards to the desert.

The moon glared down upon the army now, seemingly

eager to watch the next phase of its torment. Wargallow and the leaders consulted.

"Should we begin the descent quickly and make our stand on the road below?" Wargallow asked.

"Aye," said the fighting men. "Better to have something at our backs and not the stairs."

THE DESCENT BEGAN at once, and as it did so the first of the enemy ranks appeared. This time they had goaded strange creatures to the fore of their forces, creatures that had been drawn up from far below the city. Brannog recognized some of them: they were far more powerful than the fleshworm he had killed, and they seemed more agile. Wriggling forward, they rushed upon the tail of the army. Following in their wake came the creatures of Xennidhum, and there was about them now a frenzy, a maniacal will to destroy. Within moments the two forces were locked together, milling like ants, and so closely packed was the fighting that it was impossible to use a sword. The terrible beasts that had been unleashed ran amok, turning upon their own masters just as eagerly as upon the army, and as they tore great swathes into the locked masses, scores of the retreating army were able to get away down the stairway. A strong line of defense held the topmost stairs, while Wargallow led the flight down. Ratillic watched the jungle for signs of life, but the fires that Korbillian had unleashed on the upward journey and the work of Naar-Iarnoc had devastated what grew there to such an extent that nothing moved now.

Sisipher clung to Brannog as they raced down the stairs, close to falling many times. Above and behind her she could hear the awful din of battle, and she felt a stab of guilt that so many men were fighting to secure her escape. Brannog knew what she was thinking and tried to comfort her.

"Some of us must get back," he said. "Wargallow, Guile, Ratillic. And you and I. If others are to come here, they will need rallying."

"But how many must die?"

"You must not think of that."

The frantic journey down the stairs ended, but the race down the road became even more breakneck. Those that still had horses rode, so that a party of them were far ahead of the retreating army. They paused to look back.

"We cannot desert them," said Guile. "Morric was right. I cannot sacrifice men when I am not prepared to fight."

"This is no time for sentiment!" snapped Wargallow. "My own men are dying up there. But we have to get clear." He pointed his killing steel at a Deliverer who had escaped with them. "You! Tell them what has happened. Guard our backs. We will make a break for the open desert."

The man obeyed at once.

"Ride on!" Wargallow called. He spurred his horse down the road alone, and moments later the others had followed. There were about fifty of them; soldiers to protect Guile, Deliverers, Earthwrought, a handful of Strangarth's men. None of them spoke, all knowing the likely fate of the army.

Ratillic caught up with Wargallow. "Be careful!" he called. "There may be others below us." Wargallow acknowledged with a wave, but he rode on scarcely less quickly. The heights of Xennidhum dropped behind them, and they heard nothing now but the thunder of the horses. Down into the deep canyon they rode, the moon blotted out by the heights above them.

A cry behind them made them turn. One of the warriors had fallen, his horse dropping under him. Guile swerved back in spite of protests and picked the man up. His men joined him, puzzled at his recklessness.

"Come on," Guile shouted at the man. "I've lost enough of you." The others had raced on ahead.

"Sire, you cannot carry me. This is too dangerous."

"Nonsense! Hold still." Guile goaded the horse harder, and his men feared that it would collapse as the soldier's mount had.

It was not until Wargallow's leading party had reined in above the desert floor that Guile caught them. Wargallow was scanning the desert. He turned as Guile and his men rode up.

"Any pursuit?" he said tersely.

"Not yet."

"There's nothing below," said Ratillic.

"The domes?" said Sisipher, but Ratillic shook his head.

"Gone."

"Then Wargallow's right," said Brannog. "We'd better see that we get across. We owe them that."

"Sire," called one of the soldiers. "We need water for the horses. My men have none left. Nor supplies."

A quick check taught them that they had hardly any water between them. "Korbillian said the pools here could be purified," said Ratillic. "But without his power—"

"We'll never reach Cyrene without water," said Wargallow. "Is there none we can use?"

Sisipher pulled at Ratillic's sleeve. "Ratillic, the dome-plants survived. They must have taken water.",

"Yes, but their structure is not like ours."

"Naar-Iarnoc survived," she persisted.

He nodded. "I don't know."

They rode downward to the basin below, and as they crossed the rocky slopes they looked up at the plateau. There was still no sign of pursuit, but each of them felt sure it would come.

"Are you sure we cannot reach Cyrene without water?" said Brannog.

"If we did not travel by day," said Ratillic. "Perhaps we could. But we dare not rest. The hordes of Xennidhum will follow, heedless of their own death." They had reached a place where dome-plants had lived. Here there were small craters where the plants had broken free of their root system, and nearby was a large pool. It glistened in the moonlight. Ratillic studied it.

"Dangerous," he breathed. But he thought of Korbillian, and of how he had tried to drag him away from the Opening. He had paid for that with the scorching of his hands, and yet, he had touched him. "I will see what can be done." He stooped to the water and before anyone could stop him he had scooped up a handful of the brackish substance. He gulped it down and stood stiffly, eyes closed. He could feel it coursing through him.

"Is it safe?" said Wargallow.

Ratillic felt the onset of the first cramp and doubled up. But he fought back the pain and straightened himself. "No. Not yet. But get a container. I may be able to do something with it."

"Has it poisoned you?" said Sisipher.

He shook his head. "I can change it within me. Little harm to me. Bring the container." One of the soldiers brought a large water sack, and Ratillic sliced it in half, making a crude dish out of it. Once this was filled, he rolled up the sleeves of his robe. His hands were badly burned. "Watch the road," he warned them, and guards were posted at once. The plateau remained silent. Ratillic dipped his burned arms in the water. He closed his eyes and spoke softly in the darkness. When he had finished, he had the water poured into another container. Three times he did this, filling as many of the containers as he could.

"Can we drink it?" said Wargallow.

Ratillic nodded. "Safe enough. Drink sparingly." He filled the bowl he had made a last time and put his hands into the water. This time his back arced. The faint power was used up. His suffering was clear.

"Ratillic!" Sisipher cried. "Stop him! We have enough."

Brannog tried to pull Ratillic's arms from the water but could not. He stepped back, about to kick the container over rather than have Ratillic suffer more.

"Wait!" Ratillic cried, and Brannog held back. "It is ready." Ratillic stood aside as the water was poured into a last container. He wrapped up his hands, but Sisipher had seen that they were raw and blistered.

"You should have enough to get you to Cyrene," he said.

Brannog grabbed him as he slumped forward. He felt extraordinarily light, as if the flesh on him had dried up to nothing. "Ratillic!"

Sisipher leaned over him. Gone now was the revulsion she had once felt for him. "What have you done?"

"Guile's fifth finger," he grimaced. "The water is safe."

"You fool!" snapped Brannog.

"Ride!" Ratillic hissed back. "I did not do this lightly. You must get across. Wargallow, get these fools away."

Wargallow put his hand on Brannog's shoulder. "Leave him."

Brannog turned, anger flaring in him. All his past fury at the death of his people and the countless other deaths rose up in him like bile. He cursed, as if about to drag out his axe.

Sisipher read his mind and thrust herself in front of Wargallow, shielding him. "No, father! We lose everything if we quarrel now. We must ride. Put Ratillic on his horse."

Brannog stared at her for a long moment, but then grunted. "This place warps anger to killing fury," he said, and Wargallow nodded, but said nothing.

They gathered their precious water containers and put Ratillic, who was already unconscious, upon his horse. As they rode out from the rocks and down to the first of the sand wastes, they heard a roar from behind them. There were lights on the road, and whether it was the remnants of the army or the creatures of Xennidhum, they could not tell. Quickly they rode across the shallow sand, and before long they had been swallowed by it.

All night they rode, pausing only to try and see from the higher ridges if there was any pursuit. Shortly after dawn they saw a cloud of dust and knew there was a pursuit, but even now they could not be sure what it consisted of. In spite of the murderous heat, they could not risk stopping, so moved on, more slowly into the embrace of the desert. Several of the horses died, and men had to ride double, which slowed them even more, but Wargallow was ruthless enough to force them on. Brannog wondered whether the man was a curse, or whether his determination to succeed at any cost was the factor which would get them through this ordeal. Wargallow spoke to every man, whether they were Deliverers or not, and told them if they could not keep up the pace, they must drop behind. None fell back.

Brannog rode with Ratillic before him now, but he had known for some time that he must have help soon. He said nothing to the others, for their spirits were frayed enough, but he sensed the Sisipher knew how Ratillic faded. In silence they rode on, only vaguely aware that they were travelling in the right direction to find Cyrene. If they missed it, they would not survive.

What followed was like a fevered dream for them all as day became night and then day again. Men died, and other horses fell, the party slowly depleted. Already the water ran low, but they made it last. Behind them the scouts reported that the dust cloud drew ever nearer, and estimated that in another day it would draw level with them.

When Brannog finally saw what he took to be the valley of Cyrene, he thought perhaps it was a mirage. Exhausted, the party crested a ridge and looked down. They had found the city of whispers. But as they came upon it, they heard a drumming of hooves. Within moments they were surrounded. Weakly, Brannog dragged out his axe. He found himself staring into a face that would not focus. But he heard a great shout not of anger, but of joy.

"Brannog!" came a voice. The face was less blurred, and after a long moment he realized that it was Ruan, and about him was a compliment of fresh troops. Brannog leaned forward to clap him on the shoulder, but the desert reached up and smothered him.

When he came to, he was in a cool stone room, within the city. Water bathed his brow and he looked up to see his daughter smiling down at him. He tried to rise but had no strength left.

"Be still," she said.

"The others?"

"All are safe, though Ratillic is unconscious," she said.

"The pursuit?"

"It comes. But Ruan is ready."

While Brannog fell back into sleep, Wargallow was sufficiently recovered to seek out Ruan. The latter had taken command of the soldiery. He had brought a thousand men across the great Silences, and he was proud of his ability to command them. He had acted swiftly when the party fleeing from Xennidhum had been found, deploying his troops defensively, seeing to the well being of Brannog and the others. There had been no time to discuss with them what had occurred in Xennidhum, so he was relieved now to see the Deliverer approaching.

"Elberon died fighting," said Wargallow, knowing the young man sought news of the warlord first. "He fought like a dozen men, but you cannot imagine what we had to face." He went on to give an account of how the others had fallen.

"And you are *all* that survived?" said Ruan, appalled. He was watching the cloud of dust that came ever nearer from the east.

Wargallow nodded at it. "Unless that is the army. But I think not."

"How is Ottemar?"

"He'll live," said Wargallow. "And is he to be the man you will crown as your Emperor?"

"We'll need to rebuild the army. We could not take Goldenisle with what we have left. And without Elberon, well, he was irreplaceable."

"But you must replace him." Wargallow turned from the young man, leaving him to his troubled thoughts. As the Deliverer watched the desert, he called men to him. "Are my eyes playing tricks? What is that to the north? And there to the south!"

Ruan had rushed to his side when he heard him shout. "The dunes! The walls that rose against us. But without Korbillian—"

Ogrond and a number of the Earthwrought were also watching. "We are safe in Cyrene, masters. The dunes will not come here. The things within them fear this city, even now. But there is enough to satisfy them out in the desert. The pursuit is loud, is it not?"

An hour later the dunes had massed and moved inexorably closer to each other. At last, long before the great cloud of dust that heralded the pursuit had reached the city, the banks of dune had closed in on it. Night fell, and while every soldier shrugged off sleep, watching the sand, prepared for battle, there was only the silence. As dawn brightened the panorama, they saw that the dust cloud had gone. There was no sign of the dunes.

"It is done," said Ogrond, who had not moved.

"Then it is safe to go back?" Wargallow asked him.

"Aye," he said solemnly. "I will take my people at once. We have found delvings that have been neglected for many years. We have much to do." He said no more than that, but scurried off to prepare the Earthwrought for the parting.

Wargallow went indoors to where Brannog and Sisipher were talking softly at Ratillic's bedside. The two men faced each other and for a moment Sisipher thought the enmity between them would flare.

"We seem to have won free," said Wargallow.

"At what a cost," nodded Brannog.

Wargallow seemed to be trying to find the words to say something that was troubling him. He looked at the unconscious Ratillic, grunting. "There has been much blood spilled. I recall your village, Brannog. If I have wronged your people, I regret it. The ways of the Deliverers must change. Grenndak has much to answer for, but so have I, and all those who stood by his Abiding Word." He held out his killing hand. The sun sparkled on its polished curves. "You have been wronged. I have been used, just as Korbillian was used." He put his arm across the heavy wooden table that had been pulled alongside Ratillic's bed.

"What are you doing?" Brannog asked.

"Take your axe. Remove this evil."

Brannog gasped and Sisipher clutched at her throat. "Father, you cannot—"

"Silence girl!" snapped Wargallow, his face white. "Do it, Brannog. You have the right. It is the hand of a murderer."

Brannog shook his head. "No."

Wargallow looked up at him, stunned. "Why not?"

"Your crimes may be many. I cannot remove them so

easily. You must carry that arm with you. Let it be a reminder of what has been.''

Wargallow sagged back. He nodded. "So be it.''

For a time there was silence. Wargallow again broke it.
''Where will you go now?''

"To find other Earthwrought tribes," said Brannog.
''Their rulers must be taught to trust us.''

Sisipher leaned over Ratillic. ''He wakes.''

Ratillic's hand unexpectedly found hers, but his grip
was very weak. Ruan entered and stood watching them.

''What must we do for you?'' Sisipher asked the Hierophant.

''Nothing for me. For yourselves. Your strength is in
your concord.'' He tried to form more words, as though
there was something he wanted to say to the girl, but the
effort was too much for him. There was a brief shudder
and it was over.

Sisipher sat back, shaking her head.

Ruan had come forward and he pulled a blanket over
Ratillic while the others looked on in silence. ''Strange to
think that he and Korbillian, men from another world,
gave their lives for Omara. It is a difficult mantle they have
passed on to us.''

''Are we worthy of it?'' said Brannog.

Wargallow motioned Ruan to him, and the young man
went. Wargallow pointed to another room. There were
steps down in to it and a tiny fountain that the Earthwrought had repaired. Beside this sat a solitary figure,
gazing across the square outside the room to where the
sands curved away. It was Guile.

''You think him fit to rule an Empire, Ruan?'' Wargallow asked softly.

Ruan and the Deliverer moved away discreetly, leaving
Guile to his thoughts. ''He carries the hopes of more people than you might think,'' replied the soldier. ''But he
must decide now. We built slowly under Elberon.''

Wargallow permitted himself an understanding grin.
''You will go on, I am sure. At least you have allies now.
Korbillian achieved that for us.''

Sisipher also wanted to be alone for a while, and found

herself drawn by the gentle play of the fountain. She did not see Guile until she was almost upon him. At once she made to leave.

"Wait!" he called, noticing her, and she turned, though she would not look at him. He searched for the words he had to say to her, struggling. "You will never forgive me for killing the boy," he said at last.

He thought at first she would pour scorn upon him, seeing the anger in her face, but then she gave a great, shuddering sigh. "It is done. Xennidhum filled us all with something dark, turning it upon each other."

"I fear," he replied, "that it drew from us the darkness that already dwelt within us. For me, that was true. I can see myself now. Elberon despised me for what happened—"

"I don't think so," she said gently, for the first time able to feel sympathy for him. "None of us is so pure. I was also to blame for Wolgren's death."

He began to protest.

"No, listen," she insisted. "I knew how much he loved me. I enjoyed his worship. I even used it a little. Not once did I make it clear to him that I could never return his love. Xennidhum was like a living thing that knew all our thoughts. It used them cruelly. It used Wolgren's jealousy to begin the fight that killed him. Had he known his love for me was wasted, he would never have become so jealous."

"Then perhaps you can forgive me for his death."

She nodded, her hands touching the waters of the fountain. "I must."

"There is another thing," he said, hesitantly. "But I do not ask forgiveness for it."

"We were all manipulated."

"Yes, but you must hear me. After the boy's death, I tried to throw an Empire at your feet, out of fear. I sought to flatter you with a lie. I understand now how it insulted you."

To his great surprise, she smiled, tossing back her dark hair. She was a woman, but how easily he could see the goddess in her, those powers that were her inheritance. "I was furious," she agreed. "But an Empire! Few women would turn down such a gift."

"I am glad that you spoke as you did."

"Let's not talk of it again," she said more seriously. "But what will you do now?"

He looked out at the desert. "Where to begin? Golden-isle is sick, doomed to collapse, unless Quanar can be overthrown. If only the Empire could be made strong, the world would not need to fear Xennidhum again. But it will take time. My destiny is there, though without Morric, I despair." He closed his eyes for a moment.

"Take heart," she said as she left him. "The worst must be over."

Wargallow and Ruan were deep in conversation with her father when she came across them. She smiled and left them to their fresh plans, going to the waiting wolves.

"One day soon," she overheard the Deliverer say, "I shall ride back to Xennidhum."

Brannog nodded. "When you do, be sure to have word sent to me."

Epilogue

A YEAR HAD PASSED since the survivors of the flight from Xennidhum had returned. Sisipher leaned on a balustrade, high up in the tower that was one of the many built by the Earthwrought not far from the edge of the Silences. She watched the skies, knowing that the great white owl, Kirrikree, would be here to make the rendezvous soon. As she looked, seeing the familiar heat haze rising from the desert, she reflected on the terrifying events of her journey to and from the city of the remote plateau. She and the survivors had worked tirelessly since their escape to ensure that the desert was closely watched. Kirrikree brought monthly reports of how the perimeters of the desert were patrolled, and of the difficulties there were in policing them. The circle of the watch had almost been closed.

Sisipher thought of those who got away, and of the army that had not returned. She thought also of her father, who was now far to the south, guided by the little folk from tribe to tribe, Earthwise to Earthwise, spreading the word of the battle and of the danger yet in Xennidhum. Already the first of the Earthwrought tribes were beginning to venture to the surface, although it would be many years before the "overmen" would be trusted by them, or before many of them could accept the little folk.

Behind the girl, the three wolves who had spread themselves in the shadows like hounds to avoid the heat, lifted their heads and growled uniformly. Sisipher soothed them with a gentle word, knowing by their thoughts that Kirrikree was near. In a moment he dropped from the sky and was beside her. They did not exchange pleasantries, even though they had not met for a month, but there was no need; between them now passed an unspoken understanding, a deep bond.

"The work progresses well," he told her. "There are now very few areas of the desert edge that are not watched constantly. We have found very little hostility on the far eastern slopes of the Silences. Already there is strong evidence that the seeping of evil power has ceased. In places it has retreated. Korbillian spoke of an illness: now he would speak of convalescence."

"That's wonderful!" said Sisipher.

"I hear word that your father has established another village above ground. The Earthwrought nation is far greater than had been realized. Brannog complains that he is no god, though his name goes before him."

Sisipher laughed. "Which is why I would not go with him. I think that all of us who came back from Xennidhum are considered more powerful than we are. How does Guile fare? And Ruan?"

"If Guile's men continue as they are doing, they will soon have raised a city on the Camonile delta! They have found an excellent site. Trade flourishes, particularly with Strangarth. And here is news that will cheer you: there is a rumor, and I think it is more than that, that Ruan is to wed one of Strangarth's daughters. Certainly Ruan has visited the king far more often than one would have thought politically necessary. And Strangarth's brood are all hot-tempered and fierce! If Ruan is wooing this vixen, he must be much taken with her!"

Again Sisipher laughed, and the owl reflected on how beautiful she looked now. She should spend more time in these new kingdoms. Visiting the towers, watching the desert was no task for such a girl. She seemed afraid to face herself, hiding her thoughts from him.

"You approve, Kirrikree?" She had to repeat the question.

"Of course! Such a union will strengthen Guile's position here. Ruan has become a young man of some stature.

He controls men with the same natural skill as did Elberon. In years to come, he will not be unlike him. Already the warriors respect him, even the veterans of Xennidhum.''

"Does Guile still speak of Goldenisle?''

"Neither he nor Ruan are eager to go to war. This is a new world. New trading routes are opening up with the lands to the south. But Guile yet has it in mind to overthrow his cousin. Xennidhum acted on him like a poison, but his system is clearing itself. When he is ready, I am certain he will move. Men still come from the west, and they stay in the new city.''

"Has it a name?''

"Yes. They call it Elberon.''

Sisipher nodded, delighted with his news. After a pause, she turned to glance at the mountains behind her in the west. "And Wargallow?''

"I have visited him. The Direkeep remains a place apart, but Wargallow has the most onerous task of all, to bring the Deliverers away from the dark faith of Grenndak. But he is strong and has many followers.''

"Perhaps he was the strongest of us all.''

"In time, perhaps, he will allow himself to emerge from his grim mission. He maintains contact with Guile, and with Ruan. Strange, but he and Ruan share a certain respect. It is no bad thing.''

"What of his ambitions, Kirrikree? What is his real goal?''

"I have often thought that Wargallow's world suffered a greater shock than any of ours. Once, like Guile, he sought to use Korbillian's power, certainly to gain by it. But he sees the changing world. I do not think he will became an enemy.''

I could look, she thought, inadvertently. See what will become of us all. No, I have taken an oath never to use my gift.

"And you, mistress?''

She stared at his intense gaze. "I think I will leave this tower soon, and go on a journey," she told him. "If there *is* to be a wedding, I want to be there.''

Kirrikree saw her laugh once more, staring up at the clear skies, and something moved within him, a weight passing.

Sisipher glanced down at the desert. She had seen the face there, the face that haunted her dreams once with its pain, but it had been no more than a mirage, and the huge figure that she had watched climb up out of the rocks was a trick, a shadow. It could be no more than that. Her vigil was over.

At that same moment, Simon Wargallow also looked up at the skies, from a high tower of the Direkeep. His own work was almost complete, although he wondered if it would be possible ever to rid the place of Grenndak's presence. Too many Deliverers remained silent about Grenndak's passing, now an open truth. Wargallow could not hope to win them all. Even so, perhaps one day he would see the keep levelled. He yet thought of the Preserver with deep bitterness. It was a hatred that stretched back many years to the time when he had been little more than a novice in the fellowship of the keep, before he had earned his purifying steel. He had first learned then how Grenndak the god enjoyed mortal girls, and how some of those girls had disappeared when he had finished abusing them. His own sister—he saw her yet. But he snapped off the memory. Now was a time for hardness. But he had avenged her, his one regret being that he had not made the first cut. Slowly his dark mood shifted as he thought of Sisipher, reminded of her by his sister's memory, for the two were not unalike. He wondered how the girl fared. Kirrikree had visited him since his return to the keep, and although he could not communicate with the magnificent bird, he sensed that it meant him to see it as a reminder of what had passed and that he had obligations to Omara before himself.

I must visit Guile and Ruan soon, he mused. They may yet plan a campaign against the Chain, though it will be some time before they have the troops. Yes, a private visit. First, though, Wargallow had to ensure that his position here was strong. The last of those who would use Grenndak's death as a weapon to oust him must be removed.

The direct methods still had to be applied. He held his killing steel close to him beneath his robe. Ah, Brannog, you should have cut it from me. Its work is not yet done. But then, where there is poison in the blood, a surgeon must cut it out.

He looked again at the sky, as he did so realizing that it was in the hope that the great white bird would come gliding down again. He could think of no more welcome sight.